UNTAMED ISLES

The Path Awakens

AARON HODGES

Edited by Genevieve Lerner
Proofread by Sara Houston and the Untamed Isles Beta Reader Team
Cover illustration by Hazal Graham
Typography by Nikko Marie

ABOUT THE AUTHOR

Aaron Hodges was born in 1989 in the small town of Whakatane, New Zealand. He studied for five years at the University of Auckland, completing a Bachelors of Science in Biology and Geography, and a Masters of Environmental Engineering. After working as an environmental consultant for two years, he grew tired of office work and decided to quit his job in 2014 and see the world. One year later, he published his first novel - Stormwielder.

FOLLOW AARON HODGES...

And receive TWO FREE novels and a short story!
https://aaronhodgesauthor.com/newsletter

PROLOGUE
GOZZO

The ship rocked beneath Captain Gozzo Sigurd's feet as it rose on a swell, then plunged down the other side. Water crashed over the stern and lightning flashed. Men screamed, helpless before the storm's wrath. Captain Gozzo clung to the tiller as darkness momentarily gave way to light. Sailors stumbled in its glow, grasping at ropes and loose cargo, anything that might save them from an icy plunge.

Another wave swamped the hull and swept the deck, collecting broken rigging and men alike in its wake. The captain watched, helpless, as his people were dragged through the broken gunwales and into the waters of the Northern Sea.

The lightning faded, plunging them back into darkness, but the desperate faces of his crew remained stark in Gozzo's mind. The ocean roared and thunder boomed. Men screamed.

The storm had come upon them suddenly, appearing on the distant horizon and racing across the Northern Sea, turning calm waters to whitecapped waves before the crew of the *Blackbird* could flee. The rains had struck first, drenching every soul aboard the beleaguered ship. The winds had soon followed, tearing at the sails, slashing them to pieces. Last had come the waves, crashing upon the hull of the *Blackbird*, smashing oars from sailors' hands and hurling men from their feet.

Now, caught in the grips of the storm, there was nothing the crew could do but cling to their ropes and pray to the divine for salvation.

The captain alone fought on, hands locked on the tiller, desperate to see his crew to safety. Remnants of the sails still flapped from the mast, gifting the *Blackbird* just enough momentum for him to steer. Miles from shore, there would be no escaping to a shallow cove, no safe berth in which to shelter. And so Gozzo watched the darkness, seeking the next rolling behemoth.

Again and again, he directed their ship into the maw of those beasts, sending the *Blackbird* to scale the great mountains of water. His arms ached and the icy air burned his lungs, but still he sought to save those he could—even as yet another loyal sailor was washed to his doom.

He stumbled as the ship crashed down from the crest of the wave. Spray whipped across his face, stinging like a thousand tiny stones. Gozzo gritted his teeth against the pain.

A flash of lightning revealed the next wave. It rolled towards them, white waters breaking at the peak, threatening to come crashing down upon the fragile vessel.

The *Blackbird* rocked as Gozzo threw himself against the tiller, and ponderously, the ship adjusted course. Holding steady, Gozzo closed his eyes, sucking in fresh lungfuls of air. This was it, the end of his strength. The power of the storm had drained his energies, leaving him empty, listless, all but spent. How much longer must he hold on, pitting wit alone against the endless fury of the ocean?

Another scream cut through the thunder. Water swirled, and another young sailor was gone, vanished into the icy depths. Desperately, Gozzo sought out survivors. There were startlingly few—less than half of the fifty who had set out with him just a week before.

"Bastards!" Enraged, Gozzo hurled a curse at the capricious Gods.

In that moment, he cared nothing for their wrath. What more could the fickle Gods hurl at his tiny vessel, which had not already been unleashed?

Boom!

The world turned to white as lightning struck the *Blackbird's* bow. The crackling of flames followed. Smoke swept across the deck and the stench of burning wood and scorched iron filled the air, though the rain still poured down. Another *crack* followed. This time the lightning struck the ocean, sending a geyser of boiling water across the decks. The flames hissed as they were extinguished, even as another flash turned the world to white.

Boom. Boom. Boom.

Gozzo clenched his eyes closed, but still the light seared them. His ears rang and he slumped against the rudder, bowed before the wrath of the Gods, his defiance seared away by the fury of salt and flame.

Boom. Boom. Boom.

The world rocked. Caught in the grips of nature's wrath, Gozzo squeezed his eyes closed and fell to his knees, no longer able to stand, to even think. Storm and ship and men, all were forgotten before the thundering, until all that remained was the burning, the ringing of thunder, the stars dancing before his closed eyes...

Silence.

The shift was so sudden, long seconds passed before the captain realised that the world had changed. Even as he blinked his blinded eyes, he was convinced the end had come, that as he'd crouched in terror, the storm had taken him and he had passed across the valley of death.

Finally though, his senses returned and he tasted the ash upon the air, felt the feathered touch of a breeze against his skin—and knew he had survived. A chill filled his lungs as he drew breath, the last of the stars fading from his vision. The remnants of his crew stood amongst the ruins of the rigging, between the shattered foremast and scattered rope. Each of them stared out into the darkness, at a world suddenly, impossibly becalmed.

Gozzo's fear turned to confusion as he stepped away from the tiller, looking to the sky. The storm had vanished as though it had never been, leaving the ship so still they might have been docked at port. Stars stretched across the sky, thousands upon thousands, the night clearer now than any he had witnessed in all his sixty years.

A half-moon had risen while the storm raged. Now its light carved the darkness. Heart still racing, Gozzo took another step and stumbled as the ship seemed to shift unnaturally beneath his feet. He found himself disorientated, as though he'd just stepped foot on solid land after weeks at sea.

Frowning, Gozzo lowered his eyes to the becalmed seas, seeking sign of survivors. Beyond the railings, he could see the brilliance of the moon and stars reflected in the still waters, except…those waters were too still, too quiet.

A shiver passed through Gozzo. Something had banished the storm, some power beyond mortal understanding. A boon, but one that could not be trusted. They needed to hoist what remained of their sails and limp back to harbour, before the storm's wrath—or something worse—appeared.

Leaving the tiller, he stumbled towards the nearest of his sailors. Blood ran from a gash across the man's forehead and he stared blankly into the distance as Gozzo approached. Clasping the man by the shoulder, Gozzo gave him a gentle shake.

"Mike, you okay?" he rasped, his voice rough from the salt spray.

Blinking, Mike turned to look at his captain. "What…?"

His eyes remained unfocused and Gozzo realised the stunned sailor would be of no use for the moment. He turned to the next. One of the youths who'd recently joined the crew crouched against a fragment of the gunwales. The man rocked back and forth, muttering something beneath his breath. The captain caught only snippets, but he knew even before he reached the sailor that he would find no help there either.

Gozzo's frustration began to build. He was about to attempt the rigging himself, when he glimpsed again the reflection of the stars upon the waters. He paused, watching the way the light played across the ocean.

So calm, he thought, even as he wondered…

Turning from the railing, he cast his eyes around in search of a lantern, but all he could see lay broken amidst the debris. There was one he kept back at the stern, inside his cabin. It might have survived.

He stumbled through the ruin of the *Blackbird*, his heart beginning to race. Suddenly he feared they had not been saved at all, but rather plunged into one of the seven hells. Some of his men were finally beginning to rise, groaning as they tested injured limbs, but Gozzo ignored them now. He reached his cabin door and dragged it open, then fumbled blindly for the unlit lantern he kept alongside the door.

When he found the handle, he lifted it from the ring, out into the night. The glass remained blessedly intact, the pilot light still burning cheerfully within. He twisted the knob, feeding fresh oil to the flame, and light blossomed.

Struggling to swallow a lump lodged in his throat, Gozzo stepped towards the gunwales. His eyes were wide, straining to pierce the murky darkness, to make sense of what lay below.

But there was no sense to be found.

The *Blackbird* had not come to rest on becalmed waters. Beyond the railings of the ship, there was no water at all. The moonlight reflecting from all around came not from the sea, but land. A land of jagged, broken slopes of shining crystal, stretching out in all directions.

Where before had only been the raging Northern Sea, somehow they had become stranded upon an island, without a drop of water in sight.

In Gozzo's hand, the lantern began to gutter as the last of the oil was consumed. He stared out at the dark land in which they had been marooned, waiting for the night to return to darkness. When it did, silence fell across the ship.

And somewhere out amidst the endless crystal, a beast howled.

ZACHARY

Crouched atop the walls of the palace, Zachary Sicario watched as the lanterns in the grounds flickered into life. His keen eyes tracked the path of the young servant as she scurried through the manicured gardens, passing from one lamp to the next with hardly a pause for breath. Bit by bit, the night was pressed back by the shimmering lights, until the palace formed a bubble of luminescence against the oppressive gloom of Leith under darkness.

"Palace" might be overstating things a little, Zachary thought to himself as the servant retired, her task complete for the evening.

In typical aristocratic fashion, the noble owners had done their best to replicate the grandeur of the royal palace back in Londinium. But Zach had visited those grounds himself on a number of occasions, albeit in a less than official capacity. He knew a cheap knockoff when he saw one.

The fountains might fill these gardens with the same joyful whispers as in Londinium, but he could see where the paint was flaking from the "marble" statues that adorned their waters. Neither did he see the same careless displays of wealth typical of the capital. No golden inlays around the windows and doors, no bejewelled eyes on the sculptures for passing thieves to filch. Even the gardens lacked the same carefully manicured touch as those found at the royal palace.

But then, that wasn't so surprising. Zach had tried his hand at gardening since retiring; he knew well the difficulty of finding good help this far north. The dark spots infecting several of the rosebushes should have been trimmed days ago.

Breathing in the sweet scent of the flowers, Zach stifled a sigh. He'd enjoyed the quiet of his garden, the homely feel of the cottage in the highlands, far from Leith and its dark underbelly. He had thought this world behind him. But alas, fate had other plans.

"Mansion" is probably more appropriate, Zach thought at last, returning to the task at hand.

In addition to the palpable absence of true wealth, the grounds of the mansion lacked one other key feature. Security. Zach had spent the past few days canvasing the noble's property. There were just two guards patrolling the outer gardens—and on this cold winter night, both had already retreated to the burning hearth in the guard house. Tonight would be like stealing gold from, well, a noble.

Still, years had passed since Zach's last job, and he lingered a while longer in the shadows, watching for something he might have missed. Even with these rich aristocratic sorts, one had to take care.

Especially with these sorts, he reminded himself. Not even Zach's reputation would survive being caught by the likes of Roy Whitfield.

Truth be told, he'd been surprised to find the man's name on his list, given so many of the others were less than exemplary citizens. But then, the aristocracy always had considered themselves above the rules. It made sense that at least a few of their kind would be interested in the Anomaly.

Three months had passed since the storm that had wreaked havoc to the eastern seaboard of Riogachd. Most of the fishing fleet had been lost, either destroyed at sea or sunk in harbours across the nation. Not even those citizens further inland had been safe, as storm surges broke through seawalls and rivers flooded lowland villages.

The storm of the century, people had called it. Yet even as the battered communities of Riogachd struggled to rebuild, the King's Royal Navy had been deployed not to the cleanup, but to a blockade deep in the Northern Sea.

After that, it hadn't taken long for the rumours to circulate. Whispers spread about strange lights and disappearing ships, though the King's Council refused to acknowledge the Anomaly. Which of course meant that half the populace was convinced the Council were covering up some grand treasure out in the Northern Sea. No one could quite decide on the nature of that treasure—some claimed it must be a sunken galley carrying gold bullion from the bank of Londinium, others that the princess's ship had gone missing on the raging seas.

As the days turned to weeks and the Council maintained its silence, the rumours had only grown in size, though not in logic. Now the people spoke of portals to other worlds and islands of gold risen from the depths, of magic and sorcery, of the power to fulfil a man's greatest desires.

It was the last that had caught Zach's attention.

Some had already tried to slip past the naval blockade. Amateurs for the most part, those with access to a skiff or steamer that had survived the storm. Some had been caught, and after a public trial, hanged. The rest had never been seen again.

Now three months had passed, and the amateurs had finally given up seeking the secrets of the Anomaly.

It was time for the professionals to take a shot.

On the wall of the mansion, Zach drew in a calming breath. A cloud drifted across the half-moon, darkening the sky but doing little to dim the lanternlight in the grounds below. But it finally stirred Zachary into action. He made one last check of the knives hidden on his person. They might not be as effective as the modern revolvers carried by the upper echelons of society, but they were reliable in a pinch. And quiet.

Finally satisfied he was ready, Zach stepped from the wall. He dropped to the ground, landing with a soft *thump*, then quickly crossed the lawns, slipping from shadow to shadow, keeping as far from the lanterns as he could. Only once did he stop, when a sudden sound came from overhead. A flash of white feathers was all he glimpsed of the owl as it dove; a moment later it rose on languid wings, the dark body of a rat clutched in its talons.

Frozen in the shadow of a plum tree, Zachary held his breath, waiting to see whether the creature had drawn the attention of the guards. Seconds slipped by and he found his mind drifting back to those first whispers he'd caught of the Anomaly. He had a nose for a mystery, and he'd needed the distraction, something to divert his mind from his...other problems. So he'd gone looking for answers.

Even in retirement, Zachary was more resourceful than most of those clinging to the underbelly of Leith. It hadn't been hard to find a soldier on leave from the royal navy. Most of those in the blockade spent their off-duty days in Leith. After 'encountering' the man at a local tavern and shouting several rounds of mead 'for his service', he'd had the truth straight from the source.

It wasn't just strange lights and fog that had appeared out in the Northern Sea. An entire *island* had risen from the depths. Sadly, apparently not one of gold. Even so, its appearance had caused much consternation amongst those back in Londinium, for it spoke of great power, one outside the Council's control.

But when the armada tried to investigate further, a mist had appeared around the island. Those ships that drifted too close had been swallowed up, vanishing without a trace.

The soldier had seen the lights himself, great flashes of white and green and blue in the darkness, but his ship had thankfully escaped unscathed.

The entire island was a mystery wrapped in impossibility.

Just the sort of false hope a dying man could cling to in his last days.

Satisfied the guards had taken no notice of the owl's late-night snack, Zach departed the shadow of the plum tree and darted the rest of the way across the lawn before slipping into the alcove of a servants' entrance. There he drew out a set of picks and went to work on the door's lock. Thankfully, like the gardeners, good locksmiths were rare commodities this far north, and the lock was of a simple design.

His mind continued to drift as he worked, lingering as it so often had these last months on the mysterious island. Its appearance had proven propitious for the master thief, but one thing was still missing. The means to reach the island itself.

His answer had come steaming into the harbour just a week past—one of the great ocean steamers from Londinium. A great ship meant a great voyage, but the crew had remained unusually tight-lipped about their destination. Which of course meant the entire city had surmised its destination.

Unfortunately, when Zach had gone looking for passage, the vessel had already reached capacity.

A minor inconvenience for the likes of Zach Sicario.

The lock to the servants' entrance *clicked*. Zachary caught the door to keep it from opening unexpectedly. Reaching into his rucksack, he drew out a can of oil and carefully applied a drop to each hinge. Anything servant related tended to be lacking in upkeep, and he wasn't about to be given away by squeaky hinges.

Allowing the door to swing open, Zachary took his first step into the mansion of Roy Whitfield. His had certainly been the most prominent name on the list that Zach had recovered from the expedition's secretary. That in itself had been a simple task—every good smuggler knew to keep records. A few bribes later and he'd been knocking on the right door. A bit of casual intimidation had gotten the list from the secretary, but not even a sharp knife had been enough to add his name. The passengers had each been given a token to verify their place on the expedition.

With the ship set to leave port again in a matter of days, there was no time to make a replica. So Zach had been forced to resort to somewhat desperate measures. Thus he found himself slipping through the gilded hallways of the Whitfield Palace.

Definitely not a palace, he reminded himself as he spotted a poorly painted portrait of the master of the house.

His padded boots made no noise on the stone floor and only a single lantern burned in each corridor, casting long shadows from the antiquated suits of armour standing at each corner. The palaces in Londinium had long since replaced these displays with marble sculptures carved by the great artists of the time. Their aristocrats wouldn't be caught dead with such outdated decorations.

Zach had "borrowed" a plan of the manor from the local chapter of the builders guild the same day he'd taken the list from the secretary. Now he made his way quickly through the long corridors, making for the personal chambers of Roy himself. The man had left earlier in the night—off for a last visit to one of his many mistresses before the expedition departed on the morrow, no doubt. The wife would be in her own chambers if Zach's source was to be believed. And they usually were.

Drawing to a stop outside a door, Zach paused only long enough to check his mental map of the manor's floorplan before entering. There was no need to oil the hinges here—no noble worth his name would allow his private chambers to be so poorly maintained—and the door swung open without a whisper.

Darkness greeted the midnight thief. Zach drew a device from his pocket that he'd picked up at a stall on the docks. Imported from the continent, the brass "lighter" crackled as he flicked the trigger. A tiny flame appeared, casting faint light throughout the room. He found himself grinning at the invention. If he'd had something like this in his days before Margery...

Zach shook himself. Now was not the time to get lost in old memories. The light revealed an empty poster bed in the corner. Breathing a sigh of relief, Zach slipped further into the room, stepping around a pair of satin upholstered armchairs and making for another doorway within the chamber. His light revealed a second room, this one furnished with a mahogany desk and great crystal doors leading out to a personal balcony.

He went to work immediately, pulling each drawer from the desk and checking them for hidden compartments before moving to the next. Most were filled with documents and other papers, no doubt of great import to the running of a noble family. In a secret bottom of one drawer he found a small collection of gold crowns, but Zach knew a diversion when he saw one. It took another ten minutes to locate the true hiding place for the man's treasures.

Not the desk at all, but a hollow compartment in the leg of its matching chair. Within, he found a rolled-up scroll, but when he drew it out, a circular token made of brass slipped from the papers. At first glance it looked like a large coin, but in place of the king's image was a seven-pointed star. He grinned to himself and slipped the token into his pocket, then stood to leave.

Which was the exact moment Roy Whitfield chose to return to his chambers.

Zachary froze as he found the middle-aged man standing in the entrance to the office. Roy Whitfield was not an impressive man, despite the satin waistcoat and breeches he wore. Not even the top hat perched on his balding head could give him the regal look that he so obviously desired.

The revolver he pointed at Zach, however, was the real deal.

"What in the name of the Old Gods are you doing in my chambers?" the man asked, his tone surprisingly polite given the circumstances.

"Ahh, would you believe I'm with the local tax collector?"

"Tax collector..." the man repeated, his brain still obviously trying to process the discovery of a stranger in his bedchambers. His eyes drifted to the broken chair lying at Zach's feet and anger finally replaced his confusion. "Lying bastard, you're a thief!"

Zach flinched as the gun in the man's hand lifted an inch, but thankfully Roy's finger did not slip. Carefully, Zachary raised his hands.

"Okay, okay, you got me," he said. "Easy, wouldn't want us to be having any accidents, would we?"

The scowl Roy wore suggested he wouldn't mind at all. He advanced into the room and jabbed the revolver in the direction of the chair.

"Where is it?" he snapped. "Hand it over now, or I'll put a bullet between your eyes."

Judging by his trembling hand, Zach doubted Roy could make that shot. But at this range, he would certainly hit *something*, and Zach wasn't ready to die just yet.

He had at least a few months more, if the physicians were to be believed.

"Do you think the rumours are true, Roy?" he asked suddenly, surprising even himself.

The question certainly surprised Roy Whitfield. "What are you talking about, man?" he snapped.

Arms still raised, Zach attempted a shrug. "About the magic," he replied. "So many rumours, some of 'em have to be true, don't you think? I know, I know, I'm clinging to straws, but the damned physicians aren't exactly overflowing with solutions, ya know?"

This time several long moments passed before the noble replied. "Are you mad?" he asked, before a sneer crossed his lips. "Only fools believe in magic. Still, I'll have my token back, thank-you-very-much. Whatever *is* out there, the Council will pay me handsomely when I bring it to them."

"I'm sure they would," Zach replied, his hands dropping an inch, fingers bending towards the hidden knives in his sleeves.

"They will," Roy replied, licking his lips. His eyes shone with excitement. Confident he had the situation under control, he was hardly paying attention to his unexpected guest now. "When I return, my exile will be reversed. I will finally be able to leave this hellhole of a city."

"Oh, I don't know, Leith's not so bad..." Zachary began, when a voice carried to them from the corridor.

"My lord, are you alright? I heard voices!"

Scowling, Roy glanced in the direction of the unseen hallway. It was all the distraction Zachary needed. Roy's mouth was already open, but whatever he'd been about to call out never left his lips as a knife slammed into his chest. A surprised look crossed the noble's face and he staggered slightly, his gaze falling to the hilt embedded in his waistcoat. Belatedly, he fumbled for the handle, before the last of the strength left him.

Zach darted forward and caught the body as it fell, lowering it gently to the floor instead. Rising, he quietly cleared his throat before adopting his best impersonation of the dead man's voice.

"Yes, everything is fine in here, ma'am," he grunted. "Please, close the door and leave me be."

A long moment passed as Zach held his breath. "Yes, my lord," finally came the reply.

Somewhere in the adjoining room, the door to the corridor clicked closed. Silence returned to the night. Breathing out his relief, Zach turned his attention to the body at his feet.

"Well that was sloppy," he admonished himself. The infamous Zachary Sicario would have never let an old aristocrat sneak up on him like that.

At least the maid had chosen now to check after their lord. Zach was in no shape for a game of cat and mouse with the city watch. As it was, he doubted many would mourn the loss of Roy Whitfield. And he had what he'd come for.

Yes, altogether not a bad outcome, he thought to himself as he crossed to the balcony doors.

Whistling softly to himself, Zach slipped out into the night.

2

LOGAN

Logan Kaine was puffing hard by the time he arrived at the port. A flurry of sound greeted him as he stumbled to a stop. Sailors shouted from the docks and wooden wheels rumbled across the bricked streets, loud enough to drown out the thundering of his heart in his ears.

Bending in two, he struggled to recover his breath, and choked as the unpleasant combination of rotting fish and tar assailed his senses. Eyes watering from the stench and the morning chill, he forced himself to straighten. Thankfully, the passersby had not noticed his distress, concealed as he was in the shadows of an alleyway. Even so, Logan's father had taught him to be better composed.

A gentleman must always maintain his poise, the oft-repeated words were a mantra to him by now. *Doubly so for those of us of new bloodlines.*

Logan straightened and puffed out his chest. He took a moment to straighten his woollen overcoat before allowing his hand to fall to the cavalry sabre he wore on his belt. His father's weapon, the same one he'd used in the Battle for the North, when the king's forces had quelled an uprising amongst the rebel clans. For his father's heroics that day, their family had been awarded land and invited into ranks of the gentry class.

Logan could only hope to one day live up to that legacy.

Stealing the blade from his father's mantle probably wasn't the best of starts, but at least it *was* a start. As his father was so fond of saying, true men seized their own opportunities in life. And the Old Gods knew, Logan had waited long enough for an opportunity to prove himself.

The tall buildings that lined the harbour cast long shadows across the street, the winter sun still hidden behind their bricked exteriors. Studying the wagons and occasional motorcoach parked along the docks, he finally spotted the one belonging to the Kaine family. A man in an overcoat that fit far more comfortably than Logan's own stepped from the vehicle.

Logan ducked back into the alley as his brother's gaze swept the street. Had Dustin noticed his pursuit? Surely not— Logan hadn't even been following most of the way. He'd lost the motorcoach in the busy streets of Leith and been forced to cut through the back alleys to arrive here in time. Unless…

Reaching into his pocket, Logan toyed with the brass token he'd taken from the packet of documents in Dustin's desk. Had his brother noticed its absence? According to the papers that had accompanied the token, it would grant its holder passage on an expedition set to depart today. Unless

Logan was mistaken, that meant Dustin would be turned away from the ship sitting at the docks below.

And Logan would be able to board in his brother's stead.

His heart quickened at the thought. Dustin would be angry at the subterfuge. But Logan hoped he might also earn his brother's respect with this escapade. Afterall, whether he was fighting off pirates in the Northern Sea or winning commendations for his work with the highland clans, Dustin Kaine was as much a hero as their father.

And Logan was tired of living in their shadows.

Glancing out from the alley, he saw his brother leave the coach and head down the steps to the docks. A line had already formed beside the giant steamboat with '*The Rising Tide*' painted on its side, the other voyagers obviously eager to set off. Two muscled sailors stood beside the steamer, checking each passenger's token before waving them past; Dustin would be in for a shock when he discovered his own missing.

Logan slipped from the shadows as his brother joined the queue. He strode across the street, doing his best to blend with the crowd as he searched for a better vantage point.

Finding a dock that neighboured the steamer, Logan settled on a half-sunken fishing ship. Like many of the vessels in port when the great storm had struck, its hull was cracked open like an egg and half its deck was submerged in the waters of the harbour. Even three months later, the clean-up continued across much of the kingdom. Those vessels deemed irredeemable had been left to rot while efforts were focused on better prospects.

Clambering onto the section of boat still above the water-line, Logan looked across at Dustin's vessel. The steamer dwarfed the fishing ship, its twin smokestacks stretching to the height of the terraced townhouses lining the shore. Black smoke was already puffing from both chimneys as the crew stoked the engines. The great wheels powered by those engines were still, but even these loomed over the other ships in port.

A shout carried across the waters, drawing Logan's attention back to the passengers waiting to board the ocean liner. A woman stood before the pair of sailors, gesturing wildly in their faces. Logan couldn't pick out her words on the wind, but the reaction of the guards was all the interpretation he needed. While one remained at his post, the second caught the woman around the waist and hoisted her onto his shoulder.

A high-pitched shriek echoed from the nearby buildings as the woman was sent flying, followed by a splash as her unexpected dunk disturbed the calm waters. There was a moment's silence as all eyes in the harbour turned to where the woman had disappeared, before she finally surfaced, coughing and spluttering.

"Guess she didn't have her ticket," Logan murmured, a smile tugging at his lips as he saw Dustin approaching the front of the line. He reached into his pocket and drew out the token, running it between his fingers in anticipation.

At twenty years of age, he should have had the chance to prove himself long ago.

The line of passengers kept their eyes carefully averted from the woman as she dragged herself onto a neighbouring dock. Closer now to where Logan hid, he could see this was not a woman of class. Far from the lavish gowns of the aristocracy—or even landed gentry such as his family—she wore a pair of men's pants and tunic, with a dagger on her hip.

Logan frowned as she stalked past his hiding place. Those on the docks with his brother looked to be a rougher crowd as well, their clothing tattered and hair unkempt. Most carried knives or sabres, even the odd pistol, but they certainly weren't soldiers. Doubt touched Logan. The papers on his brother's desk had said little about the expedition itself. He'd assumed it was another voyage into the highlands, where Dustin had spent much of the past few years.

It must be, he reassured himself. *They're probably highlanders themselves, returning north Dustin.*

He rested a hand on the pommel of his father's sabre, but it did little to calm his nerves.

On the other dock, Dustin finally reached the front of the queue. The guards barred his path while he searched the satchel hanging over his shoulder, presumably for his papers and token. Even from a dozen yards away, Logan could read the confusion on his brother's face. Despite his doubts, he found himself grinning again. Surely if he could outmanoeuvre his famed brother, he could survive a little expedition in the north.

Finally, Dustin looked up from the satchel and spread his hands. The guards exchanged a look before advancing on him. Dustin didn't even try to avoid them. His voice rang out as they grabbed him.

"Cordelia Leif!"

The name froze the pair of guards in place. After a moment's hesitation, they released Dustin and stepped back, doubt now etched across their meaty faces. The elder of the Kaine brothers only folded his arms, one finger tapping at his elbow.

No, no, no…

Logan's heart was suddenly thundering. Surely Dustin couldn't sweet-talk his way out of this one.

A woman appeared at the railings of the steamship. Dressed in a woollen trench coat with a sabre on one hip, revolver on the other, she looked more the part of pirate than sailor. The tricorn hat holding her greying locks in place only served to enhance the image.

Her gaze lingered on Dustin. He stared back, the hint of a smile tugging at his lips, before finally she waved a hand in a curt gesture. Immediately, the guards snapped to attention and stepped aside. Nodding his thanks, Dustin strode up the ramp onto the steamship.

Logan slumped to the wooden boards of the broken fishing ship. So much for outsmarting his brother. Just as he always had, Dustin was one step ahead. Cordelia was obviously the captain of the vessel; he must have arranged passage with her personally. Typical.

The token rang like a bell as it slipped from Logan's fingers and struck the deck. He watched it spin, before finally settling against the wooden boards. He wanted to hurl it into the harbour, but he hesitated, glancing back at the ship.

Dustin was just disappearing down a stairwell beneath the deck.

Maybe...

The guards didn't appear to have a list of passengers, only the tokens. If Logan boarded while his brother was below, no one would be the wiser that he didn't belong. And if he avoided his brother's notice until they were out to sea...well, by then it would be too late to turn back.

His heart thrummed to the beat of the distant steam engine as he plucked the token off the deck. Leaping back to the docks, Logan set off at a run. The passengers waiting on the opposite berth had dwindled to a trickle now, the last of them moving quickly to present their tokens and board. Pounding up the steps to the street, Logan darted along to the next set of stairs.

Only there did he slow, taking the chance to compose himself again. Straightening his overcoat, he squared his shoulders and set his jaw. He would need to be convincing if he wanted to pull this off. Ahead, the twin chimneys of *The Rising Tide* puffed black smoke as the great paddle wheel began to turn.

You can do this.

He lifted a foot, only for a dark cloaked man to push past him.

"Sorry, kid," a voice called back as the stranger thumped down the wooden steps. "In a bit of a rush!"

Thrown off-balance, Logan scowled after the man, before the sounding of a horn snapped him back to his more pressing concern. Men and women dressed in the tatty clothing of sailors raced about the steamship, readying ropes and raising the mainsail that would complement the power of the steam wheel.

It looked as though the ship would be departing any second. Cursing, Logan abandoned all pretence of dignity and raced down the dock. Ahead, the dark-cloaked man produced his token with a flourish. The guards paused only long enough to inspect the metal disk before waving the stranger aboard. They were about to follow, when the sound of Logan's approach must have caught the attention of one.

He turned back as Logan stumbled up.

"Got a...token...for one." His chest was heaving and he barely managed to get out the words.

The guard who'd lingered raised an eyebrow as Logan presented his token. "Little young, aren't you lad?" Even so, he reached out and took the coin. Logan noticed two of the fingers from his right hand were missing.

Logan nodded his thanks but did not respond to the question. He was used to people questioning his age. Unlike his father and elder brother, he didn't have the muscular physique of a born warrior. Seven hells, he barely had a beard. He was relieved when the man waved him aboard.

Only as he stepped onto the metal ramp and felt the harsh vibrations of the steam engine beneath his feet did Logan's earlier reservations come rushing back.

Suddenly his heart was racing and needles were prickling his scalp. What was he doing? He wasn't a hero like his brother or father. He didn't even know how to use the blade he wore at his waist. He had no place on this expedition, not with dubious sailors who threw women into the harbour, nor the passengers and their knives and swords and guns.

"You coming aboard, kid? Don't know about you, but I'm fairly eager to see the back of this city."

The voice had come from above. Logan's head jerked up and found the dark-cloaked man from earlier leaning against the iron railings. He wore a condescending smile on his lips as he waved for Logan to hurry up.

Logan's stomach twisted itself into a knot. Three times in as many minutes now he'd been called a kid, or worse. That was how everyone had viewed him his entire life. Dustin, his father, even this stranger, they all saw him as a child.

It rankled. Logan might lack the natural charm of his brother, might not possess the strength of their father, but he was a man grown. Flashing the man a glare, he continued the rest of the way up the ramp and boarded *The Rising Tide*.

It was past time Logan chose his own path.

3

ZACHARY

Leaning against the gunwales of *The Rising Tide*, Zach watched as the young man disappeared into the crowds lining the deck of the steamship. He shook his head. The kid's pale tufts of facial hair suggested he wasn't long out of his teen years. What was he doing on an expedition like this?

The close-cropped blond hair and cavalry sabre he wore might offer some suggestion. Both were popular among the gentry class, especially the children of the military sorts. Another young man looking to make a name for himself, no doubt. Not in itself a dark mark against the kid, but it certainly wasn't a glowing commendation. His parents might have worked their way up from more humble origins, but the children of gentry tended to be a mixed basket, fluctuating from wildly arrogant to surprisingly down to earth.

The Rising Tide rocked gently as the last two sailors on the docks removed the last of the mooring ropes and leapt across the widening gap to re-join the rest of the crew. If

Zach was disappointed with his fellow passengers, he was less than impressed with the ship itself. The 'great ocean steamer' had turned out to be less ship, more a collection of rusted steel panels held together by rivets. The paint on the hull was bubbling in patches, flaking in others, revealing the copper corrosion beneath. And the harsh vibration beneath his feet felt worryingly like the engine was about to fail—or worse. He feared the entire vessel might fall to pieces the second they hit open waters.

Yes, all and all, he was less than impressed.

On the other hand, they were away.

Zach found himself smiling as the port of Leith drifted away, satisfied with his night's work. Any number of eventualities might have thrown him off-schedule, not least of which was the body he'd left behind in the Whitfield manor. He'd half-expected the authorities to be waiting at the docks, but clearly no one else in the household had known of the missing documents that would have pointed them to *The Rising Tide.*

He moved to the stern and leaned against the gunwales for one last look at the city. Tall towers loomed at either end of the harbour, protection against the pirates that had once roamed the eastern seaboard, while the spires of castle hill rose in the distant sky. Terraced houses lined the shore. Their slate roofs and narrow living quarters were more characteristic of the south than the thatched cottages of the highlands. Each stretched up three or four storeys to overlook the quiet waters. He and Margery had once considered renting one of those upper apartments, with their pristine views and morning sunshine, before they'd settled on the cottage in the countryside...

Six months.

The words of the physician cut through the cheerful memories. That had been three months ago now, a few days before the great storm. He'd gone to the woman when he started coughing up blood, at Margery's insistence. He regretted that now. Better not to know, to live his last few months in peace, than to suffer the torture of waiting, of knowing.

Shivering, Zach gave his home city a final nod, then forced his thoughts to the path ahead. He had few misgivings about the likely fate of this expedition. The other passengers on *The Rising Tide* might believe they were setting off in search of treasure and riches, but that was the problem with relying on gossip and rumour. They had a habit of sending men to early graves.

But Zach's gravestone had already been inscribed, its date set just a few months hence. The physician had said he needed a miracle. Well, he would find it on this mystical island.

Or die trying.

The other passengers packed the main platform of the steamship, but there was a raised upper deck that looked to be quiet, so Zach made his way towards a nearby stairwell to escape the jostling. The numbers surprised him, given the uncertainty of their destination. He would like to meet whichever captain had convinced so many to part with their hard-earned gold on such a gamble. They were clearly a man after his own heart.

Climbing the stairs, Zach found there was a third level to the ship, though this was smaller, consisting only of the bridge from which the captain steered. Large glass windows looked out in all directions. He glimpsed a shapely figure behind the glass, hands on an enormous wheel.

A woman, then, he thought to himself, tucking that information away for later.

For now though, Zach took advantage of the quiet of the upper deck to move to the front of the vessel. The hull lifted as the steamship rounded the rocky point that sheltered the harbour and made for open seas. Cries followed as the ship dropped into the first of the ocean swells, sending water splashing over the sides and drenching those standing nearest the gunwales.

Zach chuckled at the chaos. He recognised a few of the passengers from his days in the underground, but many others were new to him. He'd been out of the game too long. Studying the dark-cloaked rogues that would be his rivals, Zach couldn't help but feel a pang of jealously. Those below still carried the energy of youth, their beards untouched by age, their lives stretching out far in front of them. While Zach...

With an effort of will, he forced his attention to the smaller cluster of men and women which had gathered near the stern. Dressed in expensive overcoats and furs, these were the landed gentry along with a sprinkling of nobility. He spotted the kid near the front; one of the few standing alone.

The ship was chugging along at a decent pace now, the harsh thrumming of the engine radiating up through his boots. The whirr and clanking of the giant wheel drowned out the crashing of the waves as it propelled them forward.

Zach allowed his mind to drift. Despite the clear morning, fog marred the eastern horizon, the heavy clouds hiding any hint of their destination.

The impossible island, Zachary thought to himself, then snorted.

It still seemed a fantasy. If not for the quality of his sources, he wouldn't have given the rumours a second thought. Even now he wasn't sure what to believe. Maybe they would slip beyond the lines of the naval blockade, only to find the entire thing a fiction, an invention by the King's Council to distract from the disaster of the storm.

What a disappointment that would be, Zach found himself thinking. *Then you'd have to go back.*

Back to Leith, back to those he'd abandoned, to his responsibilities.

Back to a slow, protracted death.

Finding his jaw clenched, Zach reached for his pipe. No point lingering on what he couldn't change. Drawing out a small container of tobacco, he filled the pipe and lit it with the brass lighter. He found himself watching the crew below.

Not your average sailors, he thought to himself.

The crew of *The Rising Tide* were well-muscled and scarred. Several were missing limbs or fingers. Ex-soldiers, he suspected. Or mercenaries, hired as extra muscle for the expedition in case any passengers proved difficult. Zach couldn't blame the captain; having seen the manifest, he wouldn't trust most of the names aboard as far as he could throw them. Which he supposed could well prove literal, given the earlier incident with the woman in the harbour.

Away to starboard, the sun rose slowly through the clouds as *The Rising Tide* steamed northward. According to the captain's secretary, they would continue all day along the eastern coast, before veering east towards their true destination under the cover of night.

Puffing on his pipe, Zach considered his fellow passengers. What could have drawn so many on such a voyage? The rumours of new lands to explore were tempting, it was true. For the young and eager of the gentry class, the chance to make a name for themselves was strong motivation.

As for Zach's former associates…well, members of Leith's underground were driven by baser needs. They could sniff out the opportunity for gain like a bloodhound to the fox. The fact the Council had involved themselves, using a naval blockade to keep the people of Riogachd from the Anomaly, well, that would only have encouraged Zach's former comrades to investigate.

Clanging came from nearby as another passenger climbed the iron steps. A woman appeared on the landing, hesitating as she saw Zach. Her ocean-blue eyes narrowed, watching him from beneath a fringe of scarlet hair. After several heartbeats, she finished her ascent and crossed to the opposite railing, her tall Hessian boots clicking loudly on the metal floor. Like the other women Zach had seen so far onboard, she wore men's trousers and a functional greatcoat. Unlike the other women—most of whom had come as part of larger groups—the parting of her coat revealed the hilt of a pistol worn on her belt.

The sight of the weapon made Zach's fingers twitch, but he offered her a polite nod rather than reaching for his knives. Given the unusual mix of classes aboard, tensions were already high. No need for misunderstandings before they even set sight on the island. The captain had already demonstrated her readiness to deal with unruly customers, and the swim would be much farther now than that of the last passenger to cause a scene.

"Fine morning, ma'am," Zach greeted the stranger instead, adopting his best imitation of a gentleman.

The woman flicked him a second glance but did not reply. Judging from the fiery hair and pale skin, she probably came from the highlands. Most clans spoke the national dialect nowadays, but those farther north still kept to themselves, holding to tradition and trading only occasionally with the south. They'd been behind the uprising twenty years ago. He was just beginning to wonder whether the woman hailed from one such group when she finally spoke.

"It would be finer without the company," she said with a gesture at those huddled below. Her accent, each word running together without pause, confirmed her highland origin.

Zach took a last puff from his pipe then emptied the bowl and tucked it back into his jacket. Below, some of the crowd had dispersed—presumably to their cramped quarters in the hull—but plenty of others lingered. They crowded the railings, eyes fixed to the east, as though the Anomaly might appear from the clouds at any moment. Zach chuckled as another surge of water splashed over the side, drenching the unwary.

"I'll admit, our fellows don't seem to be of the greatest renown," he replied, allowing a touch of highland twang into his words. "Though I am sure what they lack in experience they more than make up for in their youthful enthusiasm."

"Opportunistic thieves and treasure hunters." The woman's response was curt and to the point.

"The usual sort, in my experience," Zach replied, then narrowed his eyes, casting another glance at the woman. "You, however, appear to be something of an anomaly. What brings an esteemed lady of the highlands into the presence of such rogues and scoundrels?"

The hint of a smile tugged at the woman's lips. It slipped away as her gaze drifted eastwards. "There are questions for which I need answers," she said at last. Zach frowned, but the woman shook herself before he could press the point, her eyes returning to him. "And what of yourself, stranger?" she asked, stepping away from the railing. "In general, I find southerners easy to read. But you…are not like the others."

Zach's pulse quickened under the woman's scrutiny. There was a glimmer in her eyes, a hint of darkness, of understanding. He quickly pasted a false grin on his lips.

"Oh you know, just another thief from Leith looking to make a name for himself," he said, taking on a commoner's accent now.

"I see." The woman eyed him a moment longer. "And what is your name, lowlander?"

Zachary hesitated before giving the answer. "Zachary Sicario."

"Willow of Dìonadair," the woman replied, then leaned her head to the side, as if curious. "Tell me, Zachary Sicario. What are you running from?"

A chill breeze blew across Zach's neck. He froze in place, heart suddenly racing as he found those sapphire eyes watching him. A denial was already on his lips, but those eyes told him she already knew the truth—or at least a part of it. How had she seen through his façade?

"If I am running, it is from a fate from which I cannot escape," he said at last, finally managing to shake himself. Though he could not regain the easy smile.

"No fate is set in stone, lowlander," came the woman's reply, "though perhaps you would do better to throw yourself from this ship, than to face what waits for us within the storm. There are tales of our destination, amongst your people, and mine."

"What are you talking about?"

"Your legends speak of a war amongst the Gods, yes?"

"I'm having some vague flashbacks to some old priests and their sermons," Zach replied, only half in jest. Some thieves left a coin every week at their local shrine to Edris, the Old Goddess of theft and mischief, but he'd never been the religious sort. "This war, it was the reason they left our lands, right? After the enemy was destroyed, burned in the seven hells, they retired to some other realm. Paradise or something." He frowned. "I didn't think you highlanders followed the Old Gods?"

"We do not accept your Old Gods, no," Willow replied, "but our legends also speak of a war amongst our peoples, against a clan steeped in dark magics. But in our stories, the enemy was not destroyed, but banished from our lands."

Zachary shook his head. "What does this have to do with anything?"

"I do not know, lowlander," she said in answer, her eyes turning to the eastern horizon. "Only that we are warned to watch for their return."

She fell silent at that, and Zach found himself thinking of the mythology of his own people. Weren't the southern priests always warning of the return of the Old Gods? There'd definitely been something about wrath and retribution against the unbelievers when the priests had been preaching to the children of the streets.

He shook himself. Magical islands were one thing, fearing the vengeance of mythical Gods that had not been seen in a thousand years was another thing entirely. A hush hung over the ship as it rose on the ocean swells. Sea spray fell between them, but the woman said no more. Finally Zach shrugged.

"I will leave you to your watch, ma'am," he said, refining his accent once more and offering a nod.

He cast her words from his mind as he turned away. There was enough to worry him without concerning himself with the affairs of Gods. He set his eyes instead on the stairs to the bridge.

It was time he met whoever was in charge of this madness.

❦ 4 ❦

LOGAN

Standing on the bow of *The Rising Tide*, fear and excitement warred in Logan's heart.

A part of him could hardly believe he'd done this: slipping away from his family, smuggling himself onto a ship, setting off on an adventure for lands unknown.

It was exhilarating.

And terrifying.

Watching the vast waters, Logan found his knees trembling. Blood pounded so loud in his ears that he feared it would deafen him. Each *thump* of a wave upon the hull, every lurch, even the harsh cawing of the gulls had his heart clasped in a vice. Only the white-knuckled grip he maintained on the railings kept him from crumbling.

He'd kept his head low while boarding *The Rising Tide*, lest his brother discover him before they left the port. What a disappointment that would have been, being sent back to the family manor before the expedition had even begun.

Now it was all Logan could manage to keep himself from running to his brother with his tail between his legs.

Another wave crashed over the bow. Logan winced as icy droplets lashed his flesh, crouching lower against the meagre shelter offered by the gunwales. Unlike the paying passengers, he had no cabin to which he could retreat—not unless he truly wanted to announce himself to his brother. And whatever his fears, Logan wasn't that desperate. Not yet.

Drawing his overcoat closer about himself, he huddled against the gunwale and tried to ignore the shivering that had begun in his extremities. The sun was dipping lower on the western horizon. Winter solstice was fast approaching and the days were unbearably short now, even when he'd had the warmth of the family solar to enjoy.

With each passing hour, seawater seeped slowly through his coat. It wouldn't be long before what remained of his excitement turned to misery.

Logan tried to concentrate on his fellow passengers. He'd placed himself near the fore of *The Rising Tide*, where other members of the landed gentry had gathered. In their colourful silk and cotton clothing, it hadn't been difficult to distinguish them from the ruffians who mingled around the rest of vessel. Though Logan had to admit, many of their outfits seemed somewhat impractical for an expedition. The thin cloaks worn by many had not lasted long in the harsh winds before their owners had been forced below deck. Logan's woollen overcoat might not have been the latest fashion, but it was certainly practical in the chill climate.

At least they weren't soldiers. Much as Logan wanted to prove himself, finding himself in the middle of a pitched battle wasn't how he wanted to start.

The pair standing closest to Logan seemed better equipped than most, with heavy felt cloaks and hoods lined with fur. Each wore a longsword sheathed over their shoulders. Unlike most other passengers, these two had remained at the railings long past the point when Logan's fingers had lost all feeling. Wondering what madness could keep the two out in these conditions, he quietly edged his way closer to them.

A frown creased the woman's pale features as she stared towards the east, blonde locks fluttering beneath her hood. Logan recognised the tension she carried about herself, the way her delicate fingers tapped at the railing, the tightness to her lips. Every thump of the ship as it fell down a wave caused her to flinch and her eyes to flicker closed, before she bared her teeth and forced them open again. She was trying to hide her nerves, but her expression made it seem as though she expected at any moment for a kraken to rise from the depths and swallow them whole.

Her companion, however, could have been her opposite. He kept his hood off, revealing jet-black hair carefully styled into spikes. Logan wondered if that was the reason he kept his hood off, though surely that would be madness in these conditions. As much as it screamed out his common blood, Logan had long since pulled the woollen cap from his knapsack to fend off the chill.

However, it was not the man's lack of sensibilities that contrasted with the woman at his side, but his wild grin. He showed none of the woman's fear as he looked to the east with a glean of excitement in his eyes. More than that, there was…expectation in that look.

"I'm telling you, Amilyse," the man's words carried on the wind. "This is it. This time we'll find it, I can *feel* it..."

Logan stumbled as another wave rocked the ship, and missed whatever the man had been about to say. By the time he righted himself, they'd already returned their eyes to the distant clouds. The woman's face was hidden now by her hood, but her hand had risen to her shoulder and lingered now at the hilt of her sword.

Logan was about to interrupt their contemplations to ask what they were searching for, but at that moment, a voice spoke from behind him.

"So it *was* you, brother. I must say, I am impressed."

The hairs on Logan's neck stood on end as he turned and found his older brother settled at the railings alongside him. Dustin was several inches taller than Logan's five-foot-seven, and better built as well, his shoulders and arms well-muscled. No surprise there. He took after their father, after all.

Little Logan took after their mother's slim figure.

Swallowing his surprise, Logan forced himself to look into his brother's blue eyes. He expected to see anger there, but Dustin wore an easy smile on his striking features. His finely chiselled cheeks and long black hair had won him plenty of female admirers in his teen years. That, at least, Dustin had gotten from their mother—their father might have fought in a dozen battles and dragged himself up through the ranks of the army, but he was a long stretch from good-looking.

"Wh...what?" Logan managed at last, caught off-guard by his brother's grin.

Dustin laughed, the sound full of mirth. "When I found the token missing, I wondered. But in truth, I did not think you had the nerve!"

Logan stood gaping at his brother, his wits lying in shredded fragments. "I...you're ah, not angry?"

"Not at all, brother! It's past time you left the nest." He paused, eyes lingering on the sabre Logan wore on his waist. "Though Father might be...less pleased."

"Ah..."

"Relax, brother!" Dustin replied easily, slapping Logan on the back. "Such are worries for another day. Tell me, how are you enjoying your first adventure?"

Dustin's words finally pierced the fog of Logan's surprise. "You wanted me to come?" He'd hardly seen his brother the past decade, not since Dustin had left on his first campaign. That hadn't been long after the plague that had swept through Riogachd...

"Of course." Dustin's face grew serious, losing his familiar smile. The light was beginning to fade, the sun setting behind them, staining the horizon red. "I am sorry, brother," Dustin continued at last. "I should have visited more often, after Mother..."

His words surprised Logan. "You were busy...being a hero," he said softly.

"A hero?" Dustin chuckled. "I've been many things, brother. I'm not sure a hero is one of them. Truth is, I practically fled Leith after Mother passed. I felt I had become a stranger in my own city. It wasn't until I left on my first expedition that I found some meaning in my life."

Logan hesitated at his brother's words. "What *was* your first expedition? I have heard the stories of the pirates…"

Dustin chuckled. "Greatly exaggerated, I assure you." He paused. "My first expedition was nothing so grand as that. The college in Leith had organised a dig in the highlands, on an island in one of the lochs up there. There is great interest back in Londinium about the past civilisations of Riogachd. One I have come to share. Though back then, I was mostly excited about seeing action. Not that there was much expectation of that. Father suggested I join as an extra pistol and sword, in case of unrest amongst the clans."

A lump lodged in Logan's throat. Their father had never made even the hint of a suggestion that Logan try something similar.

"They were long, cold days and nights, brother," Dustin remarked, as though reading his thoughts. "You haven't missed much."

"You said you found yourself up there."

Dustin scratched his chin. "I suppose I did," he said, then grinned. "Ah well, better late than never, right?"

Logan nodded, though he couldn't bring himself to smile. His heart fluttered as he looked out over the dark waters. The winter winds howled through the chimney behind them and shivering, he drew his coat tighter.

"So where are we going now?" he asked.

The smile fell from Dustin's face and he looked away—though not before Logan caught the glint in his eyes.

"That first expedition changed my life in more ways than one, little brother," he replied, the softness gone from his tone. "I met friends, comrades, and…others. Without any fighting to be done, the researchers had me help with the dig itself. And one day, I uncovered something…"

With the words, Dustin drew his hands from his pockets, lifting something up to the light of a nearby lantern. Squinting, Logan leaned closer, struggling to make out what his brother held. It was a piece of crystal—maybe quartz—its clouded surface flickering in the firelight.

"What is it?" he asked, curiosity piqued.

"That's just it, isn't it? No one knows. Long ago, there was an ancient people who lived on the highland lakes. They built houses on stilts over the waters, single chambers large enough to home entire families. But a thousand years ago, all trace of their presence vanished. Without the people to maintain them, their houses collapsed back into the lakes, forming tiny islands—and tombs in which their secrets remain hidden to this day. I found this on that first expedition, in the ruins of one such island."

Logan looked from the stone to his brother. "Shouldn't it be in a museum somewhere?"

"Probably," Dustin replied with a shrug, the smile still fixed to his face. "It's quartz, but of a sort unlike any found in the highlands. It seems to have been shaped and polished by human hands, so its owner obviously held it in some value. But there is a flaw in the crystal, something inside that caught my attention." He passed it to Logan.

He hesitated before taking the artefact. There was a slight warmth to the stone, leftover no doubt from Dustin's pocket. It was pleasant with icy wind whipping across the deck, cutting into his bare hands. Clutching the crystal tighter, he held it up to the light. Only then did he see what his brother meant, the shadow within the crystal facets. More than a shadow—there was a shape inside, something with form.

"It's a fossil," he realised at last, looking at his brother for confirmation.

"Yes," Dustin replied.

"That's not possible, is it?"

He'd found a fossil himself once, when he'd been just a child on a rare trip to the southern coast of Riogachd. In the sandstone cliffs which lined the beaches there, he'd noticed the strange pattern and investigated, finding the remains of an ancient sea creature, the spirals of its shell barely discernible amidst the layers of stone.

But as far as he was aware, fossils formed in stone, not crystal.

"I would agree with you," Dustin replied, "if not for the artefact in your hands. I have never been able to determine what manner of creature was preserved within."

Logan raised the crystal to his eye again. The last light of day had faded now, and the great ship surged its way on through the dark seas, steam engine thumping in the night. Light flickered from a nearby lantern, but its glow was dim, not enough to light the railings before them, let alone the murky depths of the crystal.

Even so, Logan noticed something he had not before. The light that shone from the crystal facets…it seemed too bright to come from the lantern.

"Is it…"

"Glowing?" Dustin nodded. "That…is a more recent development."

Logan lowered the stone, his heart beginning to race. What was he holding in his hands? "How recently?"

The easy smile slipped from Dustin's lips. "As I said, on my journeys I have developed an interest in the arcane. But all these years, I have learned nothing of this artefact. I had given up, and was using it as a paperweight on my desk in Londinium," he admitted. "That is, until late one night a few months ago, when it suddenly lit up like the sun. Only for a few seconds, but when it died, well, that glow remained."

Logan shivered, following Dustin's gaze out over the dark waters.

"The storm?" he whispered.

Dustin nodded.

Finally, Logan realised what he'd missed earlier: the sun had set behind them. As it had fallen and their conversation had stretched into the night, *The Rising Tide* had changed course. They were no longer heading north into the highlands, but east—towards the clouds.

Towards what had been dubbed the Anomaly on the streets of Leith.

Suddenly cold, Logan tried to pass the stone back to his brother, but Dustin shook his head. "You hold onto it for me, brother. Perhaps fresh eyes will help to unlock its secrets."

"What does it mean?" Logan whispered, looking at the crystal in his hands.

Dustin laughed and clapped him on the back again. "That's what we're going to find out, little brother."

❦ 5 ❦

ZACHARY

Zachary paused at the entrance to the bridge, Willow's words still lingering in his ears.

What are you running from?

He hated it when people saw through his façade—even when that someone was clearly a madwoman. What had all that nonsense about the Gods and ancient civilisations been about? Still, there was no point lingering on the encounter. He wanted a better understanding of who was organising this expedition, preferably before they reached the Anomaly. That way he could plan his next steps for the island.

Steeling himself, he pushed open the door to the bridge. A cloud of tobacco smoke billowed out to greet him. He swallowed a mouthful before he could stop himself, and the coughing fit was upon him. A fiery pain wrapped around his chest as he hacked up what felt like half his lungs. A taste like iron filled his mouth and gasping, he struggled to draw breath between wheezes. It was a long minute before the bout finally left him.

Drawing a handkerchief from his pocket, he surreptitiously wiped the blood from his lips, aware of the pair of steel-grey eyes that watched him.

The captain of *The Rising Tide* looked to be a woman in her early fifties, her hair streaked as much by grey as the black of her youth. The parting in her trench coat revealed both a revolver and sabre on her broad hips. Just now, her hand was resting on the hilt of the first. Despite the smoke inside the bridge, she held no pipe, though the ends of a cigar lay in a tray beside the tiller.

"I'd apologise for the smoke," she said, narrow eyebrows lifting to crease the wrinkles of her brow, "but passengers aren't meant to be in here. Do I need to call one of my boys to show you to your cabin?"

Offering a sheepish smile, Zach spread his hands. "I come in peace." With a flourish, he drew his pipe from his coat. "And bearing gifts, if you'll share a little warmth."

The woman's eyes narrowed, but ignoring their steely glint, Zach crossed to the brazier burning in the corner and stretched his hands towards the heat. The winds outside carried the chill of winter.

"Not as young as I once was," he explained, "the ice seems to get into my bones nowadays." He flashed a grin over his shoulder. "But I'm sure a young lass like yourself isn't bothered by the frailties of us old men."

The captain chuckled. "Still the platitudes, Mr. Sicario. There is at least as much silver in my curls as your own."

Zachary froze. Their gazes locked from across the room and he felt the weight of the woman's appraisal, even as he inspected her in return.

"I am afraid you have me at a disadvantage, ma'am," he said finally. "You know my name, but I do not know yours?"

The woman raised an eyebrow. "Are you telling me the famed Zachary Sicario does not even know whose ship he has smuggled himself onto?"

Zach's heart, which was already pounding at her earlier words, truly began to race now. Even so, he kept his voice cool as he held her gaze.

"I'm afraid time was rather short. I did not uncover much about who had organised the expedition," he replied, even as his hand dropped to the knife he kept at his belt, the largest of his collection. "Now I'll ask again: how do you know my name?"

"Now, now, Mr. Sicario, there's no need for threats," the captain murmured, even as she stepped around him and shifted the tiller a degree towards the east. She moved with the rolling gait of a sailor—unlike much of her crew.

Through the windows of the bridge, the sun had reached its winter zenith and now crept ever closer towards the western horizon. As the ship moved, Zachary glimpsed a shadow beneath the door—one of her men, or perhaps several, were waiting outside.

Completing her adjustment, the captain leaned against the wheel. "I thought you were offering an old lady a smoke?"

Zach's mind raced over her words, trying to decipher their meaning. This woman knew who he was. If she'd wanted him disposed of, he would already be resting at the bottom of the ocean. Of that he had no doubt.

That left only one conclusion—she wanted something from him.

Outwardly, he kept the easy smile on his lips. Greed he could use. "Apologies, Captain, I seem to have forgotten my manners."

With another flourish, he added a measured finger of leaf into the bowl of his pipe, then drew the beloved lighter from his pocket and offered it to the captain. "Would you do the honours…?" He left the question dangling, hoping to finally get a name from the secretive captain.

"Cordelia," she answered, "Captain Cordelia of Leith, to riffraff like yourself," she added as she took the offered pipe and lighter. Igniting the tobacco, she raised it to her lips and inhaled. "Now," she continued, exhaling a smoke ring, "what are you doing on my ship, Mr. Sicario?"

Zach leaned back against one of the windows, contemplating the question. Now that he knew her title, he could put together a few of the missing pieces. The infamous Cordelia of Leith had a few exploits of her own, not the least of which was smuggling a shipment of supplies to the king's forces during the civil war twenty years ago. It was rumoured she'd then done the same for the rebellion.

Recovering his pipe from the captain, he drew in a lungful of the pungent smoke, still appraising the woman at the tiller. It burned his throat, but prepared for its acrid taste, he resisted another bout of coughing.

Cordelia was a smuggler who played both sides—that suggested she didn't intend any outright treachery. She would simply be looking to maximise her return from this expedition, wherever the wild winds of the Northern Sea brought them.

"Hoping to pass unnoticed, for starters. I guess that's out the window."

Cordelia chuckled. "Well, when you go around threatening secretaries, that tends to attract some attention."

Zachary snorted. "I barely touched her."

"She said you held a knife to her throat."

"Yes, well, I left her a gold crown for the trouble."

"Oh?" Cordelia raised her eyebrows. "The little tramp didn't mention that."

"Ah…" Zachary hadn't meant to report on the poor woman. "Anyway, I never told the woman my name."

"No, but the description was enough to pique my interest. And when word reached me of the…events at the Whitfield Palace, well, the deeds matched your reputation."

"It was really more of a manor…" Zach muttered, then shook his head and levered himself up from the wall. "An unfortunate incident, I'll admit. Though honestly, I was surprised to find nobles in your manifest."

"They tend to have the gold to compensate for their passage," Cordelia replied, "unlike certain stowaways. Tell me, Mr. Sicario, how *do* you intend to pay for your place on my ship?"

"I thought I already had," Zach replied with a lopsided grin. "Having a man like Roy Whitfield onboard would have cost you far more in trouble than his fare was worth." He hesitated. "Which, regardless, I believe you collected in advance."

Silence fell between them. The two eyed each other as the engine thrummed beneath their feet, the light outside slowly fading as the short winter's day came to an end. Then abruptly, the captain burst out in laughter.

"Oh, I like your style, Sicario," she said at last, wiping an imaginary tear of mirth from her eye. "Tell me, would you like to know why you're still standing here, rather than at the bottom of the ocean?"

"I'd like to think it's because of my winning personality," Zach replied.

As quickly it had appeared, all hint of humour drained from the woman's face. Jaw hardening, she took a step towards him, hand dropping to the pistol on her belt, one finger tap-tapped at its hilt.

"Let me rephrase that, Mr. Sicario," she said, an edge creeping into her voice. "Why should I not call my men in here right now and have you thrown overboard?"

Zach swallowed. Despite her earlier cheerfulness, the glint in Cordelia's eyes was deadly serious. He looked out the window, towards the clouded eastern horizon. He hadn't come on this voyage to make enemies.

"Information," he said at last, turning from the hidden visage to answer the captain. "That's what I can offer you, Cordelia."

The captain said nothing, only raised an eyebrow, waiting for Zach to continue.

Zachary obliged. "You still don't know what it is we're looking for out here, do you?" He watched her as he spoke, registering the slightest crease that wrinkled her forehead. "You know it's got to be important, with the King's Council protecting it. You wanted in, so you organised this expedition, right?"

The hint of a smile tugged at Cordelia's lips. "Just go on, Mr. Sicario. I'm waiting to see whether you have a point to all this, before I see the weights attached to your ankles."

Zach was thrown off by her reaction. Was he wrong? Did she already know what the Council was protecting? It hadn't been *that* difficult, getting the truth from the soldier, but then, such were the rumours spreading through town, it was difficult to sift fact from the fictions.

"Whatever your reasons for putting this expedition together," he continued, throwing caution to the wind. "I don't take you as a woman who settles for crumbs when a feast is on the offering. If even a fraction of the rumours are true, the Anomaly could be the key to untold wealth. You must want a part of that treasure."

A chuckle rasped from the back of Cordelia's throat. "And I suppose you'd be willing to share?"

"Share?" Zach smirked. "What makes you think I'm interested in the treasure at all, captain?"

"You expect me to believe you've become a philanthropist in your old age, Mr. Sicario?"

"Let us say that in my advanced years, I no longer care for what worldly riches we might find on the island."

Cordelia's eyebrow, which was already arcing high enough to wrinkle her forehead, rose until it all but disappeared into her greying locks.

"You and I are of a similar age, Mr. Sicario...." The captain trailed off, her eyes narrowing as the import of Zach's words sank in. "Island, did you say?"

Zachary allowed his grin to spread as his gaze returned to the cloud bank to the east. Now that the light had faded from the day, he thought he caught flashes of light amongst the grey.

"Surely you did not set out on such a venture without first learning the truth about your destination, captain?"

The floor scuffed beneath Cordelia's boots as she joined him at the window. "If your information is correct, your resources are greater than my own. Too many rumours on the streets to know which are true. An island of gold, the edge of the world, gateway to another realm, all of them seem fanciful. Not even the aristocrats have managed to drag that secret out of the Council."

"It is an island," Zach confirmed, then hesitated, thinking of the other story the soldier had told, of the disappearing ship.

He looked at the captain from the corner of his eye, still trying to judge what manner of woman Cordelia was. Clearly not one afraid of a little danger. Still, an entire naval galley had vanished into the mist. That was enough to give even a bold woman second thoughts.

"More than that, not even my source knew the details," he said at last.

Silence answered his words. Zach forced himself to keep his eyes ahead, fixed on the distant clouds, lest his indecision give him away. If she sensed he was holding something back, that the danger posed by the Anomaly was greater than anyone suspected…well, this little adventure might end before it ever began.

"Very well, Mr. Sicario," Cordelia said at last, "you have earned a reprieve—at least for now."

Grasping the wheel, she turned it clockwise, the mechanisms within clacking as it spun. Zach stumbled as the ship rocked, surging over a wave as they turned sharply eastward. Shadows flickered on the decks below, the lanterns set around the ship rocking wildly with the movement. The cloudbank loomed ahead as they straightened out.

Most of the passengers had already disappeared into their quarters. Only a few remained, silhouettes against the dying light of the sun. As the shadows lengthened and the night's mists crept their way over the bow, Zach found he could no longer distinguish between the thieves and the gentry.

"And if I require more than a simple reprieve?" he asked suddenly.

Her lips thinned at his words, though she said nothing, eyes dancing in the light of the brazier. Beyond the panes of glass, the night was pitch-black…except, were those lights out in the darkness? The Council's blockade? At his side, Cordelia remained quiet, though he noticed now her crew moving about the deck, extinguishing lanterns.

Zach let out a long breath. He could keep quiet, land on the island alone and without allies. He still had his knives, his wits. They had been enough for him in the past. And yet, Zachary had no desire to spend his last days battling for his life. And if there was a magic on the island that could save him…well, he would need allies to uncover that secret.

Outside, the ship was dark; only a single lantern remained to light the way, shuttered to direct its light on the waters ahead. Beyond the silent ship, there was no mistaking the lights of the blockade now, their lanterns burning in the dark. Zach shivered, imagining the eyes of the soldiers that must search for them, the ears that listened. In the quiet of the bridge, the thrumming of the engines seemed incredibly loud, but beyond their cocoon of warmth, the crashing of waves drowned out all other noise.

"I would like your protection," he said as Cordelia rotated the wheel a degree. There was no trace of hesitation in the woman's eyes as she navigated the blockade—this was her life, her livelihood. "Whatever of value I find on the island is yours to keep. I want only to go about my way unhindered once we arrive."

Silence answered his request. The captain still watched the ocean, but her eyebrows had knitted into a frown as she contemplated his words. He could see the suspicion in her eyes, the doubt, and finally she shook her head.

"I don't get it, Zachary," she said, dropping the formalities, "what's your angle? Why are you here, if not for power or riches? What do you get out of all this?"

Those words rang within him, echoing the strange woman's earlier enquiries.

What are you running from?

Somehow, he kept the smile plastered to his face. "They say only the boring grow old, Cordelia," he said in answer.

I'm here to save myself.

But that was a lie too, wasn't it?

"I've lived a good life. Now I'd like to meet the Old Gods on my own terms—preferably after some rousing adventure."

I'm running away.

"One has a reputation to uphold, after all."

Running from the pain in her eyes.

Swallowing the memories, Zach offered the captain of *The Rising Tide* a final nod, then turned and stepped back into the cold embrace of night.

He made it only a few steps down the stairs before the strangeness of the night brought him to a halt. Frozen, he looked around, trying to determine the source of his unease. A stillness hung over *The Rising Tide*. Though the ship still rocked beneath him, there was something missing now to its rhythm, as though something had vanished. A voice rose behind him, muffled by the bridge, but he recognised Cordelia's cursing...

Then it struck him.

Silence.

The harsh thumping of the engine, of the furnaces as they burnt their coal, of the great wheel as it propelled them onwards, all of it had gone still, leaving only the quiet of the night.

And the pounding of waves upon the hull.

Zachary cried out as the ship pitched violently beneath his feet. Caught without power, *The Rising Tide* became a leaf against the power of the ocean. Before Zachary could brace himself, he found himself hurled off-balance. Throwing out a hand, he reached desperately for the railing, but his fingers closed on empty air.

Then he was falling, blind in the darkness.

A cry tore from Zachary's lips as the icy water enveloped him.

6

LOGAN

Logan cried out as the ship pitched wildly beneath his feet. He had just a moment to see the excitement on his brother's face turn to shock before the deck lurched again—and suddenly the railing he'd been holding was torn from his grasp.

Suddenly he was airborne. The darkness spun, and raising his arms, Logan braced for impact—only to find cold waters swallowing him up. A second scream turned to bubbles billowing around his face. Saltwater rushed to fill his mouth. Stars burst across his eyes and his lungs screamed. He thrashed, boots slipping against the currents, the bag across his shoulder and sword on his belt threatening to drag him down.

The sea swirled around him, pushing, twisting, spinning him until Logan could no longer tell up from down. All was darkness. Weakness spread through his limbs as he struggled. His eyes burning as he tried to pierce the murky depths, to find—

There!

A light flashed in the dark, golden, brilliant. He kicked out, fingers clawing at the water...

Logan gasped as he burst through the surface and sucked down desperate lungfuls of air. Red filled his vision and his stomach churned, oblivion threatening. He forced himself to breathe, clinging to the fine thread of consciousness, even as his teeth began to chatter.

Waves crashed around him as he trod water, still threatening to force him back down. The stars faded and his mind cleared, though that only brought home the significance of his peril. Something had happened to *The Rising Tide*. Somehow, he'd been thrown overboard...and so had his brother.

"*Dustin!*" he screamed, struggling to lift his voice above a croak as he turned this way and that, searching the seas around him.

There was no sign of Dustin, but to his surprise Logan found there *was* a source of light. It came from his hand, where he still held the stone Dustin had passed him. He stared at the crystal. He hadn't even realised he'd been holding it in the depths. Its light had grown, casting enough of a glow that he could see a few feet.

There was no sign of *The Rising Tide* or Dustin. He was alone, a hundred miles from land, from any sort of help. Mists hung over the waters, aglow with the light of his stone and the halfmoon beyond. Already he could feel the cold seeping into his bones, draining away his strength.

Another gasp of breath turned to a half-sob. Terror clawed its way up Logan's throat, threatening to drown him as surely as the ocean in which he floated. His heart hammered painfully in his chest. Part of him wanted to scream and scream until he could scream no more, until his brother found him, until his father came and rescued him.

He could just imagine the look on the man's face, the judgment. Heroes like his father and brother did not need to be rescued. Heroes found a way to survive, whatever the odds.

And so stifling his sobs, Logan drew in another breath, and finally managed to slow the racing of his heart. He couldn't afford to panic. The waters were cold, though not as cold as he'd expected for the depths of winter. And he was a good swimmer. He and his brother had often snuck away to the local swimming hole as children. Even in summer, the stream had been colder than the water now. A strange phenomenon, but not one he could afford to question now.

Sweeping out his hands to keep him afloat, Logan flinched as his fingers encountered something in the water. A moment later, he struck another object. Lifting his light, he saw that all around, debris bobbed in the darkness, wooden boards and broken beams and pieces of cork capped in steel.

The wreckage of a ship.

A chill that had nothing to do with the water spread through Logan. Surely it couldn't be *The Rising Tide?* He grasped one of the boards to use as a flotation device and struggled to think of some other explanation. The ship had been rocking perilously on the waves, but the steamer was so large, surely it could navigate the conditions. He hadn't seen any rocks either, not out here in the middle of the Northern Sea.

His heart was beginning to race. Logan drew another calming breath. He could do nothing about the fate of *The Rising Tide*. He couldn't even help his brother. All he could do was try and survive long enough to reach land…

Choosing a random direction, Logan started kicking—anything to distract himself from his likely fate. Now that he had the wooden board, the weight of his father's sword no longer bothered him, nor the pack slung over his shoulder. Hopefully the oilskin lining of the bag had kept its contents dry. If he somehow reached land, a change of clothing might very well save his life in the chill of winter. There was also flint to light a fire. He shivered, imagining the heat of a flame, the comfort of a warm fireplace—

A wave broke over Logan's head, driving him back into the depths. He came up spluttering, clinging desperately to the crystal with one hand, the wooden board in the other. He'd almost drifted off, almost slipped off into the realm of dream, to a place of warmth and comfort…

Logan frowned. He could see the waters ahead clearly now, the rolling waves as they emerged from the mists, their surfaces flickering, reflecting some distant light. The breath caught in Logan's throat and he lifted his gaze.

A heavy mist loomed, swallowing up the seas. In the fog, lights danced. At first he thought they must be the lanterns of the naval blockade, but…these lights were too stable for fire. They reminded him of the crystal in his hand, though they must be far brighter to pierce the heavy cloud.

The hope from the lights was short lived. Pain wormed its way slowly through Logan's body. Each stroke, each kick of his feet seemed to have less effect. Despite the unnaturally warm currents, the waters were still draining his energy, bit by bit.

The lights loomed closer, but Logan no longer paid them any attention. They were a figment, surely, of his fevered mind. What else could they be? There was nothing out here but the naval ships, and their glow had been far away when he'd stood on the bow of *The Rising Tide*, their captain steering expertly between their ranks.

Logan's eyes slid closed as weariness settled like a lead cloak around his shoulders. Exhausted, trembling, unable to even open his eyes, Logan clung to his piece of board, fingernails digging into the wood.

Darkness swirled, the lights piercing his eyelids, so that it seemed the stars themselves danced before his eyes. Lying half-stretched over the plank, he watched their shimmering glow, wishing them to become magical creatures, Gods or fae that might save him from his watery fate…

Lights spun, and Logan's pain fled as he found himself adrift in a void. The mists remained, swirling, but gone were the waters, the cold, the night. He felt a tug at his core, something within responding to the conjuration, a distant pull.

Trembling, he reached for the pinpricks of light, yearning for the promise held in their fiery glow.

Another appeared in the void, a ghost emerging from the mists. It held no form, but a part of his soul recognised the kindred spirit, the shimmer that was his brother's consciousness. Dustin's gaze was distant as he took shape, as though about to set off on another of his adventures, and Logan called out in desperation.

"Dustin!" he yelled, even as he felt a tug of the pain of his physical body, the pull of reality.

Through the mists, he saw Dustin glance back. Their eyes met across some unknown distance. A smile touched the other man's lips.

"You're alive, brother." His gaze flickered, as though searching for something else in the mists. They quickly returned to Logan. "Thank the Gods, whatever they might be."

Logan frowned at his brother's words, even as that strange realm began to fade, and the call of his body grew stronger.

"Dustin, where are you?" he cried out, panicking as his brother faded, becoming again the formless ghost.

"On the island, brother," the reply came from the mists. "Use the crystal. Find me…"

Logan gasped as he tore himself from the dream. Blood pounded in his ears, driving an ache deep into the base of his skull. His mouth was parched with the tang of salt, but he was no longer adrift. He could feel the cold stones pressed against his face, the solid earth beneath him.

He coughed and struggled to his hands and knees. Spots danced across his vision, all but blinding him, but at least they were not those strange lights of his dream. Shuddering, he clutched at the stones, grasping a handful between his fingers, still trying to convince himself they were real.

When his vision finally cleared, he found it was still night. The sky was dark and there was no sign of the lights he'd glimpsed in his fading state. The clouds had vanished. A thousand stars stretched overhead, the brilliant glow of the halfmoon shimmering in their midst—though it was fading towards the horizon as day drew near.

A look around found Logan on a rocky beach. Debris lay strewn across the stones, sheets of metal and twisted beams of wood lying dotted between spires of dark rock. Nearby, cliffs stretched towards the grey sky.

He muttered a quick prayer of thanks to Bes, Old God of good fortune. Surely the deity had been smiling upon him this night.

But where exactly had his good fortune brought him?

On the island, brother.

Logan swallowed as he recalled the dream. It had been so vivid, so real—yet it was already fading, the images sinking back into his subconscious.

He stifled a moan. His father's sword was poking uncomfortably into his side and the rest of him felt as though he'd been dragged behind a motorcoach for half a mile. He should be dead, frozen by the icy waters, sunk to the bottom of the ocean. Instead he sat on a beach that should not exist. There was no way he could have drifted back to the mainland in the space of a few hours, not after *The Rising Tide* had gone steaming out into the Northern Sea. He had heard the rumours back in Leith about the Anomaly— everyone had, but…

Now he was forced to confront reality. The debris left no doubt—their ship was gone. It had probably struck unseen rocks and been torn to pieces in the surging currents. Logan, Dustin, and everyone else aboard had been plunged into the sea. In the winter waters, it was a miracle he had survived…

Crunch.

Logan's head jerked up as the sound of footsteps on loose stones came from nearby. Something moved in the shadows of the cliff. Pushing himself into a sitting position, his eyes strained to pierce the gloom, his heart inexplicably racing. He opened his mouth to call out to whoever was there, but found the words would not come.

Crunch. Crunch. Crunch.

Step by step, the shadow drew nearer, until finally it emerged into the moonlight.

Logan swallowed a scream. The shadow was not one of his fellow passengers.

It wasn't even human.

It was darkness itself.

Beware, Outsider, you trespass on sacred crystal.

7

LOGAN

Beware, **Outsider, you trespass on sacred crystal.**

Logan flinched back from the creature, from the voice that seemed at once to come from the swirling shadows as it echoed inside his own mind. Scrambling across the gravel on hands and knees, he tried to regain his feet, and in his panic dropped the crystal fossil.

Darkness returned as the light of the stone flickered, sending shadows rippling all across the shore. The creature fused into the black, but its voice remained.

Long have we slumbered, dreaming of our revenge, it hissed from the shadows.

"Wait!" Logan yelped, the words sending spikes of terror stabbing through his heart. "I didn't...didn't mean to..." He gasped, unable to even string together a simple sentence.

The creature ignored him. ***Finally the beasts stir to wakefulness. They come. Terrible is the fate of those they find on these shores.***

Desperately, Logan scrambled through the stones of the shore, seeking the tiny spark that was the crystal fossil. A terrible darkness seemed to loom about him, darker even than night.

Their hunger fills this night. Long starved, they seek the spark of life, which for so long was denied them.

An unintelligible cry tore from Logan. He could sense the thing creeping upon him, the terrible tendrils reaching out…

Light flared to life as his fingers closed around smooth crystal, the spark in the fossil swelling to a brilliant glow, casting back the shadows. Snatching up the artefact, Logan leapt at last to his feet and swung in the direction he'd last seen the shade.

He reached for the hilt of his father's sabre, but froze as he found the creature unmoved. His blood ran cold as the light revealed the rippling shadow, a darkness that took no true form. Constantly changing, it shifted like smoke, billowing and retreating. Logan found himself transfixed, unable to look away.

"Please," he finally managed to rasp when the shade did not attack. "Please…I mean no harm…our ship…it was wrecked…" Mouth parched, he trailed off, unable to offer anything more to the embodiment of darkness before him.

The creature did not reply. Though it had no eyes or mouth or any other distinguishing feature, he could sense its attention upon him, the weight of its gaze. Unhurriedly, it drifted closer, the darkness mingling with the light of the crystal he held. Logan cringed as a rippling hand reached out, unable to tear himself away and flee.

Pathfinder... The word was spoken like the sighing of a breeze.

Something in the creature's voice sent a shudder down Logan's spine. But to his relief, it drew back from him. Regathering the tendrils about itself, it loomed tall in the lingering dark.

Forgiveness, Stone Bearer, the creature continued. ***I did not recognise your light. Welcome. Long have I guarded these shores against the unworthy, awaiting the return of the Pathfinders.***

Logan's heart was still hammering, but his terror had at least subsided somewhat. The creature before him was pure darkness, surely some demon dragged up from the seven hells, and yet...it did not appear to wish him harm...

"Stone Bearer? Pathfinders?" he whispered. "You...you called me that, didn't you?"

What might have been the shade's head inclined slightly. ***May your return herald a new Age of Heroes.***

"A new..." Logan trailed off. His mind was racing, struggling to make sense of the creature's words. He glanced at the crystal in his hand.

Could it be...? The shade had seemed angry, ready to unleash its dark powers, until Logan had picked up the crystal, igniting its light. Only then had it seemed to recognise him, naming him a "Pathfinder". He wanted to ask more, to demand what it meant, but was afraid to further reveal his ignorance, lest it withdraw the title.

"Thank you for your welcome, Guardian," he said at last, finally recalling some of his training as a gentleman. It seemed like the least precaution one could take when talking to a creature of pure darkness. "The creatures you spoke of," he continued, swallowing his fear. "This means…they will not harm me?"

The beasts will know no master. Not until the power of the isle is claimed.

"Ah…" Logan's mouth hung open, his thought unfinished. He swung away from the shade and raised the crystal, searching for the beasts it spoke of. Unfortunately, the crystal's glow wasn't enough to illuminate the entire beach. "You mean…"

The beasts will hunt you, Pathfinder.

Logan retreated a quick step and cast another glance over his shoulder. A light had appeared on the horizon, revealing the dark clouds. There was a fleet of ships beyond those clouds, he knew. Yet between him and the blockade was the raging sea, the crashing waves and icy currents. He would never make it.

He closed his eyes, struggling with the terror, the despair that swelled within him. What was he doing here? He wasn't like his brother, calm and in control. A hero. Dustin would know what to do if he was here, if he had survived the wreckage…

"Please," Logan whispered, the terror speaking now.

I cannot aid you, Pathfinder, the creature replied. *You must unlock the power of the stone if you wish to claim the island's power.*

"I don't want any power," Logan replied. "I just want to find my brother."

The shade seemed to hesitate. *Even so.*

Logan tightened his fist around the crystal, raising it before him. The shade did not move, though he could sense its attention again, its fixation on the crystal fossil.

"Then…how do I unlock the stone?"

I am Guardian, not guide, came the creature's reply. *Some secrets, you must uncover for yourself. You hold the fate of nations in your hand. Prove yourself worthy, Pathfinder, and the power will come.*

Logan was about to demand more from the creature, to tell it that wasn't enough, not when it had promised that monsters would hunt him. But before the words could leave from his mouth, something else moved in the shadows of the shore.

Heart lurching, Logan raised his crystal, expecting one of the fabled beasts to come charging from the darkness.

Instead, this time the light caught the silhouette of a man rushing towards them. Gravel crunched beneath his boots as he leapt, a cry upon his lips. A blade glittered in his hand as he raised it high. Logan flinched as the man landed beside him, stones showering in every direction.

"Back, foul creature of the deep!"

Distantly, Logan noted a second figure—a woman—racing after him, but it was the man who drew all attention as he swung his sword at the shade. The creature did not react, though its darkness flickered as the blade slashed through the shadow that made up its form.

For a second, nothing happened. Silence fell across the cove. The moment stretched out, punctuated only by the crunch of the woman's approaching footsteps. Logan had enough presence of mind to recognise them as the couple from the bow of *The Rising Tide*, though the rest of him was still fixated on the shadow creature, still reeling from its words.

A burst of sunlight from the distant clouds finally broke the stalemate. A sigh like the breath of the dead whispered across the shore as the light grew brighter. Slowly the shade faded away.

"Hurrah!" the man exclaimed, turning from Logan and the place where the creature had been to greet the woman's approach. "Sister, we did it!"

Logan stared as the two hugged. He'd been so engrossed by the shade, he hadn't even noticed their approach. They each held a shining blade of silver, which made their embrace somewhat difficult, but neither appeared willing to sheath the blades just yet. The man still wore his grin as he turned towards Logan.

"Greetings, fellow passenger," he said with a nod. "I am pleased we arrived in time to defend you against the demon."

Behind, the woman nodded her agreement, though her expression showed none of the man's excitement.

"Demon?" Logan stared at the pair, looking from their weapons to the dark cliffs, to the shadows that surrounded them still, before finally realising they were talking about the shade. "It wasn't a demon...was it?" he finished dumbly, suddenly uncertain.

Grimacing, the man stepped forward and placed a hand on Logan's shoulder. "They are cunning creatures, but they speak only lies. Tell me, what did it say to you?"

"I..." Opening his mouth, Logan closed it again, frowning as the shade's words whispered in his mind.

The creatures will hunt you, Pathfinder.

He swallowed, mouth suddenly dry. "It said there were creatures here...monsters that will hunt us," he managed at last. His words barely rose above a whisper, so that his supposed rescuer had to lean in close to hear him. "It said that we're all in danger."

To his surprise, the man chuckled. "Perhaps it told one truth then," he said with a grin, before turning to his sister. "You hear that, Amilyse?" he asked, his voice quivering with barely controlled excitement. "We were right! We've finally found it: the island of monsters!"

8

ZACHARY

*Z*achary awoke face-down in the sand, water lapping at his waist. Coughing, he groaned and forced himself up. Spitting out a mouthful of dirt, he squinted against the brilliance of the day, his sluggish mind struggling to recall where he was and how he'd come to be there.

It took a moment for the memories to catch up to his surroundings. His conversation with the captain slowly trickled back to him, how he'd negotiated her protection during their time on the island...

Zach blinked, pushing himself into a sitting position, his heart beginning to race. His head whipped around, taking in the beach on which he lay, the stark cliffs rising above, the waves crashing over rocks behind him.

I'm on the bloody island.

A curse slipped from Zachary's lips. His memories after the bridge were vague. He'd slipped, hadn't he? Fallen down the stairs? But he'd been a long way from the edge—surely he couldn't have fallen into the water? Had Cordelia betrayed him after all? His hand fell to the knife on his belt—which had mercifully remained in its sheath. If that was the case, the woman would pay…

But no, something had happened after he'd stepped from the bridge. The night had been silent. The ship's engines had failed. A sickly feeling curled around his stomach as he noticed the flotsam covering the beach.

He swore again.

So *The Rising Tide* had sunk. He'd known the steamer was a piece of junk the moment he'd stepped aboard, though the engines failing mid-voyage…it was strange, to say the least.

Gathering his strength, Zachary leveraged himself to his feet. A quick check revealed four of his five knives were still in place, but he'd lost his pack in the fall. He could recall hitting the water now, and the desperate struggle afterwards to stay afloat. Swimming had never been a strength of his, and so he'd had to lose the bag. The clothes had been a more difficult matter, but he was glad for the coat now. The thick wool kept off the wind, despite the water that had soaked it.

Zach turned his gaze to waves breaking on the reefs off the shore. He supressed a shudder. How he'd survived those churning waters was beyond him. He would have thanked the Old Gods for their mercy, if he didn't suspect this was all some cosmic joke. It would be just like those fickle entities, to save the life of a dying man.

Still, he was alive, and if he wasn't mistaken, the currents had carried him into the Anomaly itself, right to the shores of the fabled island.

He lay on a narrow stretch of black sand, edged on one side by the swirling currents of the ocean, tall cliffs on the other. The cliffs themselves shone in the daylight, formed from a kind of black crystal. Obsidian, perhaps, though there was nothing like this anywhere in Riogachd. Most of the nearby coasts were of hard gravel, the cliffs of white chalk or limestone.

Somehow, Zachary found himself smiling. He hadn't been lying to Cordelia when he'd claimed to have no interest in riches or power. It hadn't even been entirely a lie when he'd told her he was here for the adventure. Anything to keep him distracted from…other memories.

He might have survived his dip in the sea, but the waters had left him parched and his clothes caked in salt. A quick examination of the wreckage turned up only an empty flask, which he tucked into a pocket in his jacket. Hopefully he could find a source of fresh water to fill it, though he wasn't sure whether such a thing even existed on this place. This entire island had only existed a few months. Zach wasn't sure he would find anything but barren stone.

But then, everything about this place was an impossibility. Even the sun above was shining with the warmth of spring. With the thick cloud and fog hanging off the coast, he felt as though he'd awakened in another world. Might have, for all he knew.

With no water or supplies, his only choice was to make his way inland. If he was lucky, he would find a stream or spring. If not, he might encounter other passengers from *The Rising Tide*. Given the debris on the shore, he doubted many had survived the wreckage. Most had been in their cabins beneath the deck and would have struggled to escape the sinking vessel.

But if Zach still lived, he couldn't discount the possibility others might as well. Though from the names on Cordelia's manifest that he'd recognised, meeting up with other passengers wasn't high on his bucket list.

At that thought, Zach checked on his knives one last time, before setting off for the narrow track he'd spied leading up the cliffs. Who—or what—had carved the switchbacks into the obsidian was only another addition to the already lengthening list of questions he had about this place.

Thankfully, the path wasn't as steep as he'd first thought. But the cliffs were still far taller than any manor wall, and the smooth stone made it difficult for his boots to find purchase. A sharp pain soon began in Zach's chest.

He was puffing before he reached the halfway point. Blood pounded in his temples and the pain in his chest only grew with each step. It wasn't long before the first coughing fit struck and he was forced to stop. Doubling in two, he struggled to draw breath as his lungs burned. It felt as though some demon had wrapped his chest in bands of red-hot iron.

Finally the pain passed. Finding himself crouched against the obsidian walls, Zachary pressed his cheek to the crystal, drawing comfort from the cool of its touch.

What am I doing here?

Despite his best efforts, the thought wormed its way into Zachary's mind. He could taste the metallic tang of blood in his mouth again, feel the creeping weakness taking hold.

Whatever this island was, whatever its secrets, this was no place for a dying man. He should be home in his cottage, wrapped in Margery's embrace…

Zachary forced the image from his mind. Supporting himself on a jagged edge of obsidian, he struggled to push himself to his feet, when he noticed something within the crystal. Spirals had formed within the crystal, reminiscent of the ancient forces that had forged it, but here the lines ran clockwise—in stark contrast to the rest of the patterns across the cliff-face.

He leaned in closer, and a tingling sensation raised goosebumps down his arms. The pattern he had noticed wasn't a part of the crystal at all. It was some kind of creature, a fossil from prehistoric times, trapped within the facets of obsidian.

That's not possible, was his first thought.

"Well, obviously it is, Zach," he muttered to himself. "Since it's *there.*"

He exhaled, but so close to the rockface now, his breath fogged the crystal. He wiped away the condensation, then flinched as a sharp *crack* came from the cliff. Heart suddenly racing, his head jerked up, expecting the entire cliff to come tumbling down on him. After all, if this island had risen from the ocean in the space of a day, who was to say the entire place might not sink back into the depths at any moment?

But nothing came tumbling down and finally Zach allowed himself to relax. He returned his attention to the mysterious fossil. But when he looked at the rockface, he found that a chunk of obsidian had broken away.

The fossil lay now at his feet. Without thinking, Zach reached down and picked it up. As his fingers wrapped around the cold stone, a sudden light burst from the dark facets, causing him to cry out and lurch backwards towards the edge. Only at the last second did he catch himself, fingers grasping blindly at the cliff-face.

Heart racing, he sank to the ground, eyes fixed on the jagged piece of obsidian. The light was fading, but did not entirely disappear. A spark remained, shimmering in the depths of the crystal.

Zach sat for a long while, his gaze lost in the depths of the stone, in the possibilities contained in that light. He'd seen a lot of things in his fifty years of life. Vaults filled to the ceilings with gold, hidden chambers stacked with scrolls—records of the delinquent lives of half the nobles in Riogachd. He'd killed men and lost friends, and watched the life drain from the eyes of both.

But never in his life had he seen a magic crystal.

That was the stuff of fairytales, legends from the forgotten days when the Old Gods had walked the earth.

They weren't the sort of thing a thief from Leith stumbled upon.

Zachary wasn't sure whether he should pick it up, or hurl it into the ocean.

"Well, given the circumstances, what's the worst that could happen?" he muttered to himself.

Tentatively, he reached out again and plucked the stone from the path.

There was no flash of light this time, only a gentle pulsing from within the stone. It wasn't cold anymore, but carried a faint warmth. He'd half expected it to turn him to dust the second he laid hands on it, but it only sat in his palm, silent, expectant.

Holding it up to the sunlight, Zachary spent long minutes studying the artefact, but he could make out nothing further of the creature within. Neither could he identify the source of the light. He was about to put it in his pocket, when he sensed movement.

He spun, knife already in hand and poised to strike, when his eyes registered the source of the movement. Shadows coalesced before him, condensing into a formless silhouette on the path before him.

*Welcome, **Pathfinder***, came the whisper of the shade.

9

LOGAN

Logan had been lost in the woods once when he was young. It had been after they'd lost their mother to the plague, and their father had been off on one campaign or another. With Dustin occupied by sword training and marksmanship, Logan had been mostly left to his own devices. He'd taken to exploring the grounds of the manor, roaming the flowerbeds and extensive gardens of the countryside property.

Then one day in the middle of winter, he'd finally wandered off the grounds and become lost in the nearby woods. It had taken searchers hours to find the younger of the Kaine brothers. By the time his rescuers had finally pulled him from the snowdrift, Logan had been shaking so badly he couldn't even drink from a mug of hot cocoa.

Worse had been the look in his father's eyes when he'd returned from his campaign, the judgement. That had been the day Logan had realised his father would never see him as an equal. It had been the worst day of his life.

Until now.

"What in the seven hells are you talking about?" Logan whispered, looking from the man to the woman in horror.

The air was heavy with salt, the sea spray forming fine mist that hung about the cove. Waves rumbled in the distance, the sound conjuring images in Logan's mind of beasts creeping through the darkness towards them. But Logan's rescuers only frowned, their brows creased, lips pursed. The red light of the rising sun glinted on the blades they held, so that it seemed the blood of their enemies dripped from the steel.

The man was the first to break the silence. "Did you not hear me, child? This is the island of monsters."

"We've been searching for it," the woman chirped in. Her earlier hesitation had vanished with the man's announcement, and now she wore an easy smile. Certainly not the kind one would associate with an island of monsters.

"What?" he repeated.

The pair stared at him, concern appearing in their eyes.

"Did you hurt your head in the water?" the woman asked. She held out a hand. "Here, perhaps I can take a look…"

Logan took a quick step back. There was nothing wrong with his head—only their words. But with the movement, the loose stones slipped beneath his sodden boots and he almost lost his balance—no doubt adding to their concerns for his health. Thankfully, he recovered before he fell.

"I heard what you said," he said, trying to keep the panic from his voice, though his heart was about to burst from his chest. He couldn't understand how the pair could seem so calm. If that shade had told the truth, the monsters they spoke of were already hunting them.

"What you're saying," he said, even as his mind ran away in a spiral of panic. "It just doesn't make any sense," he continued, losing his battle for control. "Why would you be *looking* for an island of monsters?" he gasped. "And what the hell was that shadow, then, if you know so much about this place?"

"A demon," the man answered slowly, as though speaking to a simpleton. "Do not worry, it is gone now. The creatures of this place cannot stand before my blade."

"Your…blade?" The blood was pounding so loud in Logan's ears by then, he was sure he'd misheard the man. "You think…that thing was afraid of a sword? It passed straight through it!"

His words drew a scowl from the man and he raised the sabre as though to demonstrate its power. "I forged this blade myself. There is a furnace in Londinium, kept stoked by the priests of the Macha." Macha was the Old God of War. "He lit its flames before departing Riogachd for the realm beyond. They still carry his power. No creature of darkness can stand against this weapon."

His voice rang with passion as he spoke. There was a fervour in the man's eyes that reminded Logan of the priests at the temple back in Leith. But these two did not wear the robes of priests. He found his gaze drawn to the woman. She too held a blade, the twin of her brother's.

"Yours too?"

"It has been our family's sacred duty for generations, to hunt the monsters of the dark," she said.

"I see," Logan replied, exhaling slowly in an effort to regain his calm. "So you have faced creatures like that shadow before?"

The pair hesitated at his words, exchanging a glance.

"Generations ago, the monsters fled our lands, fleeing to their hidden realm," the woman replied. "But our family did not forget."

Logan's heart sank. For a moment he'd hoped they might be like his brother, experienced fighters, hardened by battle. Momentarily overwhelmed, he turned from the pair, struggling for calm. His mind was racing, still struggling to process the shipwreck, let alone the appearance of the creature and the pair of monster-hunting siblings. Pathfinders and monsters and magical islands...it was all too much for him.

Where are you, brother? He hurled the thought into the void. *I need you!*

He didn't even know if Dustin was alive. His brother wasn't one to let a little shipwreck get in his way, but...where was he then? Figments of the dream still clung to him, but surely it had been just that—a dream.

Logan cast his eyes over the shore. Now that the sun was up, he could see the wreckage more clearly. Twisted steel and broken boards littered the cove, and much of it looked recent. Ignoring the siblings for the moment, he wandered through the wreckage, seeking something to confirm it had come from *The Rising Tide*.

The cove was only some hundred yards wide, and it didn't take Logan long to reach the other side. He found no sign of other survivors. Dark cliffs hemmed him in, stretching out into the raging sea. Shivering, he stumbled to a stop. He was pretty sure he was in shock. Maybe the entire encounter with the demon had been a hallucination…but no, the siblings had seen it too.

The hairs on his neck stood on end as he turned to study the pair. They hadn't followed him, thankfully. They stood in the centre of the cove, heads leaned close in discussion. They claimed to have saved his life.

Logan was far from sure about that, but friend or foe, there was no ignoring the shade's warning. There were monsters on this island, creatures that would hunt him. He had his father's sabre and had received the same training as his brother. But as a child, Logan had not excelled with the blade—nor the revolver for that matter. His father had never said as much, but he knew it was yet another source of disappointment for the man.

That was why he'd taken the blade in the first place—to prove to his father that he could be a warrior.

If only he felt so determined now.

His gaze turned to the strange crystal in his hand. Its light had dimmed again, allowing him a glimpse of the fossil in its core. The shade had said that unlocking the stone would protect him, but he had no idea how to do so. And in the meantime, he was defenceless.

The siblings weren't.

Whether they'd fought monsters before or not, they seemed to know how to use the swords they carried. When the beasts came, they might at least stand a chance. Logan had no choice—he would have to join them.

Tucking the stone into his water-laden coat, he started back along the shore towards the pair. His eyes lifted to the cliffs as he walked. They loomed above, though now that it was light he saw they were not the limestone or granite of the cliffs near Leith, but a deep black crystal that shone in the light of the rising sun.

"Child!" A shout from down the beach drew Logan's attention back to the siblings. It was the man again. Logan grated his teeth at the sight, but the pair were already moving to join him near the cliffs. The man raised a finger to point. "Do you see the path?"

It took a moment for Logan to pick out what the man meant. Shadows still clung to the twisted pieces of crystal, concealing the trail that zigzagged its way up the black stone.

"Wait!" he called as they strode past him. "What are your names?"

The pair lingered long enough for Logan to catch up.

"Rob," the man answered. "My twin is Amilyse."

The woman nodded her agreement.

"You can call me Logan," he replied, his voice firm. "And I am not a child."

"In our family, one is considered a child until they have forged their own blade," Rob replied.

That brought a scowl to Logan's face, but he held his tongue. Turning his gaze to the trail, he swallowed.

"You want to go up?"

"Of course," Rob replied simply. "There are monsters to be destroyed."

"Are you sure we shouldn't wait here?" Logan asked, supressing a shudder at the way Rob casually referred to battling monsters. "There's sure to be a rescue party when people back in Leith realise what happened to *The Rising Tide*."

"There will be no rescue party," Rob said curtly with a gesture towards the ocean.

Logan followed his motion. Fog filled the horizon, stretching from sea to sky in an impenetrable wall. Lightning flickered in those clouds, casting strange lights across the water's surface. Out there, a storm was raging. Yet where they stood the sun shone, its rays strangely warm for winter.

"Those clouds have not shifted in months," Rob explained. "They surround the Anomaly in all directions. We slipped past the naval blockade in the night. No one knows we are here."

A lump lodged in Logan's throat. He stared at the man, willing him to say more, to explain why that was not a complete disaster.

"Rob, you're scaring him," Amilyse cut in at last, stepping between her brother and Logan and placing a hand on his arm. "Never fear, Logan. We will protect you from the creatures."

"Yes, now come," Rob said, his grin returning as he turned towards the cliffs. "We have monsters to hunt."

He set off up the zigzagging path without a backwards glance. Logan hesitated as Amilyse followed her brother, and they started up the first switchback together. His mind was racing, still struggling to come to terms with his situation. The shade had warned that the beasts would hunt them, and he did not want to be caught alone. He still couldn't decide if the pair were heroes or insane. But at least they were armed. And maybe, just maybe, they knew what they were doing.

Cursing beneath his breath, Logan started after the twins.

"So this place," he said when he caught them, already puffing from the climb. "You knew it was here?"

"We suspected," Rob replied. He seemed to do most of the talking for the two.

"And you came here willingly?" Logan asked, still struggling with that part. "Why would you come to a place of monsters? That's madness, you know that, right?"

To his surprise, Rob laughed. "Madness to the common man," he replied. "To us, it is duty."

At his side, Amilyse hesitated, but ultimately nodded her head in agreement.

Still no less confused, Logan fell silent. His legs were already burning and he needed to concentrate on the climb. The trail helped—without it, it would have been impossible to scale the two-hundred-foot-tall cliff. But it was still a climb of two hundred feet and Logan was already weary from his time in the water.

As they walked, he asked whether the pair knew what had happened to *The Rising Tide*, or if they'd seen his brother after going into the water. Unfortunately, the twins knew little more than him about the fate of the vessel. They'd awakened at the other end of the cove and had only noticed his presence because of his light.

Thankfully, neither had asked him about the stone in his pocket. It had a connection to this place, he knew. The shade had confirmed it.

Pathfinder.

That was what it had called him, but what did the title mean? Would Dustin know? He'd claimed to have discovered little about the crystal in all the years he'd possessed it.

A chill touched Logan as a new thought occurred to him. The shade had said the creatures would hunt any who trespassed on this place. If his brother *had* survived the crash and landed on the island, they would come for him as well.

Use the crystal, brother, the words of his dream filtered back to Logan. *Find me…*

Suddenly, those words took on a new meaning for Logan. Dustin had given him the crystal fossil, the one item the shade had promised would protect them. Would his brother be helpless without it? Dustin was a warrior and a hero, but demons were an altogether different threat than pirates.

Logan lifted his gaze. They were nearing the top of the cliffs now, close to the crest and the secrets that lay beyond. Suddenly, he was glad the pair of siblings wanted to press on. Gripped by a new sense of urgency, he picked up the pace. Whatever waited above, it would have to be faced sooner or later. For Dustin's sake, it would have to be sooner.

I'm coming, brother!

10

LOGAN

Logan stood atop the crystal cliffs and stared open mouthed at the vista that had greeted their ascent. Despite his earlier haste, he had already been standing there for several minutes. After the harsh crystal cliffs and desolate gravel beach and Rob's stories, he'd expected to find this land a twisted and broken place, the home of demons and monsters and worse.

This place just gets stranger and stranger.

Instead of desolation, a broad plateau stretched away from the clifftops. Long grasses swayed gently in the breeze. Flowers of red and blue and silver shone in the morning sunlight, blooming in the unnaturally warm air, despite the winter raging beyond the distant cloudbank. Where below the beach had carried the harsh scents of salt and sea, here the fragrance of spring prevailed, of sun and blossoms and freshly-cut grass.

The plateau seemed to stretch away in all directions, though the long grass obscured their view, making it impossible to tell where the land might fall away to the jagged cliffs. Even so, there was no mistaking the scale of the place. To the north, the plateau rose, and grass turned to the dark shadow of forest. Beyond even that, a mountain rose, its peak stretching a mile into the blue sky. A sprinkling of snow dusted the stark summit.

Just as he was about to look away, Logan glimpsed a shimmer atop the mountain peak. He stared, waiting, and some ten heartbeats later, a burst of light flared amidst the grey stone. It lasted only a second, so fleeting it might have been a flicker of sunlight against stone. But as he watched, it came again and again, a sudden brilliance amidst the barren stone, too far off to determine its source.

Shivering, Logan looked from the mountain to his companions. "This…this doesn't look like a land of monsters."

The grim looks on the faces of the siblings seemed to agree, though after a moment Rob shook his head. "The servants of darkness are masters of deception, Logan," he replied. "You have already spoken with their ambassador and did not suspect. They have no doubt created this apparent paradise to entrap the unwary."

Logan nodded slowly at Rob's words, returning his gaze to the long grass. He swallowed. The man was right about one thing at least—anything could be hiding in the vegetation. A beast could be just a few feet from where they stood, and they would never know until it made its move.

"The light," Amilyse said after a while, glancing at her brother. "What do you think it could be…"

"The source of their power," Rob replied grimly. "We must destroy it before monsters grow strong enough to reach the mainland."

"I…" Logan trailed off. He was coming to realise that criticising Rob only incited the man further. But neither did Logan have any desire to go near that light. Perhaps the man's passion could be redirected. "What about the other passengers?" he asked. "If others survived, won't they be helpless against the creatures here?" If the twins were truly heroes, they would not let their fellow men and women be slaughtered.

The smile slipped from Rob's face, his brow creasing in a frown. He glanced at Amilyse, then back down at the raging ocean.

"I'm…not sure anyone else could have survived, Logan," Amilyse said.

Logan met her eyes, refusing to back down. "Please, Amilyse. I didn't come to this place alone. My brother is out there somewhere. We have to find him before the beasts do."

As he spoke, he slipped a hand into his pocket and clutched the crystal fossil tight. Maybe Dustin would know how to unlock it, now that they'd reached the island.

"The boy is right." Logan's head jerked up at Rob's words. Squaring his shoulders, the monster hunter tore his gaze from the waters. "I suggest we follow the cliffs. If anyone else survived, they would not have stayed long on the beaches without water. In this grass they will leave tracks we can follow."

Logan's spirit lifted and he grinned back at the man. "Thank you, Rob."

As they set off along the clifftops, Logan was struck by the contrasting views on either side. Towards the sea, the mists churned and roiled, as though frustrated that Logan and the others had slipped through their grasp. The dark clouds filled the horizon, seeming to prove Rob's earlier claim that the island was surrounded.

As for the island…it was like looking on another world. Sunshine lit the long grass as midday approached. There was no denying the climate was different now. Even the breeze blowing across the clifftops carried the warmth of spring. The icy touch of winter was a distant memory.

Unfortunately, it wasn't long before their stroll between the two worlds was forced to a halt. As they moved along the cliffs, the long grass pressed them closer and closer to the edge, until even Logan was forced to admit they would need to venture further into the island.

As they stood looking through the long grass, Logan found a cold sweat beading his forehead and his heart hammering in his chest. He shared a glance with the others. There had been no sign of the creatures the shade had warned of, but that did not mean they weren't out there. A flicker in Amilyse's eyes betrayed her nerves, and for the first time, Logan realised she couldn't be much older than his own twenty years.

Neither could her twin, for that matter, though Rob showed none of Amilyse's hesitation as he drew the sword from the sheath on his back and stepped up to the long grass. A grin spread across his face as he looked at them and licked his lips.

"Come on, sis, don't tell me our friend's nerves are getting to you?"

Amilyse's face hardened. Keeping her eyes determinedly fixed away from Logan, she drew her own blade and joined her brother.

"Of course not," she said curtly before turning to address him. "Don't worry, Logan. We'll protect you."

Looking from the pair to the long grass, Logan was tempted to turn around right there. But had he not set off on this journey to face his fears in the first place? He drew a breath, hand falling to the hilt of his father's sword. He might be facing demons instead of rebelling clansmen, but he could no more turn from this challenge than his father could in the Battle for the North. He needed to find his brother, before whatever creatures haunted this place did.

Logan drew his father's sabre.

A grin appeared on Rob's face. "Welcome to the hunt, Logan."

Such were his nerves, Logan hardly noticed the man had used his name for the first time.

"Shall I, ah, lead then?" he offered.

This time true surprise showed on Rob's face, but he quickly replaced it with a grin. "You're braver than I thought," he said, slapping him on the shoulder. "Lead on, my friend."

A lead weight had settled in Logan's stomach. The blade was surprisingly heavy in his hand. A shudder ran down his spine as he imagined some shadow creature hidden in the grass, waiting to pounce. This was madness.

But there was no help for it. Where they stood, the cliffs fell sharply to the ocean without any signs of a path down. It was either go back, or press on through the grass.

So drawing in a breath, Logan pushed his way into the vegetation.

Crack, crack, crack.

Logan froze as the sharp noise carried to his ears. His eyes were drawn down. The sound had come from the grass he'd just trampled—not a soft crunching, but a harsher noise, like that of breaking glass...

His fears momentarily forgotten, Logan ignored the strange looks Rob and Amilyse were giving him and plucked a broken strand of grass from the ground and held it up to the light. The sun flickered against the green, shimmering as though it were not grass at all, but...

"Crystal," he whispered, unable to believe what he was seeing.

"What is it, Logan?" Rob asked, moving up next to him. "You're not having second thoughts already, are you?"

Logan shook his head, handing his discovery to the man. Rob frowned at the offering, but then his eyes widened as well and he looked from the strand of grass to their surroundings.

"Is it all...?"

Logan grasped a cluster of strands and crushed it in his hand.

Crack.

The sound of breaking crystal was audible for all to hear this time. He opened his hand, revealing the way the light shimmered against the crystal facets of the vegetation. Flowers were blooming amidst the grass as well. He could smell their aroma, but surely they couldn't...

...he plucked a red-hued wildflower from its stalk and held it up to his nose. A rich aroma filled his nostrils as he inhaled. Trembling, he let the flower fall from his fingers, his mind struggling to accept what his senses were telling him. The flower was as crystallised as the grass. It should smell like nothing—but his nose said it was as real as any bloom in the gardens of the Kaine manor.

He slumped to the ground, breath rasping in and out as he struggled to contain his shock. It was all too much, too impossible. The shipwreck, the mysterious island, the monsters. Now an entire meadow of crystal grass. Hells, not only the grass, not even just the flowers. The cliffs had been some kind of black crystal. And looking at the dirt beneath him, he realised the soil shone with the sun's light.

All of it, even those distant trees, even the jagged mountain.

All of it, formed from shining crystal.

"What is this place?" he whispered.

This time not even Rob deigned to answer.

"My, my, what have we here?"

Logan started as a man's voice carried through the grass. Even as he struggled to rise and search for the owner, the pair of monster hunters leapt into action. Silver rippled in the sunlight as they raised their blades, moving with surprising speed to head off the threat. They need not have wasted their energy.

Laughter carried across the plateau as a man appeared on the clifftop behind them. Logan recognised the dark-cloaked stranger immediately as one of their fellow passengers—the one who'd pushed past him on the way to boarding the ship. Like the rest of them, he'd seen better days. His cloak seemed to have dried somewhat in the sun, but several tears now marred the fabric and his face was pale, despite the strange warmth of the island. Even the grey in his hair seemed more pronounced, as though his time in the water had drained him of several years.

Despite all that, he approached them with a grin on his face. Laughter reflected in his eyes as he looked from Rob to Amilyse and raised an eyebrow.

"I thought kids these days preferred pistols to blades."

"We are not children, sir," Rob practically growled. Logan hid a smile at the man's reaction, though it fled when Rob pointed his sabre at the newcomer's chest. "And you would do well to explain your presence here."

"A shadow sent me," the stranger replied, coming to a stop at Rob's gesture. His face became serious as he looked from the sword to Rob. "You'd best know how to use that, kid, if you plan to go around threatening strangers on this island. There were other passengers on *The Rising Tide* without a tenth of my patience."

Rob did not answer the man's words, but his eyes narrowed and the tip of his sword lifted an inch, as though he were preparing to skewer the man on the spot.

"You were on *The Rising Tide?*" Amilyse spoke in her brother's place, the high pitch to her voice conveying surprise.

"He was," Logan confirmed, finally picking himself up off the ground. Seeking to disarm the situation, he sheathed his blade. Then, realising he still held a handful of crystal grass, allowed the strands to drift away on a gust of wind.

"It's all crystal," the stranger remarked.

"How is that possible?" Logan rasped, his mouth parched from both shock and dehydration.

The stranger shrugged. "The shadow would not tell me."

Logan's heart lurched as the import of the man's words finally set in. "You saw it too?"

"Where is it?" Rob spoke at the same time, swinging his sword from the man to the long grass that surrounded them. "Did it get to you?" he hissed. "Is that why you're here? To sell your soul to the demons, to make yourself their ally?" His fist tightened around his sword hilt.

"That was an option?" the stranger replied, eyebrows lifting into his greying fringe. "What do we get in return? Ultimate power? Eternal life? Please, tell me more."

An actual growl rumbled from Rob's chest and he advanced a step, until the tip of his blade touched the stranger's chest.

This time the dark-cloaked passenger did react. His hand snapped up, slapping aside the flat of Rob's blade before he could strike. The monster hunter cried out, trying to bring his sword to bare, but the stranger surged forward, cloak swirling about him. From some fold in his clothing, a dagger appeared.

Everyone froze as the blade touched Rob's throat.

"As I was saying," the stranger continued, still wearing the same friendly smile, "you really should learn how to use that weapon before you go threatening strangers, kid."

Another abrupt motion from the stranger, and Rob was lying in the dirt, gasping as he struggled for breath. The stranger swayed, as though the effort had cost him something, but the apparent weakness was only momentary. Straightening, he kicked aside Rob's fallen blade, then turned to confront Amilyse.

She stared at him, eyes wide, sword trembling in her hand. She hadn't even raised it from her side. The stranger regarded her for several moments before offering a nod.

"So you're the smart one," he said with a chuckle. He turned to Logan. "What about you, kid, want to take your shot at an old man?"

His feet seemingly fixed to the ground, Logan quickly shook his head and left his sword sheathed. The stranger laughed.

"Good choice," he said.

At that, he bent down and plucked the fallen sword from the ground. He offered it hilt-first to Rob, who had finally recovered his breath. The monster hunter did not accept the weapon; instead, he stumbled to his feet, dark eyes glowering at the stranger.

"I'm not here to ally with any demons, kid," the stranger said at last. "I'm not sure what that shadow thing was, but I don't trust it. Anyway, the name is Zachary Sicario," he finished by offering his hand.

"Then what are you here for?" Rob snapped, ignoring the man's pleasantries.

Zachary sighed. "And here I took you for gentlemen," he said. He reversed the blade again and slammed it into the ground with a *thud*. "Amongst civilised society, one offers his name before crossing blades."

Logan flinched at the insult, and even Rob and Amilyse stiffened at his words. They might be miles away from Riogachd and Londinium, but the smirch upon their families still cut deep. Any retort would only add to their dishonour, so Logan quickly stepped forward and offered a short bow.

"Apologies, Mr. Sicario," he said quickly. "I am Logan Kaine, and this is Rob and Amilyse...ah, I didn't get your last name?" he finished lamely, glancing at the pair.

"Rainer," Amilyse offered, then: "We are sorry, Mr. Sicario. We could not be certain of your intentions."

"That's quite alright, Ms. Rainer," Zachary replied. "I've seen the captain's manifest for *The Rising Tide*. You would do well to trust no one on this island."

"Does that include you, Mr. Sicario?" Rob asked, his voice still hard.

Zachary chuckled, though this time Logan couldn't help but feel the laughter did not reach the man's eyes.

"Of course that includes me, kid," Zachary replied finally, the grin still on his lips. "Now, you were saying something about demons?"

11

ZACHARY

Zach's chest burned as he strode through the long grass. From the long strands and seed tufts, it was a type of fairy grass if he was not mistaken, the sort that grew in the drier parts of the continent. Normally, it did not grow in the cold and humid conditions around Riogachd. Then again, it normally didn't grow from crystal either.

As they moved, he caught whispers of movement in the vegetation, glimpses of small shadows as animals fled their approach. His new companions were right about at least one thing—they were not alone on this island. But the creatures he'd glimpsed so far had shown no interest in attacking the larger humans. Zach offered a reluctant prayer to Edris that it remained that way.

Unfortunately, not even the strangeness of this new world could distract him from his pain. The flames in his chest were building with each step. He could feel another coughing fit coming on. They seemed to be getting worse. Maybe they were. There'd been more blood the last time.

The dehydration wasn't helping. He'd walked all morning before encountering the three young gentry and had not crossed a single stream. The metallic taste of blood lingered in his mouth and he yearned to stop and catch his breath. His body was failing him, but Zach would be damned if he let that stop him—not when fate had dangled such a tantalising prospect before him.

He shivered as the words of the shade cut through his discomfort.

You stand on sacred crystal, Pathfinder. Gateway to untapped powers, key to life and death itself.

The words promised more than he'd dared to hope for. Certainly, he'd expected to find a mystery out here in the Northern Sea. Had even allowed himself to hope the rumours could be true, that a magic might exist that could cure him. But hope was a dangerous thing for a dying man, and so he'd never truly allowed himself to *believe*.

Now…

He hadn't lied to Cordelia. Hadn't lied to the three youths either, when he'd told them he didn't trust the shade. But seven hells, they were surrounded by *living crystal*. The magic of this island was undeniable. It was enough to make even the most cynical of men believe.

Careful, Zach, he reminded himself.

He turned his thoughts to his new companions. The pair of monster hunters were far from impressive. He'd didn't believe their story for a second. Tales of "magical swords" and an ancient family of monster hunters might have impressed the young Logan, but Zach wasn't sure that was a particularly difficult feat. Logan was barely a man and had obviously lived a sheltered life. He'd fumbled several times just trying to sheath his sabre in Zach's presence. It was clear he'd never used the blade in combat.

The young man was trailing behind the others now, struggling almost as much as Zachary to match their long strides. Wherever they'd come from, the siblings hadn't lied about their training. Zach might have outpaced them in his youth, but he was a long way from those days now.

Still, he did his best to hide his weakness. He didn't want to undo his earlier work, putting the fiery Rob in his place. Catching the man off-guard had been easy. Whatever his skill, Rob was clearly arrogant, overeager for a fight. The outcome between them might have been different in a fair fight. But as long as Rob believed in Zachary's ability, that was an unlikely eventuality. The feeling of cold steel against one's throat was enough to give even the boldest of men second thoughts.

As for Amilyse and Logan, well, they would not challenge him. They were followers, not the sort to take charge.

"So, the shade appeared to you as well?" Zachary spoke up as he fell into step with Logan. He was clearly the weakest link—the girl was unlikely to side against her brother if it came to a disagreement. "Tell me, did it speak to you?"

Logan hesitated, his eyes darting in the direction of the siblings. "I…" He swallowed, then nodded. "Yes. It said that I was trespassing. That creatures would come for me."

"Truly?" It hadn't mentioned anything about trespassing to Zachary.

"It didn't warn you about the monsters?" the youth questioned.

"Oh, it mentioned the beasts," Zach replied. "And something about being a Pathfinder."

Logan's eyes widened and he came to a sudden halt. "What?" he hissed, stepping in close. "Wait, you have a stone as well?"

"Stone?" Zachary feigned ignorance, even as his fingers twitched towards the pocket in which he had tucked the fossil.

"Like this," Logan whispered, drawing out a piece of quartz.

Zach's eyes widened as he noted its glow and the silhouette within. For a moment he eyed the kid, wondering what he knew, whether his whole innocent appearance was an act. If it was, the kid was a better performer than Zachary had ever been. Hesitantly, he drew out his own crystal, though the obsidian shone with a dark light beside the quartz.

"Do you know what they are?" Logan asked, his voice hushed with excitement. "How to wake them?"

"Afraid not, kid," Zachary replied honestly. He tucked the crystal back into his pocket, nodding for the young man to do the same. "Do your friends up there know about it?"

Logan shook his head.

"Probably best we keep it that way."

A frown creased Logan's forehead. "Why? They're trying to help us."

Zachary suppressed a chuckle at the young man's naivety. He smiled instead. "That remains to be proven," he replied. "Regardless, the shade said the stones were important, that they could protect us from the things on this island. Even if they don't interest the twins up there, other survivors will want them. Best that word doesn't get out."

"Are you always this suspicious?" Logan asked.

This time Zach couldn't stop the laughter. "In my line of work, suspicion keeps you alive, kid. Things like trust, those are luxuries for others."

The kid said nothing for a time, and they continued after the siblings, the only sound the strange crunching of the crystal grass beneath their feet. They were still doing their best to follow the line of the cliffs eastward, though they had to take care not to stumble over the edge, disguised as it was with the vegetation growing right up to the clifftop. They had yet to cross paths with any other survivors.

"What line of work are you involved in exactly?" Logan asked finally.

Damn. Zach hadn't meant to clue the kid in to his past. Too late to take back the words now though.

"Let us just say I was involved with a rough crowd in my youth," he replied with a shrug and a smile. "Don't worry, those days are behind me now."

"I thought you said we shouldn't trust you."

Zachary's grin spread. "That I did, Logan," he replied. "Maybe you're not so naïve as I had thought."

"Thanks," Logan replied shortly.

"I've learnt to judge men by the company they keep," Zachary laughed, "and, well..."

Logan glanced at the pair ahead. "They seem to know what they're doing…"

Zach snorted. "Don't tell me you believe their story, kid?"

"They did scare off the shade," Logan replied, somewhat defensively.

Zachary chuckled, not caring enough to make an issue of it. The twins might be what they said, or they could be something else entirely. He hadn't entirely discounted the possibility that the King's Council had operatives on this expedition. A pair of unknown young gentry wouldn't have been his first pick as spies, but then perhaps that was the point.

"You didn't see anyone else before you found us, did you?" Logan spoke up again.

That drew a frown from Zach. He'd seen the kid board alone, back in Leith. "Were you looking for someone?"

Logan nodded. "My older brother, Dustin. He was with me when the ship went down."

"Dustin Kaine…that does ring a bell. Something about pirates?"

The kid's face tightened almost imperceptibly. "That's him."

"Sounds like a stellar brother, allowing his baby brother to join him on a mad voyage to an island of monsters."

Colour appeared in Logan's cheeks. "It was not exactly his choice."

"Oh?"

"I smuggled myself aboard using his token. He still managed to talk his way aboard though."

"Did he now?" Zachary asked, his interest piqued. Cordelia hadn't seemed the sort to bend the rules.

"Dustin can be very persuasive when he wants to be."

"An interesting man."

Concern creased the kid's features. "We were talking at the bow when the ship capsized," he said softly. "I didn't see what happened to him after we went in the water."

"I'm sorry," Zach said after a pause, "I haven't seen anyone but you three since coming ashore."

Logan nodded. "I figured as much." He seemed to pull himself together with an inhalation of breath. "I'm not worried," he said in a rush. "You don't know Dustin. He wouldn't let a little thing like a shipwreck keep him from an adventure."

"You seem to have a high opinion of him."

Logan shrugged. "He takes after our father."

Zachary found himself smiling at Logan's innocent belief in his brother. He had no siblings, but there had been times in his life he'd found himself looking up to someone. Everyone needed a hero, even a thief on the streets. Unfortunately, in real life, heroes tended to let one down. For the young man's sake, Zach hoped this Dustin really was alive, not a corpse at the bottom of the Northern Sea.

"I look forward to meeting him…"

He trailed off as a sound carried to him on the breeze. Coming to a stop, he lifted his head, scanning their surroundings. The tall grass still hemmed them in on all sides but the path Rob and Amilyse were cutting with their swords. Logan came to a stop beside him, eyes wide with sudden fear, while the pair of monster hunters continued, unaware of their delay.

Zachary ignored them all. Ears alert, he turned on the spot, straining for another hint of the sound. The breeze had died away and for a moment he could only hear the pounding of blood in his ears, the distant crashing of waves on rocky shores...

There!

Just a murmur, but this time it was unmistakable.

Grinning, he turned to Logan, who was staring at Zach as though he was about to announce their impending doom.

"Can you hear it?" he asked.

Face pale, the young man shook his head.

Zachary grinned. "Follow me."

A few minutes later, the four of them stood beside a gently bubbling stream. The narrow waters weaved their way across the plateau, the stream barely deep enough to have created its own bed, though recent rains might have swelled it somewhat, for in places the waters had flooded the roots of the nearby fairy grass.

Zach was thankful to have heard its burbling, for the little stream did not flow all the way to the cliffs. Instead, its waters plunged into a hole at their feet, vanishing into the depths of the crystal island. If they'd continued their path close to the coast, they would have missed it completely.

Not that a running stream had any business existing on the island in the first place. It had risen from the depths of the ocean just a few months ago. This entire land should be barren rock. Logically, a few pools of collected rainwater should have been the most they could hope for. But logic had been well and truly put on hold by the magic of this place.

The water shone in the sunlight, so clear he could see each individual stone on the bottom. His mouth watering, Zach knelt to drink, but a new voice interrupted him.

"Stop!"

His head jerked up. His hand went to one of his knives, before his mind caught up. He recognised the accent as belonging to the highland woman he'd spoken to on the deck of *The Rising Tide*. She emerged from the long grass on the other side of the stream, revolver in hand.

"You don't want to do that, lowlander."

✤ 12 ✤

LOGAN

"Y ou don't want to do that, lowlander."

Logan started as the woman emerged from the long grass. At the sight of the gun in her hands, he reached for his sabre.

"Don't," came the command.

He froze as he found himself staring down the barrel of the revolver. His mouth suddenly parched, he carefully removed his hand from the hilt of his blade.

"What have we here?" Zachary asked, still knelt beside the water. He sounded far too calm for someone facing down an armed highland woman. "Are you robbing us, Miss Willow?" He tisked. "After all that contempt for our fellow passengers. I'm disappointed."

Logan blinked. "You *know* her?"

Zachary chuckled. "'Know' is probably a little strong. We briefly crossed paths on *The Rising Tide*."

"Gods damnit, lowlander," the woman snarled. "I told you to get away from the water." She gestured wildly at the stream with the revolver, as though to emphasise the point.

"Actually, you told me to stop," Zachary said quietly. He rose all the same. "Why exactly are you worried about the water?"

The woman pursed her lips. Logan saw the doubt in her eyes. "I'm…not entirely sure, but—"

"By the Old Gods," Rob interrupted. "I'll not stand here listening to superstitious hogwash from the likes of *her.*" The way he said the last word made it clear he was referencing Willow's obvious roots in the highlands. Even twenty years after the war, the situation remained tense between south and north, especially for those that hailed from Londinium.

Willow's revolver came back up as the monster hunter stepped up to the stream. He stared down the barrel of the weapon. When she did not pull the trigger, he smirked, then knelt and scooped up water and drank from his cupped hands. Letting out a sigh, he sat back on his haunches.

"Ahhh, that is better," he said. "You see, woman? Nothing bad happened."

Far from looking reassured, Willow stared at Rob as though she expected him to explode. Logan stared as well, until a sharp intake of breath drew his attention to Amilyse.

"Look!" she cried, pointing to the water.

Logan obeyed, and gasped himself as he saw what she'd noticed.

The stream had come alight. A strange blue glow now came from the waters around where Rob crouched. He scrambled to his feet as light bathed his face, drawing his blade as though he expected the water to attack him.

"Dark magic," he hissed.

"Or something else," Zach murmured. He looked at Willow. "You expected this?"

She shook her head, her already pale face white in the sunlight.

Logan stared at the glowing waters. The light had spread, and now a dozen yards of the stream was lit with the strange blue light.

"Maybe its harmless," he murmured.

"I found…bodies near another stream like this," Willow said quietly. "They'd been torn to pieces. Only one was still alive. He tried to warn me, said something about the water, before…he died."

Zach swore.

In the distance, something began to bark. Everyone froze, looking in the direction of the noise. That wasn't the soft yapping of the neighbourhood stray. There was something about those cries, something sharp and unnatural that set the hairs on the back of Logan's neck on end.

A second creature soon joined in the first, then a third. Before long, a chorus of growls and baying came from the grass around them. Whatever creature they belonged to, there had to be dozens.

And they were coming closer.

Cursing, Rob leapt to a rock lying on the side of the stream, trying for a glimpse of whatever approached.

"They're coming," he said grimly.

Logan's knees began to tremble. He reached for his sword, but it took several attempts just to grip the pommel.

"You think?" Zach snapped, his normally calm voice edged with tension.

"We have to get out of here," Willow hissed. She leapt the stream to land on their side.

Logan nodded his agreement.

"They're coming from along the coast," Rob offered.

"Then we're heading inland," Zachary replied.

He shared a look with the highland woman, before the two started off along the riverbank, heading upstream. Logan was about to follow them, when he noticed Rob had not moved from his stone.

"You go ahead, Logan" Rob announced.

Logan swallowed. His insides were twisted into a knot. Whatever these things were, he didn't want to be here when they arrived. Even so he hesitated, looking from the departing Zach and Willow to the twins. The sapphire light of the stream shone from their faces, rippled from their blades. In that moment, they truly looked like the heroes they claimed to be.

But appearances could be deceiving. What if Zachary was right, and their fabled blades were only that—fables? He looked at Amilyse, beyond the hardness of her jaw, the glint in her eyes, and saw her fear. Rob might be assured of their destiny, but his twin was not.

Making up his mind, Logan took a step towards the siblings. "Rob!" he called. "We have to go after them!"

The man frowned. "Flee with them if you wish, Logan," he snapped. "We will not be turned from our destiny."

"But we need you!" Logan insisted. "Without your protection, the rest of us are helpless. Is it not your family's duty to protect those who cannot defend themselves?"

Rob's grin faltered at Logan's words. His eyes flickered in the direction Zachary and the highland woman had vanished. Uncertainty warred in his features before he let out a violent curse and stepped down from his rock.

"Come, sister," he practically spat. "Let's make sure the old man and the highland fool are safe."

He set off after the others without a backwards glance, leaving Logan and Amilyse frozen for a moment by his sudden change of heart. The young woman let out a muffled sigh and offered Logan a hesitant nod before another howl sent her scampering after Rob. His heart pounding, Logan followed fast on her heels.

They caught up with Zachary first, as he lagged behind the highland woman. Rob wore a terrible scowl on his face now, though he did not try to turn them back. The stream grew wider as they raced inland, its waters deepening. The barking grew more distant but did not die altogether.

Logan shuddered at the thought of the dark creatures reaching the clearing where they'd stood. In his mind, they appeared as giant wolves with fang and claw, though that was just his imagination, surely. Not even Rob had caught a glimpse of the things before they'd fled. For that, Logan was glad. He doubted this was a case of the bark being worse than the bite.

Rob kept flashing glances over his shoulder as they ran, a look of frustration on his face. Some of the fear had faded from Amilyse's eyes now, but she showed no desire of turning back to face the monsters.

They only stopped once the barking had died to distant whispers. By then the tiny stream had become a river, too deep for them to wade across—especially with the beasts still prowling. They'd obviously been attracted to something about the glowing waters.

Exhausted from their flight, Logan slumped to the ground, his hands shaking. Despite never seeing the creatures, he felt he'd never come so close to death.

Well, not until last night, he supposed, when he'd fallen into the icy waters. Zachary and Amilyse soon joined him. The older man had lost most of his colour and was panting hard. Logan found himself wondering why a man his age would come to such a place.

Rather than rest, Rob began to pace, every so often casting dark glances back in the direction they'd come from.

The highland woman remained standing as well, though her eyes were not to the south, but the north, lingering on the snowy mountaintop. Light still flashed near its peak. Watching that glow reminded him of the light in the stream and despite his thirst, he scooted back a few more feet from the water's edge. Maybe Rob was right about this place after all.

"Well, thank you for the warning, Willow," Zachary said at last. "If only some of us had listened." He flashed Rob a glare.

The monster hunter bristled, but Logan quickly stepped between them. "Fighting won't solve our most pressing problem." When the two men only stared at him, he swallowed and gestured at the stream. "If those things are going to chase us every time we touch the water, how are we going to get a drink?"

Zachary pursed his lips, his eyes taking on a distant look. "The other group you encountered," he said at last to Willow. "You think they were drinking from the stream as well?"

When the woman nodded, he reached into his jacket and drew out a metal flask. "Did any of them have one of these?"

"No." Her brow furrowed as Zachary stepped towards the river. "Wait, what are you doing?"

Zach paused, then offered a sheepish grin. "Hopefully something dashingly intelligent," he replied, then when the rest of them only stared at him in confusion, elaborated further. "Okay, I have no idea if this will work, but we'll have to try it sooner or later, and I'm thirsty. Just be ready to run."

Then he knelt beside the stream and carefully dipped the mouth of the flask into the running water. The rest of them held their breath. Air bubbled as the flask filled, until finally Zach lifted it back out with the same care not to let the water touch his fingers. They all watched the waters for another long minute before releasing a collective sigh.

"How did you know?" Willow asked.

"I made an educated guess," Zachary said. "The shade said something about a spark of life. Figured that might have something to do with us."

Logan frowned. The words had a ring of familiarity about them, but he couldn't follow the man's logic.

Zachary eyed the flask warily before taking a swig. When no light appeared within and barking didn't follow, he offered it to the others. When his turn came, Logan accepted it gratefully. As he drank, the words of the shade finally returned to him.

Long starved, they seek the spark of life, that which was so long denied them.

He still didn't entirely know how Zachary had made the connection, but it seemed there must be something about humans themselves that the beasts hungered. Something that had transferred to the stream when Rob touched its waters.

"I will leave you now," the highland woman announced suddenly.

"You're leaving?" Logan asked.

The woman was already turning away, but she paused at his question. "Yes."

Zachary grunted as he levered himself back up from the rock he'd perched himself on. "Are you sure?" He gestured to where Amilyse and Rob lingered nearby. "We've got a pair of monster hunters on hand," he said lightly.

Willow eyed the pair. Rob stared back, his eyes hostile.

"I believe so, yes," she said eventually.

"There might be safety in numbers with those things."

Willow hesitated. "Perhaps, but I will move more quickly on my own."

Zachary looked like he would like to argue further, before seeming to think better of it.

"Your questions?"

"The shade answered some," came Willow's reply, surprising Logan. As far as he was aware, it had only appeared to himself and Zachary. Did that mean Willow had a fossil as well?

"Other questions still need answers," the woman added.

A silence lingered at her words, before Zachary offered a nod.

"Wait!" Logan burst out, before the woman could turn away again.

A frown creased Willow's forehead. "What is it?"

"The others you mentioned…" Logan paused, swallowing. He wasn't sure he wanted to know the answer to his question. "Did any of them have long black hair, blue eyes?"

The woman's frown deepened. "On the ship, I saw you standing at the bow with another man. Is this the one you seek?"

Logan nodded, his heart lodged in his throat. "My brother," he rasped.

Willow shook her head. "I did not see him there."

With that, she turned and disappeared into the grass.

Logan slumped back to the ground with a long breath. His brother hadn't been amongst the dead. Of that he could at least be thankful. Though that still left him questioning whether Dustin had even made it to the island. The more time passed here, the more his questions grew. His brother would have answers, when they found him.

If we find him.

Rather than linger on the thought, Logan pushed himself to his feet. His brother was out there somewhere.

He had to be.

❧ 13 ❧

ZACHARY

Zachary's hands were trembling as he reached for his lighter and pipe. He would never admit it, but the incident with the stream had left him shaken. It had been a long time since he'd been pursued. And he was no longer the man he'd once been.

Most of his tobacco had been lost during his midnight swim and he'd left the rest drying for a special occasion. Now seemed as good a time as any. But as he flicked the lighter, no spark came from the contraption. He struck it again and again, but it must have been damaged in the water, for the flame did not appear.

He tucked the pipe and lighter back away with a muttered curse. His hands were still trembling. It wasn't just from the fear, he knew. Age had slowed him today, but even that was not the entire story. The six months the physician had given him were already halfway gone.

So little time.

A terrible loneliness gripped him as he sat beside the river. He'd barely noticed during their flight, but it was strange how its waters had grown as they moved upstream. Most grew larger towards the coast, as other waterways joined together and grew. He looked at the waters again, noticing now some dark patches across the bed. Leaning closer, he saw that the currents formed tiny whirlpools in those places.

That was why the waterway shrank towards the coast. Its waters were slowly draining away, disappearing into little fissures in the riverbed. Vanishing into the depths of the crystal island.

Zach shivered despite himself. Imagining the darkness below their feet, his regrets returned. What was he doing here, so far from home? This island, with its monsters and crystals and shades, it was a place for the young. Better that he'd left this voyage for the likes of Rob and Logan and Amilyse. Naïve they might be, but how else did one learn than by facing the dark things of this world.

There was no place here for an aging thief. He should have accepted his fate and stayed like Margery had wanted, stayed with the one person who'd ever loved him.

No. Feeling the tears welling in his eyes, he forced the memories from his mind and levered himself to his feet. *No, there is power here. You will find a way.*

He shivered. Instincts long honed by a life of crime told him not to trust a thing the shade had said, but there was no denying the magic of this place. It remained to be seen whether it could help him. But they would find no answers resting here beside the river. The sun was already falling rapidly towards the unseen horizon. Despite the unnatural warmth of the island, it seemed the short winter days still prevailed.

"So you were the source of all the commotion, Mr. Sicario." A woman's voice interrupted his contemplations.

Zachary's head jerked up. For a moment, he thought Willow had returned. Instead, it was Captain Cordelia of Leith who parted the tall strands of grass. She was followed by half a dozen of her hulking sailors, each armed with a rifle. His heart sank. Despite their agreement, the woman and her crew were yet another complication. The island was quickly becoming crowded.

Rob and Amilyse seemed to think the same. They reached for their blades at the sight of the newcomers' arms. Zach stepped between the captain's group and his own, arms raised to see off any violence.

"A fine afternoon to you, captain," he greeted her with a smile. "I'm pleased to see that you and your men survived the accident with your dear ship."

The captain came to an abrupt halt. "Yes, I thought you'd perished for sure," she said, her eyes narrowing.

"Seems the Gods aren't done with me yet."

"The engine failed just after you left the bridge."

Zach didn't miss the suggestion in her voice. "Then gladly I could not have had anything to do with it, being so far from the engine room," Zach replied with an easy grin. "That does, of course, leave the question as to why so fine a ship would fail." He paused, letting the words sink in. Others were likely to be asking the same question. "A discussion for another time, I'm sure. Let me introduce you to my latest compatriots."

The others still wore a mixture of expressions when he turned to them, from suspicion to surprise to anger. He ignored them all and began to make introductions.

"The lovely siblings here are Amilyse and Rob Rainer. Monster hunters, apparently. Think they're destined to save the world or some nonsense."

"Careful, old man," Rob growled. After a moment, though, he sheathed his blade in a show of peace and offered a polite nod to Cordelia. "Greetings, Captain," he continued. "It is good to see you survived. We are in dire need of competent allies to combat the demons of this land."

Amilyse said nothing. Nor did Cordelia for that matter.

"Yes, all very proper, these two," Zach said, before pointing to the kid. "And this is Logan. Not half as interesting as the monster hunters, I'm afraid."

Logan nodded a greeting to the captain, his eyes clearly nervous. Zachary laughed inwardly. The kid was no liar, that was for sure. Guilt at his illicit embarking on *The Rising Tide* was written plainly across his face.

"I'm beginning to think you know everyone on this island," Logan muttered after shaking hands with Cordelia.

His words earned a chuckle from the captain herself. "Yes, despite his name not being on my manifest." She paused, eyeing him closely. "Which, it occurs to me, neither was any Logan."

"I...er...ah..." Logan stammered, his face going a beet red.

"Like myself, Logan acquired his token through a less than legal manner," Zachary supplied when he thought the kid had suffered enough. "However, he only stole from his brother. It seems a case of no harm, no foul though, as you let his brother board anyway."

Cordelia started, her eyes snapping back to Logan. "Your brother is Dustin Kaine?"

Logan's eyebrows knitted together in a frown. "You know my brother? Have you seen him?"

"Like I said, I put together the manifest," Cordelia said quickly, dismissing the question and moving past the kid towards the water. "Good, you found water, we were growing desperate…"

"*No!*" Zachary and Logan exclaimed in unison.

Cordelia froze. Brow furrowed, she stared at them. "Why?"

Zachary quickly explained what had happened after Rob had drunk from the stream earlier. Her eyes narrowed as he spoke, while the men behind her shifted nervously on their feet, casting glances at the long grass.

"These creatures, you didn't get a glimpse of them?"

"No."

"Then how do we know they're even dangerous?" She gestured at her sailors. "A few shots are bound to scare them off."

Rob snorted. "Your modern weapons will not harm these demon spawn."

Cordelia turned smouldering eyes on the young man. "And I suppose your little knives will?" She laughed.

It was the wrong move.

Rob's face darkened, his knuckles turning white as he clenched his fists. "Enough of this," he snapped. "Sister, come. Let the fools slink and hide behind their guns. It is time we finally proved ourselves worthy of our family's name."

He started towards the water, face set with determination.

A curse slipped from Zachary's lips and he started towards the man, but Cordelia was faster still.

"Duncan, Junayd."

At a gesture from the captain, two of her sailors slung their rifles over their shoulders and leapt at the young man. The heavily muscled sailors had Rob overpowered before he knew what was happening. Growling, he struggled in their grasp, trying to draw his sabre. When that failed, he demanded his sister come to his aid, but Amilyse stood frozen. She allowed herself to be disarmed by another of Cordelia's men without a fight.

"Well that's useful," Zachary remarked when the twins were under control.

Cordelia grunted. "What about Mr. Kaine?"

"The kid is fine," Zach replied, glancing in Logan's direction. His face was pale. He stared at the twins as the sailors bound their hands with strips of rope.

"So what do we do about the water?"

Zach tossed her his flask by way of answer.

"Gah!"

They both spun back to Rob as one of the sailors hit the ground. Blood now streamed from the man's nose. Growling, he reached for his fallen rifle, even as the other sailors raised their weapons and took aim.

Zach sighed. He might have known the foolish young man would meet his end like this. But before a shot could be fired, Logan stepped between Rob and the riflemen. His face was pale, his eyes wide. He made no attempt to draw the sabre on his hip, but raised his empty hands instead.

"Wait!" he cried. "Please, don't shoot!"

A groan rasped from Zach's chest. He closed his eyes. He had no desire to see the kid gunned down alongside the fool. But to his surprise, the hail of gunfire he'd been expecting did not follow. He looked from the sailors to Cordelia, and saw that the woman had raised a hand to stay their bullets.

"Get out of the way, Logan," Rob said softly. He moved alongside the kid and place a hand on his shoulder. "This is my fight."

Zach shook his head. The young gentleman truly had a death wish.

"No," Logan surprised Zach yet again. "You're only here because I convinced you to help protect us. You don't deserve this."

"The young fool is right, Mr. Kaine," Cordelia snapped. "Now is not the time to play hero. If this man wishes to die, I am only too happy to appease him."

"Your weapons do not scare me, captain," Rob growled, raising his sabre. The rattle of fingers reaching for triggers whispered around the clearing.

Zach stifled another sigh. *Why me?* he wondered, even as he stepped forward to join his companions.

"Gentlemen, gentlemen. Esteemed lady," he said, his hands raised to show his intent. "I'm sure we can come to some agreement."

"I said I was done talking," Rob replied.

"You'll be done breathing if you don't do what I say," Zach hissed, unable to keep the anger from his voice. A knife appeared in his hand, shining red in the light of the setting sun.

The blade seemed to make more of an impression on Rob than the six rifles combined. He frowned, glancing from the knife to Zach to Cordelia, then back to Zach.

"What do you propose?" Rob asked.

At his side, Logan visibly relaxed at the man's words. Zach took a step closer to the young man, hands still raised.

"A truce, if only for this night," he said with a gesture at the setting sun. Darkness was already sliding its way across the plateau, the shadow of the mountain drawing nearer. With it, the unnatural warmth of the day was fading, heralding winter's return. "Let's set camp here," Zach continued, "see what manner of food we can put together between us. Maybe even enjoy a fire, if we're feeling bold. In the morning, if you and your sister are determined to continue with this madness, you can go on your way without us and summon monsters to your hearts' content."

Rob hesitated a moment longer, but it was clear the battle was already won. At last he gave a curt nod. Sighs of relief spread around the clearing as he lowered his weapon. Even Zach found himself relaxing, so much so he almost missed the signal Cordelia gave.

He spun back, but it was already too late—a sailor raised his rifle and brought the butt down on the back of Rob's skull. The sharp *crunch* of the blow finally drew a reaction from Amilyse, as with a shriek she leapt at them. But already disarmed, she was little threat and another of the sailors caught her before she could reach her brother. Logan stumbled back as the sailor straightened and pointed the weapon at his chest.

Zachary turned to the captain. "Do you really think that was necessary?"

"I'm not one to take unnecessary risks, Mr. Sicario," she replied before turning to her men. "Bind that man before he wakes. The sister too, if she keeps up like that." She seemed to hesitate when it came to Logan. "What about you, Mr. Kaine?"

Logan hesitated, glancing at Zach before swallowing whatever objections he might have had. "You won't harm them?"

"So long as they don't have any more ideas about summoning these monsters of yours," was the captain's reply.

To his credit, the kid glanced again at Rob before offering a nod. His loyalty was impressive, though the twins had hardly done anything to earn it. Again, Zachary found himself wondering at the missing older brother. It was impossible to assess what manner of man this Dustin was, but he sensed the reality might differ significantly from the picture Logan painted.

"And you, Mr. Sicario?" Cordelia queried, turning to Zachary. "Any objections?"

"None at all," Zachary replied. "Now, I believe someone said something about some food?"

❧ 14 ❧

ZACHARY

The sun set quickly over the crystal island, plunging the company into the icy chill of a winter's night. With the onset of darkness, the personality of the land changed. The whispering of the wind through the long grass became a sibilant hiss, as if demons had truly ascended from the seven hells. As the moon took its place in the sky, the stark mountain peak appeared as a shadow against the silver light, a dark presence looming above.

Zachary shivered as he watched the change. It was like the subtle distortion of a dream, the picturesqueness of day shifting in subtle ways to a landscape borne of nightmares.

Then came the first flickering strands of light in the dark. It began as a spark, a dull blue in the depths of the river, in those dark caverns he had noticed in the day. Like the flames of a freshly lit hearth, those sparks did not take long to spread. He watched the river come to life, until the entire waters burned like an unholy reflection of the moon above.

His heart lodged in his throat, Zach waited for the howls to follow, for the terror to freeze his muscles, for that awful sense of helplessness. To his surprise they did not come. When he finally looked around, Zach was unsurprised to see the others also staring at the stream.

"Do you think we should leave?" Cordelia asked.

Zach shuddered as he looked from the woman to the swirling currents. His first instinct was to say yes, but he forced himself to approach the matter logically. When Rob had drunk from the stream earlier, the barking had begun almost immediately. This…this seemed to be part of some natural phenomenon, some part of the island's laws, perhaps. Turning from the river, he looked across the plateau, watching, waiting…

Out in the darkness, other lights appeared, some blue, others green, yet others a deep scarlet. They stood there for a time, until finally Zachary expelled a breath.

"No," he said. "If it was the light the creatures were attracted by, they'll be everywhere tonight. And this is the only water we've found."

Cordelia considered that for half a moment before nodding and gesturing to her men.

"Duncan, set up a perimeter. Junayd and Byron, you're taking first watch. Reeves, Ioan, Peck, fish out those oatcakes and whatever other food we recovered from the shore and pass it around."

The men leapt to obey. Cordelia looked like she was about to join them in some task, but Zachary gestured for her to wait. Crossing to a boulder that had been split in two by some unknown force, he sat near the water's edge and waved for Cordelia to do the same.

"Thank you for sparing the young man," he said as the woman settled on the other half of the boulder.

Rob sat on the other side of their makeshift camp, hands tied behind his back and mouth gagged after he'd woken and begun to curse them all with threats of violence and death. His sister had been left free for now, though without her weapon.

"You know their family is noble blood, right?" Cordelia remarked. "Weren't you the one claiming their lot are more trouble than they're worth?"

"I stand by that statement," Zachary replied, "but the kid isn't so bad. It would have been a shame to see him caught up in the crossfire."

He watched the woman closely as he spoke, seeking some reaction to the mention of Logan, but she said nothing, only stared at the shimmering waters. The soft tones of music drifted from the camp behind them. Zach glanced over his shoulder and saw that one of Cordelia's men had a harmonica at his lips.

"Byron's quite the musician," Cordelia said, following Zach's gaze.

"Let us hope it doesn't draw the beasts."

"What are they?" the captain asked after a pause.

Zachary hesitated. "As I said, I do not know what they look like," he replied, "only what I heard. Their cries were like this place: unnatural. There was something unnerving about them. Made me feel as though I were a spring lamb waiting for the slaughter. I haven't frozen like that since...I can't remember when."

"Maybe you're just getting old, Sicario."

"Maybe," he murmured, then changed the subject. "So was there anything left of the ship?"

"If there is, it lies at the bottom of the Northern Sea," Cordelia muttered. "I can't explain it. Something happened to the engine. It just stopped. In those swells...she never stood a chance."

Zach grunted. "Are you sure it wasn't sabotage, one of your engineers maybe?"

"They all went down with the ship, so I rather doubt it, Sicario," she said it in a bland tone, but he noticed that the edges of her lips tightened at the mention of the lost men. "So did my box of cigars, for that matter." she continued quickly. "Don't suppose that pipe of yours survived."

Nodding, he drew out the pipe and lighter. "Enough for one last smoke."

They had decided against a fire in the end, though there was more than enough driftwood lying amongst the grass— presumably leftover from when the island had risen from the depths. It just wasn't worth the risk. So Zach hadn't tried his lighter again. He tried it now, but it remained stubbornly dead.

"Don't suppose you've got a light?" he asked.

"Here," Cordelia replied, drawing a box of matches from her coat.

She must have kept them someplace sealed, for they were not sodden like everything Zach had carried into the water. Taking the box, he struck a match against the phosphorous on the side, but nothing happened. He tried again, and again, until the match snapped. He went through several more before giving up.

"Water must have gotten to them?"

"Damn," she muttered, taking back the box. "Well, if you find any working ones, consider them included as part of our bargain. I could use a bloody smoke after today."

Zachary nodded, though his chest clenched at her words. He'd suddenly become uncomfortably aware of the crystal fossil in his pocket. He'd told Cordelia anything he found on the island was hers. It was a good thing he'd told Logan to keep quiet about the stones. Given their apparent importance, Zach wouldn't part with it willingly, but the arms Cordelia commanded wouldn't exactly give him much in the way of choice.

"The kid's brother," he said instead, "he said you let him board without a token?"

Cordelia looked away at that, but Zachary was done with dancing around the secret. He leaned closer, allowing the sound of the sailor's music to cover his words.

"Why?" he pressed. "Who is this Dustin to you?"

"A man I would very much like to find," Cordelia replied, her voice dropping to a growl.

Zach raised his eyebrows in surprise.

"That man is the reason any of us are on this cursed island, Sicario."

"What?" Zachary's surprise deepened. "I thought you…" He trailed off, recalling the look the woman had given him back on the bridge of *The Rising Tide*, the amusement in her eyes. "You didn't organise this expedition at all, did you?"

"No," Cordelia replied grimly. "I sold the extra spaces, sure, but Dustin Kaine was the one who fronted the expedition. Paid well for it too, or I never would have considered crossing the Council. You know how big that flotilla is out there? Most of the southern armada must be camped beyond those cloudbanks." She paused. "Probably a good thing. From what I've heard, we've already outstayed our welcome. Peck's a decent huntsman; he should be able to get some driftwood burning tomorrow, with or without matches. We'll make a signal fire even those blind naval sailors won't be able to miss."

Silence fell between them as she trailed off. Zachary was only partly listening. His gaze was focused across their makeshift camp, where Logan Kaine sat with the young Amilyse. Had he misread the young man? Had he been manipulating them all along, playing Zachary to some unknown ends? But no, he knew enough to know the innocence in the kid's eyes was genuine.

Dustin can be very persuasive when he wants to be.

That was what Logan had said. He'd thought it the naïve belief of a younger sibling in their elder, but perhaps there was more to it. Who was this man, who had so readily risked the wrath of the Council?

And what does he want? Zachary wondered.

"If you'll excuse me," he said abruptly, rising from his rock.

Cordelia nodded and he left her beside the shimmering river, making for where Logan and Amilyse sat in quiet conversation. Cordelia rose behind him.

"Byron, you think that's a good idea?" she asked as she approached where her men sat.

The sailor with the harmonica smiled sheepishly and tucked the little instrument into his jacket. Scars criss-crossing the backs of his arms. Several of the other men sported similar marks and one was missing several fingers from his left hand. Where had Cordelia found these men?

The kid looked up at the sound of his footsteps, eyes widening to find Zachary standing over them. Amilyse tensed, her eyes flashing as she rose and faced him. Gone was the timid girl from earlier. Love was like that sometimes. It cut through the fear, bringing out the fire within.

"You said we had an accord," she snarled, teeth bared, golden hair shining in the moonlight. "I demand you let my brother go free."

"I also warned you not to trust me," Zachary replied easily. "So when you think about it, this is really all on you."

A growl rumbled from the back of Amilyse's throat and Zach leaned back, fully expecting her to leap at him. But Logan spoke before either could react.

"Amilyse," he said softly, "don't. These people aren't the patient sort."

To Zach's surprise, Amilyse paused at the kid's words. Her eyes flickered to where one of Cordelia's men stood. His hard eyes were fixed on the girl, one hand resting on the butt of his gun. Smiling, Zachary allowed the moment to stretch out, for the weight of the girl's predicament to fall upon her, before clearing his throat.

"If you'll excuse me, Miss Rainer, I would like to speak with Logan alone."

Amilyse's eyes flashed daggers at him, but she made no further advances against his person. She spun on her heel and stalked across to where her brother lay under guard.

Zachary watched her go for a moment. She had a shapely figure, if the whole insanity about monster hunting could be ignored. Logan's eyes lingered on her as well and Zach smiled to himself.

Ah, to be young again, he thought. *I remember looking at Margery like that, once upon a time.*

"That was a brave thing you did," he said instead, taking a seat beside the young man, "speaking up for her brother."

"Thank you," Logan replied after a time, "but I know it was foolish. They would have killed us both if you hadn't intervened."

"Yes, it was quite the lapse in judgement, wasn't it?" He laughed. "Don't worry, I won't let it happen again."

A frown replaced Logan's grateful look. "You saved our lives."

"I saved the life of a *noble*," Zachary replied. "Believe me, kid, that's a dumb move."

"You just said it was brave."

"The two are not mutually exclusive," Zach said, before offering a sigh. "Think about it. Would a man like Rob have done the same for you, if your positions were reversed?"

"He already has," Logan said simply, then seemed to hesitate. "Why do you think he stayed with us when we fled the beasts."

Zachary frowned. He *had* wondered about that, but had assumed Rob's courage had failed him in the end. "Why?"

Logan glanced in the direction of the twins. He swallowed. "Because I asked him to," he said quietly.

It took a moment for Zach to understand. He laughed when it clicked. "You didn't think he could really fight them, did you? Sorry, 'slay' them is probably the proper term."

A scowl replaced Logan's doubt. "I only thought it prudent we stick together."

"So you told poor Rob we needed his magic sword to defend us," Zach surmised.

"Yes," Logan admitted. "And how did we repay him." Anger crept into the young man's voice. "How did *you* repay him?"

Zach let out a sigh. "The pair might be genuine, kid, but they're still fools," he replied at last. "We couldn't allow them to draw the creatures down on us—Cordelia couldn't trust them not to try."

"He gave his word."

Zachary only stared at the kid, until Logan was forced to look away. "I believe we already spoke about trust being a luxury."

"That sounds like a lonely life."

"It is," Zachary replied truthfully, even as a face drifted before his eyes.

Or at least it was, until Margery.

Silence fell between them. "You should know, the captain plans on returning to the coast and signalling the navy tomorrow," Zach said at last.

To his surprise, the kid didn't react to his words. Logan's eyes were fixed on the darkness beyond the halo of the river. The plateau was still lit by a thousand tiny pinpricks of unknown lights. But as Zach watched, one of those distant pinpricks flickered out.

He frowned. "What was that?"

IN THE DARK OF NIGHT, THE WIND THAT HAD SWEPT ACROSS the plateau died suddenly. An unnatural stillness settled over the island, the silence of expectation, of a thousand creatures holding their collective breaths.

The first tendrils of mist formed over the quiet waters of the hidden lake. They gathered quickly, forming a dense fog that swept down onto the plateau. Lights that had shone from the waters and trees and dirt were smothered, winking out.

The mists swept on, gathering about the grasslands. A power went with them, a dark whisper, a call to those that still slept.

In a burrow in the earth, the call reached one such slumbering mind. The creature stirred as the cool tendrils wrapped about it, carrying with them a long-forgotten scent.

The scent of humanity.

Eyes snapped open. Great paws clawed the earth. A monstrous body hauled itself from the earth.

And a howl that had not been heard in a thousand years rent the night.

15

LOGAN

Logan watched as the lights in the distance died one by one. Bit by bit, darkness returned to the night.

"It's getting closer," he said finally.

Beside him, Zachary nodded. He still wasn't sure of the man, after his betrayal of Rob. But just now, beggars couldn't be choosers. Behind them, Cordelia and her men had noticed the phenomenon as well. They stood, weapons clutched tight, waiting. Zach's hand fell to the knife on his belt. Logan did the same with his father's sabre, but he drew no reassurance from its cool touch.

Soon the last light on the plateau blinked out, leaving only the glow of the river, a sapphire oasis amidst the black.

The camp waited, silent, for the darkness to claim them too.

Abruptly, a fog came rolling forward, swallowing the long grass surrounding the camp, creeping onwards to claim them as well. Logan shuddered at the sudden cold. So heavy were the swirling mists, he found himself struggling to make out the others in the gloom. Only Zachary's features were clear, standing directly beside him. The man wore a grim look as he watched the mists swirling about them.

Abruptly, the man chuckled, the tension fleeing his body. He turned to Logan and grinned.

"Relax, kid. It's just a little fog."

For a moment, Logan wanted to believe the words.

Then a shadow coalesced from the mists before them.

Beware, Pathfinders. The shade rasped, its dark tendrils mixing with the mists. ***A Thoona stalks this night. You must wake the stones, or you will surely perish.***

Logan's heart began to race. Such was his panic at its first words, it took him long moments for his sluggish mind to piece together the rest of its words.

"*How?*" he gasped, reaching out a desperate hand to grasp the creature. His hand passed straight through the shadows. The thing had no more substance than the mists around them.

I am a Guardian, not guide, Path—

"Yes, you said that before," Zachary snapped. "Maybe you should consider a change of occupation."

A distant sound carried to them through the mists. At first, Logan thought the cheerful sailor Peck had begun to play his harmonica again. But no, he glimpsed the man through the drifting tendrils, not far from where they stood. He clutched his rifle tight to his chest, eyes wide as he stared at something off in the mist.

The sound came again. This time it was unmistakeable. Someone—or something—was playing music out in the mists. But the soft chords didn't come from any instrument Logan recognised. They hung in the air, as though the music were a part of the fog itself. It gathered strength, its volume rising as its source grew closer.

The song wound its way into Logan's consciousness, the sweet notes carrying him away to a time long ago. He smiled as warmth embraced him, as he looked up into the face of his mother, felt her arms holding him tight. The song was her voice carried from the distant past, a gift brought to him from beyond the grave, a—

Logan started as a sudden heat flared against his chest. He jerked, surprised to find himself lying facedown in the dirt. The fire still burned against his chest, and he scrambled to pull the crystal fossil from his pocket. He was surprised to only find it warm when he clasped it in his fist.

Only then did he think to look around. He blinked, surprised to find Zachary lying on the ground beside him—though as he watched, the man stirred. With a curse, he rolled to his side, fumbling for his own crystal.

Logan looked at the stone in his hand. It had woken him. But how had he fallen asleep in the first place? The last thing he remembered was the mists, the music...it had stopped now, but his heart began to race as he stood and looked around. Cordelia and the sailors, even Amilyse and Rob, they were all on the ground.

He stumbled towards them, and the glow of his stone brightened. By the time he reached them, something in its light had already woken them. He moved from one to another, checking each was alert before looking for the shade again.

But the creature had vanished, leaving them alone in the mists.

They hadn't had a chance to ask what in the seven hells a Thoona was, but he sensed it had something to do with that music.

"What is that thing?" Cordelia demanded as she stood, looking at the stone in Logan's hand.

But Logan was in no state to answer the woman's questions. He watched the mists, struggling for a glimpse of whatever the shade had warned them of, but the tendrils were too thick to see more than a few yards beyond the river's light.

"Please, you have to free us!"

Logan jumped as Amilyse's voice carried through the night. He found her struggling with the man guarding her brother. Before he could interfere, a shout from Cordelia cut through the mists.

"Duncan, cut them free," she growled, "and give them their swords. We might need them."

Bellowing commands, the woman strode through the mists. Alert again, she pointed at her men, gathering them in a defensive circle facing outwards, ordering them to ready their weapons. Logan wondered how she could appear so calm. They'd all just been put under some kind of spell, sent into a deep slumber. Whatever was out there, it didn't obey the rules of nature.

Wake the stones, or you will surely perish

He looked back at the crystal in his hand. It shone a brilliant white, the fossil at its core shimmering, casting its own shadow upon the ground. He clutched it tight between his fingers, willing it to reveal its secrets, but there was no change in the pale quartz.

"Let them come," Rob snarled, diverting Logan's attention from the stone. The monster hunter strode through the mists, blade in hand. He came to a stop beside Logan and nodded to his sabre. "You'd best draw that, Logan, or get out of the way. Demons are not known for their mercy."

"For once I agree," Zachary replied.

"Did I ask your opinion, traitor?" Rob snapped.

Zachary only chuckled. He drew the knife from his belt—and a second from some secret compartment in his sleeve. "Save your anger for another time, Rob," he responded. "It's time to find out if these monsters of yours bleed."

"They will," Rob snarled. "Come, sister. Destiny awaits us."

The breath caught in Logan's throat as Amilyse stepped forward. Their eyes met as she passed him by. He saw the fear there. But this time there was no hesitation as she joined her brother. Lifting her chin, she stared out into the mists, seeking the beasts.

"Foul beasts of the dark!" Rob bellowed, raising his blade high. "Come and meet your end!"

As though in answer to his challenge, a roar shook the night.

Despite his attempt at bravery, a moan slipped from Logan's lips and he found himself retreating a step. Even Zachary seemed shaken—yet somehow Rob and Amilyse stood strong, silver blades held at the ready, waiting for the creatures to appear. Somewhere behind them, the captain was shouting, ordering her men to hold the line, to wait until they saw the creatures before firing.

Logan shuddered, his entire body trembling. He looked from the twins to the crystal he still gripped in his free hand. It hadn't changed—if anything, its glow had dimmed. He struggled to hold back a scream. Silently, he begged for it to save him, to come to life and destroy the creature that stalked the mists…but nothing happened.

Logan closed his eyes, fear giving way to terror.

Fool, fool, fool!

What was he doing here? He'd thought himself ready for an adventure, to finally prove himself a hero like his brother, like their father. How wrong he'd been. At the first signs of danger, he had become a coward, trembling behind the blades of better men.

This was his brother's world, not Logan's.

"I hope you two are right about those blades."

Logan's eyes snapped open. That had been Zachary. For the first time, he heard an unmistakable note of fear in the man's voice. It did nothing to improve his own terror, but… it was somewhat reassuring, to know he was not the only one to feel fear.

After a moment, he finally reached for his sword and moved to stand with the others. A muffled silence hung over the night, the mists seeming to swallow up all sound, so that it seemed they stood alone in a ring of empty white. The music did not come again, even as the minutes stretched out, until it seemed that perhaps the Thoona—whatever that was—had passed them by.

"Very well, demon of the night," Rob said suddenly. "Amilyse, protect Logan and these other fools. I will find the beast."

He stepped into the mists before any of them could argue. The white tendrils parted momentarily before swallowing him up. Amilyse gave a little hiss and took a step after him, before she caught herself. Logan saw that her blade was trembling, but couldn't gather the strength to offer any words of reassurance. He could barely keep the sword from falling from his shaking hand.

He clenched the stone tighter with his other hand, willing it to grant him courage—if nothing else.

Abruptly, a scarlet glow lit up the mists, so bright it cut through the night like a razor. It burned like a bonfire, the source just out of sight in the fog, though Logan sensed there was no heat about this light. It was like what the crystals emitted: cold, a light without life.

"Back, demon!" Rob's shout carried through the fog. A shadow flickered near the scarlet light. "You cannot stand —" His voice cut off abruptly.

"Rob!" Amilyse cried, her blade wavering as she stared into the eddying mists. Then, before anyone could stop her, she darted away.

Logan's heart gave a violent lurch. He looked at Zachary. The fear was open on his face now. Terror crawled its awful way up Logan's spine.

Then a woman's scream carried through the darkness, and something within him snapped.

Without thinking, he leapt into the mists after Amilyse, his father's sabre raised before him. He caught a curse from behind, then the crunch of footsteps as Zachary followed.

The mists swallowed them up.

Logan stumbled as the world was plunged into white. The red light had already vanished, fading back into the fog. The long grass pressed in around them, the mists and darkness making it all the more difficult to see a foot in front of their faces. As they left the light of the river, the fossils they each held became their only source of light, though even that was unreliable. Logan's flickered in his hand like a guttering lantern. He feared it could go out at any second.

Thankfully, Zachary's dark fossil produced a steady light.

"You better not get us killed, kid," he muttered.

They froze as a scream carried through the night. Amilyse. Logan started in the direction of the sound.

"I don't remember asking you to come."

"Blame it on my generous spirit."

Silence fell between them. Amilyse had fallen silent again. There had been no further shouts from Rob. Logan swallowed, the hairs on the back of his neck prickling. He imagined eyes watching them from the darkness, great teeth closing about his throat. The red glow did not return.

They found Amilyse crouched in the dirt, her soft sobs carrying through the night. The magical sword lay discarded at her side. A second lay shattered on the ground before her. Her slender frame was bent in two, cradling something in her lap. Logan's heart fell into the pit of his stomach when he realised what it was.

Or rather, who.

Rob's eyes were still open, though they stared blankly into the void. A look of shock was upon his face, as though even in his final moments, he could not believe it had ended as it had.

"By the Old Gods," Logan whispered.

Zachary said nothing. The grimace on his face were all the words he needed. As Logan stood fixed in place, Zachary crossed to where Amilyse crouched. She looked up at his approach, her eyes stained red, tears still streaming down her cheeks.

"It...this...wasn't supposed...to happen!" she gasped between sobs.

"Did you see what did this, Amilyse?" Zachary asked, his voice not unkind.

But Amilyse did not seem to hear the words. She buried her face in her brother's chest, hugging him close, as though if she could only protect him from the night, he might yet survive.

That was a futile hope, even in this mystical place. Blood no longer flowed from the terrible wound that had torn out Rob's throat. The flickering of Logan's crystal caught the sheen of blood on the ground beneath the man.

"Seven hells, girl," Zachary snapped suddenly, "get up before the same thing happens to you."

The woman's head jerked up at that, her eyes wide, the last of the colour draining from her face. She looked around, eyes wide, as though finally remembering where she was.

"Come on," Logan said more gently than the older man had managed. He stumbled forward and offered his hand.

She took it after a long moment, as though her mind was still struggling to process words. Only as he drew her to her feet did she resist, her gaze falling to the body at her feet.

"I can't...I can't leave him."

"You don't have much choice, girl," Zachary all but snarled.

"Here, take her," Logan said quickly, "I'll bring him."

Amilyse's eyes widened at his words, while Zachary's brow knitted into a scowl. He said nothing though, only took the young woman's hand, drawing her away from the body—though not before he picked up her fallen sabre.

Swallowing his fear, Logan turned back to Rob. He had no desire to touch the dead man, but...he understood Amilyse's pain. The thought of Dustin lying out here somewhere, his body left for the beasts to defile...

...forcing the images that thought conjured aside, Logan sheathed his sword and crouched beside Rob. Reaching out a hand, he slid the man's eyes closed. He shivered as he felt the body's warmth. He'd only ever seen one death before—his mother, when she had succumbed to the plague. The memory was a cold dagger in his chest, but he let it go and carefully scooped Rob up from the ground.

Grunting, he struggled to lift the man to his shoulders. The noble was by no means light and Logan was far from the strongest of men. When he finally managed it, he clenched his teeth and turned to seek the dim light of the creek. Thankfully, Zachary and Amilyse had lingered, and with a gesture from the older man, they set off back into the mists.

They hadn't gone far from the stream, no more than a hundred yards, yet to Logan that walk seemed a hundred miles. Rob's bulk pressed him down, sapping his strength. He tried not to think about how the dead weight he carried had been another human just a few minutes before, alive and full of strength, eyes aglow with excitement as he chased his destiny.

Logan's anger stirred on behalf of the dead man, at the lies he'd been fed from the hands of his family. Rob had believed himself invincible, destined to battle the evils of this world. Now, despite his courage, he was dead, his silver sword broken.

And evil still stalked this night.

By the time the three of them stumbled back into the glow of the stream, Logan's strength was all but spent. Cordelia and her men still stood in their ring, rifles at the ready, eyes on the swirling mists. Cordelia raised her weapon at their appearance, but quickly lowered it again when Zachary led the way from the fog. The two of them stepped away. Whispered words passed between them, leaving Logan to stagger forward and carefully lower the body to the ground.

His heart was pounding, the blood roaring in his ears from the fear and exertion, but he felt a small measure of pride as Amilyse knelt beside her brother and reached out to stroke his cheek. At least he hadn't run. At least he'd done something worthwhile, however small, to help ease Amilyse's pain.

The sensation did not last long.

Ahhhh-ooooo!

Logan and the others in the camp froze, turning slowly to face the darkness.

Within the fogs, a scarlet light bloomed, shifting, moving, coming closer.

And the mists parted to reveal the beast.

Teeth bared, copper eyes aglow in the moonlight, the beast advanced on all fours towards them. It moved like the lions he'd once seen on a visit to the Londinium zoo. Those beasts had fascinated and terrified the young Logan in equal measure.

This creature even had the mane of a male lion, but in place of two eyes, four glared at them from the dark. And it was far larger than the beasts back in Londinium, standing as tall as any horse, its jaws large enough to swallow a man's head whole and have room for seconds. Claws the size of knives tore the ground, leaving great grooves in the earth. Its jagged tufts of fur stood on end, the scarlet light rippling from the creature itself, staining the night bloodred.

Opening its terrible jaws, the creature howled. The sound cut through the silence, shaking Logan to his very core. His gut twisted in a knot and iron bands squeezed his chest tight. He struggled to breathe through the sudden terror. When he finally did manage to inhale, the stench of rotting struck him like a solid, physical thing. If he'd had anything in his stomach, he would have undoubtedly hurled it onto the crystal soil.

His sword still hung from his belt where he'd sheathed it to carry Rob. He didn't bother to draw it. No sword could harm this creature.

Nothing could.

❦ 16 ❦

ZACHARY

Zachary swore.

He was surprised he could say anything at all. The creature's roar had filled him with such terror, it was all he could do to keep himself from fleeing. The monster before them was worse than any pack of hounds, worse than any creature upon this earth. It loomed before them, its four eyes burning with a copper light. In their metallic depths, Zachary could sense its rage, its hunger.

Screams came from all around as Cordelia's men scattered, but no gunshots sounded. Even beneath the weight of his own fear, Zachary had enough presence of mind to realise the strangeness of that.

He cast a glance over his shoulder. Cordelia stood a few yards behind them, eyes on her rifle rather than the beast. She was cursing violently. It was clear something had gone wrong with the weapon—with the others as well.

"Zachary!"

Logan stumbled beside him. He turned his attention to the beast. Its attention had turned to the pair on the ground— Amilyse, still knelt beside her brother. Face pale, she stared up at the monster. He felt a pang of pity for the woman. He'd seen that look many times in the faces of men. Shock had set in, stealing away her wits.

He could feel his own fear, the adrenaline pulsing in his veins, and drew a calming breath. Panic would not help him, nor the girl, though she was already probably beyond help. Maybe it was for the best. She'd almost gotten them killed once already this night, going after her brother.

But one look at Logan was all it took to know he would go to her rescue. He seemed to be growing a habit of putting himself in danger on behalf of those unworthy of the risk.

He was also the only reason Zach had followed the girl into the mists. The kid's brother clearly knew something about this place. In Zach's experience, keeping one brother alive was generally a good way of gaining the other's trust. And since Logan looked about ready to throw himself between the girl and the monster…

A curse slipped from Zach's lips. He looked at the mysterious crystal in his left hand. It was meant to be the key to everything. So far it had proven about as useful as a night-lamp. He would have to resort to traditional weapons.

His gaze turned to the sabre he carried in his right hand. Amilyse's blade. He didn't for a second believe in the stories the twins had told about their weapons, but it had a better reach than his knives. That was important against a creature so large.

Though Rob's death had already proven its deficiencies.

Still, with no better options, Zachary darted forward. Logan shouted out behind him, but Zach ignored the kid. For the first time in days, his breath came cleanly in the chill night air. His vision was clear as he neared the scarlet glow that was the monster. Fear added speed to his movements, the adrenaline pumping in his veins granting him desperate strength. The silver blade rippling in the bloody light, he raised it high.

Zachary gave no battle cry, no bellowed words as he aimed his sabre. That was the way of the warrior, the soldier. Not the dark forces that stalked the night. His blade fell in silence, the razor point slashing for the creature's throat.

Crack.

The harsh screech of breaking steel broke the silence of the night. Zachary staggered back from the creature, the blade still clutched in one trembling hand. With an almost morbid fascination, he watched as a spiderweb of cracks spread through the silvery steel. Belatedly, as though the fabric of the sword had finally caught up with its reality, the blade shattered. The steel pieces rang like bells as they struck the stony shore of the river.

Zachary stared at the useless hilt he now held.

The others stood in stunned silence.

Slowly, Zach's gaze shifted from the broken blade to the scarlet beast, and he saw what he'd missed. What they had all missed.

Like the cliffs and grass and the dirt beneath their feet, this creature was not of flesh and blood. Bulging muscles of crystal rippled as the giant head shifted, its fur shining. The crystal clinked as it moved, rock hard, impenetrable. No wonder their weapons had no effect. It seemed to know it too. There was no fear in the copper eyes as it inspected the humans, only that burning rage, only hunger.

Throwing back its great head, the beast howled.

The sound shattered the spell that had held the humans enthralled. With cries of panic, they scattered.

"The rifles aren't working!" a man cried out somewhere behind Zach.

The beast reacted to the sound, its copper gaze snapping to the owner of the voice. A sound rumbled from its throat, not the growl or roar one might have expected from such a terror, but a soft, joyous tone. The sailor froze. Swaying on his feet, a dazed smile came across his face and his eyes became glassy, as though his mind was someplace far away.

He stood like that until the beast leapt. Only as the crystal fangs closed upon him did the spell break. A scream rent the night, quickly cut off as the terrible jaws snapped closed.

Zachary watched on in horror. He was used to death. On the streets, in the underworld, it was an old rival, one you knew would inevitably overtake you, but you fought to your last breath. But this...

Rob had gotten off lightly.

Even so, he found himself unusually calm. Cordelia was screaming at her men and still struggling with her rifle, as though that might save them. Idly, his mind pondered the failure of the firearms. Had no one thought to check that they were functioning? No shots had been fired in their earlier conflict, and now he found himself wondering...

His skin tingled as he made the connection, his mind racing back to the wreckage of *The Rising Tide*. Had that only been last night? The engine had failed—that was what Cordelia had claimed. But she'd been unable to say why.

But that was not all, he realised. His lighter had failed since coming ashore. And Cordelia's matches.

Zachary shivered as he looked at the monster.

Something was very wrong on this island.

Rob had been right about that at least.

Out in the night, something howled. Not the beast they fought, but another still in the fog.

Zachary swore as he saw a second glow approaching. Not scarlet this one, but a darker shade of violet. Strangely, he felt no fear now. It had been a long shot, coming here anyway. At least he'd tried. At least he'd fought, instead of lying down and accepting his fate.

A cry from across the clearing. Logan had reached Amilyse's side and was struggling to drag her to her feet, but the woman was resisting. Zachary cursed as the creature's attention turned on the pair. The music came again, but unlike the sailor, Logan seemed unaffected. He had a fossil, like Zach.

The thought drew Zachary's attention to the stone in his hand. The piece of obsidian pulsed, and for a second, he thought that something moved within. Dark light spilled over his hand. Heart suddenly racing, he raised it towards the monster.

"Come on, you stupid stone," he snarled, "wake up, save me!"

The dark glow continued to ebb and flow, the shadow within shifting, but still nothing happened. Cursing, Zachary lowered his hand again. Logan had managed to get Amilyse to her feet, but still she resisted, reaching for her fallen brother. Step by step, they stumbled towards the tall grass, seeking to disappear into the vegetation.

But their struggles had already drawn the monster's attention. It stalked across the clearing towards them.

They weren't going to make it.

Standing calmly to the side, Zachary saw all this, and more. He saw Cordelia taking command of her men, mouth wide as she screamed for them to flee. Saw the sailors casting aside their arms and turning to dart into the long grass.

Zachary could have followed them. He was on the opposite side of the clearing from the creature. He could slip away, flee. No one would blame him. This battle could not be won, not against these creatures.

But then what?

There was no escaping from this place. It was clear now only one thing waited for them on this island.

His old rival, death.

"Hey!"

Zach's bellow carried across the clearing, cutting the silence like a dirk through flesh. The pale faces of Logan and Amilyse turned in his direction, but Zachary ignored them, focusing instead on the creature. Its scarlet glow still lit the night, drowning out the blue of the stream, the silver of the moon somewhere above the mists.

A shiver ran down his spine as its copper eyes met his gaze. Grimly, Zachary reached for one of his knives. He barely had to aim, so large was his target, so monstrous its size. A harsh *crack* sounded in the night as the blade struck the beast's throat and shattered.

The creature didn't even flinch. An awful silence followed. Zach could see the end staring from those copper eyes.

"I'm sorry, Margery," he whispered to the wind. "I should have stayed."

He drew another knife from its hidden sheath. There was a *thump* as it slammed home. It did no more damage than the first, but now the beast's attention turned fully on Zachary. Strange notes sounded from the depths of its throat, but the crystal warmed in his hand and he felt no effect.

Growling, the beast started towards him.

"Well that did it," Zach muttered.

Turning, he sprinted into the mists.

17

LOGAN

Fear had all but robbed Logan of reason. Only instinct kept him on his feet. He needed to escape, to flee into the night. If Amilyse hadn't been lying between himself and the tall grass, he probably would have left her. As it was, her sobs had cut through his terror, causing him to pause.

Now, as he watched the Thoona stalk towards him, he found himself wishing he'd left her behind. Her cries as he'd pulled her from her brother had drawn the creature's attention. With the world stained by its scarlet light, it seemed they had already been plunged into the seven hells.

He might have released Amilyse and fled. Driven mad by the loss of her brother, she still struggled in his grasp, making flight all but impossible. His own strength was barely enough to hold her, but still he did not let go.

He would not abandon her.

Not like…not like Dustin had abandoned him.

"Hey!"

A voice cut through the darkness. Logan's eyes widened as Zachary stepped into the bloody light, obsidian fossil in hand. When the beast did not turn, his spare hand whipped up, a knife appearing in his palm. He hurled the blade. It flashed across the clearing to strike the beast with a *clang*.

The strange music of the creature cut off as it turned from them, its four eyes fixing on the dark-cloaked man. Silence followed as beast and man stared at one another. Logan swallowed. What was Zachary doing? The shattered sabre had already proven the thing invulnerable.

That didn't seem to deter Zachary, as another knife hissed through the night to strike one of the copper eyes.

That got the creature's full attention. A growl rumbled from deep in its throat. It started towards the knifeman.

Zachary seemed to hesitate for a moment. Eyes wide, he watched the creature stalk towards him. Then he turned and disappeared into the mists.

And the beast chased after him.

Logan stared in disbelief. The creature still lit the night, its red glow spreading through the long grass like a flame, but already it was dimming, the mists pressing closer again, swallowing them up.

Sweet relief swept through Logan. Zachary had deliberately drawn the creature away. But his relief lasted only seconds. What now? Surely Zach couldn't outrun that thing. He certainly couldn't fight it.

Unthinking, Logan released Amilyse and took a step in the direction Zachary had disappeared. Suddenly though, Cordelia was there, barring his path. The woman had ordered her men to flee, but it seemed she hadn't run herself. Anger twisted her face and her fist flashed out, catching him in the cheek.

Stars burst across Logan's vision and before he knew what was happening, he was on the ground.

"Where in the seven hells has your brother brought us?"

His ears ringing, Logan struggled to understand the woman's words. What did the captain know about his brother? Lights danced in his vision as he struggled to push himself up, before rough hands caught him by the coat and dragged him to his feet.

"Wh…*what?*" he gasped as she shook him. Cordelia wasn't making any sense.

"Where is your damned brother is hiding!" she hissed, teeth bared, steely eyes wild.

Suddenly there was a pistol in her hand. He struggled to break her hold and escape, but the woman only laughed, madness in her voice. Lifting the weapon, she cocked the trigger and pointed it at Logan's face.

"I should blow your brains all over this damned crystal," she hissed.

Logan stammered a plea, even as he fumbled for the hilt of his blade. "Please, no, don't—"

Click.

His heart fell into his stomach as the hammer fell and he squeezed his eyes shut, expecting the end. But nothing happened. Bellowing her laughter, the captain tossed the weapon away.

"If only the damned things would work," she snarled, "but then, you knew that. Stepping in front of our guns like that, made you look real brave, didn't it? Did your brother tell you? I swear, when I find him, I'll gut the man like a fish." A savage grin appeared on her lips as she drew her sabre. "Guess I'll have to make do with you for now."

"I…no…please, I don't know what you're talking about!" He stumbled back, but her hand caught him by the collar. Strengthened by years working on ships, her grip was unbreakable. "Dustin didn't tell me anything about this place! He didn't know anything himself!"

"So you say." Cordelia snorted. "I say otherwise. Dustin was the one who organised the expedition in the first place."

"*What?*"

By way of answer, Cordelia's fingers tightened on his coat. Off-balance, he stumbled, and a kick from the woman swept his feet out from under him. Before he could recover, Logan felt the cold touch of a blade against his throat.

"Don't play dumb with me, Mr. Kaine. Your brother led us through the door to the seven hells; I want to know why!"

"I…" Logan started to deny her, to tell her it wasn't true, but…

His mind returned to that night on the ship, the excitement in his brother's eyes when he had spoken of the fossil coming to life on his desk. That had been the night of the great storm, months ago now. Would Dustin really have waited patiently for some random smuggler to organise an expedition into the Northern Sea?

Or would he have taken things into his own hands?

Logan met Cordelia's eyes. They stared at one another, then her scowl hardened and the pressure against his throat increased. He swallowed, feeling the blade slicing his flesh.

"I don't know why my brother brought us here," he said, taking care not to move lest the steel cut him further. "But he wouldn't have led us to our deaths, not deliberately. There must be a way to fight these things."

Cordelia shook her head, glancing at her remaining men. Her eyes took on a distant look. "Maybe it would be better to run," she murmured. She no longer seemed to be talking to him. "The coast isn't that far. Those waters were bad, but not so bad as this place…" she trailed off, her eyes flickering in the darkness. "Damn…"

Logan followed her gaze and swallowed. A new light had appeared in the clearing. Removing her blade from his throat, Cordelia turned towards the glow, sabre raised, though they both knew the futility of her action. Still on the ground, Logan scrambled to his knees, desperate for a glimpse of the newcomer.

Tendrils of fog parted before a new creature.

It was…much smaller than the first.

More fox than lion, it moved on all fours from the long grass, its triangular-shaped head barely reaching their knees. Its eyes were silver, but there were only two, and they lacked the rage of the earlier crystal beast. Its violet glow pulsed, the bushy tail swishing back and forth. It took a hesitant step towards them.

Cordelia hesitated, sword still raised. "Well, maybe I can kill this one."

The creature seemed to understand her. Dropping into a crouch, it gave a low hiss, the sound more snake than fox. And its colour changed, shifting from violet to emerald, as though the alteration was no more difficult than a change of clothing for these creatures.

Gathering himself, Logan climbed to his feet and drew his father's sabre. Cordelia cast a glance in his direction. They had both seen what the other beast had been capable of. The sailor they'd lost had been caught in some kind of trance. With power like that, and their seemingly invulnerable flesh, even a tiny creature like this could prove deadly.

Cordelia swore suddenly. Taking her sword in a two-handed grip, she advanced towards the creature. Growling, the fox-like beast crouched lower, baring row upon row of crystal teeth, each as sharp as a razor. The sound had no physical effect on them, thankfully, but that didn't mean the thing was not dangerous.

Gritting his teeth, Logan forced himself after the captain. Whatever their earlier dispute, they needed to work together if they were to survive. He still had the crystal fossil. Its glow had softened with the appearance of the creature, but it was no longer cold to the touch. Was its warmth from his own heat, or was the power within finally waking?

A cry carried through the night as Cordelia leapt at the crystal fox, her sabre sweeping down. Logan braced himself for the *crack* of its impact. Surely it would do no more damage against this beast than Zachary's blades had against the scarlet monster.

But to his surprise, Cordelia's sword struck only the soil at her feet, as the creature vanished.

They had only a second to stare, bewildered, before it reappeared.

Now there was not just one, but a dozen of the crystal creatures. They stood in a ring around the captain, short fur standing on end, their emerald light casting her features in a sickly glow.

Cordelia staggered as a collective rumble came from the creatures, spinning one way, then another as she tried to pick which would attack first. Logan gripped the fossil and his blade, unsure how to react. Should he strike at one with his sabre, or try to use the fossil as the shade had suggested?

The creatures had not yet attacked. They stood in their circle, each crouched low, poised as though to strike.

Finally Cordelia seemed to make a decision to go on the attack. Screeching a battle cry, she leapt, her blade striking at one of the creatures. Again Logan expected a *crack* from the impact, and again he was disappointed. This time, Cordelia's sword passed straight through the beast...which flickered, then slowly faded to nothing.

Logan stopped midstride, staring at where the beast had vanished. Did this fresh threat have some way of teleporting? Or...

Understanding came as the ring of creatures advanced, moving in perfect unison, as though they each shared a single mind—or were all a reflection of one. He opened his mouth to shout a warning to Cordelia—

"Enough, Caspar!" A man's voice carried from the fog. "Stop tormenting the poor wench."

Puffing heavily, an elderly man stepped into the light. Wrinkles creased his face and he walked with a pronounced limp, the remains of his silver hair plastered to his scalp.

Seemingly responding to his command, the crystal foxes flickered and vanished, until only one stood before Cordelia. It gave a final growl at the captain, then turned and trotted over to the old man. He reached down and ran an age-speckled hand through its fur.

"There, Caspar, see, the wench ain't our enemy," he said, now clearly addressing the creature. "Guess the Thoona go' away." Giving the beast one last pet, he swept his emerald eyes across the clearing. They settled on the body of the sailor. "Ah, but ol' Gozzo was too late." He shook his head. "Guess we'd best introduce ourselves to the new blood."

He started towards them, but Cordelia raised her blade before he could take two steps.

"Who the hell are you, old man?" she growled. "And if you call me wench one more time, I promise you we'll go straight from names to digging your grave."

The old man froze. He stared at the blade in her hand for a long time, brow furrowed, as though he were struggling to recall a distant memory.

"I am called Gozzo," he said at last. "I was shipwrecked here…a long time ago." The smile returned to his lips as he spread his arms. "Welcome to my home."

❦ 18 ❦

ZACHARY

Zachary had been hunted before. Many times, in fact. Once, when he'd scaled the walls of a *real* palace back in Londinium, he'd found himself on the receiving end of a pack of hounds. Those had been difficult to shake, even when he'd made it into the woods that bordered the city. A terrifying night of hide-and-seek had followed. Zach had only survived on raw wits and speed.

But the baying of those hounds had been nothing compared to the howls that chased him through this night. The beast, the monster, the Thoona or whatever the shade had called it, followed him still.

He staggered in the darkness, tripping on the uneven ground. Throwing out his arms, he struggled to keep himself upright. He managed—barely. The mist swirled as he corrected himself, holding the black stone high to light his way.

Heart hammering, he cast another glance over his shoulder. It was still there. The burning glow, the looming presence of the monster. Death. Gasping, he fixed his gaze ahead and ran on.

But the pain was returning. The momentary respite had ended and now his chest heaved, his lungs burning as they struggled for air. It sapped his strength, shortening his strides.

How long could he keep this up? His flight left a clear path through the tall grass. Any fool could have tracked him, and there had been an intelligence behind the beast's gaze. Maddened, enraged, starved, but still intelligent.

A howl broke the stillness of the night. The crystal pulsed in Zach's hand, urging him on. Desperate, he ran faster.

Faster than he'd run that night long ago, when the hounds had hunted him through the woods of Londinium.

Faster even than he'd run from Margery all those nights ago, when the physician had given him the news.

It still wasn't enough.

The first Zach knew he'd reached the forest was when the yielding grass was replaced by a decidedly unyielding tree. Unable to stop his flight, he twisted midstride and his shoulder struck the bark with a muted *thump*.

He crashed to the ground, vision spinning, lungs heaving as he tried to catch his breath. Stars danced across his vision as he lay there. His stomach lurched, threatening to evacuate itself on the spot. Clenching his teeth, Zach closed his eyes and dragged in another mouthful of air. He could feel the scratching at the back of his throat but forced himself to sit up before the coughing fit could take hold.

Stumbling to his feet, he clutched the crystal close, its glow now the only light amidst the mist. Well, the only light if he did not look back. The scarlet beast still stained the distant tendrils—it was not far behind.

A cough tore from Zach and the world spun. He clasped at a tree for balance, and felt the smooth crystal beneath his fingers. The surprise hardly registered at this point. Crystal, stone, metal, what did it matter, so long as it could support his weight.

Gasping, he spat out the iron taste that had filled his mouth and straightened. He could not stop. Now that he'd reached the forest, maybe he had a chance. The trees would not leave a trail like the grasses. He just prayed the creature could not follow his scent. If so…

He forced the thought away, trying to remember the position of the trees in relation to the plateau. In the darkness and fog, he'd picked a random direction and run for all he was worth. Only now did Zach realise how foolish that had been. He could have just as easily run off one of the coastal cliffs as into the tree.

From memory, he recalled the forest stretching towards the north, up into the foothills of the mountain. It would have to do. He could linger no longer. Gathering his strength, Zach set off at a jog.

The ground beneath the trees was clear of shrub, and Zachary found the going easier now that he no longer had to force his way through the grass. The mists were lighter here too, as though the trees held back the tendrils.

However, the darkness remained, the thick canopy blocking out all hints of the moon's light. He had to raise the obsidian fossil high to see the way ahead.

With the easier pace, his breath slowly returned and the pain subsided. Bit by bit, the glow of the beast fell behind, its howls growing more distant. His panic eased, and Zachary began to think he might yet survive the night. At last, he slowed to a fast walk, and began taking note of his surroundings.

The crystal trees seemed to stretch in all directions. Their dark trunks formed silhouettes at the edges of his vision, more than once startling him, thinking the shade had returned. It had vanished after its somewhat useless warning. If it came again, he had a few choice words planned for it.

His gaze was drawn to the fossil. How to unlock its secrets? Perhaps the elusive Dustin knew. After all, he'd had one of these artefacts sitting on his desk for years, according to Logan. He'd even arranged this entire expedition. Surely he'd had a plan to protect himself once here.

Thinking of his abandoned companions, Zach found himself wondering if his efforts to distract the beast had saved them—or if that second light he'd glimpsed had caught them before they could flee. The last he'd seen of Logan, the kid had been struggling to get Amilyse to run. Zach could only hope he'd been intelligent enough to give up on the girl.

"Fat chance of that," he muttered to himself.

The kid's naïve faith in his fellow man wasn't meant for a place like this. He would die before abandoning one of his companions.

Would a man like Rob have done the same for you?

He already has.

Zachary shivered. Perhaps it was he who no longer fit. Had he become too jaded in his old age, too distrusting for this world?

"Fat chance of that as well," he said to the dark trees.

No, the world had only gotten darker in his time away. And trust would get a kid like Logan killed, sooner or later.

He might already be dead.

"Keep moving, Zach," he said, shaking himself, "that thing is still out here somewhere."

His best hope was to evade the creature until morning. The mists had only appeared with the darkness—maybe the Thoona would vanish along with them when the sun returned.

And so he kept on, moving slowly through the forest now, the weight of his exhaustion pressing down on him. His legs ached and the flames crept slowly back into his chest. Pain ran its way up his spine, until it seemed a thousand tiny needles were stabbing into his skull.

Every step only drove them deeper, until no matter how tightly he clenched his teeth, the agony would not leave him, until his vision spun, and the darkness reached out for him, carrying him away in cushioned fingers…

Images flickered through Zachary's vision, memories of Leith, of distant Londinium, of years left long behind, and others not so distant past. He found himself surrounded, battling men and women on all sides, swirling in the dark, his cloak tangling in an attacker's blade, his own finding flesh.

The image changed, and he lay in a warm embrace, a woman's lips pressed against his own. Truly, he had never deserved a woman like Margery. The darkness within him was a stain on her purity.

Yet she alone had seen through the swagger, through the criminal façade, and recognised the man within.

Zachary clung to that image, to the memory of her heart beating beneath his ear, to the rise and fall of her breasts. In the warmth of the dream, he could almost believe he was there, that he had not thrown this all away, had not abandoned her.

That he had not run.

He shuddered as the image changed. Pain shone from Margery's eyes as she stood in the doorway of their cottage. Zachary screamed at his dream self to stay, to go to her, but instead he turned and walked away.

And the world faded to black.

Zachary flinched awake, surprised to find himself on the ground. He sat up quickly, the beginnings of panic taking hold as he realised he'd lost consciousness. His head whipped around, searching for the beast.

Night still gripped the land, but a light had appeared in the forest now. The soft blue glow of a burbling stream. Stifling a groan, he pushed himself up and crawled to where the trickle of water wound its way through the trees. He still had his flask, and after carefully filling it in the current, he drank deeply. He wasn't sure if touching the already glowing waters would attract anything, but there was no point in risking further disaster.

He crawled to the nearest tree and placed his back against it before closing his eyes. There was no telling how much time he'd lain unconscious, but surely morning could not be far off by now. At least some of his pain had eased. When morning came, he would try to follow the stream, in the hope it might lead back to their camp. If anyone had survived, he would find them there.

Crunch.

Zach opened his eyes as the harsh sound carried over the gentle music of the stream. Beyond the sapphire light, the forest remained dark. He strained to pierce the shadows, seeking movement. There was no sign of the red glow of the beast, and for a second he wondered if someone else was out there, another passenger, maybe, who'd escaped the disaster…

The shadows shifted, and Zach's breath caught in his throat as the Thoona stepped into the light. It was the same beast that had hunted him across the plateau, he was sure of it, but it no longer glowed. Its colour had faded, its fur changing from red to a deep black, tinged with orange hints of its earlier flame. The bronze eyes did not seem to have noticed him, for it approached the stream in silence and lowered its head.

Zach watched on, breath held, as the beast drank deeply of the glowing waters. He couldn't tell whether it was the water the beast sought, or the light. The unseen beasts they'd encountered earlier in the day seemed to have been triggered by the light. But that was light from Rob's touch. This glow came with the night. Was there a connection?

The stones shifted beneath him as he tried for a closer look. It was only the slightest movement, but the crunch of shifting soil was enough. The creature's head shot up, the four eyes swivelling to where Zach lay in the shadows. Immediately, its colour changed back to the burning scarlet, as though it were one of the chameleons Zach had seen in the markets of Londinium.

Except where those had been harmless, the change in this creature promised death.

It didn't bother with the music now. It knew that would not work with the crystal in Zach's hand. He could see the knowledge in its eyes.

Zachary used the tree to push himself to his feet. He would not die sitting down.

I'd prefer not to die at all.

But it was too late for that. The Thoona advanced a step, claws digging deep into the damp earth. He could sense its rage, the simmering tension it carried on the air before it. This beast did not want him here, did not want any of his kind on this island. It would kill them all, if it could.

There was nowhere left to run. Zach knew he had to fight. His knives were useless, but he felt better as he drew his last blade from its sheath. Its weight was reassuring, like an old and loyal friend. His knives had never let him down before. Until this night, of course.

His gaze was drawn to the fossil. His magic stone. What a let-down *that* had turned out to be. He could feel the power of the thing, could see the shadow of the fossil. It seemed to shift within the crystal facets, as though something was struggling to get out...

Zachary's heart suddenly lurched in his chest. It couldn't be that simple, could it? The beast was just a few steps away now, so close it could probably have leapt and killed him already. But beneath the rage there was something else in its eyes, in the way they stared at him.

Or the way they stared at the fossil.

"Gotta be worth a shot," he whispered to the silent forest.

He lifted the fossil high above his head, then slammed it against the crystal tree trunk he stood beside.

LOGAN

Logan stood in a world of crystal darkness. The multifaceted walls shimmered as he tried to orient himself, but the world shifted with each turn of his head, rippling, glowing with some impossible light. Finally he squeezed his eyes closed as his stomach began to churn.

"So you're alive, brother."

Dustin's voice broke the silence. Logan's eyes snapped open, but to his surprise, the crystal world had vanished...no, not vanished—changed. The hairs on Logan's neck stood on end. He was in his father's sitting room, complete with pair of leather armchairs and decanter set on the corner table. Candles burned in the chandelier, casting shadows about the room...reflecting from the crystal.

All of it was crystal now, the chairs and mahogany desk, the decanter and woollen carpets. It was as though someone had cast a replica of the room in the living crystal of the island.

Except for his brother.

"Dustin," Logan croaked, his heart thundering in his chest. Dustin had taken a seat in their father's armchair. "What is this place? Where are we?"

Grinning, Dustin rose and drew Logan into a hug. "I thought perhaps you would find it comforting," he said as they drew apart. Crossing to the decanter, he ran a finger around the rim of a glass, but made no move to pour the amber whiskey.

"I…" Logan stammered. "What…you created…this place? It's not real, is it?"

"No, brother," Dustin replied, his face turning serious. "Eiliah gives me some power to soul cast, but for now it is limited."

"Eiliah? Who…you're not making any sense, Dustin!"

A chuckle rasped from his brother's throat and he clapped Logan on the shoulder. "That is because you have not woken your stone," he replied. "All will become apparent soon. For now, our time is running to an end. I will see you on the island, brother."

"Dustin, wait—"

Logan couldn't finish the sentence. A burst of light tore through the room, shattering the crystal walls. The chairs and desk lost their form as it passed through and Dustin vanished, leaving Logan standing again in that shimmering world of crystal…

Gasping, Logan woke to find himself lying on the cold ground. For a moment, images of the dream lingered, the strange replica of his father's sitting room, the excited grin on his brother's face. But already it was fading, the crystal glow giving way to the chill reality of the morning light.

He lay there for a few heartbeats, focusing on what Dustin had said. He no longer doubted the dream had been real, not after everything he had witnessed on this island. But his brother's words had been brief, offering little clue as to his next move—other than waking the crystal fossil.

And how do I do that, brother?

His frustration bubbling over, he came to his feet. What he *really* wanted was to get the hell off this island. A cold sweat broke out on his forehead as he recalled the terror of the night, of the monstrous Thoona stalking towards him, blood dripping from its crystal fangs. As he saw again Rob's body on the ground, his empty eyes staring…

Logan shuddered. He was lucky to be alive. Drawing in a breath, he looked around the clearing. At first glance, little seemed to have changed from the night before. The stream still burbled its way past where they had set their camp. The waters had lost their glow with the rising sun and the others were staying well clear, lest their touch reignite the light and draw some fresh terror down upon them.

With daylight, the island had returned to a paradise. The sun was warm upon Logan's face, and he closed his eyes, breathing in the still of the morning. An earthy scent lingered on the air, as of broken ground, with a whiff of salt from the ocean. They had seen no birdlife on their first day, but in the distance Logan heard the harsh cawing of a seabird. He wondered how long it would take other life-forms to find this place.

His stomach rumbled, reminding him he had eaten only rations in over a day. The stream had solved their immediate problem of thirst, but hunger would soon begin to set in.

Cordelia and her five remaining men had already risen, while Amilyse lay nearby, her eyes open, but staring unseeing into the distance. There was still no sign of Zachary. A lump lodged in his throat at the thought. The man had saved them by leading Thoona away from the camp. But now Logan feared the worst.

Would they even find his body? Two already lay dead. The bodies of Rob and the dead sailor, Byron, had been placed at the edge of camp, their faces covered with scraps of cloth. It was all they had been able to manage in the night.

Inevitably, Logan's gaze was drawn to the strange man that had appeared from the mists. He sat on a boulder beside the river, his eyes distant. Cordelia had spoken with him the night before, but Logan had been too exhausted to participate in the exchange. Now he found himself wondering about the stranger.

He moved towards the stream, taking the opportunity to examine the man. From his wrinkled features and grey hair, he appeared older even than Zachary. A scar slashed across his nose and right cheek, all the way to his jaw, leaving a hairless streak through his unkept beard. There was a grizzled look to his features, like the stone of a cliff-face at the edge of the ocean, its surface pitted by the steady erosion of time. His tattered clothing only added to the impression.

The man had called himself Gozzo the night before. Even stranger, he'd been accompanied by the small, fox-like creature. That was why it had not attacked, and why it had retreated upon his arrival. Logan saw no sign of the creature now though.

Logan paused as he caught sight of a crystal lying in the hands of the stranger. Or rather, the crystal that *floated* before the stranger. An emerald the size of a man's fist hovered before Gozzo's face, a soft light seeping from its facets.

"How...how are you doing that?" The words slipped from Logan without thinking.

The stranger looked up at his voice, eyes widening momentarily in surprise before a wild grin replaced the expression.

"Why that's Caspar, 'course."

Logan stared at the man, barely understanding his accent, let alone the meaning of his words. The man had mentioned Caspar the night before, hadn't he?

Seeming to realise Logan's confusion, Gozzo's grin only spread. He tapped a finger to the floating crystal. Light burst from the stone and Logan staggered back, raising a hand before his eyes to fend off its brilliance. By the time he opened his eyes again, the glow had vanished.

Where the crystal had drifted now stood the fox-like creature from the night before.

This time Logan more than stumbled—he leapt back from the beast. Unfortunately, the stones were loose beneath his boots and his ankle twisted, sending him crashing down beside the river. His heart froze, and he scrambled back from the edge before he ended up in the water itself.

Laughter carried to his ears. He looked up to find the old man still seated on the stone. One hand now rested on the head of the beast, which stared unblinking at Logan, its silver eyes aglow in the daylight.

"Oh, don't let old Caspar bother ya," the man cackled. "Wouldn't 'arm a soul."

"Wh…what is it?" Crouched amongst the stones and dripping water, Logan struggled to get the words out.

"Caspar's one of the Pluff. Means fox, in the old language. Tricky buggers. Can't trust ya eyes with 'em around."

Logan struggled with the man's words, still trying to piece together his accent. It was even thicker than some of Cordelia's sailors. Definitely from the south.

"You said your name was Gozzo?"

"Gozzo Sigard."

"I'm Logan." He took a cautious step towards the man and his beast, and when it did not move, offered his hand.

"Pleasure to meet ya, matey." They clasped palms.

Logan returned the greeting, though he couldn't keep his gaze from drifting back to the creature. "What *is* it?" he whispered again.

The smile faded from the old man's face. He pursed his lips, looking from Logan to the beast. "Now there's a question," he murmured. "Never knew I was incomplete until the day we bonded. Couldn't really describe it to ya better than that."

His words made little sense to Logan, but he nodded anyway. "Where did it come from?"

"You tell me, Pathfinder."

Logan's head jerked up at the mention of Pathfinders. "Where did you hear that word?"

"From the shadowy bastard that's always hanging around this place," Gozzo grunted. "Likes to follow those with the fossils."

"How…how do you know I have a fossil?"

"Old Caspar told me. Can sense it on you, 'parently."

"How…wait, it *talks* to you?"

The old man chuckled. "More like he sends impressions."

Logan swallowed at this new piece of information, but put it aside for the moment, focusing instead on the man's earlier words. He'd seen the shade, knew about the fossils and the Pathfinders, whatever that meant…

"So…Caspar, he came from a fossil?" he asked hesitantly.

"Ay, matey, that he did."

Logan reached into his pocket and drew his own stone into the sunlight. Gozzo's eyes settled on the stone. Within, the shadow was still, its glow died to a spark.

"How do I get it out?" he whispered.

"They come when your need is great."

Logan frowned. "I'd say things are pretty desperate."

The crooked smile returned to the old man's face. "Oh, things aren't so bad down here. Wait until you see the mountain."

"The mountain?" At its mention, Logan's gaze was drawn to the distant peak. He watched as the light flashed amidst the dark stone.

"Ay," the old man murmured. "That's where we were wrecked. If you think a little Thoona is bad, wait until you see the terrors that wait up there." He shook his head. "Enough to make ya flesh crawl. Tis why me and Old Caspar keep to the lowlands."

"How long have you been here?" Logan whispered.

"Oh...not so long." Gozzo's eyes took on a faraway look. "Time...passes differently, when you're trapped. Was a terrible storm, must be months ago now? Thought we were done for, but someone musta been smiling on the old *Black-bird*. Island rose right beneath our bloody feet."

"What...happened to the rest of your crew?"

"A dozen of us survived the crash," the old man replied softly. "The others are all gone now."

Logan shivered, sensing the pain in Gozzo's voice. The great storm had been three months ago.

"All this time you've been alone?"

The man smiled and rested a hand on Caspar's head. "Not quite alone."

Logan nodded. He had a hundred other questions about the strange creatures, but before he could ask any, a voice carried across the camp.

"Right lads, enough with ya lounging. Byron wouldn't want y'all moping around on his account. Up with ya!" Cordelia stood in the middle of the camp, sabre in hand as she waved it about her head. "We're not spending a day longer on this Gods forsaken island!"

🕸 20 🕸

ZACHARY

The forest was never truly silent. Zachary had realised that as he sat through the night, watching the darkness turn slowly to light. Leaves rustled as they shifted in the gentle breeze, and even here in this place of crystal, there was life. Twigs crunched beneath the feet of unseen creatures. Harmless, he hoped, though he was not without protection now.

Even the trees themselves had their noises. A gentle groan as trunks expanded, a high-pitched shriek as one of the unseen animals bit into crystal bark, the whisper of roots as they spread through the soils. He found himself wondering if those back home made the same sounds. Would he have noticed then? He had spent long days in the gardens, cultivating his flowers, but had he truly ever listened to the plants?

Or was it only now that he could hear them?

His gaze slid to the crystal in his hands, to the dark glow that seeped from its opaque depths. Something shifted within, the shadow he'd once thought of as a fossil. Now made real, brought to life. He squeezed the crystal tight between his hands, then allowed it to fall.

The obsidian flashed, its light expanding, becoming a cloud of liquid light. Bit by bit, it changed, edges sharpening, until a crystalline creature took shape from the light.

It was smaller than the creature that had pursued him through the night. It only came to his chest when he stood. And it was of a different sort. It still stood on four legs, but where the Thoona had been all bulging muscle, this creature was slim and nimble, built for speed. The jaws were wider, but in place of enormous fangs were hundreds of tiny teeth. Twin tails stretched out behind it, strangely stiff, as though they might serve a purpose beyond wagging.

It sat before him, the elongated eyes watching him in expectation. Their copper sheen was the only similarity it shared with the Thoona. The beast itself had fled at its appearance, turning tail and disappearing into the dark trees.

Leaving him alone with the creature that had emerged from his stone.

There was a bond between he and it, an energy that had formed the moment the crystal had shattered. Zach had spent the night trying to piece together the mystery of its presence, but he was still no closer to anything close to understanding.

Zach shook his head. He could tell the energies pulsing between them. It was as though this creature were feeding off his own energies in some way. But if that were the case, then where was the fresh strength *he* felt coming from? His every muscle, every vein and sinew thrummed with a strange power, banishing his weariness, his weakness. He hadn't felt this good in years.

Yet there he sat, alone, his fate unchanged.

The newfound energies had done more than give him strength. The bond with the creature had expanded his senses, allowed him to witness the glory of the forest, to hear the trees, to observe the life all around him.

But it was not just the forest those senses allowed him to observe.

The new power could also be turned on himself.

And despite his new strength, despite the power of the creature crouched before him, Zach's disease remained.

He could see it now, visualise it with his new senses—a black, twisted thing inside him, wrapped about his core, filling his lungs with poisonous tendrils. They had spread even beyond that, to his stomach, his heart, his brain.

Closing his eyes, Zachary held back a sob.

He'd been so close. For a heartbeat, it had seemed his greatest hope had been realised, that he'd found a magic that would heal him.

In the end, all it had done was allow him to watch the thing that would kill him grow slowly larger, to stand helpless as the cancerous tendrils spread, until he eventually succumbed.

Zachary exhaled sharply. He could sense the concern from the bonded creature. It knew his despair, felt his pain. The colour of its coat changed, becoming a mottled brown. A reflection of its concern, he knew instinctively.

Without thinking, he reached out a hand to stroke its head. The crystal fur was stiff and unyielding, but it bent rather than shattered as might have been expected from such fine crystal. He shivered as the giant maw turned and nudged at his hand.

This creature was nothing like the enraged beast that had hunted him. He could sense its mind, like images through an opaque window. There was an ageless quality to that mind, a sense that it had been waiting a long time, dormant in its crystal casing...waiting for *him*.

Zachary pushed the sensation aside and levered himself to his feet. He would worry about the strange bond later. This might not be the magic he'd hoped for, but at least it was something that could protect him from the dangers that stalked this island.

The copper eyes followed Zachary as he stood. Despite their connection, that gaze was strangely unnerving. The intelligence behind them was unmistakable. He was about to order it back into crystal form when a woman's voice called out from the nearby trees.

"Well met, lowlander."

Tensing, Zachary spun towards the sound, before he recognised the shapely form of Willow emerging from the trees. He let out a long breath, struggling to calm his nerves. The night's excitement and his lack of sleep conspired to make him jumpier than a newborn foal.

The creature that followed Willow from the shadows didn't help with that.

Immediately, his own beast grew tense, a growl rumbling from the back of its throat as the other creature came to a stop at Willow's side. It was a different sort than his own again. Standing on all fours, this beast was built like a boar, though its bulk was enough to make even the greediest of swine squeal with envy. And unlike a hog, the four legs this creature stood upon ended in great paws rather than hooves. Its claws were hidden, but Zachary could sense their presence. Its crystal coat had darkened to black, though in some places it was speckled brown.

Willow frowned as she looked from her own creature to Zach's, which seemed just as agitated as the newcomer. "They don't seem to like each other much," she remarked.

Still tense, Zach struggled to exhale. He could sense his creature's mind, its distrust of the other.

"No," he said finally, glancing at his beast. "She's a friend," he said to his creature, though he suspected it was unnecessary with their bond. "So is her...what did you call it?"

Willow chuckled. "I call her Zahra."

She gave no order to her creature, but it fell silent all the same. Zach frowned. He hadn't given his a name yet—he hadn't even thought about his next move, for that matter. As he touched a hand to his creature's head, it began to glow, the light swelling before it shrank and changed back into a piece of crystal. It drifted slowly up to hang alongside his shoulder.

"It might be easier to talk without the distraction."

Nodding, Willow did the same. Zach noticed her creature turned into a crystal the colour of sulphur.

"Where did you find it?" he asked.

"I might ask you the same thing."

He raised his eyebrows at that. "In the cliffs when I first arrived. I thought it was a real fossil, not...whatever these things are."

The woman frowned, though after a pause, she finally answered his question: "It was passed down to me by my clan," was all she said.

Interesting, he thought to himself, *and Logan's brother found his fossil in the highlands. What is the connection?*

He said nothing out loud though. Stones crunched as Willow crossed the clearing and knelt beside the stream. She had found a flask of her own somewhere, and after filling it, she drank deeply, then wet her face with the rest.

Zach watched as she washed herself, still wondering at her presence here. She claimed to have questions. Now it turned out she had a stone of her own. Did that mean she knew more about this place than she'd been letting on? Or was it only a coincidence?

He snorted softly to himself. On the streets, you learned quickly not to believe in coincidences.

"So you survived the night, lowlander," Willow said at last, rising and turning to face him. "What about the others who were with you?"

Zach grimaced. "Rob is dead. The fool rushed out into the fog after one of the beasts. The others..." He trailed off, glancing in the direction of the camp. "I'm not sure. I distracted the beast. But I think there was another. I don't know if Logan and the others survived after that."

"The others?"

"We found Captain Cordelia and some of her men."

"I see," she said softly. "Did any of these others have fossils?"

"Only Logan," he replied, then paused before asking: "So what are they then, these things?" He gestured unnecessarily at the stone hovering beside his head.

Willow shook her head. "Too many questions," she murmured, "but this place has answers too, I know it."

Zach grimaced. "You're a strange one, aren't you?"

"Driven," she snapped, turning her back on him. "You would be too, if…" she said, before changing track. "Keep that creature of yours close if you plan on sticking around. I would not have survived the night without Zahra."

Zachary nodded. "Nor me. Where will you go now?"

"To the mountain," Willow replied immediately, her eyes turning towards the unseen peak. "I will find my answers there."

Zachary shivered at her confidence. Since arriving on the island, he'd stumbled from one near-death situation to another. Now, with the fresh energy of his creature burning within, he found himself looking at the treetops, towards the unseen mountain beyond. The light atop the stark peak promised power. Perhaps he would find what he sought there.

An image flickered into his mind, not of Margery, but of Logan's earnest face.

A curse slipped from Zachary's lips. He'd left the kid with Cordelia. The woman wasn't the forgiving sort. She had already lain the blame for this entire expedition at Dustin's feet. Even if Logan had survived the night, he might not live much longer if the captain got her hands on him.

Zach offered a nod to the highland woman. "Then I will bid you farewell. Good luck with your answers," he said. "I hope we meet again."

Then against his better instincts, he turned and started in the direction of the camp.

21

LOGAN

"We can't leave!"

Logan stood before the captain and gave his best impression of a determined look. He still wore his father's sabre—useless as blades had proven against the crystal beasts—but he didn't dare reach for it. Not with the glint in Cordelia's eyes as she stared down at him.

"And why is that, Mr. Kaine?" she asked, her voice low, dangerous.

Logan swallowed. "My brother is still out there." He tried to sound confident, but his voice came out more as a whisper than a growl.

"Your brother?" Cordelia asked. She took a step towards him. "You think I care about your damned brother? The only reason I'd hang around for that bastard would be to have the pleasure of killing him myself."

Though he tried to hold his ground, Logan found himself retreating before her anger. She still thought Dustin was responsible for all this. He'd barely had time to consider that claim last night. Now he found himself reassessing her words.

"You claim Dustin brought us here, right?" he said, thinking on his feet. "That he funded this entire expedition?" If Dustin had really managed that, it had been without their father's help. Logan wasn't sure how that was possible, but he pressed on with the train of thought anyway. "Don't you think a man with those kind of resources would reward you handsomely for coming to his aid?"

Long seconds passed as Cordelia said nothing. Slowly though, her expression changed from anger to a look of contemplation.

"No amount of gold is worth my life, nor the lives of my men," she said finally, before a grin spread to her lips. "Though, something *did* just occur to me." She advanced a step towards him.

"Wha...what's that?" Logan stammered, his heart suddenly racing. He retreated another step.

"That there might be another way to recoup my losses," Cordelia replied menacingly. "As you said, the Kaine family is obviously one of means. I'm sure they would pay a fine ransom for the safe return of their son, don't you think, Logan?"

Logan tried to deny the claim, to tell her that he didn't know where Dustin had found such wealth, but words would not flow.

A grin spread across Cordelia's lips as she gestured to one of her men. "Duncan, keep a hold of Mr. Kaine for me. Make sure no harm comes to him. He'll be coming with us."

The sailor missing several fingers from his right hand stepped forward at her command. "Sorry, lad," he said, resting his meaty hand on Logan's shoulder.

Before he could say more, however, another voice piped up.

"My, my, what a pickle y'all have on ya hands."

Cordelia spun as the old man rose from his boulder. The green crystal floated beside him, pulsing with a dull glow, but the beast did not appear. Even so, its presence had Cordelia's attention, and she waited as Gozzo limped towards them.

"Ah but the old bones do hate these chill mornings," he complained, coming to a stop beside the captain. "Now, what seems to be the problem, lass?"

"We're leaving, Mr. Sigard," she replied. "You can join us if you wish, or not. But Mr. Kaine is coming with us."

"Excuse an old man, lass, but where do y'all think you'll leave *to*?"

Cordelia hesitated, her eyes narrowing, as though she suspected the man of a trap. "We'll head back to the coast and build a signal fire. There's plenty of driftwood lying about we can burn. There's a whole armada out there in the Northern Sea. Someone is bound to notice the light."

"An admirable plan!" Gozzo cried. "To think, old Gozzo never thought of it!" Cackling, he waved his hand and turned away. "Come back and find us when y'all are done; old Gozzo will be waiting."

He wandered back to his rock and resumed his seat. For a moment, Logan, Cordelia and everyone else in the clearing stared at the old man. Even Amilyse had looked up. She watched the man with her fiery eyes, the slightest hint of a frown creasing her forehead.

The moment passed. Scowling, Cordelia strode up to the old fisherman.

"What, old man?" she growled. "You've tried lighting a fire?"

Gozzo snorted, looking up at her from his rock. "Can't light a fire here—not from the driftwood. Only crystal burns here—the trees and grass and such. Dunno why. Doesn't matter anyway. Ain't no light that gets through them clouds." He made a wild gesture in the direction of the cloud-stained horizon that surrounded the island. "Whatever magic controls this place, it doesn't want anyone leaving."

Cordelia pursed her lips, but she said nothing for the moment. Logan shifted nervously on his feet.

"What are you saying?" Logan said at last, anything to break the strand silence. "That—"

"That your damned brother has doomed us all," Cordelia snarled, swinging on him.

Suddenly there was a knife in her hand. Logan hadn't even seen her draw it. He stumbled back from the woman, but before she could advance on him, light flashed. Suddenly Gozzo's beast crouched between them. Fur bristling with a golden hue, a growl rumbled from Caspar's throat. The woman took a quick step back.

"Now, now, lass, let's not fight amongst ourselves," Gozzo chuckled. Shuffling forward, he leaned a hand on the woman's shoulder and grinned. "Gods know, there's 'nough on this island tryin a kill us, without adding each other to the mix."

Teeth bared, Cordelia shrugged off the wrinkled hand, but to Logan's relief she made no further move towards him.

"Looks like you get your wish, Mr. Kaine," she snapped instead. "All of us stuck here with you. But know this: if your brother lives, I *will* find him. And whether it's in his blood or his gold, I *will* have payment for my ship."

Logan swallowed at the burning in her eyes, but he said nothing. Instead, he forced his gaze to Gozzo. The man had survived here for three entire months. Surely, in all that time, he had come up with a plan to leave this place.

"You said the magic wants us to stay here?" he said, steadfastly ignoring the daggers Cordelia's eyes were flashing him —and the actual dagger in her hand.

"Ay," the old fisherman agreed, "and to butcher anything not made of crystal."

Logan drew in a breath. "Then how do we turn that magic off?"

That seemed to surprise everyone. Gozzo paused, mouth already open, as though he'd had a response for another question lined up. Cordelia's scowl did not change, but he saw the sudden uncertainty in her eyes.

"Mmm, this place…it's unnatural, matey. The weather never changes, not the sunshine, not those clouds out there. Old Gozzo's been all over this island and not found an off switch for any of it." He hesitated, the wrinkles at the edge of his eyes crinkling as he turned towards the north. "Well, everywhere but…"

"…the light," Logan finished for him, following the old man's gaze to the light atop the mountaintop.

Gozzo had said his ship had been wrecked up there, but that the creatures had forced him to flee.

"You told me last night that the beasts up there were even more dangerous than down here," Cordelia interjected.

"Ay," Gozzo replied, his aging Adam's apple bobbing up and down.

Logan shivered. What could be worse than the Thoona, with its burning eyes and haunting call? Just the thought of facing one of those things again sent a tremor through his very soul. But…staring at that light, Logan knew one thing with a sudden certainty. That glow was the source of everything magic on this island. And if Dustin still lived, that was where he would be heading.

"How do we reach it?"

"Reach it?" Cordelia asked. "Do you just have a death wish, Mr. Kaine?"

"I'll go."

The three of them looked around as Amilyse spoke. Unnoticed, she had left her brother's body and now stood before them. Her eyes were still red from crying, but she fixed her jaw in a look of determination.

"Don't be a fool, Ms. Rainer," Cordelia snapped. "Those things cut through us like a knife through butter—"

"I said I'll go," Amilyse snapped, turning from Cordelia to Gozzo. "Whatever this place is, my brother was right. It is evil. If…if there's a chance to destroy it," she paused, taking a moment to draw breath. "Your creature, you said it could protect us?" she demanded.

Cordelia snorted. "That thing could barely protect itself from my sword," she sneered. "You expect us to believe it can fight off one of those monsters?"

"Old Caspar?" Gozzo scratched at his balding hair, before offering a shake of his head. "Nah, too many of 'em up there." His eyes lingered on Logan. "We'll need others."

"Then how do we get the damn things?" Cordelia said. "That one we saw earlier didn't seem interested in being tamed. Too busy ripping out throats."

"You think so?" a new voice called out.

Logan's heart clenched. He recognised the newcomer's voice. Zachary's name was on his lips, but instead of the thief, it was one of the crystal beasts that stepped into the clearing. Fear spread its icy fingers through his veins. It wasn't the Thoona, but something else, more dog than great cat. Its copper eyes burned as it stalked towards the cluster of humans.

A growl came from Caspar. It stepped between the humans and the beast, but now Logan could see just how small the creature was compared to its rivals. The creature that approached was smaller than the Thoona that had killed rob, but was still easily twice Caspar's size. That didn't seem to trouble the little Pluff though, as a dozen replicas of the fox-like creature sprung forth from its crystal body. They darted forward, moving to encircle the other creature.

"Woah, there!" the voice came again, and on the other side of the clearing, the grass parted to reveal Zachary, hands raised before him. "Let's not go starting any monster fights between friends, hey?"

22

ZACHARY

"What other option do we have, Cordelia?" Zachary snapped, his frustration getting the better of him.

Cordelia glared back at him, hands on her hips, threateningly close to the hilt of her sabre. Firearms might have proven useless on this place—the sailors had tried without success to get the weapons firing again—but there was nothing wrong with a bit of sharp steel. Zach's fingers twitched, drifting towards where his one remaining knife was concealed, until he forced himself to stop.

"I don't see certain death as an option, Sicario," the captain retorted. "And I don't trust that old man. There has to be a way to signal the outside world."

"We need supplies at least," he insisted. "Gozzo says he has a stockpile. You won't get far without food."

"I'll go hungry for a few days if that's what it takes to get off this Gods forsaken island."

Exhaling, Zachary allowed his eyes to drift closed for a heartbeat. He prayed for calm. He should be relieved—he'd been surprised to find anyone alive in the first place. Though of course, not everyone had survived...

His gaze was drawn to the edge of the clearing, where Logan, Amilyse, and the sailors were still raising the cairn beside the river. The old man's creature, the Pluff he'd called it, had helped to dig the grave in the crystal soil. The cairn had been Logan's idea.

Zachary suppressed a sigh as the group went about their task, collecting stones from the river's edge and piling them in a little tower. Here they were, surrounded by danger on all sides, and they were wasting their strength on a grave marker.

What are you doing here, Zach?

He looked back at the captain. At least the distraction had given the pair a chance to speak in private. He'd already learned from Logan her plan to ransom him back to his family, if they ever made it off the island. Not as bad as it could have been, given Dustin's responsibility in stranding them all here, but still...

"Cordelia, please, see reason—"

"Reason?" she snapped. "Reason would be stringing that kid up by the neck for his brother's crimes."

There it is, he thought, cringing.

"Don't be a fool, Cordelia," he said wearily. If he couldn't speak to her sense of reason, perhaps her avarice would listen. "Can't you see? This place is everything we hoped for.

Sure, there's been some missteps along the way, but this thing…"

He trailed off, glancing at the crystal that floated beside him. The shadow, barely discernible in the obsidian, shifted within, seeming to respond to his attention, but he did not reach out to summon the beast. Just a glimpse of the crystal beasts was enough to unsettle his companions after the events of the night.

Gozzo had called his creature a Brackis. Where the night-marish Thoona used its haunting song to lure its prey to sleep, the Brackis were somewhat more…deadly. Apparently Gozzo's own beast, Caspar, had had a few encounters with the creatures, and had barely escaped in one piece.

"These stones, they have power," he said at last, turning back to Cordelia. "It is more than just a beast, more than a pet or companion. Since it woke, it's like all my senses have been expanded. I feel stronger, better than I have in years."

His gaze fell on the light atop the mountain. *So far.* How many days would it take to cross the plateau, to travel through the forest and up those stark slopes? He would need to sleep, to carry supplies and to protect himself from what-ever new threats this island had in store for them. Alone, he would fail.

His fingers twitched, reaching for his pipe. It was an old habit, more than a craving. He hadn't felt the desire for its harsh smoke since the bond had formed. Drawing it from his pocket, he twirled it between his fingers as he considered his predicament.

Logan and Amilyse were committed to the old fisherman's plan, but they were far from the most reliable of allies. The girl was blinded by grief and rage, while Logan was…well, life still had a few harsh lessons in store for the kid.

"I don't doubt your magic stone has power, Sicario," Cordelia replied finally. "I just fail to see how that benefits me."

"I think Gozzo is right," he replied. He didn't trust the old fisherman either, but he'd already had his own suspicions. "Whatever is keeping us from leaving, whatever lifted this place from the sea and put those clouds in place, the source of it all is up there."

"That might be true, Sicario," Cordelia said. Some of the anger had left her voice now. "But as I said, it's not just my own fate on the line. My men trust me with their lives. *Me*, not you or some half-mad fisherman. How can I trust that you have our best interests at heart, Sicario? I don't even know why you're here—and before you start, don't give me that rubbish about a noble death. I didn't buy that on my ship and I don't buy it now."

Zachary eyed the woman. He was surprised to hear the sincerity in her voice when she spoke of her men. Cordelia might be a smuggler willing to play both sides for a profit, but it seemed she had a soft touch for her people. No wonder they had followed her so loyally into this nightmare.

"I'm dying," he said at last, the words barely a whisper on his lips. "Cancer, the physicians tell me. Only have a few months to live, unless I can find an impossible cure." He looked pointedly at the mountaintop.

A silence hung on the air. Cordelia watched him, eyes narrowed, as though she were looking for some sign that he had lied. She probably was. Who could blame her for being suspicious? They both knew the lives the other had lived. He spread his hands, as though to say he had nothing more to hide.

"That…explains a few things," she said at last.

Zach waited a heartbeat before asking, "And?"

She sighed. "It doesn't change much, Zachary," she said, then gestured to the floating crystal. "I see now why you're willing to risk it all—you have nothing left to lose. But I'll not take my men on a suicide mission. Hell, you heard the old man—even two of those beasts won't be enough up there."

Zachary hesitated at her words, his gaze flickering across the camp to where Logan stood with Amilyse beside the now-finished cairn. Shaking himself, he looked back at Cordelia.

"And if there were another?"

The captain's eyes narrowed. Her eyebrows lifted a fraction as she followed his gaze.

"The boy?"

Zachary inclined his head.

Cordelia hesitated, before letting out a snort. "You cannot be serious, Sicario?" she exclaimed. "Would you really put our lives in the hands of a boy who's barely cut his chin with a razor?"

The words hung for a moment between them. He knew she was right. Logan was still just a kid. They couldn't trust him with such a responsibility, not with so much at stake. He knew what he had to do.

"I'll talk to him."

23

LOGAN

Ahead, Cordelia and her sailors paused before they entered the trees. Logan slowed with them, casting a glance at Amilyse who walked at his side. It had been a quiet journey from the river, the woman saying little as they cut their way through the long grass. Logan didn't press her. He couldn't begin to imagine what it must be like to lose her brother...

Not unless Dustin really is dead.

He swallowed, shoving the thought aside. Ahead, the others were just starting into the trees, Zachary and Cordelia in the lead. He didn't know how the man had convinced her to join them in this mad quest instead of returning to the coast, but there had been no more mention of ransoms. For that, at least, he was thankful.

Flashes of light came from ahead as Zach and Gozzo summoned their creatures. Logan was a little irked that the old fisherman seemed to have forgotten his existence since

Zachary's appearance. There was much he still wanted to ask the man about the crystal creatures—and the fossil that weighed down his pocket.

But his questions would have to wait, as together, the pair of creatures and their owners entered the shadows beneath the trees. Drawing in a breath, Logan shared a glance with Amilyse.

"Ready to see what's in there?" he asked, finally breaking the silence.

Amilyse blinked as they started forward. It seemed to take several moments for his words to seep into her consciousness, and when they did, the perpetual frown she wore only deepened.

"I am ready to avenge my brother," she said, her voice hard as her eyes returned to the path ahead. "Whatever it costs."

A lump rose in Logan's throat. He tried to speak, but could not find the words. At last, he could only shake his head.

She was right about one thing. None of them knew what this gamble might cost. The island had already stolen two lives, and if the beasts only grew stronger the further inland they travelled...

He slipped a hand into his pocket and clenched his fingers around the fossil.

They come when your need is great.

So the old fisherman had claimed, but why then had it not helped against the Thoona that had attacked their camp? Only Zachary's quick thinking had saved them from suffering the same fate as poor Rob.

He glanced again at Amilyse. She no longer wore the sabre her brother had claimed would protect them. Both blades had been lost in the encounter with the Thoona, shattered by its crystal flesh. Without her weapon, she no longer looked the fierce monster hunter, but an ordinary woman, her eyes wide as she faced the shadows. And despite her words, there was fear in those eyes.

"You don't have to do this, you know," he said, the words blurting from his lips. "Rob, he would have wanted you to be safe—"

"Safe?" Amilyse interrupted. "Safe? We were born, raised, to hunt monsters, Logan. There is no 'safe' for a Rainer." Her gaze drifted to their surroundings. It was dark in the forest, the deep shadows beneath each crystal tree whispering of hidden dangers. Only above was there hint of light, a soft, emerald glow as the hidden sun filtered through the crystal leaves.

"I would bring shame upon my brother's name if I fled, Logan," Amilyse finished, her voice dropping to a whisper.

"But…" Logan swallowed, not knowing what to say.

Thankfully, Zachary appeared in time to spare him the awkward words. He stood at the side of the path they were following, arms crossed and leaning against one of the crystal trees. Logan looked around for his creature before spotting the floating crystal. Apparently he'd been waiting for their appearance, for as the last of Cordelia's men passed him, he pushed himself up and fell into step with the pair of them.

"Hello, kids, enjoying this fine morning, are we?"

Logan frowned at the man's overly friendly greeting. Since his return with the crystal creature, Zachary had been a changed man. His face had lost its pallid tone, and he no longer struggled to keep pace with Cordelia and her sailors. The obsidian crystal floated alongside him, its soft glow lighting up the nearby shadows.

Amilyse stared at him, lips parted as though to say something, but in the end she only set her eyes straight ahead and continued walking

"Ah. Still upset about the dead brother I see." He nodded, as though agreeing with himself. "Understandable. That's the detriment of family, isn't it? They can be the most ignorant, toxic sack of coal this side of the channel, and you've still got to love 'em—"

Zach broke off as Amilyse swung on him, her fist flashing out to catch the older man square in the cheek. The blow seemed to catch Zachary by surprise, for he staggered back from her, eyes wide. His hand lifted slowly to touch his cheek, and his mouth parted, though no words flowed.

A stunned silence followed as Logan looked from Zachary to Amilyse. Beside her brother, she had seemed timid and inexperienced. It had been easy to forget this woman had received the same training as Rob. Or perhaps it was only that she'd been forced to step into the vacancy he had left.

"Well that seemed a little uncalled for," Zachary murmured.

"You called my brother a sack of coal!"

The dark-cloaked man raised an eyebrow. "Was I wrong?" he asked, calmly advancing a step.

This time he seemed taller, looming over the woman, making her seem small. His eyes flickered, and Logan glimpsed the darkness there, one he'd almost forgotten the man possessed.

"My brother was…he was a hero," Amilyse rasped, though her words lacked the same force as just moments ago. "He was fearless."

"Exactly," Zach replied. Turning, he started along the trail after the others, leaving the two of them behind. "Come on, before we lose them. I don't know where the old man's campsite is, and I don't want to spend half a day blundering around this forest trying to find it."

Logan cast a glance at Amilyse. Anger and confusion warred on her face. Ignoring him, she strode after the departing thief.

"What are you saying?" she demanded.

Zachary sighed. "I thought I made myself pretty clear. Your brother was a reckless fool, Amilyse. His death does not change that fact."

A growl like that of a feral cat rumbled from Amilyse's throat as she swung at Zach again, but this time he was ready. The man brushed off the blow, then stepped forward, catching Amilyse off-guard with a push that sent her sprawling.

Logan quickly stepped between them, but already the woman was dragging herself up. A shove sent him stumbling out of her path. Teeth bared, she jabbed a finger at Zach's chest.

"Rob was the bravest man I knew!"

"I thought you said he was fearless," Zach replied. His voice was soft, but there was still an edge to it. "One cannot be both."

"What's the difference?" Amilyse's face was turning red and it seemed she was only moments away from launching herself at the man again.

"What's the difference?" Zachary shook his head and glanced at Logan. "And here I thought you were the naïve one, kid." He gave an exaggerated sigh. "I've known many brave men in my life, Amilyse. Ay, and women. Some feared the ocean, others great heights. One even feared the world beyond the four walls of his home. Each morning he struggled just to set foot outside his doorway."

"He does not sound brave to me."

"Enough with your ignorance," Zachary snapped, his patience apparently spent. "Those men knew fear; they faced it every day of their lives. Their courage was not some fleeting thing, but something forged in the fires of their terror, tempered in their dread, and made all the stronger for it."

Turning her head, Amilyse sniffed. "At least my brother was not a coward. At least he did not run away."

Breath hissed between Zachary's teeth as he came to a stop. Amilyse advanced another few paces before turning back to him, a smirk on her lips. Logan stilled, finding himself between them, but Zachary did not rise to her bait.

"I would rather any of those men at my side today than your brother," Zachary replied, his voice cold. "Fear is but a tool. It warns us of danger, gives us an edge. Lacking fear does not make you brave. It makes you a fool."

"My brother was not a fool!"

"Oh?" Zach snapped. "Was I hallucinating last night when Rob went blindly charging into the mist after the Thoona?"

"I..." Amilyse started, then trailed off as she stared into Zach's eyes, the scream dying on her lips. They stood facing each other for a moment. The pain in Amilyse's eyes was obvious, but Zach's words seemed to have stolen the fight from her.

"Whatever your love for him," Zachary said at last, "you cannot deny it was Rob's own actions that got him killed. They almost got *all* of us killed. Because he went out there, we three had to follow him, risking ourselves by leaving the camp. *That* was brave. I saw your fear. You followed your brother into the mists anyway. To help him. But Rob..." He shook his head. He didn't need to finish the sentence.

"Enough!" Amilyse burst out. The anger had drained from her face now, leaving it pale beneath the shadows of the forest. "I'll not hear any more cruel words from you. My brother died trying to save us!"

"He died playing the hero," Zach said coldly.

Amilyse didn't try to strike him this time. Instead, she spun and stalked up the path after the others. Flashing Zachary a glare, Logan made to follow her, but the man raised a hand to bar his path. He tried to shove past, but the man held him back.

"Leave her a minute, kid."

"What did you do that for?" he snapped, his own anger bubbling over.

"She needed to hear it," Zachary replied, glancing in the direction of the departing woman. "However much it hurts." He shook his head, as though to dismiss the thought. "And besides, I wanted to talk to you in private."

❧ 24 ❧

ZACHARY

Zachary lingered until the girl had disappeared between the trees before gesturing for Logan to continue. The kid flashed him a glare before obeying. Zachary stifled a sigh. He regretted the way he'd spoken to Amilyse, but also knew they couldn't afford having another Rob on their hands.

Taking the lead, Logan set off at a pace Zachary would have struggled to match just the day before. That thought brought a smile to his face. The shadow of his doom might still lie within, but at least he could now enjoy the time he had left. Using his newfound strength, he set off after Logan.

The strange trees pressed in around him as he walked, the scent of pine and fir trees strong in his nostrils. Zachary could not begin to explain the strangeness of that. That crystal could have a scent, for starters, was an impossibility. But even the presence of pine in the warm, humid climate of the island was another idiosyncrasy.

Then there were the individual trees themselves. Earlier, he'd finally taken the time to inspect one up close, and had found the slight transparency of the bark allowed him to see what lay within. Hidden within each tree were tiny tubes of crystal, each bubbling with the movement of water from the earth below to the leaves above. What happened there, not even Zachary could guess.

He caught another glare from Logan as they walked, and noted the way the kid's eyes lingered on the crystal that hovered of Zachary's shoulder. He'd known Logan would be curious—another reason he'd wanted Amilyse out of the way.

Reaching up a hand as they walked, Zachary tapped a finger to the obsidian. Light swelled as the creature woke, expanding until it formed a sphere. The shadow within shifted, before the light receded to reveal the beast Gozzo had named a Brackis.

His Brackis.

A tingling sensation began at the nape of Zach's neck as he felt the connection between them strengthen. Its waking mind pressed against his own, the twin copper eyes looking left and right, inspecting the shadows as though suspecting some attack. Perhaps it was. They still knew so little about this place.

"Have you named it?"

Logan's question directed Zach's mind back to the task at hand. He gave the kid a frown. He'd meant to ask Willow about her own, and had yet to speak privately with the old fisherman. But the kid was right. The creature was a fearsome beast, and fought now at his side. It deserved a name fitting of its presence.

"A good question," he said, turning to the crystal beast at his side. "*Do* you have a name?"

The copper eyes narrowed. He sensed a hesitation across their link. For just a second, he felt he stood at the edge of a precipice, a wealth of knowledge stretched out before him. These creatures, they were not like humans, of flesh and blood. Crystal survived, crystal prevailed. How long had this place rested beneath the seas? How long had the creature at his side slumbered, only now to wake?

Despite their bond, Zach felt himself retreating a step from the Brackis. Thankfully, the sense of enormity was already dissipating. Confusion took its place. The Brackis stared at him, burning with the faint glow of its kind. When he reached out again through the link, Zachary realised not even this creature understood that vast knowledge. There were holes in its memory, like a puzzle missing half its pieces.

"You can't remember," he mused at last. "Well, we can't just keep calling you 'monster.'"

He sensed a pulse of agreement from the Brackis and chuckled.

"You can talk to it?" Logan asked.

Zachary shrugged. "In a way," he replied cryptically. "These things, I think they're ancient. They probably predate our modern language."

"That shadowy thing spoke with us easy enough."

"True," Zachary murmured, eyes narrowing as he looked around. "I wonder where our shadowy friend has gotten to. Have you seen it since the Thoona attacked?"

Logan shook his head, and Zachary shrugged. The shade seemed to have a particular interest in their stones. What had it called them...Pathfinders?

"Keep an eye out," he said. "I'm sure we haven't seen the last of it. Now," he continued, turning back to his own creature. "What are we going to do about my dazed little friend here?"

A rumble came from the Brackis's throat as it paced at his side. Its coat took on a scarlet sheen, revealing its irritation. Logan was right—it didn't have any problem understanding them. It was communicating its own thoughts that it struggled with.

"What about that then?" Logan cut across his thoughts. When Zachary only frowned, the kid gestured at the Brackis. "What about Daze?"

Zachary laughed. "Not the most creative, is it?" A rumble of agreement came from the creature. "I don't see you coming up with anything better," Zach admonished, then: "Daze it is!"

The rumbling increased in pitch and they both burst into laughter. Light flashed as Daze returned to its crystal form. A sense of irritation lingered across their bond, like a bitter taste on the back of Zach's tongue, but it was easily dismissed.

"Knew you'd come around," he said, addressing the chunk of obsidian.

The pair of them continued in silence after that. It took several minutes before Logan asked the question Zach had been expecting.

"How..." The kid trailed off, as though unsure how to proceed. "How did it happen...Daze, I mean? Your crystal...how?"

A sigh slipped from Zachary's lips, quickly stifled. He forced a smile in its place.

"You haven't figured it out yet?"

Logan dropped his eyes. "Gozzo said the fossil would wake when I needed it most, but I couldn't get it to do anything when the wild Thoona attacked."

"Wild Thoona? I like that," Zachary mused, momentarily distracted. His eyes drifted to Daze's floating crystal. "What would that make ours then—Tames?"

"Huh? What are you talking about?"

"We need a name for these creatures, right? Why not Tames?" He chuckled as Logan just stared at him, and another pulse of irritation came from Daze. He could practically picture the creature's eyes rolling in its head. "It's going to catch on, just wait. Anyway, what were you saying about Gozzo?"

"That the fossil would only wake if I was desperate."

This time Zachary found himself pursing his lips. It had seemed simple enough, breaking the crystal to free Daze from its stasis. But then, he *had* been pretty desperate, confronted with the wild Thoona.

You were quaking in your damn boots, Zach, he admonished himself.

Was that why it had worked? It seemed strange that their state of mind might impact the ancient creatures locked within the crystals. Or rather, it would have seemed strange had it not been for the connection he had forged with Daze. There was still much they did not know about these Tames. He resolved to corner the old fisherman later and question him about the creatures.

Letting out a sigh, Zach glanced again at Logan. The kid wore an eager expression as he stared at Daze's crystal, waiting to hear the truth about the mystical creatures. Zachary felt a pang at the sight of his enthusiasm.

"You know, kid," he said suddenly, "I've been thinking. Cordelia and her men, none of them have a Tame of their own. They're dead weight. If we really want to reach that light, maybe we should leave them behind. They'll only slow us down in the long run."

It was against his better judgement, making the offer. He might not exactly *trust* Cordelia, but now he understood her motivations, well, he could trust her intentions at least. Logan was a wild card, unreliable, unpredictable, naïve. Yet here they were.

To his credit, Logan truly seemed to consider the offer. His eyes took on a distant look and they walked in silence for a time. Zachary supposed the captain hadn't exactly done much to inure herself with the kid.

"They'd be in danger if we left them with only Gozzo and Caspar for protection," Logan said at last, then shook his head. "No, we should work together. We're stronger that way."

Zachary had expected no less. "You know what your problem is, kid?" he asked abruptly, then continued before Logan could reply: "You believe in others."

"Some might call it a strength," Logan said defensively.

"It'll get you killed some day."

The kid furrowed his brow at that, but he offered no further argument.

"The stones, these creatures, they're a big responsibility, you know?" Zachary said after a pause. "They're our only protection in this place."

"I know," Logan said, his voice growing eager. "That's why I need you to tell me how you woke Daze. So I can help everyone."

Zachary sighed. "The process seemed simple enough to me," he said, forcing a smile. "I can show you, if you like."

"Really?"

Zachary struggled to keep the smile plastered to his face as he nodded.

You're better than this, Zachary.

He shivered at the memory of Margery's voice. She had always expected him to be better than he was. But where had that gotten her? Abandoned on her front porch while he walked away. He shivered at the last glimpse he'd had of her, the pain in her face. With the memory came the pain, a flame that swelled in his chest, burning, simmering. He stumbled as some of the strength that had fuelled him dwindled.

"Are you okay?" Concern replaced Logan's excitement. He reached out a hand to steady Zach.

Zachary shrugged off the offer of help and straightened, still struggling to understand what had happened. He glanced at the floating crystal. Daze still pulsed with its familiar glow, but the connection between them seemed to have weakened.

He shook off his weariness. He could not expect the power to completely isolate him from the illness.

"I'm fine," he said as they started off again. "Just a little heartburn."

Zach spotted movement on the trail ahead. Cordelia had lagged behind the others and now lingered in the shadows beside the trail. Logan didn't seem to have noticed her. Zachary turned to the kid. If he wanted to get back to Margery one day, this was the only way.

"Now, what were we talking about? Oh yes, your fossil. Here, let me see it." He held out a hand, waiting.

Logan hesitated only a heartbeat before drawing the piece of quartz from his pocket. The stone had brightened since Zach had last seen it. After another pause, he placed it in Zachary's hand.

"Thank you," Zach murmured, lifting the crystal to inspect it.

The quartz was just cloudy enough to obscure the fossil. He found himself wondering what manner of Tame might be contained within. Would it be another Brackis like his own? Or perhaps the fox-like Pluff like the old fisherman's. Or yet something else they had still to encounter? The possibilities could prove endless.

"So how do I wake it?" Logan asked.

Zach blinked, aware he'd allowed his mind to drift. A frown replaced his smile as he lowered the stone. It was cold in his hand. His fossil had been warm, even before it woke. Was there a reason for the difference?

"Is that it?"

They both looked up as Cordelia's voice interrupted their exchange. Logan's eyes revealed his surprise, while Zachary nodded. The woman stood staring at the stone in Zach's hand with undisguised greed in her eyes.

You don't have to be this person, Zach, Margery's voice whispered from his past, repeating her oft spoken words.

Zach thought of the challenges that lay ahead, the beasts and magic and whatever other threats the island might throw their way. Logan had done well to survive this long, but the kid couldn't handle what would come next. He'd almost gotten himself killed against the Thoona, trying to protect the foolish Amilyse. They couldn't trust him with such responsibility.

Closing his eyes, Zachary sent out a silent apology to his wife.

I do if I want to see you again.

"Here," he said, turning to Cordelia and tossing her the stone.

"Hey—"

"Quiet, kid," Zach snapped, eyes still on the captain.

"How do I wake it?" she repeated Logan's earlier question.

He hesitated, thinking of what the captain had told Logan. "We're not entirely sure yet. I broke mine when the Thoona had me cornered, but there might be more to it. We'd better talk with Gozzo before you try anything."

"What…why…that's mine!" Logan was still spluttering when the pair turned suddenly to face him. He broke off as Cordelia drew her sabre and rested it against his chest.

"Easy now," Zach said, stepping forward and placing a finger to the steel, forcing the point down. "That wasn't part of our agreement."

The captain allowed her blade to fall, but she did not take her eyes from the kid. "I'd drop the protests, Mr. Kaine, after the crap your brother pulled. I'm taking this stone as a payment for my ship." She paused before her voice took on a lighter tone. "Believe me, its for the best."

"But…it's mine," Logan rasped.

Zach felt another pang in his chest, like the pain from earlier, but deeper this time, as though a piece of his soul had been cut. He shuddered, struggling with suddenly weak knees, and drew in a calming breath. He'd done the right thing. If he hadn't acted, Cordelia would have taken the fossil by force.

"And now it's mine," Cordelia said. She held up the stone with a grim smile. "That's how the world works. Now, since we're done here, you'll excuse me. I have an old fisherman to interrogate."

She strode away, taking the stone with her and leaving the pair of them alone on the trail.

"Why?" Logan rasped when she was gone.

Zachary found himself unable to look him in the eye. He could understand Logan's anger. But it mattered little now. Calmly, he drew his last dagger from its hidden sheath and held it up to the crystal light. Logan still had the sabre on his hip, if he cared to use it. But Zachary knew he would not.

"Sorry, kid," he said, shaking his head. He opened his mouth, intending to explain, to tell Logan how this would be better, that Cordelia would protect them both now. But the words felt weak even to him, and they turned to dust on his tongue. Instead, all he said was: "I warned you not to trust me."

With that Zachary turned and started after the others. He didn't look back to see whether Logan would follow. After all, without the fossil, the kid had no other choice.

But you did, Zach.

Despite his best efforts, Margery's voice chased after him.

25

LOGAN

Logan sat on the edge of the lake and looked out over the glistening waters. It had taken them most of the day to navigate the shadowy forest, but the journey had been blessedly uneventful. They had arrived on the rocky shores with the fall of dusk, in time to witness the lights appear deep within the waters. They had begun with the same deep blue as the river, but soon other shades had joined, scarlet and beige and emerald, violet and auburn and every colour between.

The rainbow waters stretched far into the distance, so bright there was no need for torches or even their own stones. The brilliance reflected even from the sky above, forming a shimmering aurora that would have made the Northern Lights cringe with envy.

In all of Logan's short life, he had never witnessed such a glorious sight, never imagined a land so magical, so mystical. But as he sat on that beach, he felt no glory, no wonder at the rainbow lake.

All he felt was misery.

His father's sabre lay across his lap. The blade that had won their family a place amongst high society. There was no magic in the silver steel, no power but that of the man who wielded it. Logan had taken it, intent on finally showing his father he was ready, that he was worthy of the Kaine name.

Instead, all he had done was bring shame.

Dustin had trusted him to look after the fossil, to protect it —and Logan had foolishly given it away.

How could you be such a fool?

He could hear his father's words now, the sneer in his voice. In a single instant of madness, Logan had proven his father's every doubt about his younger son correct. He hadn't even fought for the stone, but given it up meekly, allowing Cordelia to walk away with it. He'd even followed meekly after her, no better than a beaten dog trailing its master.

Laughter carried down the shore as Cordelia and her men joined in on some private joke. No doubt it was at Logan's expense. He clenched a fist around a handful of stones, wishing he'd had the courage to fight. All of Zach's fine words, his talk of fear and courage, all of it had been meaningless. He should have never trusted the man, whatever his fine words.

Fool. Coward. The words twisted insidiously in his mind.

Dustin, he would have never fallen for Zachary's tricks. He would have seen through the man in seconds.

A shiver passed through Logan. Looking out at the shining lights, he finally allowed himself to wonder if Dustin was gone. Surely if he'd survived the shipwreck, they would have found some sign of him by now.

A tear streaked Logan's cheek. Despite his best efforts, another followed. His eyes burned and he squeezed them closed against the beauty of the lake. How Dustin would have loved this place. The magic, the creatures, the mystery. It would have all been one great adventure for his brother. Despite the danger, that was the sort of man Dustin had been.

Who he is, Logan reminded himself.

But there was no denying the doubt at the back of his mind.

Opening his eyes again, he allowed his gaze to be drawn beyond the lake, to the stark slopes on the far shore. No forest there, nor long grass—only patchy tussock. Even from a distance, the mountainside seemed to radiate a dark purpose, as black as the lake was bright. Recalling Gozzo's words, he wondered what manner of beasts they would find there.

His gaze continued higher and he watched as the beacon flashed atop the mountain. They were closer now, though still not close enough to make out the source. That light had drawn them all to this place.

It will be your death.

The words whispered in Logan's mind, fuelling his doubts. Yet he could not deny them. This place, it was his brother's dream. Not his. Logan was too fearful, not brave enough for a place like this. Zachary was right: he was out of his depth.

"Hey there, matey."

Gozzo's voice carried down the shoreline. Logan was surprised to see the man limping towards him, lit by the flickering red glow of the fire beyond. The old fisherman had assured them the flames would not attract the beasts. Nothing from outside would burn within the limits of the island's influence, so they'd collected branches from the crystal trees instead. The sailor, Peck, had been a huntsman in another life, and had used a bit of his old craft to get the flames burning.

"Mind if I join you?" Gozzo took a seat alongside Logan without waiting for a response.

Irritation prickled Logan, but he pushed it down. Gozzo had been nothing but kind to him. He'd even invited the group here to his camp. Admittedly, that had proven to be little more than a few pieces of canvas strung between trees just beyond the beach, along with a random collection of items he'd scavenged from the coast over the months he'd been trapped here.

But Logan's loss was not the old man's fault. He only had himself to blame for that. Well, himself, and Zachary.

The old fisherman let out a groan as he lay back against the stones, the Tame curling up at his feet. Logan sensed no danger from the little Pluff, not like the larger Brackis that Zachary had bonded with. That thing was monstrous, with its enormous jaws and rows of teeth.

"Old Caspar says you no longer have the stone," Gozzo said softly.

Logan's head jerked up, but he didn't immediately reply.

"The lass was asking me how to wake 'em," Gozzo continued. "Seems ya crystal has switched hands. That by your choice?"

Of course it wasn't my choice! Logan wanted to scream the words, to haul himself to his feet and march up the beach and demand Cordelia hand the crystal back.

But he did none of that, only sat on the hard stones and clutched his father's sabre tighter.

"Maybe it's for the best," he croaked. "I'm not much of anything. At least Cordelia will be able to protect us."

Silence answered his words. He glanced at the fisherman. Gozzo sat staring out at the lights, his eyes distant, the colours shimmering against his emerald eyes, reflecting from his pale skin.

"I was nothing once," he said at last, his voice as distant as his eyes, as though recalling some distant memory. "They called me a dreamer, a romantic. Said I would never amount to anything." He shrugged, suddenly shaking his head. He ran his fingers through the crystal coat of the Pluff, as though it were a hunting dog. "That's what the world likes to do to us dreamers, matey. Put you in a box and tell you thems ya limits. Up to you if ya believe it."

Logan swallowed, looking back at the fire. Cordelia stood near the flames, speaking softly with one of her sailors. Duncan, he knew from the missing fingers. Her second in command. The man must be twice Logan's size, all muscle and brawn. His heart sank. Even with the sabre, he didn't stand a chance against Cordelia and her men.

Then he spied Amilyse. She stood to the side of the others, dark eyes fixed on Zachary. He could sense her anger, even from here. *He* couldn't fight them, but maybe if he gave the sword to Amilyse...she'd caught Zach off-guard before. Maybe she could again.

He began to rise, but it was at that moment Cordelia decided to turn. Their eyes met across the gravel shore. A smile twisted her lips, a look that dared him to give it a try, to attempt whatever he had planned.

Logan sank back to the hard stones. Amusement shone from Cordelia's eyes as she dismissed him. She hadn't even needed to lift a finger, and he was defeated.

"How did you survive three months in this place?" Logan rasped. He was ashamed to hear the tremor in his voice.

The old man shrugged. "Didn't 'ave much choice, did I?" he replied. "The island, its power, it trapped me here. Ain't any choice but to perish or persevere."

"I would have perished," Logan whispered.

"Ya think so?" Gozzo asked.

When the man did not continue, Logan looked up and found two sets of eyes on him. Caspar had lifted its crystal head, the twin slits of silver watching him in the darkness. He shivered at the intelligence there. Zachary had claimed his 'Tame' was confused, its mind cracked and disjointed. That didn't seem to be the case with Caspar.

"I'll let you in on a little secret, matey," Gozzo said at last. "Those stones, Caspar and his ilk, they don't just choose anyone."

That got Logan's attention. "What do you mean?"

"Wasn't the only one of my crew to find one of 'em stones," Gozzo replied. "Pathfinders..." he paused, head leaning to the side as though to listen for something. "What is that?"

At his feet, Caspar slumped suddenly to the gravel, its silver eyes sliding closed. Gozzo stared at the creature for several heartbeats, forehead creased. Tentatively, he made to raise his hand and reach for the Tame, but something seemed to hold him back. He swayed where he sat.

"Damn..." he muttered before toppling gently backwards. Gravel crunched as he slumped against the shore.

"Gozzo?" Logan croaked, confusion turning to panic as he shook his companion.

The old fisherman snorted and mumbled something, but did not stir. Heart suddenly racing, Logan stumbled to his feet and swung around. This was just like what had happened when the Thoona first came for them, but there had been no music this time. And he and the others were untouched by whatever had affected Gozzo.

Then he turned to look out over the lake. Mist rolled towards them across the still waters. A cold wind followed, sending tremors down Logan's spine. Within the fog, new lights appeared, a burning scarlet that drowned out the rainbow of the lake. Churning within the icy tendrils, it moved towards them.

"Gozzo!" he shouted, still trying and failing to wake the man. Caspar lay still beside him, equally unconscious.

In desperation, Logan turned to the others standing around the fire. They still hadn't noticed the approaching mists. He steeled himself for what needed to be done.

"Zachary, we have a problem!"

26

ZACHARY

"Zachary, we have a problem!"

Logan's call carried up the beach. It took a moment for Zachary to realise the kid had been calling to him. He turned toward the voice and cursed as he found his eyes blinded by the firelight. That had been careless. It took precious moments for them to adjust. By then the scarlet lights out on the lake were already growing near.

Down the shore, the old fisherman lay on the ground beside Logan. He didn't move as a chilling howl echoed through the night, ringing out across the still waters.

Zachary cursed. The kid was right. Something was very wrong.

"What's got the kid so agitated?" Cordelia appeared at his side.

"I imagine it's got something to do with that," he replied, pointing to the approaching glow.

With the angry red came a familiar fog. It swept down the mountainside, tendrils churning, boiling, concealing the beasts within. The rainbow lights of the lake dimmed before its approach, then winked out entirely as the fog swallowed them up.

Cordelia cursed. She reached for her stone, but Zach raised a hand.

"Not yet," he said, eyes shifting to the unmoving fisherman. "Something's wrong with Gozzo."

As he spoke, he was already starting down the shore. Logan glanced back at his approach. There was no fondness in the kid's eyes, but Zach ignored him, kneeling instead beside the old man.

"What happened to him?" he asked quickly.

"How should I know?" Logan snapped, anger getting the better of him. He paused, eyes darting out to the lake then back to Zachary. "He just dropped, right when the fog appeared. His Tame too."

"Like with the Thoona," Zachary bit back a curse and rose.

"Sicario, it's getting closer," Cordelia chipped in. She held the fossil in her hand like a shield, knuckles pale as she clutched it tight.

Noticing how Logan's eyes lingered on the stone, Zachary quickly stepped between them, then touched a hand to his own crystal. Light blossomed, forcing him to turn away.

When he looked back, Daze stood in its place, its rows of deadly teeth bared, copper eyes lighting up the shore. The

Brackis's coat had taken on a dark streak down its back, while its legs were a snowy white.

Zach followed the Tame's gaze as not one, but two creatures stepped onto the gravel shore.

The first stood tall like a stag on long legs, its antlered head lifted proudly. The crystal hooves strode across the water as though it were solid ground, ripples racing out across the calm surface with each stride.

Cast in a burning red glow, Zachary found himself shivering at the sight of the sharpened antlers. And they were just what could be seen. What other unseen powers might it possess. Something that could knock Gozzo unconscious, even from a distance?

The second creature did not float upon the waters like the first, but rather burst from the depths. Water sprayed across the stones as it landed. Its face was like that of a pug, stretched wide with large teeth peeking from behind swollen lips. Beady copper eyes watched them with a burning anger. Its body was squat and bulky, almost as small as the old fisherman's Pluff, though in place of fur it was protected by a leathery hide.

Strangely, while the front half of the beast was doglike, its rear sported a tail and dorsal fin like a fish. Indeed, it had seemed more graceful in the waters than on the shore, as its stumpy legs stumbled on the loose gravel. As it recovered, it snarled and let out a harsh bark, not unlike the ones they'd heard back on the plateau.

Stones crunched behind Zachary as the sailors advanced down the beach. Five remained. Their faces shone with a fear he could well understand. None of them understood this place, the rules by which this world was governed. They were strong men, ex-soldiers he was sure, and were used to facing enemies with sword in hand, testing their skills against a wily foe. Here, those skills availed them nothing. And still they moved to defend their captain. Zachary was impressed by their loyalty.

"I'd say this is a pretty desperate situation, wouldn't you, Sicario?" Cordelia muttered.

Zach grimaced, his eyes falling on Logan. The kid said nothing, but there was no doubt he'd heard Cordelia's words.

"I'd say so," Zach said before turning to Logan. Down on the shore, the creatures howled in unison and charged. "Do whatever you can to wake the old man."

Finally he looked to Daze. There he hesitated, unsure what to do. Before, the Thoona had fled his Tame's wakening. He had no idea how to command the creature into battle.

Thankfully, Daze didn't seem to need all that much commanding. The Brackis turned to face the creatures, a growl rumbling from deep behind the rows of razor-sharp teeth. Zach felt its anger filtering through the bond between them as it started down the shore, felt its burning hatred for the wild creatures. It seemed a reflection of their own, as though there was some great rivalry—

Zach gasped as his perspective shifted. Suddenly he was low to the ground, looking up at the antlered beast as it bared teeth that looked disturbing in the deer-like face. He stumbled—and felt stone crack beneath his taloned feet. A rumble sounded from his throat, and for the first time he felt the terrible power within him...

No, not him. Daze. He had merged with the Tame. A distant sense remained of his own body, a tug from across their link. Looking back, he could see himself on the beach behind him, eyes glassy and staring, mind...departed.

Another howl drew his attention back to their foe. The energies of the Tame surged again, exhilarating, intoxicating. A man could get used to that sense of power.

On the shore below, the antlered creature lowered its head and charged.

Zachary watched it for a moment with contempt. This creature dared to challenge him? He stood for a moment in the body of Daze, watching its approach, before the human part of him surfaced, shaking off the reckless arrogance.

Where had that come from? Even as he asked the question, he realised the answer. Daze. Their two minds shared the same body for the moment. The Tame's mind was fractured, but a sharp pride cut through the fog. It was ancient, these beasts newly formed. Far beneath its power.

Or at least, they should have been.

From Zach's perspective, the energies radiating from the wild beasts was an equal to those burning within them. He feared the Tame's broken mind had made a miscalculation.

A fear that was confirmed a moment later as the antlered creature struck them with the power of a runaway locomotive.

Crystal groaned and shattered as fiery pain lashed Zach's mind. Screaming, he sought to retreat across the link to his own body, to flee that terrible agony...

...but found himself trapped within the torn body of Daze. Hurled backwards by the force of the blow, they struck the ground hard. Stones

flew up around him, drawing cries from the humans further up the shore as they were pelted with rocks. They scattered, seeking shelter.

Zach hardly heard them. Stunned, he tried again to flee the agony, but something bound his consciousness to the Tame.

A bellow from the wild creatures snapped him out of his confusion. He could ponder the strangeness of his quandary at a later date. For now, he and Daze apparently needed to fight as one.

He surged onto his four legs with a roar. The second creature darted towards him, seeking to take advantage of his distraction. Thankfully, the half-dog, half-fish creature was smaller than Daze and not half as vicious. Their talons struck the creature a blow, sending it tumbling backwards into a nearby bank of mist.

Growling, Zachary swung around, expecting the other to be barrelling down on him. But the stag seemed to be struggling after its first attack. It shook its antlered head as though stunned, before finally straightening and setting its copper eyes once more on Daze. Hooves pawed the gravel shore as it readied for another charge.

Where the hell is Cordelia? *Zach thought desperately, but he could not call out from Daze's form.*

He had no knives to hurl now, but Daze's teeth and claws seemed deadly enough. Thankfully, the blow from the stag-like creature didn't seem to have slowed him.

It was time to attack.

He launched himself at the beast. The power with which the Brackis sprung surprised even Zach, hurling him several yards across the shore in a single bound. The monster reared in response, hooves flailing for his face, the disturbing fangs bared.

A blow from the crystal hooves struck him in the shoulder with a crunch of breaking crystal, but it didn't carry the same momentum as before and Zachary managed to shrug it off. They dropped into a crouch, then sprang, his jaws fastening upon the creature's throat.

Crunch.

Screaming, the stag tore itself loose from Zach's grip. A chunk of crystal broke away from the beast as it staggered back. No blood flowed from the wound, but the injury had clearly taken a toll on the creature. Growling, he moved in to make the kill.

A flash of red was his only warning before the dog-like creature launched itself from the darkness. Zachary cried out as teeth sank into his shoulder, leaving a row of tiny piercing marks. He turned burning eyes on the beast. It was half the size of Daze and should have shrunk before him. It tried to take another bite instead.

A swipe of Daze's paw sent it tumbling back into the dark.

Shaking off the lingering pain, Zachary turned in search of his main foe--

Boom!

The world shook as thorny vines exploded from the gravel around Daze. In an instant, they had wrapped around the form of the Brackis. Barbs like daggers tore into his crystal flesh, drawing a bellow from the depths of Daze's throat.

Red and green lit the night. Through the tendrils, he saw the antlered creature approaching. By its twin colours, he knew instinctively the vines were its doing. And it was not finished with him yet. Now the antlers began to glow, a fiery gold gathering at their points. Lowering its head, the beast pawed the ground—and charged.

Frantic, Zachary fought to tear himself from the vines, but the crystal strands were as strong as any steel. Each movement only drove the thorns deeper, only tightened their grip about Daze.

The world turned to white as the creature struck.

Zachary screamed as he found himself back in his body. For a moment, he gasped in the cold night air. Stars danced before his vision and swaying, he sank to his knees. The weight of his body did nothing to reduce the agony flowing across his connection with Daze. He could not escape it. His chest constricted, wrapped in bands of iron.

Voices were cursing nearby, but he could not make out their faces through the stars, couldn't understand what was happening. He knelt on the hard gravels, paralysed by his bond with the Tame. A hiss escaped his lips as he tried desperately to sever the connection, to flee.

Instead, it drew him slowly back…

He could feel the pieces of himself breaking on the golden antlers. Crystal crumbled from the wound. That blow had left Daze terribly injured. Zachary had no concept of a Tame's anatomy, but his insides were swirling like molten metal. He struggled to hold back the pain.

To his relief, though, the thorns had at least fallen away. As the crystal tendrils faded, Daze was left alone on the rocky shore. The Tame's mind swirled, barely clinging to consciousness. The attack had broken something within the beast. Zach sensed if not for his presence, his own meagre strength, the Tame would have already fallen.

He didn't want to know what would happen then.

Growling, he forced the Tame to its feet, determined to fight on. A fire still burned within, diminished, only a fraction of what might have been. It would have to do.

Their foe had retreated along the beach. It was already preparing for another charge. No thorns this time, only the golden glow of its antlers. He sensed a new emotion from Daze.

Fear.

They would not survive another such blow.

Along the shore, the stag-like creature lowered its antlers and charged.

27

LOGAN

"**W**hy won't it break!"

Cordelia's curses rang through the night. Logan was knelt beside Gozzo, still trying to wake the old fisherman, when he became aware that something was wrong. He looked up, surprised to find the captain on her hands and knees, scrambling for something on the ground. Crystal light flickered as she clasped the fossil and slammed it against a piece of stone. There came a sharp wrenching sound, like nails on a chalkboard, but the crystal remained stubbornly intact.

Beyond where she crouched, Zachary stood unnaturally still, his eyes staring into the distance.

"Damnit, Sicario, snap out of it," the woman snarled, clutching the stone and standing. "What in the seven hells am I doing wrong?"

The stones will not be used by the unbonded.

Logan flinched as the shadowy tendrils of the Guardian formed before him. His heart thundered as he half rose to his feet, reaching instinctively for his father's blade.

You must take back your burden, Pathfinder, or all here will be lost.

This time the words pierced the fog of Logan's panic. He stared at the swirling smoke, mouth suddenly parched.

"Bonded?" he rasped. "What are you talking about? It's hers now, she took it!"

But the shade did not respond. It hovered for a while longer, tendrils swirling above the gravel shore, before fading from view. Logan cursed. What the hell was he supposed to do now? Cordelia wouldn't just give him the stone. It was the only thing that could protect any of them in this damned place. But apparently it was useless in her hands.

Gritting his teeth, he levered himself up. Gozzo and his Tame would not stir. There would be no salvation there. He had to assume one of the monsters fighting on the beach had cast some spell over the pair. Though if that were true, he couldn't understand why the rest of them had been unaffected?

Another round of curses came from Cordelia. She stood now with sabre in hand, the fossil lying before her on a piece of stone. Screaming a battle cry, she brought the blade down on the quartz. Light flashed at the impact, followed by a *boom* of energy unleashed. The weapon was torn from the captain's fingers and went skittering across the beach.

And came to rest at Logan's feet.

He stared at the sword for a long moment before looking up at Cordelia. Her eyes were wide, her mouth parted, as though she were about to demand the weapon's return. Swallowing his fear, he placed his boot on the flat of the blade and drew his father's sabre. This would be his only chance. Her men had retreated into the forest when the battle had begun. Amilyse had gone with them.

It was just Logan and the captain now.

For the first time in his life, the leather hilt of his father's sword felt comfortable in his hand as he pointed it at the captain.

To his surprise, a smile spread across Cordelia's lips. "So the pup has a bite after all," she murmured, reaching down to pluck the fossil from the rock at her feet. Light flashed as she tossed it in the air, casting shadows across her face before she caught it again. "Are you sure this is the path you want to take, Mr. Kaine?"

A shiver spread down Logan's spine. He looked again at the sword in his hand. The blade shone in the crystal light. His father's blade. His family's legacy.

"You should return that to me, Captain," he said, "before it's too late."

"Is that a threat, Mr. Kaine?" Cordelia laughed. The mirth was short-lived as her face darkened. She advanced until the tip of his blade rested against her chest. "Go on then," she hissed, "do it."

Logan's anger swelled at the challenge. Cordelia was just like everyone else in his life. She thought he was weak, that he didn't have what it took to stand amongst the adults in the room. His grip tightened around his father's blade as he pressed it forward. The razor edge sliced through the threads of Cordelia's bodice.

"Well?" The woman did not so much as flinch. "I'm waiting."

Looking into her eyes, Logan saw the challenge there, the unyielding strength. She would never give in. Only in death would she admit defeat.

A lump lodged in his throat. Was this really who he wanted to be? The sort of man willing to cut down an unarmed woman, however deserving, to serve his own ends?

"Please, Cordelia," he said softly, "you have to give me the stone, or we're all going to die here."

At that moment, an agonised scream carried through the night. The two did not so much as blink, though Logan felt his heart clench. That sound had not been produced by any human. Shrill and piercing, it was what Logan imagined a voice of crystal might sound. Another shriek followed, and finally the pair flinched, turning towards the sound.

Zachary's Tame had been engulfed by emerald vines. As they watched, the deer-like creature charged, its golden antlers slamming into the helpless Brackis.

Cordelia cursed, her attention snapping back to the crystal in her hand. She raised it above her head.

"It won't work," Logan said quickly.

That got her attention. "What are you talking about?" she snapped, hand still raised.

"It's bonded to me," he replied. The stone pulsed in her hand, as though in response to his words. He felt a tug in his core as though something had brushed his soul. "Only I can use it."

Cordelia's eyes narrowed. "Do you think I am a fool?"

"No," Logan said. He lowered his sword and stared at the blade for a long moment. Then swallowing his doubt, he tossed it aside. "I'm not a fighter, Cordelia. My father always wanted me to be…so much so, I convinced myself I wanted to follow him." He swallowed, struggling with the words. "You're the better choice to protect us—any fool can see that. That's why Zach chose to give the stone to you. But it wasn't his choice to make. It has to be me."

Another cry carried through the night, though it was fainter now, as though its owner was fading. Their eyes locked, neither looked away.

"Have you ever been in a fight?" Cordelia asked suddenly.

"Not in my entire life."

A sigh slipped from Cordelia's lips, her eyes sliding closed. "The Old Gods help me."

Already looking like she regretted the decision, Cordelia tossed the fossil to Logan.

He almost fumbled the stone as it tumbled through the air. But as his fingers closed around the flickering stone, the light within stabilised—then flared to blinding life. Cordelia cried out and Logan almost dropped the stone again as its warmth spread through his fingers. Something reached out to brush his mind, and he shivered, sensing the question there.

Instinctively, he knew there would be no going back once he answered. He embraced it anyway.

Yes!

He raised the fossil above his head and brought it down upon a nearby rock.

Light burst from the stone and coalesced instantly, changing, solidifying, growing, until a beast of crystal stood before Logan.

It was a Thoona.

He shivered as the four burning eyes of copper settled on him. In that instant the connection was formed, the bond that could not be broken. And he understood Zach's words from that morning. The vastness of the creature's mind was matched only by the distorted jumble of images flashing before Logan's inner eyes.

A rumble from down the shore snapped the images into crystal clarity. For a heartbeat, Logan found himself in an enormous chamber. A great crystal lit the darkness, and a rumbling filled the world, though he could not see the source. The energy pulsed, spreading from the crystal, filling the chamber, the island, the world.

Instinctively, Logan knew the truth.

This was the light atop the mountain, the power that held them to this place.

Then he was back in his body. Time stood still as power flowed from his Tame into his body, stimulating his every sense. In that moment, he saw all. Saw the fear in Cordelia's eyes as she watched the battling monsters. Saw the sailors in the trees, their faces cast in shadow. Saw Amilyse crouched in the gravels, hand clutched tight about something that burned. Saw the antlered creature readying itself for the final blow.

And he saw Zachary and Daze, united in their futile battle with the wild beast.

A roar came from Logan's jaws as he found himself merged with the unnamed Thoona. The shift hardly gave him pause. Daze and Zachary were in peril. The man might have betrayed him, but he did not deserve death. Logan charged.

Along the shore, the enemy paused mid-stride at Logan's cry. Spying the new threat, it changed directions and leapt to meet him. The crystal antlers shone with unnatural light. He could sense its rage—and joy— at Zach's suffering. Now it sought another victory.

But this beast had not been left untouched by its battle with Zachary. Crystal had been torn and shattered around its throat—a mortal wound for any creature of flesh.

But not this beast. Antlers lowered, it bore down upon him. Fear clawed at Logan's insides, screaming for him to flee, that he was not strong enough to face this beast, that he would perish on this shore, defeated and alone.

"Courage is not some fleeting thing, but something forged in the fires of their terror, tempered in dread, and made all the stronger for it."

They were Zach's words, spoken in reprimand of Amilyse and her reckless brother, but Logan clung to them now as though they were a lifeline thrown in stormy waters.

He settled into the body of his Tame. His claws extended, digging deep into the gravel shore. The power in this creature was like ecstasy, its strength beyond anything he could have imagined.

The enemy bore down on him, antlers lowered, a roar unsuited to its deer-like appearance ringing across the waters. He could see its rage, made visible by its burning scarlet. And he could see its weakness. The crumbling crystal where Zachary had struck it earlier.

At the last moment, he moved, human mind and crystal Thoona moving as one. In a rush of power, they leapt, an enormous paw sweeping out to strike the chest of the enemy creature.

The harsh crackling of breaking crystal followed.

Logan reeled back as the point of an antler slashed across his furry mane. Thankfully the attack did not pierce further than that, as the creature reeled back. Cracks spread across its chest where Logan had struck it, growing like a rapidly spun spider's web. The scarlet glow of the creature faded, to be replaced by a sickly green. For a heartbeat, Logan tasted its fear, the panic on the air.

Then with a final crack, *the beast shattered into a thousand pieces.*

Stunned, Logan stayed with his Tame, watching as the creature turned to dust. At last only the emerald glow remained where the crystal stag had stood. The light hovered in the air, before it surged across the shore into Logan—or rather, his Tame.

He cried out as fresh energy surged through his crystal form, sizzling as it spread to every limb, every fibre of the Thoona. Limitless power. That was how it felt, for the briefest of seconds. The images swirled again within his mind's eye, clearer this time, slower. He felt that understanding was just beyond his reach.

But the ecstasy did not last long.

Consumed by the memories, the second beast had gone unnoticed.

Until it came barrelling at him from the mists.

✲ 28 ✲

ZACHARY

His mind still merged with Daze, Zachary watched as the stag shattered into a thousand pieces. Chunks of crystal went skittering across the gravel and the scent of burning metal carried on the air. Light bloomed where the beast had stood, before going rushing into the other Tame.

The Thoona. Its four eyes glowed bronze as it stood tall, jaws parted, crystal fur glistening with the absorbed energies. He could sense its joy, and the joy of the human soul within. Instinctively, he knew this was not Cordelia, but Logan. How had the kid convinced the captain to give up the stone? He didn't believe for a second that Logan could have taken it from her.

Their respite did not last long.

With a cry of unbridled rage, the dog-like creature burst from the mists. Gravel showered across the beach as it launched itself at Logan's unnamed Thoona.

A cry rang out in Zachary's mind as razor-sharp teeth sank into the other Tame. Squealing, the Thoona bucked and twisted until the beast *was dislodged. With a swing of one great paw, Logan sent his new enemy tumbling across the shore.*

Watching it disappear into the swirling fog, Zachary was perplexed. Was it his imagination, or had the thing been larger this time? It had definitely been brighter, scarlet in its rage. The creature was obviously infuriated by the ease with which they rebuffed it.

That thing took a chunk out of me.

The words rang in Zach's mind. For a second, he thought it must be Daze. Then he saw the eyes of the other Tame, and realised it was Logan. How had the kid figured that one out? Instinctively, he reached out in return.

Did it seem larger to you?

Logan did not reply. Snarling, the creature burst from the fog again. This time Logan was ready for it. Spinning, the great teeth of the Thoona sank into crystal flesh. A shake of his head sent the creature reeling, great chunks of crystal crumbling from the wound. Yelping, it fled again into the mists.

Definitely not my imagination, *Zachary pulsed to Logan, a sense of urgency gripping him.* **That thing is getting bigger.**

I'll deal with it.

The Thoona turned from him with the words, its copper eyes scanning the mists. Zachary cursed as Logan stepped into the icy tendrils. There was something strange about this enemy. It didn't seem bothered by its repeated defeats.

The creature attacked again. It was almost as large as Daze now, though still smaller than Logan's Thoona. Bursting from the fog, it latched onto Logan's hind leg before he could react. Roaring, the Thoona bucked, struggling to bring teeth and claws to bear. But like a true hound, the creature clung on, growling even through its mouthful of crystal.

There was no doubt now. Where before the Thoona had handled it easily, now even a direct blow from one of Logan's paws was not enough to tear the beast loose.

It was growing stronger with each defeat.

Logan, wait...

He started to give a warning, but at that moment the Thoona rolled, catching the creature beneath its bulk. That was finally enough to break the beast's hold, though a chunk of crystal went with it as it was dislodged. Howling, Logan's Tame regained its feet and spun in search of the enemy.

It had already vanished again into the mists.

Damn, where did it go?

Kid, I think—

You think too much, *Logan snapped.* **I'm going to tear that thing apart.**

Zach cursed as the Thoona turned away. This wasn't the passive and cautious Logan he'd come to expect. Then he recalled the sensations that had swept through him as he merged with Daze. The sense of power, the arrogance and indifference to the enemy. Those sensations had faded now, fled with the first blow the enemy had struck them.

What must it be like for a young man, new to the world, let alone this place?

The dog-like creature attacked again before Zachary could talk any sense into the kid. The Thoona roared a challenge and turned to meet it.

This time though, the balance had changed.

The enemy had doubled in size, growing larger even than Logan's Thoona. Caught off-guard, Logan went down, practically flattened by the greater bulk of the monster. Teeth that were no longer tiny gleamed as they sank into crystal flesh.

The Thoona screamed, the sound haunting amidst the mists. Emerald light burst across the shore as Logan's golden glow fled. An aura of terror swamped the shore as the Thoona tried and failed to recover. Claws the size of daggers slashed at the hound creature, but they no longer penetrated its crystal hide.

Teeth flashed again, and crystal flesh crumbled.

Needles spread across Zachary's flesh as his hair stood on end. He could feel the weakness within Daze, their dwindling strength. Pain still radiated from the gaping wound the first beast had left. It was a struggle just to stand.

Now they would have to fight.

Gathering their legs beneath them, man and Tame lifted themselves from the ground and felt some of their energy return. Wounds and pain did not seem to affect these crystal creatures the way it did humans. There was no way Zachary could have stood so soon after the beating Daze had taken.

Perhaps it was the wounded pride he sensed from his Tame. It had been shown up by these wild creatures, almost brought to an end. The creature he'd named Daze could not let that stand.

In a burst of speed, they bounded forward. There was no time to hesitate with Logan at the creature's mercy. The enemy was larger than Daze now, but its back was turned to them.

Zachary moved to strike. As he did so, he became aware of something within the Tame whose body he inhabited. A memory of power. Something stirred. Energy flushed through Daze, gathering...gathering in its twin tails...no, not tails at all. Stingers.

Snarling, he struck out with the twin barbs. The razor-sharp points sank deep into the hounds flesh, tearing through its crystal hide. A scream rent the night as the enemy reared, spinning and tearing the barbs loose, seeking its assailant and releasing its hold on Logan.

Zachary felt a rush of relief, but it was short lived as the burning eyes turned on him. Fiery red burst from the leathery skin, lighting up the nearby trees. He glimpsed the horrified faces of Cordelia's men standing in the shelter of the forest.

Then before Zachary's eyes, the enemy creature doubled in size. Its rounded figure swelled, the jaws stretching wide, razor-sharp teeth growing to the size of daggers.

Cursing, he leapt back. Daze wouldn't survive a blow from that thing, not after the punishment they'd already taken. Thankfully, the hound's new size had robbed it of some speed. Its short legs struggled for traction in the gravel, giving them a chance to retreat.

And for Logan to recover his feet.

A stillness came over the Thoona as it stood there, before a haunting music emanated from the Tame. Zach shivered. He knew that sound. And while it was not directed at him, he felt a tug in his soul, a remembered terror from the Thoona that had stalked them the night before.

Unfortunately, the music did not have the same calming effect on this creature as it had on the humans. Shrugging off the magic of the song, the four short legs of the hound sank deep into the gravel. Zachary shivered as he sensed a power gather about the beast, retreating a step. The *air began to vibrate. Sparks flew from the leathery skin, sizzling as they gathered force.*

Boom!

Sparks burst from the hound, racing outwards in all directions. Zachary flinched back, but there was no avoiding this attack. Caught in a web of burning electricity, Zach expected the end. Daze was too weak to survive another blow.

He stiffened, electricity surging through their crystal channels. But to his surprise, this time there was no pain. Instead, a tingling spread through Daze, starting in their core and rushing outwards until it had reached every limb, every inch of the Tame.

The brilliance faded and Zachary exhaled in relief. Or rather, he tried to. Daze's body would not respond. Jaws and legs and stingers… nothing moved. The electricity had left him paralysed.

As the light faded, the enormous creature stood still on the shore of the lake. Gravel crunched as it took a ponderous step. A rumbling like laughter came from its chest as the copper eyes examined its foes. Zachary saw that like him, Logan's Thoona had been frozen by the blast.

For a moment, time stood still. Then the hound started towards Logan. In his body, Zachary sensed the sudden thrumming of his heart. He watched, helpless, as the monster closed in on Logan's frozen Thoona. It was so large now, a single bite would tear the Tame in two.

There was no knowing what would happen then. Zachary and Logan's souls were entangled now with those of their Tames. If Daze or the unnamed Thoona perished, would they suffer the same fate?

Zachary had no desire to find out.

He couldn't move, but as he watched the creature near Logan, he finally noticed something he'd missed. The creature's back where he'd struck no longer shone with the same vibrant red as the rest of it. Instead, the crystal had gone dull and cracked, as though...

...as though it had been poisoned.

Daze's heart quickened as the memory came rushing back. Zachary would have smiled if his Tame's jaws had been capable of such an expression. Poison. It seemed all too appropriate for a man of the underground.

The acrid venom was working its magic on the hound, but would it be quick enough to save Logan? There was no way of knowing.

Instead, Zachary dug deep. His mind sank into the crystal vortex that was Daze, seeking out power, some energy that might aid them to break free. There had to be something he could do. Heartbeats passed as the creature crept closer, and still he sensed nothing but cold crystal...

...no, not cold. There was a warmth within the Tame. The same warmth he sensed through their bond, the energy that had allowed him to hold back the symptoms of his illness. Except merged with his Tame, this sense was in reverse.

The power was not within Daze, but himself.

As his consciousness became aware of it, the power changed, rushing suddenly from his own core across their connection into Daze. As it touched the Tame's core, warmth became heat, and heat became flame.

There was a sharp wrenching within Daze as they tore themselves from the paralysis. He staggered for a moment, before righting. Their eyes fixed upon the enemy.

And still the fiery power gathered.

Until Daze could contain it no longer.

Raising their twin stingers, they unleashed that power in a burst of crackling, poisonous energy. The enemy had no time to react before the attack struck. And while it did no apparent physical damage, its effect was no less devasting. The sickly patch of crystal pulsed and began to grow, spreading rapidly across the creature's leathery skin. Where it went, the scarlet glow faded, the energies that powered the hound fleeing before its acrid touch.

Until at last, the enemy stood still. Its flesh dulled, its copper eyes fading to an empty white. Fissures spread through the dead crystal, the sharp crackling they made was loud in the night's silence, until with a final splintering, the beast shattered.

Daze slumped to the soft gravels, his energies spent by that final attack. With Zachary, they watched as the glowing light hovered where the beast had stood, then went rushing towards them—

And suddenly Zach was himself again. A wave of exhaustion swept through him, as though his own body had been suffering alongside Daze. Recalling that last burst of energy he'd drawn across their connection, he wondered if there was more truth to that than he realised. Certainly, the pain his soul had experienced had been real. It lingered still, like thorns lodged in the soft places of his mind.

But they had survived. Against all odds, they had defeated the two monsters. Flashes of light came from along the shore as Daze and the unnamed Thoona reverted to crystal form and returned to their human partners. Logan himself stood nearby, a look of astonishment on his youthful face. He stared at the piece of quartz as it came to a stop before him. There was no sign of Cordelia.

A groan came from Zachary's feet as Gozzo pushed himself into a sitting position. Confusion showed in the old man's eyes as he surveyed the scorched patch of earth left by the monster's electrical attack.

"Wha…" he shook himself and stood. "It was a bloody Skelt, wasn't it?"

It took a long moment before Zachary realised the word was the man's name for another of the creatures. He frowned. "Antlers, hooves? Looks a bit like a deer?"

"Ay, that's the one," Gozzo growled. He stood. "Where'd the bastard go, you chase it off?"

"Killed it," Zachary said absently.

Surprise showed on the old man's face. "Well, ain't that something." He cast another look around the shore, before finally noticing the crystal floating beside Logan. "And ain't that something else. Looks like y'all have some telling to do."

Zachary could only nod. His eyes were on Logan as well. Despite the battle they had just fought together, there was no missing the anger behind the kid's eyes. Zachary had a feeling there might yet be a reckoning for what he'd done in the forest.

29

CORDELIA

Cordelia stood in the shadows, looking out across the lake. Dawn's light stained the horizon. The mists had vanished with the coming of the day. All was silent but for the gentle lapping of tiny waves against the shore, the rustling of leaves in the treetops.

She closed her eyes. Her heart was still pounding, her body tensed from the events of the night. Not for her the peace of sleep. How long now since she'd last rested? Two days? Or was it three? She found that her mind was foggy, struggling to recall details. She'd stolen a wink here and there, no more than an hour at a time. Anything more, and the nightmares woke her, the image of the terrible beast emerging from the grass.

A curse slipped from her lips. She straightened and stepped away from the tree on which she'd been leaning. Last night was meant to have brought an end to those terrors. That she couldn't protect herself. Couldn't protect her people. With the stone, the helplessness she'd felt since landing on these unholy shores should have been washed away.

But she had failed.

For the stone had not woken. Not for her. Instead it had been the Kaine boy, a *child*, that had saved her crew. And by taking the stone, it was Cordelia who had almost doomed them.

That was the worst of it. She had realised her mistake in coming here that first night. All those dreams of riches and treasures had died the moment the Thoona had emerged from the grass. The second it had slain Byron. This night, she was lucky the beasts had not taken another.

Silently she drew her blade from its sheath. She might as well hurl it into the icy waters. It was no more use here than their rifles, not now that the others had their so-called Tames. What threat could a piece of iron pose with the invulnerable monsters to protect them?

Worse than the failure itself, was the knowledge she had failed her men. They had trusted her to lead them on this venture, believed she would protect them. Her men did not need to rely on prayers to Edris or Bes, nor the fickle support of the followers of the Earth God Houtu. It was Cordelia of Leith who offered broken men a second chance, who gave them purpose, kept them safe. For that, their loyalty was unshakeable.

Until this fateful voyage.

Footsteps approached through the trees. Duncan appeared, her first man and the sailor she'd placed on the dawn watch. He'd joined Cordelia's crew a few years back, after an injury in a skirmish in the north had cost him his trigger finger, along with a few others. The King's Council offered pauper's wages to soldiers injured in combat. He and his family would have been on the street within a month if Cordelia hadn't found him.

She nodded a greeting as he joined her on the shore. She had wandered down the beach away from the camp in search of privacy, but was pleased to see the man doing his rounds. They might not have many options to protect themselves from the beasts, but they could warn the crystal bearers—or the Pathfinders, as they'd been calling themselves.

"No sign of monsters, Captain," Duncan murmured.

"Glad to hear it, lad," she replied, before hesitating. "I am sorry I brought you to this place, Duncan."

The man shrugged. "Likely woulda been dead in some back alley long ago if not for you, Captain," he said. "It's nothing."

"Your life is not nothing, Duncan," Cordelia replied, then smiled. "But thank you."

Duncan nodded. "I'll resume my patrol then."

She watched him move away. His words did little to salve her guilt. How many had she lost on this journey? Byron had fallen to that terrible Thoona. He had a family too, a wife expecting his return. And the wreckage was sure to have had other casualties. She had found only half her crew on the beach when she woke. The others were likely dead, though she still held out hope.

Footsteps came from behind her. Cordelia frowned. Who else was on watch? Peck? No, she would have never heard him in a forest like this. And he should have been patrolling on the other side of camp. She was about to turn when an unfamiliar voice spoke from the shadows.

"I'm impressed. Your men are loyal, Cordelia."

Her heart pounding, Cordelia spun. A silhouette shifted beneath the trees. Her sabre gave a *hiss* as it slid from her scabbard. She advanced towards the undergrowth.

"*You*," she growled as a face appeared amongst the crystal tree trunks.

"Me," Dustin repeated, an easy grin on his stubbled chin.

All of Cordelia's rage, all of her anger, came rushing to the fore. "Give me one reason why I shouldn't run you through," she snarled, taking another step towards the elder of the Kaine brothers.

A growl rumbled from the darkness as a creature shifted in the shadows. Silver eyes glinted in the dawn light as the beast bared its teeth. Cordelia froze, goosebumps prickling her skull. The creature remained cast in shadows, but she'd caught enough of a glimpse that her every instinct screamed for her to run. She looked slowly from the beast to Dustin.

"You'd better hope your beast is quick," she said, blade still pointed towards the man. "Or we'll be seeing each other in the seven hells."

Dustin chuckled. "There'll be no need for that," he said, waving a hand. The beast faded back into the shadows. "I didn't come here to fight."

"What did you come here for?" Cordelia spat, the point of her sword trembling. She had to hold herself back to keep from running the man through then and there. "You knew what this place was. You lured us all to our deaths."

"No," Dustin replied with a shake of his head. "I'll admit, things have not gone as planned. But this place is not death, Cordelia. It's the future!"

"Tell that to my sailors," Cordelia snapped.

"I regret our rough landing," Dustin said softly, "but you were warned the journey would be perilous."

"I lost my ship and half my crew! Dozens of passengers perished in the waters. You said nothing of such dangers."

The man looked away at her words, the easy smile falling from his lips. "I did not know," he said. "I am sorry. I underestimated the protections that remain in place."

"I don't believe you."

He spun back to her. "I brought my little brother with me," he growled. "Do you think I would have put him in danger if I'd known what waited?"

"I don't know," Cordelia replied, hesitating. "I know he is in my power though."

Dustin smiled, though it did not reach his eyes. "Not after last night."

"You were there?"

"In a fashion."

Cordelia's anger returned. She tightened her grip on the sword hilt. "I still have not heard a good reason why I should not kill you where you stand."

The words hung between them a moment before the man sighed. "I admit I owe you a debt, Cordelia," he said at last. "But perhaps this will help pay it back in part, at least."

At that he reached into his coat and drew something from the inner pocket. A soft glow bathed the clearing. Cordelia's heart clenched as she recognised the blue light. A sapphire.

"Is it…"

"See for yourself." Dustin said as he tossed the rock to her.

Cordelia flinched at the action, and only at the last minute did her hand flash up to snatch the sapphire from the air. Swallowing, she held it up to the dawn light. A shadow was revealed within, the fossil trapped within the stone. Warmth spread through her fingers as the stone's glow grew brighter. Her heart began to race.

"Why?" she whispered, looking from the stone to Dustin.

"Zachary was right," came the reply. "You were the best choice for a stone. Wake the beast within. Use it to protect yourself and your people. I ask only that you protect my brother as well."

"You won't be joining us?"

Dustin chuckled. "I thought you wanted to stab me."

Cordelia said nothing, only stared at the man, until finally he shrugged. Turning, he looked out across the lake towards the stark slopes of the mountain.

"I cannot join you, not yet. There is something I must first do."

Following his gaze, Cordelia's frown deepened. "You're seeking the light? We are heading there as well."

Dustin chuckled. "So I understand. I, however, have a head start."

"You're starting from the same place as us," Cordelia replied, perplexed.

This time Dustin's laughter rang out across the shore. "Am I?"

Abruptly, Cordelia jerked awake. Heart racing, she swung her head left and right, but there was no one. She was resting with her back to one of the scraggly crystal trees. A curse slipped from her lips. She didn't even remember sitting down. Frustration built within her as she realised it had all been a dream. How desperate had she become, that the crystal fossils invaded even her sleep?

Yet as Cordelia made to stand, she felt something tumble from her fingers. Blue light flashed from the ground as the sapphire tumbled across the stones. She froze for a second, mouth agape, struggling to understand how it had come to be there. Then hesitantly, she reached out and picked it up.

The shadow within the sapphire was unmistakeable, the warmth in her hand reassuring. Her heart beat hard in her chest as she rose. Pursing her lips, she started back along the shore in search of the old fisherman. This time, she would be taking no chances. She would wake this Tame long before they had to face another of the deadly creatures.

30

LOGAN

The scent of burnt stone was strong on the air where Logan sat on the rocky shore. Watching the sun rise over the clear waters, he found his mind replaying the events of the night, the rush of sensations, the agony and ecstasy of his battles.

He shivered. The crystal was heavy in his hands. Recalling the alien mind of the Tame merged with his own, a part of him wanted to stand and hurl it into the lake. The power of the creature within terrified him. When they had merged... everything had changed. He'd been himself, battling against the wild creature, and yet...he also hadn't. There had been another presence, another soul fighting alongside him.

That mind had at once seemed ancient and terrifyingly different...and yet it felt as a part of his own mind as well, as though some timeless part of his soul had finally returned to him.

What that meant, Logan couldn't begin to guess. He only knew he hadn't acted like himself last night. The thrill of battle, the exhilaration of the kill, those were sensations he'd never experienced before. Things his father and brother had lived, for sure, but Logan? He shivered. A creature, however strange, had perished by his hands. And he had celebrated. That scared him.

Not to mention, it had been foolish. His revelry had almost cost them everything. He could still feel that sense of helplessness, of raw terror as the enormous monster loomed over his Tame. If not for Zachary, he would have been finished...

...though he would not offer the man his thanks. It had been Zach's fault they'd come so close to defeat in the first place.

Footsteps approached, slow and limping.

"Glad to see you figured it out, matey" Gozzo said as he lowered himself down with a groan.

Staring into his crystal, Logan shook his head. "The Guardian came to me. It told me about the bond."

"Guardian?"

"Dark, shadowy creature. It appeared to us first on the beach."

"Ah, yes. Just call it the shadow myself."

"It warned me that Cordelia wouldn't be able to use my stone. You knew?"

"Old Caspar might 'ave suspected. He sensed your bond with the stone that first morning we met. Was what marked ya as a Pathfinder. Reckon it was forged when the Thoona attacked."

"So why didn't it appear to protect me then?"

"Ya still need to break the damn thing, first time," Gozzo replied with a chuckle. "Good thing ya friend figured that one out."

"He is not my friend," Logan murmured.

"Suppose not."

A shiver ran through Logan. He turned the crystal in his hand, watching the shadow moving within.

"Do you feel different?" Logan asked suddenly. "Since bonding with Caspar, I mean?"

The old fisherman did not immediately answer. His fading eyes lingered on the lake, on the distant shore and the stark slopes beyond.

"I am not...the same man who was stranded on this island," he said at last.

Logan swallowed a sudden lump in his throat. He waited for further explanation.

"I have often wondered, these past...months," the fisherman continued, "if the stone has changed me—if *Caspar* has changed me. I'm a harder man than I was. Perhaps that is just who I needed to become for this place. The divine know, it's taken enough from me." He sighed. "Truthfully, I cannot answer ya question, matey."

He reached out then, touching a finger to his stone. Light flared as Caspar appeared. He rested a hand on the Tame's head, and a smile brightened his gloomy features.

"But I can tell ya I don't regret the bond," he added. "'Tis smart to be wary. It's all still new to you. But they ain't so scary, these creatures, once ya get to know em. They are but an extension of our souls, a reflection of the eternal spark within every human. They only enhance what was already there."

Despite the man's reassurance, Logan found himself shivering. He sensed the truth in the man's words. That rage, that fury, had that truly been inside of him?

"So, have you decided on a name?"

Logan hesitated, glancing at the stone in his hands. He shivered, remembering the despair of the night before, the doom he'd thought would claim them all. Yet through that darkness, their Tames had shone true.

"Hope," he whispered.

"A good name," Gozzo murmured.

He looked up as fresh footsteps approached. Amilyse came to a stop before them, hesitating as she looked from Gozzo to Logan.

"Can we talk?" she asked Logan pointedly.

Grinning, the old fisherman excused himself, and Amilyse took his place alongside Logan.

For a long while, she said nothing and they sat there in silence. The sun was stretching ever higher overhead, the unnatural warmth returning to the island. Without the darkness and mists, the opposite shore was visible now. A hundred crags and broken ridges waited, their deep shadows beckoning. Gozzo had warned them that the beasts on those shores wandered the land at all hours. Day or night, there would be no safety once they crossed.

"So, you've become one of them," Amilyse said suddenly.

Logan hesitated, looking from the woman to the stone in his hands. He shrugged. "I wasn't left with much choice."

"No, I suppose not," she murmured, her gaze distant. "I don't know who I am anymore."

"Because of Rob?" Logan asked after a pause.

A sigh slipped from the woman's lips. "In part. I miss him. Maybe Zachary is right and he was a fool, but he always meant well. I've never met anyone so full of life." She laughed, the sound harsh, raw. "We wanted to save the world together, to destroy the monsters as our ancestors did. Who knew we couldn't even save ourselves?"

"We destroyed two last night."

"By allying ourselves with those very monsters." She sighed, then reached into her pocket and drew out a glowing rock.

Logan started as purple light pulsed between her fingers. She held the piece of amethyst up to the light of the sun, revealing the shadow within.

"It came to me last night," she whispered. "When the first creature attacked, it showered us all with gravel from the beach. This landed at my feet." She shook her head. "I'm a monster hunter. How can I consider waking this thing, knowing what it is? How can I consider…what did Gozzo call it…bonding with a creature of darkness?"

Logan bit his lip, unsure how to respond. Moments slipped past, and then he reached out and touched the piece of quartz that hovered before him, in the manner he'd observed Zach and Gozzo do. Light spilt across the gravel beach as Hope emerged. He sensed Amilyse grow tense alongside him, but the Tame only settled before Logan.

Sensing its copper eyes watching him, Logan reached out and rested a hand on the Tame's head. After a moment, he felt a vibration from the creature, followed by a gentle warmth in his palm. Its coat changed colours, becoming the golden hue of joy. Smiling, he looked at Amilyse.

"Do you really think he's a monster?"

The woman hesitated. "I don't know what to think anymore," she admitted.

Logan nodded. Removing his hand from the Tame, he gestured for her to take a try. Her eyes narrowed with suspicion as she studied the creature. Hope watched her back, copper eyes gleaming in the morning sun, unfazed by her distrust. Finally Amilyse touched a hand to the Thoona's back.

A gasp burst from Logan as a prickling sensation ran down his neck, spreading quickly until his skin was tingling all over. Not seeming to notice his reaction, Amilyse pursed her lips, then gently stroked Hope's head. A soft rumble came from the Tame, and the tingling sensation grew more intense.

"Well…that…feels weird," he stammered.

Amilyse snatched back her hand at his words, but he only offered a smile. "Didn't say it was bad," he laughed.

But Amilyse didn't share his smile. Her eyes had returned to the crystal in her hand.

"I could have woken it last night," she admitted finally. "I felt…something from it as soon as I picked it up." She looked at him then, eyes wide, and he finally saw the truth. She was terrified. "I could have helped you, but I…didn't. I was afraid."

"We were all afraid," he said, trying to reassure her.

She shook her head angrily. "You don't understand," she rasped, tears appearing in her eyes. Raising a hand, she wiped them away before they could fall. "I couldn't… couldn't move. It overwhelmed me. Just like it always has." Her voice broke. "I am not my brother. I can't just stand in the path of monsters with a smile on my face. Ever since we set foot on this island, I have been terrified. And now he's gone…" She looked at him through teary eyes. "There was a test we had to pass before our family would accept us as monster hunters. My brother and I, we were locked in a pitch-black dungeon for a month. No light. No escape. No mercy. Only each other." Her voice had fallen to barely a whisper now. Her eyes were haunted. "And then…then…" she trailed off. "By the time they released us, I could barely remember what the outside world looked like. I left a piece of me in that dark place. I would not have survived without him."

"That's horrible."

Amilyse stared at him as though he were mad. "It was a test," she replied, "to see whether we had the strength to face the darkness. I failed. Only my brother saved me from my shame. But the truth remains. I am a coward, Logan. I always have been."

Logan shivered. Her words were the same ones she'd hurled at Zachary. He could understand her reaction now, her need to appear fearless, to cling to the myth of Rob's courage. It had given her strength in an uncertain world. Now, faced with true danger, with a peril that had already taken her brother, she found herself floundering.

"You're not a coward, Amilyse," he said, eyes drifting out over the waters. "It's like Zachary said, being afraid doesn't make us cowards. It's what we do with that fear." He smiled as a memory came to him, one he'd buried deep. "My mother used to say something similar. When I was young, I feared there were monsters under my bed."

At his feet, Hope lifted its head. Logan glimpsed understanding in the creature's eyes. He smiled. "*Those* weren't real," he said.

"What did she tell you?" Amilyse asked.

"That fear is the true monster. If you run from it, allow it to rule you, it will only grow until it consumes you. But turn and face it, master it, and it becomes a loyal hound."

Amilyse sighed, returning her gaze to the crystal in her hands. For a while neither said anything, only sat and watched as the red light of dawn faded from the horizon.

"My brother would curse me if he knew I held this," Amilyse said suddenly.

"Rob is gone," Logan said gently. "We have to do what's necessary to survive."

Amilyse pursed her lips. "I know."

A shadow fell across them then. Logan frowned as he found Cordelia standing beside them. Before he could ask the treacherous woman what she wanted, her eyes settled on the crystal in Amilyse's hands. His heart lurched and he stumbled to his feet, prepared to summon his Tame to protect his friend, if necessary.

But Cordelia only waved a hand dismissively. "So you found one as well, Ms. Rainer," she said instead to Amilyse. She held up a sapphire of her own, its depths stained by darkness. "Good. Let's go find the old fisherman then. It's about time we ladies got some muscle of our own behind us."

❧ 31 ❧

ZACHARY

The roses glistened in the morning sunlight, the reds and violets and blues set aglow by its distant brilliance. The bushes were nestled amongst the trees, several dozen yards along the shore from where they'd taken shelter for the night. Zach wasn't sure how he'd missed them earlier, but he sat beside them now, breathing in the richness of their aroma.

Their crystal beauty was a stark contrast to the horrors they'd faced in the night. It amazed him they had all come through unscathed—at least physically. The mental scars he'd accumulated in the desperate battle would take longer to heal. Suffice to say, his plan with Cordelia had been an utter disaster.

He shivered, a hand drifting to his chest as he recalled the wound Daze had taken. Echoes of the Tame's agony still haunted him. He wondered how far their connection went. Power passed back and forth between them; of that much, he was sure. But if the Tame perished, if Daze fell while they were joined…

Thankfully the kid had saved him before Zachary had learned the answer to that question.

He sighed, eyes drifting closed. He'd thought he'd been doing the right thing, taking the stone from Logan. That's what he'd told himself. When surrounded by enemies with only two swords to go around, you didn't give the second to a kid. Cordelia should have been the right choice. But this place didn't play by his rules.

Zachary felt a pulse across his connection with Daze and found the creature's copper eyes watching him. He sensed concern from the Tame. It didn't understand his pain, the doubt that had infected his soul. How could it?

The sun was rising higher now and the overhanging branches returned the roses to shade. Like those in his own gardens outside of Leith, several of the flowers had wilted. Amazing, that the crystal plants of this world behaved so similarly to their own.

Kneeling alongside the nearest bush, Zach drew his last knife from its sheath. Unlike the Tames, the crystal stems did not resist the razor-sharp edge. He set to work removing the dead buds from each plant.

It was a waste of time, he knew. No one in this dark place had time to stop and smell the roses. He did it anyway. If these roses truly behaved the same as those in his garden, removing the dead buds would redirect the plants energies to growing fresh flowers. Plus, it was tidier.

There were plenty of dead heads to choose from, and so the task kept Zachary occupied for some time. As he worked, he caught the distant chattering of voices from the direction of camp. He figured he should probably head back soon. He needed to apologise to Logan for what he'd done, help to plan their next move.

Instead, he continued with his flowers, knife moving methodically from bud to bud, removing the waste, so each plant could grow anew. His mind drifted as he worked, returning to a time not so long ago when his knives had gathered dust in the bottom of his dresser, when he had enjoyed the warmth of Margery at his side, her laughter in the summer sun.

Zach's hands stilled on a rose. Just as with Logan and the stone, he'd told himself he was doing the right thing, leaving her, returning to the underworld. That was his only hope, after all. They'd already explored every other avenue. The physicians had all said the same thing—that he needed a miracle.

Why are you really leaving, Zachary?

Margery had whispered those words the night he'd left. Her chestnut brown eyes had watched him as she stood in their doorway. She had pleaded for him not to go, that they would get through this together.

Closing his eyes, Zachary let fall his tears, long held back. They had both known the truth as he'd walked away. That he wasn't really leaving in search of a cure. He had left because he couldn't stand to see the pain in her eyes any longer, because he couldn't stand the agony he caused her.

In the end, Zachary had left because he was a coward.

He had turned his back on his wife, thrown away their last few months of peace, and for what?

To return to a life of crime, of murder and betrayal?

Suddenly the knife was heavy in Zach's hand. He opened his eyes. Shadows clung to the blade, its deadly edge glinting from a sliver of light that pierced the overhanging branches. With this in his hands, he was a deadly man. Yet in this place, his skills had been found wanting. Not just with the blade. Everything he'd learnt in the underworld.

Logan might have been a naïve kid, but at least he'd approached this place with an open mind. Not with the distrusting lens through which Zach viewed the world. Despite his years with Margery, he remained stuck in the past. He'd thought that was what he would need here, to survive against the odds.

But where had it gotten him? What had his knives and distrust achieved?

He found his gaze drawn again to Daze. The copper eyes watched him still. Zach swallowed. There was a weight in those eyes, an expectation.

He looked at the knife in his hand and with a final exhalation, let it fall beside the rose bushes. Whatever happened next, he needed it no longer. That world, the darkness of his past, it would serve him no longer.

It was time he tried a different path.

The voices along the shore had grown in pitch now. Rising, Zach wandered back towards the others. He spotted Cordelia, returned from her scouting. No doubt she'd spent the night suffering her own misgivings. What was her place here, without a Tame to protect her?

The thought trailed off as he saw the stone glowing in her hand. His heart clenched. It couldn't be, could it? Where had she found another fossil? Yet as he neared, he saw the captain was not alone. The young woman Amilyse held one as well. Her gaze darted from Cordelia to Gozzo, indecision writ across her features.

"What have we here?" Zachary asked as he strode up to them, adopting a light-hearted tone despite the angry glares cast in his direction. He was momentarily surprised by the venom in Amilyse's glare, until he recalled their conversation in the forest. *Oops.*

Cordelia, however, wore a smile as she nodded a greeting. "Mr. Sicario, welcome back. We were just discussing how we might avoid any further confusion around the ownership of these crystals."

"Oh?" The others said nothing, though he didn't miss the glare from Logan. He would have to speak with the lad later. The girl too. For now, he looked to the old fisherman. "Is there a reason they can't just break the crystals now, like I did with Daze."

"It won't work," Logan spoke up. "I get a sense of it from Hope. This crystal form, their dormant state before we woke them, it's not...natural? They need something to help them. The connection is a part of it," he hesitated. "They need more than that though...desperation? Terror? Anger? I'm not sure, but it's more than just forming a bond with one of us and breaking a crystal."

Zachary scratched his chin as he considered the young man's words. The behaviour of the creatures intrigued Zach. Was there something special about their Tames, something that meant they'd slumbered on, while other creatures had woken to hunt the unwary humans. Why did the wild beasts hate humans so much, for that matter, while the fossil creatures chose instead to form a bond.

A tingling sensation raised the hairs on the back of Zach's neck. He was close to something, some missing piece to the puzzle of this place. On a whim, he tapped Daze's crystal to summon the Tame, then moved to the waterline. The others said nothing as he crouched, but a collective cry came from around the circle as he reached out to cup a mouthful of water in his hands.

The light was instant this time, the glow starting on the water's surface and spreading slowly until a section of water some three yards across was affected. The others backed away, wide eyed as they looked from the shimmering light to the trees, waiting for the barking.

Zachary ignored them and looked instead at Daze. He could sense the creature's sudden tension across their link. But it was not madness that inflicted the Tame, but a hunger. Its elongated eyes stared at the water, its entire body quivering.

Then the Brackis turned, its gaze meeting Zach's. Seeing the question in their copper depths, he nodded. Letting out a delighted bark, the Brackis leapt into the lake, sending glowing water splashing in all directions.

The others stared, while Zach only smiled. The Tame's colours had dimmed since the battle in the night, and while the gaping wound had closed over, there was still a fragility about the Tame. Now he could feel the energy pulsing once more across their bond as the Brackis's strength flowed back into him.

In seconds the waters were dark again. Not enough time to summon any nearby creatures, apparently, for no barking had followed. But as Daze stepped back onto the shore, all could see the sheen had been restored to its crystal fur. There was no sign of its wound now.

"What…" Logan murmured.

"They need our energy to survive," Zach explained, though he'd only just worked it out himself. "What was it the shade called it: the spark of life? My guess is there are three ways they can take it."

"The bond," the old fisherman offered, nodding slowly to himself.

"Our bodies," Amilyse's voice was strained, barely lifting above a whisper. "When they kill us."

Zachary nodded grimly.

"And the…water?" Logan asked, confusion still writ across his face.

"That lake isn't natural," Zachary mused when the others fell silent. "There's no way so much fresh water could have all accumulated in a few months."

"And?" Logan snapped, his irritation showing through.

"There must be something about it that amplifies our energy," Zachary explained. "It acts like a catalyst, reacting with that spark inside of us and creating something greater...a literal feast for our monster friends here."

Daze rumbled something that might have been agreement.

"What does this have to do with anything?" Logan asked.

The question surprised Zachary. "You were saying the fossils needed something from us to wake them. I think that's what this place has been all about—gathering our energy, using it to feed the creatures here..." he trailed off, eyes drifting to the mountain peak. "And maybe something more. Something important."

There was a silence after his words. Blinking, Zachary looked back at his companions. Cordelia's face was her usual reserved self, while Gozzo's eyes were on the mountain, a frown creasing his features. Of them all, only Logan met his eyes.

"No," the young man said softly, "that's not important, Zachary. What's important is that we all have a way to protect ourselves—so we don't have to rely on you. What's important is waking Amilyse's crystal." He didn't mention Cordelia. The captain obviously hadn't escaped Logan's bad books either, despite giving him back the fossil.

Zachary stared at Logan for a long while, surprised by the uncharacteristic outburst. But then, the danger of the night had pressed them all to their limits. The strain was written clearly on the young man's face.

"Oh," Zach replied, his voice unnaturally calm. "I see." Tucking his thumbs into the waistband of his trousers, he turned to the two women. "And you're sure that's what you want?"

Cordelia met his eyes and nodded. Amilyse hesitated a heartbeat longer. He could understand her doubts, after her and her brother's attitude towards the creatures on their first day. That was done now though, and finally she nodded as well.

"I take it you have a solution in mind, Sicario?" Cordelia questioned.

"I do," he replied with a grin, "and this time it will cost you nothing, Captain."

He turned to Daze. The merge was instant this time and he found himself through the Tame's eyes at the pair of women. They were still looking at his human body, rather than Daze. It was strangely disorientating, looking at himself standing there, eyes staring sightless, hands hanging limp at his side.

But he hadn't merged with Daze to examine himself. Turning, he stepped towards the women. Their eyes immediately swivelled in his direction. Zach stretched the Brackis's enormous jaws into a grin.

Cordelia and Amilyse took a joint step back.

Laughter rumbled from Zachary. It came out as a growl.

If these two needed a jolt to wake their Tames, well, it was Zach's duty to deliver.

Throwing back his head, he unleashed a howl, and leapt towards them.

And twin stars of light erupted on the shores of the great lake.

❧ 32 ❧

LOGAN

L ogan's heart was still racing as the light of the twin fossils faded. Hope had appeared at Daze's howl, leaping to place itself between Logan and the threat. But it had been yet another trick, a game by Zachary to manipulate events.

And now there were two more Tames. The creatures stood alongside their human partners, copper eyes blinking in the day's light. Cordelia's was scaled like an armadillo, though the overlapping plates had a duller look, more like stone than crystal. It stood on four short legs, its body hanging low to the ground, and Logan imagined its movements must be like those of a lizard, swaying side to side as it advanced. A thick tail swished across the stones, while its jaws were all serrated edges rather than teeth, though Logan had no doubt its bite would be no less dangerous for it.

"Well, that was easier than I expected," Gozzo observed. He limped forward and gestured at Cordelia's creature. "That's a Pango," he continued. "Tough buggers. Old Caspar's never managed to break that scale armour when we've encountered one in the wild."

"Damn, Captain," one of Cordelia's men spoke up. Logan thought it was the one called Duncan. "It's got your rocky personality and everything."

To Logan's surprise, the woman grinned at the joke. He was pretty sure that was the first time he'd ever seen her smile. Well, at least the first time one had reached her eyes. It faded as she looked from her creature to the fisherman's Caspar.

"Their eyes…" she murmured. "Every creature we've seen so far has copper eyes. All except yours and…" she trailed off, watching the old man expectantly.

Logan frowned. He hadn't noticed that before, but the captain was right.

"Ay," Gozzo nodded. "Old Caspar's were copper too once. All that energy last night, what you absorbed from the beasts you defeated, it builds over time. Eventually we pushed past some threshold, and his eyes changed to silver. Suddenly battling the monsters this side of lake weren't so hard."

"What about mine?" Amilyse spoke up. Her voice was tense, though Logan could not tell whether it was from excitement, or fear.

He swallowed as he looked at her Tame. It was the same sort they'd fought last night, the deerlike creature with the antlers and hooves.

"That's a Skelt," Gozzo supplied the answer. "Tough things as well, especially those antlers."

"Found that one out the hard way," Zachary muttered.

He'd returned to his own body now. Logan found his irritation returning as he looked at the man. Over the past few hours, he'd tried to put aside his anger at the man. But each time he thought the matter left behind, Zachary would speak again, and all the rage and feelings of betrayal would come rushing back.

"So, there are five of us," Cordelia mused, studying the old fisherman. "You said the land beyond the lake is dangerous, that there'll be more of the wild creatures." She paused, seeming intent to let those words sink in before continuing. "Will five be enough?"

"It'll have to be," Zachary replied for the captain, "unless you have any more fossils tucked away wherever you found these two?"

Cordelia shuffled on the spot, her eyes dipping slightly, but she said nothing. Before Logan could question where she *had* found her stone, he was distracted by a strange tingling sensation across his link with Hope. Turning to the Tame, he saw the Thoona and Amilyse's newly awakened Skelt had grown close. Muzzles extended, they sniffed at one another.

Logan found himself grinning as he looked at the former monster hunter. Lips parted slightly, Amilyse stood wide eyed and staring at the pair of Tames. She didn't appear to have heard anything they had been saying.

"Told you it felt weird," he laughed.

Her head jerked up, and red tinged her cheeks. "Sorry," she murmured, then visibly shook herself. A frown replaced her look of wonder. She set her eyes on Zachary. "Sorry," she repeated, though now her tone was touched by anger. "Why would we listen to a word you have to say, Zachary?"

Logan nodded. "I can't help but agree. In fact, I think its past time we parted ways."

"Amilyse, Logan—" Zachary started, but Amilyse cut him off.

"Oh, so now you know our names?" she snapped. Scarlet light washed across the beach as her Tame's colours shifted to match her mood. "What about Rob's name? You remember him? Or is he still just a 'fool' to you?"

The older man backpedalled a step at the woman's fury. "I'm sorry for what I said," he murmured, raising his hands in surrender. "For what I did. I never should have taken the stone. I don't expect either of you to understand—"

"No, Zachary, I understand perfectly," Logan cut in. "You think I'm naïve, that I'm not tough enough for this place. You already made that perfectly clear."

"I was wrong."

"You were," Logan agreed, "just as I was wrong to trust you. Either of you," he added, his eyes falling on Cordelia. "Why would we travel with either of you, after what you did. What's to stop you from stabbing us in the back the next time an opportunity arises to better yourselves?"

"Your brother," Cordelia said softly.

Logan started. "What does Dustin have to do with this?"

The woman gestured to her Tame. "That's where he came from, Mr. Kaine," she replied. "I cannot explain it, but last night I dreamed of your brother. He offered me the fossil, and asked that I protect you. When I woke, the stone was resting on my chest."

She fell silent, though her eyes did not leave Logan. He hardly noticed. Blood thundered in his ears, drowning out every other sound, all other thought.

Dustin was alive.

Relief swept through him like a spring flood and he struggled to keep the tears from falling. Twice his brother had come in his dreams since arriving on the island, but until now they'd been just that. Dreams. For all he'd known, they'd been the conjurations of a mind desperate to believe Dustin still lived.

Now, with a few words, Cordelia had confirmed his fragile hope. And Dustin had given her a Tame.

"I am truly sorry that we tricked you, Mr. Kaine," Cordelia said formally. "I'm afraid it's somewhat of an occupational hazard in our line of work."

Logan drew in a breath, struggling to force his mind back to the present.

"Okay," he said at last, "so Dustin visited you. Good," he exhaled, turning to Zachary. "What about *him*?"

Cordelia frowned. "What about him?"

His heart still pounding, Logan advanced a step towards Zachary. He sensed from the corner of his vision the change that came over his Tame, and knew Hope had taken on the scarlet of his rage. It pounded within his skull, surging along his bond with the Tame and reflecting back. It seemed to gather strength with each pulse of his heart, until at last he could contain it no longer.

The words burst from him in a rush. "Did my brother say anything about needing this good for nothing *thief?*"

The woman hesitated, looking from Logan to the dark-cloaked Zachary before bowing her head.

"No."

Logan met Zach's gaze. "Then this is where we part ways, Zachary Sicario."

Zach pursed his lips. "Don't be a fool, Logan. You need me. You saw how that Skelt manhandled Daze. How that hound almost destroyed your own Tame. Alone, we die. We're stronger together."

Logan shivered as a trickle of ice slid down his spine. Zachary's words conjured memories of the night he would rather forget. Angrily he forced them aside. It didn't matter that Zach had saved him last night. They would have never been in such peril had the man not betrayed him in the first place. One good deed did not erase the black mark.

"I'm sorry, Zach. I can't trust you."

"You're trusting Cordelia."

"I'm trusting Dustin," Logan snapped.

"Oh yes, your elusive brother." Anger flashed in Zachary's eyes now. He advanced until they stood eye to eye. Growling, Daze too took on the scarlet rage of his Tamer. "Where is he then? If he cares so much about you, why is he not here?" He spun on Cordelia. "I don't suppose your employer had an answer for that, did he?"

The woman pursed her lips, but said nothing.

"Dustin will have his reasons," Logan cut in.

Zachary threw back his head and laughed. "Oh I'm sure that he does, kid" he said, a sneer appearing on his lips. "Only, you've never stopped to ask yourself what they are. Do you really think his motives are any less selfish than my own?"

"Of course."

"Then why am I here, trying to protect your foolish skin, while he is nowhere to be found."

Zach's shouted words rang out across the lake, before fading to a hushed quiet, to a silence taut with expectation. The others said nothing, only watched as the pair faced off, waiting.

"I don't know, Zach," Logan rasped finally, his throat inexplicably parched. "But no one asked you to be here. So leave. Go chase whatever selfish reasons brought you to this place. You're not wanted here."

There was a long pause, before Zachary gave a curt nod. "Fine."

Without another word, he turned and walked toward the trees. Cordelia and her men parted to let him go, but not a word passed between them.

Logan watched the man crunch his way up the shore, a lump swelling in his throat. Doubt touched him, but he shook it off. This was the right decision. The man was a rogue and a thief and worse. Zach himself had warned them not to trust him. He was only taking the man's own advice.

Only at the treeline did Zachary pause. He hesitated in the shadow of the trees before glancing back. Their eyes met across the distance, and Logan saw the pain in the man's face.

"I'm dying, kid," the words carried down the shore. "That's why I came, the reason I'm here. So that one day I can go back and hold my wife close." He paused, allowing the words to hang in the air, before giving a final nod. "Good luck, kid. Be sure to keep one eye over your shoulder, with that lot."

Then he turned and disappeared into the trees.

33

LOGAN

The company lingered after Zach's departure, some wandering off to rest their eyes, while Cordelia's sailors set about breaking down the camp. Gozzo's supplies were already dwindling under the demand of the larger group, but they would be enough for a few days yet, having been scavenged from his fishing ship. Logan had no desire to try eating anything of crystal origin—whether it be one of the crystal plants, or the any number of tiny creatures he'd caught glimpses of in the shadows.

Though if they were stuck here long enough, Logan supposed they'd eventually be forced to cross that bridge.

They struck out east along the lake as the sun approached noon. A later start than the past few days, but the sleepless nights had finally caught up with them. Zachary's last words played on Logan as they walked.

I'm dying, kid.

Another attempt at manipulation? The man had *seemed* sincere...and Zachary *had* seemed ill their first day on the island. Logan had assumed the man's coughing fits were from the long ocean swim after the shipwreck. But perhaps there was another explanation...

He shook his head angrily. Even if that were the truth, it didn't change Zachary's actions. The betrayal of his trust could not be so easily forgotten. Could it?

He also saved your life. Twice.

His mind continued to rerun their final confrontation as they continued along the lake. To their right, the trees remained dense, the forest unbroken, but on their left the opposite shore grew slowly closer. The lake had an elongated shape, making it longer than it was wide. It was several hours before they found themselves drawing near to the lake's far end.

But as the stark slopes neared, Logan found himself no closer to a resolution around Zachary's betrayal. Should he have forgiven the man or not? Not that it mattered now. Zachary was gone.

"You look worried," Amilyse said, interrupting his thoughts.

Logan attempted a smile, though he feared it did not reach his eyes. Amilyse's Tame was in its physical form, and he felt a probing from Hope, before the Thoona appeared at his side. Joining the Skelt, the Tames continued along the shore ahead of the pair.

"Have you named it yet?" he asked, making a clumsy attempt to change the conversation.

Amilyse smiled. "Delilah," she replied. "After an old tabby we used to have at our estate."

The Tame looked around at that and gave a soft snort.

Logan chuckled. "A fitting name for a terrible monster."

"You were right," Amilyse said after a while. "They're not monsters at all. Delilah…it's like she was always a part of me, only…"

"Older?" Logan nodded. "It's strange, isn't it?"

"It is," Amilyse mused, then: "so, what is preying on your mind, Logan?"

He chuckled. "Where do I start? This place? The Tames? The monsters? My missing brother?

"Probably with Zachary."

"Yes, probably with Zachary," Logan agreed with a sigh. "I've been trying to figure out why just the thought of him makes me clench my fists with rage…and yet, I already seem to have forgiven the captain."

Amilyse pursed her lips. They continued in peace for a time. The shore had changed as they walked, the gravel giving way to harder stone beneath their feet. Waves lapped gently at the shore, and somewhere in the depths of the nearby forest he heard insects buzzing. Logan wondered if they were creatures of the island, or if other creatures from the outside world had discovered this place.

"It's a matter of trust, really," Amilyse said at last.

"What do you mean?"

"You could forgive Cordelia because you didn't trust her in the first place. Zach..." The corners of her lips crinkled as she frowned. "Whatever his pretty words, he did all he could to gain our trust—then set it alight at the first opportunity he had for gain. That's what hurts, why it cuts deeper."

Her words were an arrow sent straight to the heart of Logan's rage.

"And yet he still expected us to forgive him," he practically spat the words.

"Of course he did," Amilyse replied matter-of-factly. "He thinks we're children, easily manipulated. Do you really believe a man like Zachary Sicario has a woman waiting for him? He understands nothing of love."

Logan cast a long look in her direction, hearing the tension in her voice. Amilyse kept a careful mask over her grief. It was easy to forget what she must be suffering, with Rob's death still so recent.

Before he could inquire further, however, Logan noticed a rumbling in the distance. The others continued on, unaware, but he came to a stop, trying to discern the source. Amilyse stopped with him, a frown creasing her features before she too heard the sound. They shared a look. It was coming from the direction they were heading, but ahead the shore curved away from them and the trees cut off their line of sight.

They chased after the others, intent on warning them, but they need not have bothered. As they rounded the bend, the source of the noise was revealed.

The lake had narrowed so much now that the far shore was no more than a hundred yards away. Unfortunately, those hundred yards were no longer the still waters of a lake. Unnoticed, they had turned to a river. The waters raced past where they stood and rushed out over the great cliffs of the coast.

Though they stood several yards from the water's edge, Logan found himself taking a step back. A cloud of mist swirled up from the nearby cliffs and swept towards them on gusts of wind. Thankfully, it was not the haunting stuff of the night, but rather a natural mist that dissipated as it met the warm air of the island.

For a moment, no one said anything. They stood together at the edge of the river, entranced by the sight of all that rushing water. Logan wondered how it must look from the bottom. The sheer enormity of the waterfall was surely greater than anything that existed back in Riogachd.

"Why did you bring us this way?" he asked finally, turning to Gozzo.

"Why?" The old fisherman frowned. "To cross, matey."

"Cross that?" Logan gaped. "Are you insane? No man could swim against that current."

"Swim?" Gozzo seemed genuinely confused. He again gestured to the waters. "Why would you swim, when there are steppingstones."

"Steppingstones…" Logan trailed off as he finally saw what he'd missed.

A line of boulders, spaced maybe a yard apart, lead across the river. Slick from the mist and the water lapping at their sides, they were a death trap if ever Logan had seen one. Which, admittedly, he hadn't.

"You can't be serious?" It was one of Cordelia's men who spoke this time.

"What? It's simple."

Before anyone could stop him, the old man hobbled to the edge of the river. Then showing far more agility than he had in the past two days, Gozzo leapt to the first of the stones. Twisting in the air, he landed easily, the crystal Tame alighting beside him. He paused only long enough to turn and wave at them before continuing on his way.

"This is insane," another of Cordelia's sailors whispered.

The woman nodded her agreement. "Turning around is becoming an increasingly attractive proposition."

His heart pounding in his ears, Logan hardly heard the captain's words. He shared a glance with Amilyse. The woman's face was pale, her eyes fixed to the waters. As though sensing his attention, she blinked and glanced at him.

"What do you think?" he asked.

"I think this is mad," she whispered, then forced a smile. "Rob would have loved it."

With that, she drew in a breath, then stepped up to the edge. Logan raised a hand, but she was already gone, leaping from the shore to land on the first boulder. Her teeth flashed as she looked back and grinned, then she was continuing after the old fisherman, fading into the swirling mist.

"Bloody insane," Cordelia muttered. "Come on then, lads. Can't let the bloody gentry show us up."

The men grumbled their discontent, but they followed their captain. Logan watched them cross, wondering at their loyalty to the woman—if that was indeed their motivation. They didn't exactly have much choice, surrounded by beasts that would tear them apart. There was no freedom on this island without a Tame at your side.

But no, these sailors had followed Cordelia, even before she'd awakened her own stone. It said something about the woman. Perhaps that was what Dustin saw.

"Come on, Logan!" Amilyse's voice carried across the racing waters. It was barely audible through the roaring of the waterfall.

Logan's skin crawled as he imagined slipping and falling into the currents, being carried over the side.

Don't be a fool, Logan. You need me.

He clenched his teeth as Zach's words rang in his ears.

Gathering himself, he stepped up to the edge.

And leapt out into the void.

❧ 34 ❧

ZACHARY

Zachary was finally alone. Wasn't that what he'd wanted all this time? The freedom to search out whatever magic powered this fantastical place, unburdened by the children of gentry and insane monster hunters?

So why did he feel such an emptiness in his heart?

He toyed idly with his pipe, turning it carefully between his fingers. It was useless here, unless he could find some local, crystal equivalent to tobacco to burn. But he hadn't craved the leaf in days. Not since forging his connection with Daze. He still reached for it at times when stressed, but the need for the pungent smoke was gone. Strange, that.

He sat before the roaring waterfall, watching the impossible quantities of water rushing out over the edge. At its current rate, the lake should have been empty long ago. It hadn't even rained here in the few days they'd been on the island. Where was all the water coming from?

His gaze drifted towards the mountain. The pitted hollows and sharp escarpments were closer now, waiting to swallow up the unsuspecting traveller. Logan and the others had already disappeared into one such gully an hour past. Already the day was growing late, noon creeping slowly towards dusk. Zachary would need to make a move shortly if he wanted to cross under the light of day.

It's because you liked him.

That's why it hurt. However foolish, however naively he clung to the belief in his brother, Logan was a survivor after Zachary's own heart. They might approach the world from different perspectives, but the kid acted quickly under pressure—albeit not always with much foresight—and inevitably came out the better for it.

He had the makings of a master thief.

Or perhaps something more. The thoughts chased themselves around Zach's mind. *Something greater than you ever achieved.*

Twirling the pipe one last time between his fingers, Zachary tucked it into the pocket of his overcoat. It might no longer be needed, but the worn steel reminded him of fonder times, sitting in his garden with Margery in his lap.

He drew in a sharp breath at that memory, and a needling of pain emanated from his chest. If he'd had the choice to do it all again, he would have stayed, would have denied the lure of his former life and remained at their cottage in the countryside. Even if that had meant death.

He couldn't turn back the clock. That was something he'd learnt a long time ago. A man must live with his decisions.

But he could make better ones in the future.

From here on out, Zachary Sicario would be master thief no longer.

He would try to be better.

Even if he had to do it alone.

A rumble came from his side, reminding Zachary of the Tame crouched at his feet. A smile touched his cheeks.

"Okay, not quite alone."

He turned his attention to the steppingstones. Just a few days before, he would have struggled with the crossing. But energy flowed freely now from Daze, granting him the strength and dexterity he had enjoyed in his youth, and he managed it without difficulty.

Now the barren slopes beckoned, the light waiting somewhere beyond the mountain cliffs. The broken stone offered a dozen openings to choose from, some broad and welcoming, others barely more than fissures, the deep shadows promising danger. He'd watched from the other side as Logan and the others had taken a broader path, no doubt following Gozzo's directions. The old fisherman must know the island by heart by now.

But Zachary must choose a new path now. He selected another canyon at random—one of the smaller fissures, it turned out—and set off at a brisk pace. He was eager to make up some lost time before the sun set over the slopes.

Stone walls rose around him. Though of course they were not truly stone, but a sort of dark red crystal. He wondered if there were iron deposits around the mountain. That often led to a red colouration in minerals—at least back in the real world. No doubt he was putting too much thought into the strangeness of this place.

Though the canyon was dark, Daze gave off enough light to banish the worst of the shadows. He kept an eye on the scarlet walls, seeking signs of other fossils. A second Tame would help to even the odds should the creatures come at him in numbers again. Unfortunately, he saw no hint of imperfections like the one he'd spotted back on the beach.

Several hours passed as he journeyed through the shadows. The canyon branched at regular intervals, and several times Zachary was met with dead ends and forced to retrace his steps. Thankfully, no beasts appeared to harass him. He was mindful of the fisherman's warning about the creatures appearing during daylight on this side of the lake.

"He also said they'd be bigger," Zach said, feeling the need to talk. He glanced at his Tame. "Think you can take them?"

A rumble came from deep in Daze's throat and Zachary chuckled.

"Hope you're right. Don't think we'll have anyone coming to our rescue next time. Unless you've got any tricks left up your sleeve? Maybe we can figure out how to put our enemies to sleep like that wild Thoona did with us…"

The words trailed away. He frowned. Something tugged at his memory, a wrongness about…something, but he could not place it.

"Those illusions of Caspar's would be useful. Think you could manage something like that?"

But no, the old fisherman hadn't mentioned either of those when speaking about a Brackis. What Zachary *had* figured out was that the creature had some form of venom hidden in its twin stingers. That was something he would have to experiment more with, though of course the only chance for practice came in the heat of battle, when his foe was intent on tearing out his throat. Not exactly the best time for getting creative.

Not that this island would give them any choice in the matter.

Zachary froze as a roar echoed through the canyon. Light burst from Daze, its colouration shifting to black and grey. A rumble came from deep in the Brackis's throat and its stingers lifted, poised to strike.

But after last night, Zachary wasn't about to go charging into another confrontation. He was about to order the Tame back, when another noise carried down the narrow gorge. He froze. That had been a woman's voice. Had he somehow looped back onto the trail of Logan and the others?

The sounds of battle from ahead grew in pitch. Zach swore. Whoever it was, he knew he had to act.

Another scream followed. Man and Tame broke into a run. What was happening? He couldn't tell if the owner of the scream belonged to Amilyse or Cordelia. Had one been caught off-guard by a beast? If so, where were the others?

Light flashed from around the next bend in the valley. Zach raced on, glad for the fresh energies that fuelled his weary limbs. After barrelling around the corner, the pair skidded to a stop.

Ahead, two creatures did battle. Zachary's blood ran cold as he recognised the shining antlers of a Skelt. He forced aside the memories of the night. No time for that now.

The second creature was the boar-like beast he'd seen with Willow back in the forest. The woman herself crouched nearby on one knee, her face pale, breath coming in ragged gasps. As he watched, she swayed, though her eyes kept the glassy look that meant she was merged with her Tame.

Zachary came to a stop beside her, turning his eyes to the true battle. Willow's Tame—Zahra, she'd called it—was losing this battle. This Skelt was proving just as vicious as the one they'd encountered the night before. It charged at Zahra, antlers lowered. The boar tried to avoid the blow, but a final burst of speed caught it off-guard.

Twin screams came from the Tame and Willow both as the deadly antler pierced the boar. It tried to strike back, the silver tusks swinging a wild blow at the Skelt, but already it was skittering away, the long legs carrying it clear.

Zahra staggered after the creature's retreat. It only managed two steps before its squat legs gave way. A sob whispered from Willow's lips as the Tame crumpled. Before Zachary could catch her, she pitched forward to the ground.

Zachary cursed. There was no time to hesitate.

A roar echoed from the canyon walls as he merged with Daze and leapt at the Skelt. They had faced these stag creatures once already. Hopefully that would give them an edge.

The Skelt froze at Daze's roar, its scarlet rage bleeding to a deep blue. It was all the opening they needed. Leaping forward with a burst of speed, they didn't bother with tooth or claw this time. They struck instead with their twin stingers. An emerald glow gathered about their razor tips as they lashed out, catching the Skelt just as it turned on them.

Antler clashed with stingers, but Zachary felt a satisfying thud *as the blow connected. The green glow swelled, and as they retreated, he saw twin spots of emerald where the stingers had found their mark in the Skelt's neck and chest.*

He felt a rush of exhilaration at their success, but the battle was not done yet.

The bloodred colouration returned to the Skelt as it lowered its antlers. Though they stood a dozen yards away, they barely saw the next attack coming. One minute the stag stood tall, antlers glowing with a golden light. The next, it was slamming into Daze. Only a quick twist of the Brackis's nimble body saved them from being impaled a second time on the golden antlers.

As it was, the thud *of the Skelt's body as it impacted with their own was enough to hurl Daze from its feet. A scream tore from Zach, and he sensed he'd cried out back in his own body too. But they did not stay down long.*

Clawing at the hard ground, they stood. As they did so, he saw that tiny threads of green now webbed the crystal flesh of the Skelt. Turning back to take another run at them, it staggered slightly before righting itself. He hoped that meant the poison was already doing its job, though he knew Willow had likely already done some damage too.

The Skelt charged them again. This time it lacked its earlier speed and they hurled themselves aside. The beast slammed into the stone cliffs where they'd stood, sending cracks racing through the red crystal. Taking advantage of its disruption, they charged in and struck again, adding two more stings to its torso.

It swung at them as they retreated, but this time Daze was able to avoid the attack with ease. He felt a thrill from his Tame, and before he could caution against it, they were leaping forward again. This time they used not the stingers, but went for its throat with the great jaws of the Brackis.

But the Skelt wasn't defeated quite yet. With a shrill cry, it lifted onto its hind legs, then brought its hooves down against the rocky ground. Stone shattered as though struck by a hammer, sending slivers of crystal out in every direction. Zach cursed as a hundred tiny pins sliced into Daze's flesh. It staggered the Brackis. A growl came from the Skelt as it readied another attack.

Come on, bud.

Using a part of him that remained attached to his own body, he gathered his own strength and sent it rushing across the bond into his Tame.

Whether it was the energy or the encouragement, Daze responded. This time he didn't bother with a physical attack. That had been hubris— and completely unnecessary.

The effects of the four stings were clearly visible in the emerald veins that now threaded the Skelt's crystal flesh. It staggered towards them, golden light flickering in its sharpened antlers. But even if it could land another attack, Zachary realised it would not last much longer. So rather than attack, they waited for it to come, then sprang quickly from its path, avoiding a second blow.

A few minutes more of evading the Skelt's attacks, and it finally collapsed. As it struck the ground, the crystal body shattered as though it had only ever been glass. The fragments of the beast dissolved as they tumbled across the ground, and the familiar energy drifted up from the remains before streaming into Daze.

By then, Zachary was already back in his body. He swung around, seeking out Willow and her Tame. The boar-like creature had already returned to its stone form. It hung suspended over the woman's unmoving body, pulsing with a soft light. Breath left him in a long sigh as he saw her chest rise and fall.

She was alive.

35

LOGAN

L ogan found himself panting as he snapped back to his body. The world spun and he quickly squeezed his eyes closed. It took several heartbeats for his pulse to return to normal. Weariness settled on his shoulders. Opening his eyes, he looked around at his companions.

Would it always be like this after an encounter? The unfamiliar exhilaration of the battle, the sudden exhaustion afterwards, the stars dancing in his vision.

Still, he was alive. They all were. That hadn't been a certainty just a few short days before.

A man moved alongside him. The former woodsman, Peck, one of Cordelia's men. Logan recognised him by his missing left eye. He nodded his thanks as the man handed him a flask of water and a stick of jerky.

Over the past few hours, they had each settled into their new roles. The sailors had taken it upon themselves to carry their supplies. This left Logan, Cordelia, Amilyse and

Gozzo to do the heavy work protecting the company with their Tames. The sailors also managed the scouting and watch, though usually one of the Tamers would accompany them in case of attack.

This had been the third beast they'd encountered since crossing the river. Despite the division of labour, Logan could feel the exhaustion creeping upon him. This one had been a Brackis, like Zachary's Tame. Caspar had been poisoned early in the battle and forced to retreat, while Amilyse still seemed to be growing into her role.

That had left Logan and Cordelia to finish the creature. Thankfully, the beast had finally succumbed beneath the weight of their twin attacks. Neither he nor Cordelia had figured out any of their Tame's special abilities yet, and while Gozzo claimed they would come, Logan was beginning to grow anxious. The wild creatures were growing noticeably stronger now, using special moves like the poison stingers to counter the Tamers' greater numbers. They needed to do the same if they were to keep pace.

The day was growing truly late now. Logan was practically out on his feet. There wasn't much argument when Cordelia suggested to set up camp. They had finally emerged from the twisting canyons, out onto the open mountainside, and there was little desire amongst them to press on through the night.

Their one issue would be water. They had brought as much as they could carry in their flasks and waterskin—both for themselves, and as a way to heal their Tames. But between the humans and Tames their supplies were already growing short and they had found no streams since leaving behind the lake.

AARON HODGES

At least now they were in the open, they could spot wild creatures approaching from a ways off. The last Brackis had attempted to ambush them from a cave that had gone unnoticed. If Cordelia's second in command hadn't spotted it at the last moment…

Logan shoved the thought aside. There was enough to worry about without what ifs. At least he'd had Cordelia's Tame fighting alongside him this time. She'd named the rocky lizard 'Morgawr,' after a sea creature of legend from her hometown in the south.

As the sailors prepared a fire from the crystalised kindling they'd brought from the forest, Logan's mind turned again to his former companion. He supposed Zachary had been forced to turn back. The man was not a fool and would know he could not continue beyond the lake alone. He would have to wait by the coast and hope they were successful in bringing down the island's defences.

That seemed a forlorn hope. Even if they reached the light, there was no guaranteeing it was the source of the island's mysterious climate or the barriers protecting its shores. They were following a hunch, little more than that…

…and Dustin.

Cordelia had told him the full story after much urging. Apparently, Dustin was seeking the light as well, if the woman's dreams were to be believed.

What are you doing out here, Dustin?

What could be so important that his brother would leave him behind? Dustin had known something of this place, even before their shipwreck. That much, Logan knew. His

316

brother had not told him the whole truth back on *The Rising Tide*. There were gaps in his story, about how he'd found the stone, why he'd organised this expedition in the first place. But nothing pointed to an explanation as to why Dustin would be willing to risk his life on this barren mountainside.

I'm dying.

Logan shivered. Zach's last words had been chasing themselves around his head all day. What had a dying man expected to find in a place like this? Across the camp, Cordelia was directing her sailors in the tying together of sail and canvas to form tiny lean-tos against the boulders that littered the slope.

The woman had known the thief the best. Logan pushed himself to his feet and then strode across to the woman. She turned at his approach, eyebrows lifting when she saw him.

"Mr. Kaine," she greeted him. "What can I do for you?"

"Why did he do it?" That wasn't what he'd planned to ask her, but the words came out before he could stop himself.

The woman frowned at him.

"You know what I'm talking about."

Cordelia sighed. "He told me about his illness, back on the plateau," she explained. "I wondered. When we set sail, he promised to give me anything of value that we found here, so long as he was free to go about his business." She chuckled. "Seven hells, that seems a hundred years ago now, doesn't it?"

Logan didn't immediately respond. He was still considering her words. "You think he was searching for a cure?"

"I didn't ask."

Grating his teeth, Logan changed directions. "Why did he betray me?"

"Your stone was the price for my support."

Finding himself clenching his fists, Logan struggled to relax. Hearing the words out loud stung.

Zach had made him look a fool.

"So he did it for himself."

Cordelia shrugged. "Depends how you look at it I suppose. Look, Mr. Kaine, I know you're seeking a simple explanation. But this world, it isn't black and white. You might as well ask why *I* insisted on taking the stone. Was it greed?" She shrugged. "Maybe. I desired its power. But I also knew you were not a fighter. How could I put my life and the lives of my men in the hands of an inexperienced boy?"

"You might have just asked."

"People don't just *ask* for things in my line of work."

"So I've discovered."

The conversation petered out there. Logan wandered away from the others, seeking solace in the stillness of dusk. In the open now, they'd been rewarded with a view across the southern side of the island. The lake spread out beneath him, the dark green of the forest lining its shore. Beyond, the swaying grasses of the plateau shone with the red light of sunset, stretching out towards the jagged line of the coast.

There, the ever-present clouds still hemmed them in. He wondered if the naval ships still haunted the waters beyond. He hoped so. If they'd returned to Riogachd, there would be no one to spy their signal.

But that was a worry for another day.

"It's actually kind of beautiful, isn't it?"

Logan looked up as Amilyse approached. Like himself until just now, her eyes were on the view.

"It's not bad, for an island of monsters," he replied with a grin.

A smile tugged at the woman's lips. She seated herself on an outcrop of rock and they both looked out towards the horizon. The light was fading now, the rainbow aurora slowly rising from the waters of the lake.

A tingling spread down his spine as he watched the view. It took him a while to realise it was not his own. Hope had emerged from its crystal state and now lay at Logan's feet. Amilyse's Tame had joined his own. The two lay alongside each other, their fur coats pulsing a rosy hue.

He shivered, sensing the closeness of the other Tame through Hope. It felt like a warm blanket had been wrapped around his shoulders. He shared a look with Amilyse.

"Weird," they said together, before bursting out laughing. This was not the short, bitter laughter he caught sometimes from her, but heartfelt, rich in joy.

"You know, I don't think I've ever heard you laugh like that."

The smile faded from her lips. Logan instantly regretted his words.

"Sorry—"

She placed a hand on his shoulder. "It's okay," she said. "It's just been…difficult, without Rob. I know he might have been a little…rash, but, well, I miss him."

Her voice cracked on the last words. Silence hung between them, before Logan hesitantly reached out to place his arm around her waist. At his touch, the woman seemed to shatter. She slumped into his arms and buried her face in his chest.

Logan held her awkwardly as she sobbed. At their feet, the pair of Tames watched them, their copper eyes curious. Logan said nothing. What *could* he say? His family didn't talk about grief or loss. After their mother had died, their father had basically left the remainder of his and Dustin's upbringing to their teachers.

Amilyse's entire frame shook. Logan looked around, hoping Cordelia or even Gozzo could help to comfort her, but they'd walked further than he'd thought from the camp and no one heard her soft crying. Unsure what else to do, Logan gently rubbed her back, the way his mother had whenever he'd been ill as a child.

Slowly Amilyse's trembling subsided. When she finally lifted her head again, her eyes were red and her cheeks—and his coat—were damp.

"Sorry," she murmured, giving a little shake of her head, as though to dismiss her grief as foolish. "My family would be ashamed."

"No," Logan spoke up, "you lost someone. I cannot even imagine what that must be like."

Amilyse rubbed her eyes. "Gods, I'm tired of hurting. Of being afraid. This place…maybe it's not the source of all evil. But there's something about it. Something that gnaws at my soul, even with Delilah. I'm afraid I'm not strong enough. Not without Rob."

Logan said nothing for a while, allowing himself to consider her words. He recalled what Zachary had said to them in the forest about the nature of fear.

"I'm glad you're afraid," he said tentatively. "Zachary might have been wrong about many things, but he was right about that. Only a madman would not fear this place."

Amilyse snorted, before eyeing him as though she'd just realised he was serious. "You don't seem afraid."

"I grew up in a manor eating off silver platters." Logan arced an eyebrow. "You think I haven't been terrified ninety five percent of the time?"

Amilyse pursed her lips. "You hide it well."

"Maybe that's the real trick to it," Logan said, offering a wry smile. "All the heroes are just good at hiding how bloody terrified they are."

A smile touched the young woman's face. He gave her fingers a squeeze. They were warm against his palm, and he found himself studying her features, the way her golden hair fluttered in the evening breeze, the glint of the setting sun in her eyes. Suddenly there was a lump in his throat.

"I don't know what this place is either," he said at last. "But we know it's dangerous. So fear is good. It keeps us alert, so we don't just…walk into the maw of a beast. But we can't let it rule us. We have to push on, however much it terrifies us. There's something up there, something that will free us from this place. I know it."

"Because of Dustin?"

Logan hesitated. "I don't know what Dustin is looking for." He found himself looking at where their Tames still lay side by side. "But I sensed something from Hope—"

He broke off as Amilyse suddenly leaned in and pressed her lips against his. Suddenly his heart was racing. For only a second he went rigid as a tingling spread across his scalp. Instinctively, he knew their Tames had embraced as well.

Then a fiery warmth swept through Logan and he was kissing Amilyse back. A moan whispered from her throat as her lips parted and their tongues danced together to an unheard music. The taste of Amilyse was like the joy of a warm spring day, the excitement like a babbling brook high in the mountains. His heart beat so hard against his chest, Logan felt it might explode. And yet he only held her tighter, kissed her deeper. For one sweet moment, all thoughts of Tames and fears and tomorrow were washed away.

Who knew how long they might have sat there in one another's embrace. But the island had other plans.

They broke apart as shouts erupted in the night. The pair were on their feet in an instant. Crystals burst to life on the hillside. Cordelia and Gozzo's Tames. Logan shared a look with Amilyse—then they were racing across the hard stone, eyes straining to pierce the darkness that had swallowed the hillside.

A shadow loomed beyond the campfire. Snarling, Hope darted past the others, Delilah just a step behind. The sailors parted for the humans and their Tames. As they stumbled to a stop, Logan was already reaching out with his mind for Hope.

The world spun, and Logan blinked, adjusting to Hope's four eyed perspective. The Tame's senses had no problems with the darkness. Stones crunched and a shadow loomed, taller than any of their Tames. Scales glinted in the firelight and great clawed wings stretched out from an elongated body. A narrow head stretched towards them, fangs glinting in the moonlight.

Logan swallowed. This was unlike any of the other creature's they'd faced. Worst of all, its eyes shone not the weaker copper of their Tames, but the deep, pale silver of Gozzo's Caspar.

It was also a godsdamned dragon.

But no sooner had Logan taken in their foe, did Hope's sharp eyes glimpse something on the creature's back...

Logan gasped as he found himself back in his body. There was a moment of disorientation, as he struggled to adjust to having only two legs and eyes. Then, heart pounding, he took a step towards the creature. Several of the sailors cried out at the movement, but the others were already with their Tames and did not notice. No one tried to stop him.

Swallowing his fear, Logan approached the dragon-like creature. As he neared it, he saw that he'd been right— someone was slumped over the Tame's back. The last of his fear turned to panic and he darted forward, even as the others offered belated cries of warning.

Logan reached the dragon just as the figure on its back lost their grip on the crystal scales. A moan came from the man as he toppled sideways—and Logan reached out to catch him. Heart in his throat, he carefully lowered the man to the ground.

The man grimaced as his head hit the stones. "Careful, brother," he groaned, eyes fluttering open to look up at Logan. "I've taken enough of a beating for one night."

36

LOGAN

"Here, matey, give him this."

A waterskin appeared before Logan. He accepted it gladly from Gozzo's weathered hands. Dustin lay at his feet, his pale face illuminated by the light of a floating stone. The dragon Tame had returned to its crystal form after Dustin had slid from its back. Even so, its light was still far brighter than the others. The stone itself was a ruby. Its light was not harsh like the enemy beasts, but a soft, gentle pulse.

Lifting his brother's head, Logan allowed a little water to trickle into Dustin's mouth. The man was mumbling something beneath his breath, his eyes fluttering as though he were caught in the grips of some nightmare, but he stilled when the water touched his lips. He relaxed then, a sigh whispering from his throat.

Replacing the cap of the waterskin, Logan nodded his thanks and returned it to Gozzo. The old man crouched alongside him, concerned eyes on Dustin's incapacitated form.

"Don't know what he met up here, but it sure knocked the pair of them around."

The sailor Duncan approached. "Do you need any help with him?"

Logan nodded. With the man's help, they managed to lift Dustin and carry him back to the fire. The ruby crystal followed. Logan's eyes were drawn to its scarlet glow. Where had Dustin found another fossil? Or two, for that matter, if he'd truly given Cordelia her Tame as well. And how had his Tame grown so powerful as to reach silver in just a few days?

Dustin woke again as they set him beside the fire. His eyes darted around his face, as though seeking danger, before finally settling on Logan. A smile appeared on his lips.

"Brother!" He said with a groan. His face tightened as he struggled to push himself up. Logan tried to stop him, but Dustin would not be denied. "About time you caught up!"

"Caught up?" Logan could hardly believe the words coming from his brother. "Dustin, I've been searching for you for days!" His relief boiled away in the face of a sudden anger. "What the hell do you mean, *caught up!*"

"Easy, brother, easy," Dustin murmured. He raised a hand and rubbed his forehead, as though still in pain. "I jest. I have been seeking you as well, ever since I woke on the beach."

Logan was already halfway to his feet, but his brother's words gave him pause. Swallowing, he looked at his brother.

Really looked. Dustin's face was grey and there were dark rings beneath his eyes, as though he hadn't slept in days. Exhaling slowly, Logan sank back to the rock he'd been sitting on.

"What happened?"

"In the water, I heard you shout, but it was too dark to find you," Dustin said softly, his words drawing Logan back to that night in the ocean. "I woke alone on a sandy shore. Well, there were no other humans anyway. The sun had yet to rise, but there were lights. They danced around me and I heard laugher, music. When I touched one, the others all fled—and Eiliah appeared."

"Your Tame?" Logan asked. When his brother frowned, he had to quickly explain how they'd come up with the name for the creatures.

Dustin chuckled. "Not a very creative name."

"Zachary wasn't a very creative man." He paused, swallowing his anger. Zachary was the last of his worries just now. He looked at Gozzo. The old fisherman was still on his feet, watching Dustin's ruby.

"Do you have a name for that...dragon sort of Tame?"

"Afraid not..." Gozzo murmured, then shook himself. "I've not seen its sort before."

"Nor I," Dustin replied, then frowned. "I don't believe I know you, sir."

"Didn't arrive on your ship, matey," Gozzo replied. "Been trapped here a while longer than the rest of y'all."

Dustin nodded. His eyes flickered and for a moment it seemed they would close again. It seemed to cost him significant effort to force them to the others who stood nearby instead.

"Captain," Dustin greeted as his gaze settled on Cordelia.

"Mr. Kaine," she replied with a nod. "When you are done with your brother, I believe we have a few financial matters to discuss."

"You will have your fortune, Captain," Dustin said with a grin. "I swear it."

The woman raised an eyebrow, but she said no more on the matter. Logan felt a fluttering in his chest as Amilyse stepped alongside him. They shared a smile and he saw the light in her eyes, a quiet joy that he at least had found his brother alive.

"What happened afterwards?" he asked then. "You woke on sand? We came ashore on gravel."

Dustin nodded. "I saw."

"How is that possible?" Logan asked. "How is *any* of this possible?"

"I do not know, brother," Dustin replied with a grin that spoke of how fantastic he thought that. "But since forming my bond with Eiliah, I have found myself able to reach into the dreams of others. Though it was only recently that I gained enough control for more than a few words."

Logan swallowed. The explanation made no sense—by the natural laws of their kingdom at least. But they were not in

Riogachd anymore. Sometimes he felt they were no longer on the same world.

"It wasn't long before I learnt the true nature of this island," Dustin continued. "The shade appeared to warn me about the beasts, but they were already upon me. If not for Eiliah, I would have perished on that beach."

"After that, we moved inland, but were bogged down in a marsh." Dustin chuckled. "I never knew mosquitos could be so bad until I had to fend off ones formed of crystal. There were several larger beasts too, though not so strong as those on the beach. Or perhaps it is only Eiliah growing stronger. I could sense that, after each victory. So I began to seek out other creatures, seeking to become powerful enough to protect myself against anything that came against me."

"So that's what you've been doing all this time?" Logan asked, his anger breaking through again. "Playing monster hunter?"

Dustin said nothing for several heartbeats, though his eyes did not leave Logan's face. "I could sense you still lived, brother," he said at last. "But I could not find where you were. Not even in my dreams."

Silence hung between them. Logan met his brother's eyes. "Why are we here, Dustin?" he breathed, before his voice rose in tone. "Where in the seven *hells* have you brought us?"

Dustin's eyes flickered in Cordelia's direction. "So you told him."

The woman, who'd been carefully averting her eyes, cleared her throat, then nodded.

"That is disappointing."

"Disappointing?" Logan ground out the word between clenched teeth. He was truly angry now. Rob's face drifted before his eyes. "People are *dead*, Dustin, dead because of this mad voyage of yours."

"Last I checked, they *chose* to come on this journey," Dustin replied, one eyebrow raised. "None were forced—in fact, many more would have paid handsomely for the opportunity to explore the Anomaly."

"They didn't even know what this place was!"

"And you think that I do, brother?"

"You must!" Logan cried. "You had the fossil, didn't you? You arranged everything. You must have known *something*."

"Educated guesses, Logan," Dustin said. "At least, until the shade came to me again."

"What are you talking about?"

An easy smile spread across Dustin's lips. "All in good time, brother."

"Cordelia said you were seeking the light as well. What is up there, Dustin?"

Groaning, he pushed himself up and placed a hand on Logan's shoulder. "The future, brother."

With that, Dustin staggered to his feet, leaving Logan still crouched on the ground. Amusement danced in Dustin's eyes as he offered a hand. His mind still whirring, Logan shrugged off the offer. He could stand on his own accord.

But that was just it, wasn't it? Suddenly he realised that Dustin saw him just as Zachary had until that night beside the lake. As a child. Too young to be of real use, to deal with such adult matters as an island of monsters and a light in the sky. That was why he'd sent Cordelia—to babysit him.

"Seven hells, Dustin," he started, stepping after his brother. "I want to know—"

Beware, Pathfinders!

Before he could reach Dustin, the shade appeared between them. Yelping, Logan jumped back, heart suddenly racing by the creature's sudden manifestation.

To Logan's irritation, his brother showed no such surprise. Instead, he nodded a greeting to the shade.

"Guardian."

Though the creature possessed no visible eyes, Logan sensed its attention switch to Dustin.

You failed to reach the core, Pathfinder.

"I did," Dustin agreed. "The alpha's power was too great."

Your failure dangers all, the shade continued as though it had not heard Dustin's words. ***Beware! The alpha has tracked your scent. Death approaches.***

The easy smile on Dustin's lips faded. Cursing, he reached for the shining red of his ruby.

The alpha arrived before he could summon his Tame.

A dark light swept across the campsite, smothering the fire and dimming even the brilliant glow of their Tames. Dark scales rippled as the creature landed in their midst, its bulk looming above even the greatest of their Tames.

Throwing back its head, the beast unleashed its roar upon the night.

❄ 37 ❄
ZACHARY

Willow stirred as Zachary approached, her blue eyes blinking in the shadows of the canyon.

"Hey, easy," he said, crouching alongside her and placing a hand on her shoulder. "That was quite the beating you two took."

The woman groaned by way of answer. Her Tame had turned back into a yellow crystal and made no sound at all. Shrugging off his hand, Willow's head swung around. Her scarlet locks hung untidily across her face and she thrust them aside with a grunt of annoyance.

"Where-is-it?" she said, her highland accent thicker than usual. Zach could hear the exhaustion in her voice.

"Destroyed," Zach answered. "You were lucky there was only one—I don't think Daze could have handled a second."

"That *was* the second," Willow replied, her eyes fluttering close. "Zahra dealt with the first. That damned thing trapped us..."

"...in brambles," Zachary finished for her, remembering what the last Skelt had done to Daze.

Then he realised what she'd said. Shivering, he looked for the first creature. The battle had left no remnants of either, but on closer inspection, he did notice further signs of battle. Sections of the canyon walls were pitted and broken, as though they'd been struck by some great force.

Further up the slope, the canyon split in two, one half continuing upwards, the other trailing back down towards the lake. He guessed that was the path Willow had taken up the mountain.

The woman grunted again and tried to lever herself to her feet. Zach offered her a hand and this time she did not turn down the assistance. She swayed on her feet, sapphire eyes examining the spot where Daze had fought the enemy.

"Was your creature injured by the battle?" she asked.

He shook his head. "We're calling them Tames..."

The woman raised an eyebrow. "That's...a curious translation."

Zachary offered a self-deprecating grin. "I never claimed to be a genius." Turning to his pack, he drew out his waterskin and held it out for the woman. "Here, pour some into your palm until it begins to glow, then let Zahra drink it. It will restore her strength."

Willow raised a second eyebrow, but after a moment's hesitation, she did as he said. Light shimmered in the gloom as her energy lit the water in her palm, before a second glow announced the emergence of her Tame. The water disappeared into its short snout. Closer now, Zach saw that a fine spiderweb of cracks riddled the creature's hide, but after drinking the water, they slowly began to fade.

"That's a neat trick," Willow remarked.

"Something we figured out at the lake."

"We? Then you found your friends?" She paused. "Something happened?"

"Something happened," he replied with a grimace. He felt no desire to elaborate.

Despite the restoration of her Tame, Willow was clearly in no condition to journey any farther today. He was fairly exhausted himself. Apparently not even the energy fed back from their Tames was endless. Better they make camp here and prepare themselves for what might come in the night, than push on and find themselves out on their feet when the next creatures came.

"I have some crystal tinder from the forest," he said, swinging the pack from his shoulder. "And some food. I don't know about you, but I could use a hot meal. We can push on at first light."

"We?"

Now it was Zachary's turn to raise an eyebrow. The woman chuckled, and didn't raise the point again. As he began to set the fire, she crossed to a nearby boulder and perched herself atop it.

Unfortunately, lighting a fire from scratch was not one of Zachary's many skills. Without his lighter or matches, he was soon cursing his luck in the name of Bes—until he made the fortunate discovery that the stones at their feet made a spark when struck together. After that, it was mere minutes before they had the crystal wood burning merrily between them.

"How many of the beasts have you faced?" he asked at last, seating himself on another boulder.

"Enough."

"Well, they're only growing stronger. I figure neither of us will survive much longer on this island alone."

The highland woman pursed her lips. "I suppose not." She reached out a hand to rest it on the head of her Tame. "And are you still running, lowlander?" she added suddenly.

He forced out a laugh. "A thief never stops running…" The words faded as the woman's blue eyes met his own. His smile slipped away. He lifted a stick from beside the fire and stabbed at the embers a bit, before tossing it on as fuel.

"Just a few days ago, I lectured a girl about fear. We spoke of cowards and brave men who faced their terrors. Thing is, I never told her that I was a coward myself."

"I did not take you for a cowardly man."

"It's all in the sleight of hand, isn't it?" He grimaced. "But that's the truth."

"You faced the beast just now. You could have walked away, left me to die, but you did not. Those do not strike me as the actions of a cowardly man."

"Physical danger has never filled me with much terror," he admitted. "Rob and I were similar in that regard. I have always had the skills and smarts to get myself out of sticky situations." He lifted his eyes from the flames. "You see, it's living that I have spent much of my life fearing."

Wrinkles creased Willow's forehead. She crooked her head to the side. "I think perhaps my skill in your language is not so strong as I thought. How can a man fear to live?"

Zachary gave grim chuckle. "And yet I do."

"You lowlanders are truly a strange people."

"Yes, we like to complicate things." He watched the flickering tongues of fire lick at the crystal wood. "Margery was the first person to ever make me want to face that fear." Zachary couldn't have said why, but something about this night made him want to speak. "The first day I saw her, she was putting on a show in the town square, acting out some skit with chairs. She had half a dozen or so. Claimed she would stack them atop one another and climb them. They were poorly made things, some crap imported from the south—not the solid stuff you have up in the hills."

"A foolish act then."

Zachary chuckled. "Exactly what everyone in the crowd thought. She kept prolonging it too, getting distracted with one ridiculous problem or another. Legs falling off the chairs and so on. Had the whole crowd eating out of her hands, waiting to watch her fail."

"Quite the woman."

"Ay, and there I was making a small fortune from her unfortunate spectators—until she *saw* me." He shook his head.

"That never happened, not back then. I was like a ghost in a crowd. But she saw me. And bloody well called me up to help with her act. I tell you, no thief wants *that* sort of attention, but I'll be damned if I didn't find myself joining her."

"Did she climb the chairs in the end?"

"She had me hold her hat while she climbed. When she got to the top, she screamed for everyone to stop. Convinced them all they had to leave a donation for the show. They damned well filled that hat to the brim. And all the while she stood atop her chairs, grinning like this was all some grand bet against the Old Gods."

Zachary fell silent then, recalling that day. The weight of gold and silver in the hat had been more than a labourer might make in a month. He could have taken it. Instead, he'd waited until Margery had climbed down to hand it over, then asked her out for a meal.

"That was the first day in my life I dared to live," he said quietly. "Margery gave me the courage to seek out something better for myself."

The words hung in the air. Zach listened to the crackling of the fire, the soft breath of the wind through the cliffs, and wondered what Margery was doing this night.

"If this woman meant so much to you, why are you here?"

"Because life had other plans," he said, then cursed. "I am not a good man. Maybe my illness was Edris's way of reminding me that I do not deserve happiness. Or maybe Kali simply decided it was my time." Kali was the Old God of Death, reaper of souls. He laughed suddenly, the sound harsh in the darkness. "Or maybe it was a test, to see whether I would hold my nerve. If I'd stay while the cancer ravaged me. If I'd let myself end."

"If so, I failed. Like I said. I'm a coward. When life got tough, I left my wife and fled. Doesn't matter that I told myself I was seeking a cure." His voice turned bitter. "You were right. I was—am—running. Truth is, I needed to get away, had to escape that look in her eyes."

"That is why you came then? You thought you would find a cure here?"

Even now, after all they had learned about this place, it seemed a forlorn hope. He shrugged.

"I thought a lot of things before we landed on these shores." He caught the woman's eyes from across the fire. "What about you? Why *did* you come—and don't say 'answers.'"

Willow laughed. "I told you of our legends, of an ancient war amongst my peoples, and a dark power that was locked away."

"You think this island is that power."

She gestured at her Tame. "Zahra proves it. Her crystal was passed down through my family for generations, with the warning it might one day be needed should the power return."

Zachary pursed his lips, recalling what Logan had told him about his own Tame. "The kid's stone also came from the highlands. It was given to him by his brother, Dustin."

"Dustin?" Willow's head jerked up at that. "Dustin Kaine?"

"That's the one. You've heard of him?"

"We have not met." She pursed her lips. "But Dustin Kaine is known as a friend to my people. What is he doing here?"

"Maybe the same as you. No one has seen him since the ship went down. But Logan is his brother. He and the others think if they can reach the light, they might be able to destroy whatever power is keeping us from leaving this place."

To his surprise, Willow lurched suddenly to her feet, her eyes wide. "What?" she hissed. "Why didn't you tell me?"

"I didn't think to…" Zachary trailed off. "What's the big deal? You said for yourself the power was evil."

"Think about what you're saying," Willow said, speaking the words with deliberate slowness. "They plan to destroy the power that holds us to this place."

"So we can leave," he agreed.

"Us," Willow whispered, "and whatever else might be trapped on this island with us."

❧ 38 ❧

LOGAN

For a second, all Logan could do was stand and stare at the monster. It was a dragon like Dustin's Tame. Covered in crystalline scales, its dark wings blotted out the moon, but the similarities ended there. Where Eiliah was slim and majestic, the creature's bulk filled the mountainside. Its flesh rippled with pure muscle, and its talons were as long as swords. Row upon row of fangs lined the massive jaws, sharp enough to tear any of their Tames in two with a single bite.

Standing on its hind legs, the creature loomed above them. Logan could see why the shade had called this an alpha. If it was truly a relative of Dustin's Tame, this must be the supreme form of its kind.

Perhaps most terrifying of all were its eyes. Not the deep copper of their Tames for this beast, nor even the brilliant silver of Eiliah or Caspar. Its eyes shone a deep, deadly golden hue. Logan could see the intelligence reflected in those eyes. It terrified him.

"Eiliah!"

Dustin's voice finally broke the spell that had fallen over the company with the alpha's appearance. There was a burst of white, then the smaller dragon appeared. Fractures still ran through Eiliah's crystal scales—they hadn't thought to give Dustin water to heal his Tame. It didn't seem to care. With a roar that seemed hollow before the alpha, it advanced towards the enemy.

Logan's heart lurched in his chest as the golden eyes focused upon his brother's Tame. A harsh wind blew across the mountainside as it stretched its wings. Pulse racing, Logan turned to his own crystal.

Hope roared as the bond strengthened, as Logan and the Tame became one. Together they leapt to the defence of their brother. Movement came from all around as the others joined them. This time Dustin and Eiliah would not fight alone.

A rumble came from the enemy's throat as it noticed their presence. The sight of so many Tames finally gave the creature pause. They felt a flicker of satisfaction. Together, the Tames had destroyed every other enemy they had encountered. This creature, however powerful, could not match them all…

The alpha struck.

Not with claw or fang, but like a true dragon, with smouldering fire. The inferno burst from the creature's maw and swept the hillside. Rock and dirt cracked and bubbled, and a terrible heat washed over the five Tames.

Logan screamed. Even merged with Hope, he could feel the effects of the pain back in his body. The enemy had not targeted the humans with its attack—they didn't seem to pay the humans any mind, so long as a Tame was present.

But Hope was not spared. The flames engulfed them, bubbling their crystal flesh. There was no time to prepare, no chance to evade the inferno.

Only agony.

They staggered as the flame dissipated, the burning orange vanishing as quickly as it had appeared. The ground beneath their paws popped and crackled with the remnants of the heat. Desperation granted them strength—along with a surge of Logan's own energy. Hope straightened, teeth glinting as they recovered.

The alpha loomed above. Amusement shone now from its golden eyes. They felt a flicker of rage to see it. The beast was mocking them, daring them to attack.

Only Eiliah and Caspar had been quick enough to avoid the flames, each having leapt to high boulders. The others were in varying states of recovery. No cracks showed yet in their crystal flesh, but sensing the damage in Hope, Logan knew they could not survive many more attacks like that.

Dustin's Tame roared as it went on the attack. It summoned not fire like the larger alpha, but a crackling bolt of electricity. Thunder shook the mountainside as lightning burst from the silver dragon. To Logan's surprise, he recognised the attack—the hound from the lake had used it against them just the night before.

His spirits rose as the lightning slammed into the alpha.

Attack, now! *Dustin's voice pulsed into their minds.*

The Tames obeyed. Bounding forward, Hope slashed out with its claws, tearing a hunk of crystal from the chest of the alpha. The others followed. Cordelia's Tame, Morgawr, burned an angry red as it leapt, tail swinging out in a harsh blow to the enemy's skull. Caspar divided into a dozen copies to come at the beast from all directions. In the chaos, they lost track of Amilyse's Tame.

But even as their attacks struck and they leapt back in retreat, Logan could sense the futility of their blows. Teeth and claw and tail would not destroy this monster. They needed to dig deeper, to find the true powers of their Tames, like Gozzo and Dustin had done.

Before they could strike again, a tremor rippled through the alpha. With a roar, it broke free of its paralysis.

Dark wings swept down. Hope, Caspar and Morgawr were all still close as a sudden gale swept across the slope. Hope dug its claws deep into the earth, clinging to the mountainside, while nearby, Morgawr did the same. Stones pelted them, kicked up by the winds. Struck from a dozen directions, the copies of Caspar flickered and went out. The real Caspar stumbled, barely able to resist the swirling winds.

Golden eyes fell upon the fox-like Pluff. Even as the gale began to fade, the terrible claws lashed out, catching Caspar and hurling it into a boulder with a sickening crunch. Cracks spread through the Tame and somewhere on the mountainside a moan came from Gozzo. Caspar did not rise again.

Logan looked back at the enemy and found its golden eyes upon him. Only instinct saved him and Hope. A bound of their powerful legs sent them leaping to a boulder.

A second later, giant claws tore a chunk of stone from the ground where they'd been standing.

They had only heartbeats to celebrate their success, as the alpha attacked again. This time a backwards swipe of its wings caught the

Thoona hard in the side. Stars burst across Hope's vision as the blow slammed them into the ground.

Reeling from the attack, Hope struggled to rise, even as the beast loomed above. Back in his body, Logan's blood turned to ice. Death shone from the eyes of the dragon now, a rage unlike any he'd seen before. There would be no second chances with this creature.

Before it could strike though, Cordelia's Tame struck. With a flare of white light, the rocky Pango slammed into the alpha's side and actually sent it reeling several feet. Logan felt a flicker of hope. Morgawr had resisted all damage in their previous battles. Perhaps it could distract the alpha long enough for them to figure out a stronger attack.

But as the golden eyes turned on the Pango, he sensed Cordelia had made a terrible mistake. This beast wasn't something you withstood. You either avoid its attacks, or suffered.

It took only a heartbeat to prove his suspicions correct.

Roaring, Morgawr attacked again, tail arcing out in the burning scythe that had become Cordelia's favoured attack. The alpha swung to meet it. The Pango's blow found its mark, striking the dragon hard in the chest.

This time, the alpha was unfazed. Instead of staggering back, the dragon loomed above Cordelia's Tame. She had only a moment before it struck, not enough to retreat, to evade its power. The enormous jaws stretched wide as they swept down to close upon the rocky Tame.

Cordelia's scream rent the night as crystal crunched and broke. The Pango thrashed, helpless, as the deadly teeth pierced its stony hide and sank deep into its flesh. Logan watched on, horrified, as the alpha gave a violent shake of its head and sent Cordelia's Tame tumbling across the hillside.

When it finally came to rest, Morgawr lay still amongst the stones, its rocky flesh now more cracks than crystal.

Now only three Tames stood against the alpha.

Logan shuddered. It had all happened so quickly. One moment, they'd had the thing surrounded. He looked around, finding Eiliah still perched atop a boulder, out of range of the enemy's immediate attacks, while Amilyse…

His heart sank as he recognised the emerald glow that shone from the crystal Skelt. Her Tame hadn't moved from where they had begun the fight. In the heat of battle, he hadn't noticed…but now he sensed her terror.

Amilyse… *he began.* ***Are you—***

He couldn't finish the question, as with a roar, the alpha launched itself at Dustin's Tame. A curse whispered in their minds as another burst of energy lit up the night, gathering about Eiliah. A boom *followed as it leapt from the injured Tame to strike the alpha.*

Again the enemy was frozen by the attack, paralysed by the electricity coursing through its crystal channels. Logan knew that feeling all too well, after what had happened back on the shores of the lake. This was their chance to strike. But as they gathered to spring at the dragon, logic returned. Claw and tooth had barely left a mark on this foe. They needed more.

So they turned instead to the power within.

They had shied away from it before now, in truth, from the depth of that mind within, the ageless, eternal nature of that power. But as they reached for it, it responded eagerly, bubbling up along with their half-remembered images. A fire gathered, a burning power within the Thoona. And as it gathered, a memory returned, of an empty chamber and a ring of shadows, of energies gathering and released.

Hope opened its eyes. All four burned now with a terrible light. With a roar, they released the gathered power. Fiery energy burst from their four eyes, leaping across the stones to strike the paralysed alpha.

This time, the attack finally had an effect. Crystal cracked and shattered as the burning energy tore into the creature, gouging a great chunk from its scaled skin.

But it did not fall.

The alpha broke from its paralysis and unleashed a roar. The sound rang across the mountainside like Dustin's thunder, so loud in their ears, deafening, terrifying…

Logan gasped as he sensed the chill spreading through their crystal form, an absolute terror that left Hope trembling, frozen in place. A shudder began deep within as the fear reached their core, robbing them of will, even as the golden eyes turned upon them.

Unable to move, to even breathe, they looked into the creature's eyes and saw death reflected there.

A blast of energy struck the alpha. It came from above, and this time it was enough to stagger the creature again. As the energy faded, Logan saw that cracks had appeared all across the alpha's body.

***So close.** Eiliah swept past on silver wings, circling for another attack and drawing the beast away from Logan.*

But it was Eiliah that was most badly injured.

***Dustin!** Logan screamed a warning as the alpha opened its jaws, but the flames had already been unleashed.*

Even so, the warning was almost enough. Still airborne, Eiliah twisted in the sky, its slender body evading the worst of the inferno. But not all of it. A howl sounded across the mountainside as crystal crumbled. Eiliah crashed into the hillside and went tumbling across the stone, finally coming to rest not far from where the other Tames already lay incapacitated.

Eyes burning golden, the alpha turned towards them.

With a gasp, Logan's terror-induced paralysis broke. He staggered, still struggling to overcome that skin-tingling sensation of terror. His heart pounded to the beat of Hope's as they watched the alpha advance.

Amilyse? *As he called, they turned towards Amilyse's Tame and found its copper eyes watching them.* **Amilyse,** *he repeated,* **please, I can't defeat it alone.**

A shiver passed through the Skelt. Delilah, that was what Amilyse had called the creature. She was still in there. He could sense her presence in that copper gaze, her terror. This was no spell of the enemy, but something else. He recalled their conversation on the shores of the lake.

You don't need to be your brother, *he called to her.* **You don't need to be fearless. You just need to believe in yourself. Like I do.**

There was no time to say more. The alpha was already looming above Eiliah and the others. He was amazed that Dustin's Tame had withstood another blow from the beast. It truly was stronger than their own Tames. But neither Eiliah nor any of the others could take another blow, especially not if it used its fiery breath again.

Yet as Logan sought within for the fiery energy he had used earlier, he found that strength depleted. A trickle of energy was gathering, but it would not recover in time to save his brother.

So snarling, Hope lowered its head and charged.

Talons clawed at the earth, hurling the Thoona forward with supernatural acceleration. Light gathered around them as they collected their strength—then slammed into the dragon with all their strength.

An audible thud *echoed across the hillside as the alpha stumbled back. A roar tore from its jaws, and the cracks criss-crossing its enormous torso grew a fraction larger. It shook its head, as though trying to clear a daze. But if it was at all stunned, it did not take long this time to recover. Even as Hope gathered itself for another attack, the golden eyes found them.*

And the terrible claws swept down…

❦ 39 ❦

AMILYSE

All her life, Amilyse had known fear. It was the shadows that danced upon her mantlepiece on dark nights, the monsters that turned her dreams to nightmares.

Their ascension was meant to have cured those fears. The day she and her brother had emerged from the month-long darkness was to be a day of rejoicing, of children reborn, destined to claim their blades and ascend to the title of monster hunters.

Instead, the ascension had been the day Amilyse's nightmares turned to reality. The days had crept past in the absolute darkness with only Rob's voice for company. That black had become a palpable, living thing. Through the long weeks, it had whispered to her, making dark promises, and darker deeds.

By the time she had emerged, Amilyse had been a blubbering wreck, her mind fractured, her resolve broken asunder. Only

Rob's presence had saved her. His voice had held the madness at bay. With his help, she had kept her silence upon their emergence. Rob had led her through the gathered ranks of their family, back into the light. Before the eyes of all, brother and sister had ascended as one to the rank of monster hunter.

But in private, they both knew who it was that had withstood the trials of the dark. And who had crumbled.

She had known, and would never allow herself to forget.

For while the twins had escaped the darkness, it had never left her. Perhaps that was why Zachary's words had cut so deeply. She knew well the beast that was her fear, the monster it became when she ran, how it could overwhelm her. Not even the best training in the world could save her from herself.

Then had come Delilah. The Tame had filled her with light, with a radiance that made her believe she might face the beast within. That the bond between their souls might give her the courage to face the darkness.

And it had, for a brief, shining moment. She and Delilah had faced the beasts of the mountain together, standing with their friends against their enemies.

Until the alpha had come.

From her first glimpse of the creature, she had realized the darkness had never truly left her. It had lurked within, hidden in the shadows, waiting for its moment to return. And return it had.

Even as the terror pierced her soul, Amilyse had felt herself drawn across the bond. But this time the union did not wash away her fear, did not light the darkness or grant her courage.

Merged with Delilah, looking upon the hulking mass of the alpha, her terror took on new life.

So she watched, paralysed, as her friends did battle.

And fell, one by one.

Lacking fear does not make you brave.

Zachary's words rung in her mind, but they did her little good now. What good were words to a coward? She had lived with this terror all of her life. She could not defeat it. The beast had only grown since that terrible day in the dungeon. The last slivers of her self-worth had been consumed the day Rob had fallen.

Amilyse, please, I can't defeat it alone.

Amilyse shuddered as Logan called for her. She could sense his desperation, his pain. His Tame shone with the emerald glow of terror, a match for her own. But somehow, Hope and Logan found the strength to face the alpha.

In her terror, she could not understand such futile defiance. The alpha was hideously powerful. It had tossed the other Tames around like ragdolls. Even Caspar, even Eiliah had not stood a chance. She watched as Logan and Dustin attacked again—and were repelled. Her terror whispered that it was pointless, that they should flee, that *she* should flee.

Amilyse couldn't even manage that.

You don't need to be your brother. You don't need to be fearless. You just need to believe in yourself. Like I do.

Nestled in Delilah's form, Amilyse closed her eyes. If only she could close her mind as well. How could she possibly help? She was worthless. Even her brother had thought so, though he would have never said it. She was too afraid, too weak, helpless. What could she possibly do to help Logan?

A boom of clashing forces shook the world. Her eyes snapped open. To her surprise, the alpha was lurching back from Logan's Thoona. A brilliant, fiery glow was just now fading from the Tame's four eyes.

But the tables did not turn for long. The alpha righted itself and swept its great wings down. Gravel pelted Logan and Hope. The Tame struggled against the onslaught, but it was only a distraction.

Amilyse watched as the alpha drew back its massive head and opened its mouth. Flame burned in the depths of its throat. Still she did not move. Not as the fires burst from the gaping jaws. Not as flames licked Hope's crystal hide.

Not as Logan's screams reverberated through the depths of her soul…

Please…I can't…Old Gods…please…

And suddenly Amilyse was moving. As Logan's Thoona slumped to the blackened stones, its flesh scorched and cracked, she and Delilah took a step forward. Then another. Words rung in her mind, Logan's, Zachary's, her brother's.

Courage is not some fleeting thing, but something forged in the fires of their terror, tempered in their dread.

You don't need to be fearless. You just need to believe in yourself. Like I do.

The world, the family be damned. I believe in you, sis.

A spark lit within Amilyse—within Delilah. A new power, a fresh energy. Her terror shrank before it. The emerald glow of the Tame faded, and was replaced with a brilliant white and black. Instinctively, perhaps from some part buried deep within Delilah, she sensed its purpose. A new ability, beyond the antlers and hooves of the Skelt, one she had seen the wild creature use beside the lake.

As the alpha loomed above the Tames of her friends, she advanced. And with each step, the energy grew stronger, as though just the very act of facing her fear, of stepping from its shadows, fed power to her Tame. Stones crunched—then cracked—beneath the force of their hooves. The alpha loomed, claws raised to strike a final blow against Logan and Hope.

Amilyse would not allow it.

The earth rumbled as the power leapt from her. A glow lit the night and she sensed the alpha's surprise. The beast turned from its victims to regard their shining form. With a final cry, they unleashed their power.

Vines burst from the earth beneath the alpha, spreading rapidly to engulf it. A roar shook the night as, too late, it struggled to escape their grip. Instead, the dagger-like thorns bit deep into the creature's flesh, holding it tight, binding it in a grasp as strong as iron.

The sudden release of energy caused Amilyse and her Tame to stumble, but to their joy, it seemed their gamble may have succeeded. Now if the others could attack…

…her heart sank as she realised the state of her fellow Tames. Not one was on their feet. Logan was struggling to rise, as was the silver Eiliah of Dustin, but it looked like they would not be in any state to attack for a few minutes yet. The thorns might not last that long…

It's up to us.

So be it. There was another attack the wild Skelt had used with devastating effect against Zachary.

Energy crackled about Delilah as they lifted their antlers. Suddenly they were lit like a star—not a soft, distant glow, but a burning beacon amidst the darkness. With a wild cry, they charged. The alpha roared in return, wings thrashing, great claws tearing at the vines, but still it remained bound.

There was a sickening crunch as they collided with the beast. Crystal scales shattered as their antlers pierced deep, tearing a terrible wound across the monster's chest.

A howl rent the night as the alpha reared back. Their attack had done terrible damage. Light seeped from the great fissures that now riddled the monster's silver scales. For a moment, it seemed the alpha would crumble to dust right there before them.

But this was no simple beast. This creature had been tasked with the protection of the light, to defend the island's power from intruders. And as the crystal vines of the Skelt fell away, its golden eyes turned again in search of its foe.

Amilyse and Delilah had been left staggered from the power of their attack. Reeling, they stumbled as stars danced before their vision. Disoriented, they struggled to recover, unaware of the alpha's attention.

Amilyse!

Logan's cry cut through their confusion. There was fear in his voice— no, more than that. Terror.

Amilyse fought against her Tame's lethargy. As their vision cleared, they found themselves looking into the golden eyes of the alpha. One wing hung limp, its edges crumbling away, and the enormous chest looked ready to crumble. Yet still those eyes burned. Still its scales rippled that terrible, angry red.

Somewhere, Logan was screaming, desperate, in pain, seeking to reach her. He was already too late.

Amilyse felt only a sense of peace as the creature loomed above them. She might not have destroyed the alpha, but she had faced the beast within, the fear that had haunted her since childhood. She was free.

Amilyse hardly felt the claws as they closed—almost gently—about Delilah. Human and Tame were as one as they rose from hot ground. The screaming in her mind grew louder and they sensed a growing light at the edges of their vision. Amilyse did not look away from the golden eyes.

Still merged with Delilah, she felt the pressure building. Finally the pain touched them as the claws pierced Delilah's crystal hide. A howl echoed across the mountainside. Amilyse cried out with her Tame. The pain snapped them from the daze. Now they struggled against that terrible grip, to free themselves, to save themselves.

Amilyse, I'm coming!

Her heart fluttered. Logan was coming. Logan would save them. He was a hero, like her brother.

Just hold on!

Amilyse could feel their energies slipping away, seeping from the dozen punctures. She could feel the claws as well. They grated within her, tearing at crystal organs. The alpha's energies burned them as well, all consuming. Darkness spread at the edges of their vision. A whimper whispered from the Tame. They tasted burning.

Amilyse, no!

And the inferno came.

For an instant, Amilyse stood again in her body, watching as the flames swallowed up Delilah. Through their bond, she still felt the fire's kiss, felt the pain, as though her own flesh was burning. She wanted to scream, to shatter the bond she had thought such a blessing and flee, but there was no tearing its anchor from her soul. No escaping this agony. Not until...

"Oh..." Amilyse whispered.

The word was still on her lips as her Tame crumbled to dust.

❧ 40 ❧

ZACHARY

Zachary couldn't recall the last time he'd slept. At least for a full night. How long since he'd been able to simply close his eyes and rest, without monsters and shadows haunting his dreams? The days had long since blurred together.

He was so weary. Not even the energy from Daze was enough to revive him. The dark threads of the cancer pulsed in his core, sapping his strength.

They had walked all night, he and Willow, though he could barely remember why. He didn't believe the woman's story about what Logan and the others might unleash. Did he? He was an intelligent man. He didn't believe in fairy tales— even if they came in the guise of ancient legends...

But he hadn't survived half his life in the underworld of Riogachd without learning to trust his instincts. And just now, they were screaming that *something* was wrong with this island. He'd been feeling it for a while now, a sense that everything they'd encountered, the way the beasts had attacked, their discovery of the fossils, everything, there was a pattern to it. Something, or somethings, were manipulating events.

The light hung above them, pulsing in the darkness, drawing them on. They were close now. They would reach it within a few hours, just after dawn. Hopefully, long before Logan and the others. They might have had a head start, but Zachary doubted the group would have pushed on through the night.

But that still left Dustin.

Logan's mysterious brother. Though he'd never met him, Zachary didn't trust the man. He'd known plenty like Dustin in his life. Cool, confident, used to getting what they wanted. Some called them heroes. Zachary had seen too many good lives lost following such men.

But what did Dustin actually want? The man had to know more than he was letting on. He'd brought them all here, after all. Had somehow reached out to contact Cordelia, gifting her a Tame. None of them had managed anything close to that feat.

Maybe Dustin was the hidden hand behind everything. If so, learning the man's motives became all the more important. *Why* had he brought them here? What had he expected to find?

He had a feeling they would soon find out.

Dawn's glow had just touched the horizon when the pair encountered something unexpected: voices.

They found Cordelia and her sailors shortly after that. Emerging from the mouth of a canyon, Zachary was surprised to find them camped out in the open, talking quietly amongst themselves. He approached cautiously, Willow at his side, but there was no sign of Logan. They soon learned the reason.

Amilyse could have been sleeping. Her body was untouched, without a single mark on her pale skin. Only when he reached out to lay a hand upon her arm did he feel the cold, that whisper of death that told you the soul had fled.

Zachary shivered. How had it come to this? He hadn't planned to make friends when he'd set out from Leith. He'd come for one reason only: to save his own skin. Yet looking at the woman's pale face, he realised he did care.

A part of him had wanted to hate Logan and Amilyse and Rob for their youth. Their entire lives were before them. You could see it in Logan's innocence, in Rob's sense of invincibility. Even in Amilyse's blind devotion to her brother. That hate was why he'd spoken such harsh words to the young woman, why he'd gone out of his way to humiliate Rob, why he'd been so ready to betray Logan.

Now he wished he'd been kinder, better. That the darkness had taken him instead. His days were numbered. Better death take him than the young.

Swallowing, he looked to Cordelia. The captain had told him everything that had passed since they'd separated.

"Where are they now?"

Cordelia's eyes lifted to the light. "Gone," she replied. "Dustin would not wait. Said they needed to reach the light before another alpha formed. We decided to stay. Didn't seem right...leaving Ms. Rainer alone..." She shuddered visibly. "You should have seen it, Sicario. Just when I was beginning to think I had a handle on this place, that *thing* appeared."

Zachary nodded. She'd already told him about the battle. He prayed to whichever of the Old Gods still cared that the kid's brother was wrong, and another one wasn't going to appear.

"What about Gozzo?" he asked. The old fisherman was the other absentee.

A frown touched Cordelia's face. "He must have gone with the others. We were all in a bit of a daze."

Zach cursed. Gozzo had been here the longest. He'd been hoping the old fisherman might be able to offer some clues about whatever dark presence might be directing events.

The source of the light was visible now. A few hundred yards above, darkness stained the stone cliffs. Every so often, light burst from that shadow, revealing the cave. Zachary shivered. He wasn't one to be superstitious, but the place had an evil look about it.

"Sicario, I wanted to apologise."

"For what?" he asked, tearing his gaze from the mountain. A cold breeze blew across the slope, though it would soon dissipate with the rising sun.

"I should have sided with you when Logan told you to leave."

Zachary chuckled. "I didn't expect you to, captain," he replied. "No honour amongst thieves, right?"

Cordelia pursed her lips. "Right," she said. "Even so, I knew it was foolish. I am glad you survived." Her eyes lingered on Amilyse's body, and Zachary understood the part she left unsaid. If he'd been there, the girl might still live.

But then Willow would have perished. He looked around for the highland woman and found her looking off into the distance.

"What is that?" she asked as Zach approached, a frown creasing her brow.

He followed her gaze, but there was nothing there.

Willow summoned her Tame and started across the slope without looking back. Zach hesitated only a heartbeat before bringing out Daze and chasing after her. Cordelia followed, the sailor Duncan moving with her.

Stones crunched as they crossed the slope. Ahead, a great cliff rose to block their path, while the mountainside gave way to a sheer drop away to their right. The trail towards the light was farther up the mountain, winding through a cluster of boulders before emerging near the cave. It would probably take several hours to climb.

Whatever Willow had spotted, it wasn't anything to do with the magical light. She came to a stop before the cliffs. Zachary was just a step behind her when she reached a hand to her Tame. They'd healed both Tames with the last of their water, a move Zach was already beginning to regret as he licked his parched lips.

A glow started in the boar-like creature's core. Abruptly it lowered its tusks and leapt.

Boom.

Something crackled and broke as the Tame struck...something. Zachary staggered as the very air seemed to boil around them. Stars filled his vision and the world seemed to turn on its axis. Then he blinked, and the sensation vanished.

But the sense of dissociation did not. He looked around, surprised to find the great cliffs that had barred their path vanished. Then he blinked, finally catching sight of what had replaced them. Surely it couldn't be...

A ship lay perched on the mountainside. They stood in its shadow, its bulk looming over them. The sun glinted strangely off the wooden boards. It took a moment before Zachary realised why.

The entire ship had been turned to crystal.

At first glance, it looked like any other ship to Zach's unpractised eye. Sure, the mast was leaning on a precarious angle and a hole had been torn in the hull. It wasn't a steamer like *The Rising Tide*, but sails, hull, rigging, a few broken oars. Definitely a ship built by human hands.

Except on closer inspection, the 'wood', while faded and cracked, was clearly made of crystal.

He shared a look with Willow and Cordelia. "What in the seven hells?"

"Seven hells is right," Willow replied.

Cordelia pursed her lips. "This can't be Gozzo's ship, can it?"

No one had an answer to that question. Willow gestured for Zach to give her a boost up onto the deck. He knitted his fingers together and grunted as she stepped into the fold. Drawing on some of Daze's strength, he hoisted her up until she caught a hand hold on the deck. Cordelia followed, then the two leaned over the side and helped him up.

If they'd thought a ship made of crystal was strange, the sight that greeted them aboard was stranger still. They found themselves in the company of six skeletons, their flesh and clothing long gone, but their bones very much preserved. As crystal.

"This was hidden," Willow murmured.

"Caspar," Zach said softly. "Gozzo's Tame, it can create illusions. Though something like this…"

"This ship," Cordelia spoke up, "it's not one of ours."

They turned towards the woman. She stood near the stern, one hand resting on the long haft of the tiller. Her lips were turned downwards in a frown as she cast a professional gaze over the stranded vessel.

"What do you mean?" Zachary asked. "You think it came from the continent?"

"No," she said, shaking her head. "Look, it's turned to crystal, but the colouration is the same. White for bone, brown for wood. You get the idea."

"And?"

"It's all wood and bronze," Willow spoke up. She was crouched alongside one of the skeletons, inspecting it for some unknown reason.

Zachary sighed, still not understanding the significance "Pretend I know nothing of ship construction." *The Rising Tide* had been mostly steel, but it was a newer design, with its steam powered engine. Not that it had been an advantage once they'd come within the island's influence.

"We've been using steel in our ship building for decades now," Cordelia answered. "Wood might still be used in a few more basic designs...but bronze?" She shook her head. "And look," she continued, leaning over the side. "The planking overlaps. Modern shipbuilders make them flush and use caulking sealant to keep out the water, when they use wood at all."

Zach ran a hand down his face. "What does any of this mean, Captain?" he asked, trying to keep the irritation from his tone. The sleepless nights were catching up with him.

They needed to be gone, before Logan and his brother did something they might all regret. What did it matter how Gozzo and his crew had built a ship? Sure, it was strange that it had turned to crystal, but they still knew so little about this place. Organic material from the outside world did not burn here. Perhaps this was what happened to the dead if left here for months.

"It matters," Cordelia said softly, turning to face him. "It matters because this ship proves that Gozzo has been lying to us, Zach," she said, dropping the formalities. "I don't know *where* this ship came from, but I know it wasn't built this century."

❧ 41 ❧
LOGAN

Logan trudged through the dawn shadows. He no longer knew why he walked. All he wanted was to lie down and hide away from the world. To pretend he was back in his family's solar, curled up by the fire with a book in his lap.

Instead, his brother had dragged him on this insane journey. Logan only stood because of his brother, because Dustin had insisted he get back up, that they keep moving.

How he longed to throw those words back in his brother's face. But even that was beyond his dejected state.

Amilyse was dead.

How? It didn't seem possible. Not after everything they'd survived. Just a few hours before, they'd been kissing in the moonlight. Now…

…now she lay still on cold stones, the light in her fiery eyes extinguished, her life fled. Despite everything they had learnt, she had ended up just like her brother, her spark snuffed out by the cruelty of this place.

Logan could feel the tears on this cheeks. He made no move to wipe them away. What did he care if the world saw his pain? In the past few days, he'd seen more death than most saw in a lifetime. He just wanted to forget any of this had ever happened.

But he couldn't. That would mean forgetting Amilyse. And Rob. And Byron, the sailor who'd died protecting them on the plateau. And all the other men and women who'd perished aboard *The Rising Tide*. He scrunched his eyes closed as the faces of the dead flashed before his eyes, ending with his last glimpse of Amilyse.

There had been surprise in her eyes as she stood on the hill-side. Fear too. But she had lived up to her family's name, to her brother's legacy. She had faced those fears, had battled the monster, had saved them all.

Even as the alpha's claws had closed upon the helpless body of Delilah, Hope and Eiliah had unleashed their fury. Fire and lightning had burst across the mountainside to strike the great beast. And finally, finally, it had crumbled.

But they'd been too late.

Amilyse had already paid the ultimate price for her bravery.

An unseen rock caught Logan's foot, and he stumbled. A strong arm caught him before he could fall.

"Easy, brother," Dustin murmured. "We're almost there."

Nodding listlessly, Logan trudged on. Dustin led the way, traversing the winding path up and around the mountainside. They were close to the cave, no more than an hour now. He still didn't know what Dustin wanted there, what they were doing. Since Amilyse had fallen, his mind had ceased to function, to process anything beyond the tragedy he'd just witnessed.

But staring at his brother's back, he remembered how Dustin had been behind everything. But what had it all been for? He didn't even know what his brother had come here for. Surely everything they'd been through wasn't because of a paperweight on Dustin's desk. It couldn't be that simple. Logan refused to believe it.

He found himself growing angry instead.

All this pain, all this death, all of it because of Dustin.

Suddenly he was stalking forward. The cave loomed above, its shadows burning from the light within. He would have the truth from his brother before they went any further.

Dustin flinched when Logan clasped him by the shoulder. Logan gasped as well, as he felt crackling energy leap between them.

Instantly, their Tames came to life. Hope had silver eyes to match Eiliah's now. The Thoona had grown larger too. It had happened after they'd destroyed the Alpha. All that energy...it had been enough to pass the threshold from bronze to silver.

Logan had hardly noticed. He had been crouching in the jagged stones, with Amilyse cradled in his lap. The newfound power had meant nothing to him in his grief. They might have defeated the alpha, might have grown stronger, but what did it matter? Amilyse was still gone.

"Brother…" Dustin started, his voice soft.

"Tell me why, Dustin," Logan interrupted. "Why are we in this hellhole? What is it all for?"

Dustin stared at him for a long while. So long, in fact, that Logan wondered whether he would answer. Finally though, Dustin reached into his pocket and took out a watch made of silver. Wordlessly, he handed it to Logan.

"What is this?"

"Open it."

Logan hesitated. The last time Dustin had handed him something, it had turned out to be a magical artefact that transformed into a monster. Yet the object he held now didn't appear to be anything more than a pocket watch. He flicked it open with a *click*.

Inside, the hands of the clock had ceased to move, though whether that was from the seawater or the effects of the island was impossible to tell. But it was not the broken clock that Dustin had wanted to show him. Inside the lid of the watch was a photograph of a young Dustin. Beside him was a woman with black hair and a welcoming smile.

"Her name is Brandi," Dustin whispered. "She's why we're here."

Logan's heart stilled. He looked at his brother. Grief was etched across Dustin's face, grief he had somehow hidden until this moment. Logan didn't understand. His brother had never mentioned a woman, a lover, a wife.

"We met on that first expedition," Dustin continued. "She was a highland woman, helping with the dig. That was why

I never brought her back to introduce to Father. You know how he felt, after the war. And besides, she wasn't highborn." His gaze drifted down towards the lake. Its waters were far below them now. "Guess he'll like Amilyse."

"I don't understand, Dustin," Logan whispered. "What does she have to do with this place?"

"I lost her a few months before the storm," Dustin continued, as though he hadn't heard Logan. "Wrong place at the wrong time. The thief's gun went off. I don't think he meant to fire. They never did catch him. They never do, these days." He swallowed. "I looked for him myself, but I had no more luck than the detectives."

"Dustin, why didn't you tell us…" Logan breathed. "Why didn't you tell *me?*"

Dustin drew in a long breath, as though preparing for a marathon.

"Then the storm came, and the crystal woke. It dragged me from my despair. Brandi had been studying it again, before…I began digging into her research. She'd been studying the legends of her people. She had an artefact as well, though hers had been handed down through her family. She'd been so close. I pieced together the rest of the clues, the connections between her ancestors and our Old Gods."

"Brother," Logan interrupted, "please—"

"Nonsense, I know. Except that this place proves they were not. Didn't you ever wonder where the Old Gods found their power? Where they came from? Why they left?"

Logan swallowed, but did not speak. There were no words.

"It was all still just speculation, until we actually found this place. When the shade appeared, I knew."

"Knew what, Dustin?"

"That this is not the first time this island has appeared to mankind."

"What?"

"This is the land of the Old Gods, brother," Dustin whispered. "The Seven Hells as well. Every tale, every legend, all of them lead back to this place, these creatures."

"That's…" Logan heart pulsed. "That's insane."

To his surprise, Dustin threw back his head and laughed maniacally. "So I thought, until I woke on that beach and Eiliah appeared to me."

"So what are you saying? That this island is the home of the Old Gods?"

"No, brother," Dustin whispered. "I'm saying this was where they were *created*, where the legends were born. That these creatures, these…Tames, *they* are what turned men into Gods."

Blowing out his cheeks, Logan exhaled. What Dustin was saying was madness, surely. And yet…

"What does it matter?" he asked at last, the brief spirit that had fuelled him fading.

"It matters, brother!" Dustin cried, grasping him by the shoulders. "It matters because this place is the end to the natural order of things. It can be the end of death itself. The shade, it spoke of fate, of immortality. If we can reach

371

the light, Amilyse, Brandi, all the others, they don't have to stay gone. We can bring them back."

Suddenly Logan's heart was beating hard in his chest. He stared at his brother, seeing the fervour in his eyes, the desperate hope. A lump lodged in his throat. He didn't want to believe Dustin's words. They were madness, surely. He didn't need false hope. And yet...

He saw again Amilyse, lying cold and still on the mountainside. And imagined her eyes fluttering, the harsh rasp of inhaled breath, the colour flooding back to her pale cheeks. Shivering, he looked from Dustin to the shadow on the hillside. As though in response to the attention, light burst from the darkness.

Could he be right?

"Are you with me, brother?"

Dustin stood before Logan, his eyes uncharacteristically earnest. He was holding his breath, waiting for Logan to reply.

Their father's sabre still hung at Logan's waist. He clenched the hilt tight. Useless as the weapon was here, it still represented something to each of them. The bond they shared as family. Looking into Dustin's desperate eyes, Logan realised for the first time in his life, his brother needed him.

"I'm with you, Dustin."

42

ZACHARY

Zach stood with Willow looking up towards the cave. By the winding trail, it would take them hours to reach its shadowed depths. It might be too late by then. Whatever Dustin planned, wherever Gozzo was, their head start was insurmountable.

Unless Zach and Willow did something...different.

Zach found himself looking at Daze. The Tame's copper eyes glinted in the rising sun. Expectation crackled within its crystal depths. He swallowed, casting a glance at Willow.

"You sure about this?"

Willow chuckled. "Come now, lowlander, you cannot be afraid, can you?"

Zach pursed his lips in a horizontal line. "Afraid, no. Wary, obviously."

"I'm open to other ideas."

Zach shook his head. That was the thing, wasn't it? They had run out of options hours ago. The ancient, crystalised fishing ship loomed on the mountainside beside them, a reminder of everything wrong with this place. How they'd been used, manipulated.

If only they knew *why*.

"You're still determined to go?" Cordelia asked.

She stood nearby, arms crossed, one finger tapping lightly on the hilt of a sabre she hadn't drawn in days. Her Tame stood alongside her. A growl rumbled from its rocky throat. Cordelia would not be joining them. Her crew could not keep up with the pace they hoped to set, and she would not leave them defenceless.

"We don't have a choice," Zach replied.

Cordelia eyed him. "Then take care of yourself, Sicario. Just because you're dying, doesn't mean you have to go get yourself killed." She paused. "Keep an eye out for the lad. That brother of his has plans as well."

Zachary nodded, though the last time he'd seen Logan, the kid hadn't wanted anything to do with him.

"Okay, lowlander," Willow spoke up. She rested a hand on the back of her Tame. "Are we doing this?"

Blowing out a lungful of air, Zach turned to Daze. "Right, bud, you ready?"

The creature gave a rumble, as if to say of course. Zach grimaced. They were about to find out. Without any further hesitation, he swung himself onto the back of the Tame.

Energy crackled along his skin as he settled on the crystal beast, but otherwise nothing alarming happened. Standing on all fours, the Brackis stood just above his waist, so his boots were precariously close to the ground. Zach would have to lift his feet to avoid loose rocks. Beside him, Willow wasn't much better on Zahra, though she settled onto the creature's back with far more grace than Zachary.

"Ever ridden bareback, lowlander?" A grin lit up her face.

"Can't say that I have."

"Then you might want to merge with Daze for this next part."

She didn't give him a chance to respond. Her Tame leapt onto the track leading to the cave. Daze bounded after her without a word from Zach. He cursed as the shock of the creature's stride sent vibrations up his spine. Following her suggestion, his mind sank into the Tame. Based on some earlier experimentation, he knew his body would not release its hold on the creature's back. This way, he could at least escape his own pain through the ride, though the respite was only temporary. Once they reached the cave and he returned to his body, Zach had no doubt he would feel every ache and bruise received on the journey.

Looking out from the eyes of Daze, the ground raced by, each bound of the Tame's powerful legs sending them hurtling upwards. It wasn't long before they left the winding path. The Tames had no need for that. They plunged directly up the mountain slope instead, claws and hooves clinging easily to the harsh terrain.

Wind whistled in Daze's ears. Zach could feel the heat of the Tame's blood pounding through their body, sensed the harsh intake of its breath, the icy air against their face. This high on the mountain, even the unnatural warmth of the island was lessened. Far above, beyond even the cave, the snowy peak glistened. He was thankful they did not need to travel so far.

Already they were nearing the cave and its searing light. There was no sign of Logan, Dustin or Gozzo as they approached. That was disappointing. He'd hoped with the shortcut they might head off their quarry. The three must already be inside. Zach prayed to the trickster Edris they were not already too late.

For what exactly, he couldn't say. All he knew was that the pit in his stomach had only grown weightier with each passing hour since he'd left the company. Willow's warning, Amilyse's death, the discovery of the crystal fishing ship, all of it had only served to feed his sense of impending doom.

The Tames drew to a stop at the cave entrance, allowing the humans to dismount. If it came to a battle inside, they would not want them encumbered. Zach groaned as he stepped down from Daze's back, his thighs locking in a cramp. He would have fallen had Willow not caught him.

He nodded his thanks, struggling to conceal his pain. It wasn't just the ride—though everything below his waist felt as though it'd gone three rounds with a Londinium ring fighter. It was the sickness. Even with Daze's energy, he could feel it draining him. Without the Tame, he would probably have been bedridden by now. As it was—

The earth shook.

There was no warning, not even a rumbling. Just a sudden, violent quaking that threw the pair from their feet. Breath hissed between Zach's teeth as he struck the ground. A thunder roared in his ears and he feared half the mountain would come crashing down on them. Such was the ferocity of the shaking, he couldn't even lift himself up. All they could do was cling to the earth and pray the shaking would stop.

It did, eventually. When stillness finally returned, it was with no small amount of trepidation that Zachary stood. He cast a nervous glance above them, but the icy glacier showed no signs of movement. He wondered now if it was even snow, or if like everything else on this island, it too was made of crystal.

He cast a glance at Willow, meeting her sapphire gaze.

"Sure you still want to do this, lowlander?" she asked.

Light burst from the cave, catching them both in its brilliance. They stood in the entrance, looking into the cave's depths, but there was no telling what lay within.

"Are you?"

Willow pursed her lips in a thin line. "I do not have a choice."

"Nor I."

"You cannot still think to find a cure?" she asked.

Zach shrugged. "I'm not sure what I expect to find," he replied honestly. "Evidence suggests there is a centuries old fisherman running around. So who knows?"

He laughed when he saw the concerned look on the highland woman's face.

"Peace. I do not intend to release any demons upon the world," he said. He kept the smile on his lips, though it no longer reached his eyes.

"Very well," Willow said. "Then let us proceed."

Zachary nodded his agreement. Inside the cave, the light no longer came and went, but was a constant stream now. And it only seemed to be growing brighter. Whatever was happening inside, time was quickly running out for them to stop it.

Together, they walked towards the light.

43

LOGAN

Logan's heart raced as he picked himself up off the floor. Dustin was already on his feet. The quake had struck the second they'd stepped into the chamber. Logan didn't think it was a coincidence.

Down they had travelled, down the winding, looping, spiral tunnel leading into the depths of the mountain, down to the heart of the island.

And as the last of the trembling faded away, they finally looked upon the source of the light.

"So this is it," Dustin breathed as Logan joined him.

They stood on a ledge above the great chamber. To their right, a ramp led down to the cavern floor, while before them was a drop of some fifty feet. The chamber itself stretched at least a hundred yards, its ceiling taller still, the sheer walls seeming to vanish into the shadows above.

A roaring filled their ears. It was the roar of rushing waters, the rumble of an enormous whirlpool that dominated the cavern. The waters spun and churned, glowing with that impossible light they had glimpsed all over the island—before disappearing down into the unknown depths.

Like the lake, the whirlpool did not seem to be draining, though it was clear the water was racing away. Perhaps this was the source of all the water across the island. If so, it was clear now why it held such power, the reason it reacted to human touch.

Just a few feet above the racing waters hung an enormous crystal. Larger than all their fossils combined, this crystal was the size of a boulder and shone with a blinding light. The waters below were bathed in that glow, *created* from it, conjured by its sheer power. At first glance its light could have been mistaken as white. But as Logan looked, he came to realise it was not one colour, but all of them. Reds and blues and golds rippled within the crystal depths, bursting forth to bathe them all in its brilliance.

Looking upon the crystal, Logan felt himself shiver. He had seen this place. Somewhere deep in Hope's memories, it recalled this chamber, that crystal. The whirlpool had not been there then, but silhouettes, men and women standing in a ring.

But seeing it in the flesh...he could sense its power. It was an almost tangible thing. The very air thrummed with the crystal's aura, setting his skin to crawling, his every hair standing on end. The power contained within those crystal facets was beyond...beyond anything of this world.

Though, looking upon the crystal now, Logan felt that its brilliance was not so great as it had been in Hope's memories. Could this be a different chamber after all? Or had the crystal lost some of its power through the intervening years?

Shadows gathering on the floor of the chamber drew their attention. Logan watched as the Guardian of the island took shape, the darkness swirling from all around. In the brilliance of the crystal, its form seemed less substantial, as though it shadows struggled to exist here.

Welcome, Pathfinders, to the heart of my island.

Dustin wore a broad grin. "We did it, brother."

Logan found himself smiling back. They descended the ramp to the cavern floor together and joined the shade on the ring of stone that surrounded the whirlpool. Its roaring grew louder as they approached, and Logan's heart began to race. One mistake, one misplaced stumble, and you would disappear into those racing waters.

"Guardian," Dustin greeted the creature formally. "Thank you for leading me here."

The heart holds the power of a thousand sparks, the shade continued.

"How do we use it?" Dustin asked, his voice hoarse with excitement.

Logan found himself growing excited as well. Standing in the presence of such power, he couldn't help but feel a tremor of hope. He saw again Amilyse's face, the uncertain smile upon her lips. Could they really bring them, bring her, back?

The shade did not reply, only swirled in place, watching them from its place at the water's edge. Dustin grunted as he looked from the creature to the stone.

"Right, you're a guardian, not a guide," he chuckled to himself.

The power of the heart may only be touched by a Pathfinder.

"Is that so?" Dustin muttered. He looked from the racing waters to Logan. "Any thoughts, brother?"

Logan pursed his lips. The whirlpool was some fifty yards across. Even at the edges, waves lapped at the sides, threatening to drag unwary souls down into the depths. No one could cross those waters, not without being dragged into the depths. Even if one *could*, the crystal hovered several feet above the surface, well out of reach for someone in the water.

No human could reach that crystal.

But a Tame might.

"Back at the lake, we fought a Skelt that walked on water," Logan said, then seeing the look of confusion on his brother's face, added: "A Skelt is a type of Tame, like a deer. The guardian didn't tell you?" When Dustin shook his head, Logan shrugged and went on. "It only told us the name of the Thoona. Gozzo passed along the rest. Anyway, I wonder…"

Dustin slapped Logan on the shoulder. "Relax, brother," he laughed. "Eiliah can fly, remember?"

Right. His brother's Tame was a dragon. Smaller than the alpha, but he'd seen it soar just the night before. Logan's cheeks grew warm but Dustin was already turning away and touching a hand to his Tame's scarlet crystal.

The slender dragon appeared in a burst of light. Its colouration flickered as it looked upon the enormous crystal, shifting from red to pink to mottled grey, before finally settling on black edged with orange. Logan frowned. He did not recognise the emotion of that colouration.

Dustin's eyes took on the vacant look of one merged with their Tame. Eiliah spread its wings a moment later. It lifted lightly off the ground as they began to beat, carrying the slender dragon out over the swirling waters.

Logan shivered as he watched Dustin and Eiliah drift out towards the crystal. Memories tugged at the back of his mind, recollections that could only belong to Hope. It *knew* this place, though its fractured consciousness could not recall why.

"Wait!"

Eiliah was drawing close to the crystal when the shout rang out across the chamber. He spun around, finding two newcomers standing on the ledge above them. His heart clenched in his chest when he recognised Zachary and the highland woman they'd met back on the plateau. A quick intake of breath came from alongside him as Dustin returned to his body.

"What do you want, Zachary?" Logan growled, though he already knew the answer. He found himself clenching his fists, his anger rising at just the sight of the man.

If Zachary thought he could steal this power for himself…

"You have to stop," the man's voice echoed strangely in the chamber. "You don't understand…"

Logan was already turning away. He wasn't surprised by the man's appearance. Whether he'd come seeking power or to save his own skin, there wasn't much difference. Zach was here for himself, and no one else.

"I'm sorry, Logan. I never should have betrayed you. But please, kid, don't do this."

The words caught Logan off-guard. He froze, the breath catching in his throat. It took an effort of will to draw in another breath, then glance over his shoulder at the man.

"Why?" Logan asked, unable to keep the bitterness from his voice. "You think I'll let you trick me again, so you can steal the power for yourself? I won't let you, not this time. I can bring Amilyse back. I can save her."

Even from the chamber floor, he saw the surprise appear on Zachary's face. For a full ten seconds, the man did not speak.

"Logan, something is wrong here," he said at last. "Something about this island, about all of this. You must sense it." He looked around, his sharp eyes scanning the shadows. "Where is Gozzo?"

Logan paused, thrown off-balance by the unexpected question. "What does he have to do with anything? We left him back with Cordelia."

"He wasn't there when we saw her."

"Then we don't know where he is," Dustin interjected. He'd separated fully from his Tame now. "Why should we care?"

"Ah, this must be the famed Dustin Kaine. Your brother has told me many good things."

"I wish the same could be said of you. Zachary Sicario, I take it?"

Zach gave a mock bow, but when he spoke again, he addressed his words to Logan.

"Because Gozzo isn't what he claimed to be, Logan," he said softly. "His ship, we found it."

"And?" Dustin snapped, his irritation showing in the glare that twisted his face.

"It wasn't built in Riogachd. At least, not the kingdom we know. The boat is centuries old. If not older."

Logan frowned. "Then it's some other ship…" He paused, then shook his head, annoyed at allowing the conman to divert them. He drew in a breath. "Amilyse is gone, Zachary. Gone because I wasn't strong enough to protect her. I have to fix things."

Several seconds of silence followed.

"Then do it. I will not stop you."

Again the words caught Logan off-guard. He stared at the man, even as his companion swung on him. Willow's eyes were furious and outrage contorted her face. Harsh words passed between them, but were lost to those below in the roaring of the whirlpool.

Swallowing, Logan looked at his brother. "What do you think?"

Dustin bit his lip, looking from Logan to the crystal. The desire in his brother's eyes was unmistakeable, but even so, Dustin hesitated.

"I don't know," Dustin murmured. His throat bobbed as he swallowed. "I have…can't ignore…can I?" He shook his head. "Your friend…is not wrong. There is something strange about this place."

"Don't listen—"

Logan broke off as light burst from the ledge where Zachary and Willow stood. Their Tames had appeared and now stood facing one another. Zach's Brackis seemed an even match for the hog-like Tame of the highland woman, though Logan had yet to encounter one of that kind in the wild.

"Stop," Zachary's voice rang from the walls. He looked from Willow, down to where the brothers stood. Logan sensed his gaze meet Dustin's. "All of us were brought to this place by our own desires. All of us but Logan. If someone is to touch that crystal, to use its power, I say we let it be him."

A lump lodged in Logan's throat. He was taken aback by Zachary's words. But even as he struggled to comprehend the man's reasoning, why Zachary would suddenly put his life in Logan's hands, he found his brother nodding.

"Your friend is right."

"What?"

Dustin looked down at his hands. "I...I have been seeking this place for so long. My mind is not clear, brother. There is something strange here, I have felt it for days, even if I could not admit it." He looked up, meeting Logan's eyes. "But you...perhaps you can see clearly."

Logan's mouth was suddenly dry. "I thought...but I'm just...just a kid."

"No, brother." Smiling, Dustin stepped forward and placed a hand on Logan's shoulder. "I have watched you these past days, seen glimpses of all you have done. You stood up for the helpless, showed trust and courage when others saw only power and danger. You have more than earned that sword you wear."

Logan's hand fell to the hilt of his father's sword. Its leather pommel was cold to the touch. Him, worthy? None of this made sense.

Yet it seemed he would not have a choice in the matter. Or rather, the choice of what happened next was all his. He couldn't pretend to understand that look behind his brother's eyes. There was desperation, that much was unmistakeable. But there was a fear as well, a sudden doubt now that they stood on the precipice. That the oasis he had sought might after all this time be proven a mirage.

And so he had turned to Logan.

Logan reached for his Tame. The pulse of the creature's power steadied his nerves, before—

Hope blinked as they became one. Through the Tame's eyes, the cavern shone with the brilliance of the crystal. A shiver passed through the

Tame as they looked on that power. A hunger stirred, for the sparks contained within.

Without thought, they stepped from stone to the racing waters. Light spilled across the surface where Hope's paw touched down, and rather than sink, they encountered something solid.

There though, they paused. Currents raced by beneath their feet, but did not touch them. Shivering, they looked back at the humans gathered around the chamber. Memories stirred within, of other humans who'd gathered in this place…

…and they saw the difference from that time. Through the eyes of the Tame, it was obvious. The crystal was not as bright as in Hope's memories, as though even the infinite energy it contained had been lessened through the ages.

Logan could not have said why, but something about that gave him pause. He drew back from the Tame to his body. He wanted desperately to continue, to free that light to bring back Amilyse, to restore the joy to his brother's eyes. A small part of him wanted to continue just to spite Zachary, to prove the man could not manipulate him. But he was no longer the naïve boy who'd boarded *The Rising Tide* just a few days before.

And just like Zachary and his brother and the highland woman, he knew something was wrong. Some instinct, some deep-seated suspicion screamed at him to turn from this power, to flee this chamber, this island, and never return.

And so Logan turned away from the crystal.

"No," he breathed. "No, Zach is right. Something is wrong here."

A part of him broke as he said the words, knowing what they meant. He saw that same pain in his brother's eyes, the death of hope. They would not get to see their loved ones again.

But before either of them could speak, a sharp whistling sound filled the chamber. It rose even above the roar of the waters, becoming a shriek, a howling. They spun towards the sound. Forgotten in the shadows, the shade spun, its darkness twisting, reforming, taking on fresh shape and substance.

Abruptly, the howling cut off.

And Gozzo stepped from the shadows, Caspar at his side.

"Damn," he said in his gruff voice. "I was so hoping that would work."

44

ZACHARY

Zachary watched, helpless, as Logan merged with his Tame and started towards the crystal. He wanted to scream that the kid was making a mistake, to demand that he turn around, that he listen. But Zachary knew it would do no good.

It was his own fault. Zachary had failed Logan as surely as he'd failed Margery.

His eyes slid closed. That was what he'd lost in all this. That he wasn't fighting for himself, but for those he loved. He no longer cared what fate this island had in store for him, whether or not the illness took him. After all, what was the point of survival if he unleashed a threat that might destroy all he loved?

He couldn't say when exactly he'd changed his mind, but he no longer doubted Willow's tale. There was just too much that did not add up about this place.

But it didn't matter now what *he* believed.

Why did you stop me? Willow whispered to him through their Tames. He sensed the anger in the highland woman. *We must stop him!*

You think you could? he snapped. *Look closely at their Tames. Their eyes are silver. Can't you sense their power? We wouldn't stand a chance if it came to a battle.*

Logan stood still on the chamber floor, his eyes distant. At his side stood Dustin Kaine, his arms folded, eyes tracking Logan's Tame as it crossed the whirlpool. At least the brother seemed half-convinced. That had surprised Zachary. Perhaps he had misjudged the man.

Then out amidst the whirlpool, Logan's Tame came to a sudden stop.

"No."

Zachary's head jerked up as Logan's voice rung through the chamber.

"No...something is wrong here."

A lump lodged in Zachary's throat as he found the kid's eyes on him. There was still indecision in that look, as though even now Logan doubted the wisdom of his decision, but there was resolve as well.

Before anyone could speak, a sharp whistling noise filled the cave. Grimly, Zachary turned from the brothers to the converging shadows.

"Now we see what this was all about."

He wasn't surprised when Gozzo took shape from the shadows. He had already pieced together most of the mystery from his conversations with Cordelia and Willow. The shade had appeared to each of the Pathfinders, but its words had differed. Zachary recalled Logan mentioning an Age of Heroes, while Willow claimed it had promised her answers. To Zachary, it had spoken of the power over life and death.

The only part he hadn't understood was the shades connection to Gozzo. Now he knew. The two were one and the same.

"Damn. I was so hoping that would work."

"I think past it's time we formally joined the party," Zachary remarked, sharing a glance with Willow.

She nodded, though her eyes never left the old fisherman. They descended the ramp slowly. Gozzo watched their approach. His features were still those of the man they'd encountered on the plateau, but his manner had changed. He stood with his shoulders held straight and arms clasped behind his back, his posture portraying a formal air. The slight twist to his lips bore an arrogance Zachary recognised well. It was the same smile noblemen gave when addressing the peasants. It was the look of someone who knew they held power over you.

"Damn, Gozzo, what happened to you?" Zach muttered as they joined Logan and his brother.

Closer now, he saw this was not *exactly* the Gozzo they had known on the island. That Gozzo had clearly been one of Caspar's illusions. The man's features were the same, with one important difference.

Gozzo was no longer a man of flesh and blood. His skin shone, reflecting the light of the crystal suspended in the centre of the chamber. Like the fishing ship and its skeletons, his entire body had been transformed to crystal.

"I only showed you a face I once possessed, Zachary."

"So what are you then?" Logan interjected. "Some kind of Tame?"

The creature at Gozzo's side stirred at the words, a growl rumbling from its throat. The old man chuckled. "You will have to forgive Caspar. He does not like that term. Past civilisations named his kind Gods, not servants. But no, Pathfinder, I am not a Tame. I am you—only a version a thousand years past. My bond with Caspar has simply allowed me to ascend."

"Ascend?" Dustin spoke at last. His voice was soft, measured.

"Yes, Pathfinder. I told it true when I said my men and I were the first to land on these shores. Only that was a thousand years ago, when the isles first rose from the seas."

"So I was right," Dustin whispered.

Gozzo smiled. "Why do you think you were my favourite?"

"A thousand years," Logan interrupted. The young man looked stunned by Gozzo's transformation. Innocent to the last, he had not expected this. "How is that possible?"

Dustin didn't seem to hear his brother. "Favourite…" He shook his head, anger appearing on his face. "If you have lied to me…"

"I would be less concerned about its lies," Zachary interrupted. His eyes never left Gozzo's crystalised face. "And more concerned about what it wants from us."

"You wound me, Zachary," Gozzo replied, clutching a hand to his chest in feigned pain. "You creatures of flesh are such mistrustful things. That is why I put on this face, though I have not worn it for a thousand years. Long have I waited for man to return to my island, only to find all those to lift the mantle of Pathfinder to be cowards. All, except one..." His crystal eyes lingered on Dustin, before turning to the others. "The rest of you required...encouragement."

"We were going to leave," Logan whispered. "Cordelia, she was determined to get us off the island. Until Gozzo convinced her..."

"It could not be allowed to happen," Gozzo said matter-of-factly. "Such fragile, fleeting creatures you are. You have no idea of the bliss of immortality, to leave behind the base needs of the flesh."

"Yet you need something from us," Zachary spoke up. There had to a be a reason for the manipulation, why it had directed events to keep them here.

"I need nothing from you, human. That is the blessing of crystal. It does not want or need, does not perish. Time is no obstacle. It only waits, knowing the inevitability of its return." The grating laughter came again, cold, almost metallic. "No, it is not I that needs something, but all of you. Is that not why you came?"

"And I suppose you would grant us those needs, demon?" Willow spoke now. Her eyes burned as she faced the creature. "Our legends warned of your return, of the false promises that come from crystal lips."

"I offer no promises, girl," Gozzo said softly, "only power." He gestured to the shining crystal. "The power of my island's heart. Yours to take, to use as you will. If you have the courage." The glassy eyes regarded each of them in turn. "The power to restore a lost love. To return a friend to the land of the living. To restore your health, or answer the impossible questions of this world. All of this, and more, I would offer you."

Silence fell over the cavern. Not an absolute silence, for the waters still roared as they disappeared into the unseen caverns. Even as Gozzo's words rung in his mind, a detached part of Zachary wondered at that. There was no obvious source to replenish the pool, and yet it was clearly racing away, disappearing into the depths of the island. It had to come from the crystal itself, formed from its magic.

But why?

Something tugged at the back of his mind. He struggled to concentrate over the pounding of his heart. The water had to be important. It had played a part in their journey right from the beginning. The way the stream had glowed when Rob drank from it. The light that appeared in the night. The excitement of the Tames as they drank the glowing liquid.

Waterways threaded this entire island. Lakes and rivers and streams, waterfalls plunging in an endless roar into the oceans. They even disappeared beneath the earth, threading unknown passageways deep within the island.

And here, the heart of it all, a whirlpool with no source but a magical crystal.

"Why do you not take it for yourself?" Zach found himself asking.

Gozzo's eyes narrowed, but the man—or whatever he had become—said nothing.

"You can't, can you?" Zachary pressed. "That's why you brought us here, what you've been waiting for. You cannot use the power yourself. You need us to take it. But why?"

The hardened eyes continued to stare at Zachary for a moment longer, before the ancient fisherman shrugged. "Does it matter?" Gozzo asked, his voice taking on an overly casual manner. "I am offering everything you dreamed of Zachary. A second chance. Just think, you can return to Margery a new man."

Zachary swallowed, his mouth suddenly dry. But he forced himself to shake his head. "I like the man I am today."

The crystal lips hardened. Gozzo turned to the others. "What of you, Dustin Kaine? You did not come all this way to balk at the finish line."

Water, Zachary, he forced himself to concentrate. *It's all about the water. Why?*

The water fed the Tames. He'd worked that out by the lake. If they used the crystal's power, would that stop the water from forming? This must be the source, the origin of the impossible quantities they had found across the island. But why would Gozzo want that? Sure, it fed their Tames, but it also fed the wild creatures that had hunted them across the island…

His eyes widened as understanding dawned.

"The beasts, they weren't just hunting us," he whispered. "They were hunting *you* as well."

Gozzo said nothing. Zachary took a step towards the…the thing.

"That's why you brought us here. You're trapped, aren't you? This crystal is the source of the island's power, the very thing that binds you here." He paused, leaning his head to the side. "You claim to be all powerful, but are you really? All this time, I never saw your Tame harm the other creatures. Every time a battle came, you faded away, or resorted to illusions."

Still Gozzo was silent. Zachary grinned. He started to turn to the others, when a flash of movement came from Gozzo's side. Caspar shot like an arrow from the shadows. A harsh *crack* echoed through the cavern as it slammed into Daze. Before Zach knew what was happening, his strength fled before a wave of agony. Suddenly he was on his knees, a silent scream on his lips.

Daze crumpled, a spiderweb of cracks spreading out from where Caspar had struck.

"You were saying, Pathfinder?" Gozzo hissed.

Zach could taste blood where he'd bitten his tongue. Suddenly his mind was like a cloud, his thoughts drifting, unable to concentrate. Even so, he forced himself to speak.

"Okay," he gasped, spitting out blood. "I might have made a miscalculation."

45

LOGAN

Logan's heart thundered in his ears. He stood frozen in place, still struggling to process everything he'd heard. This crystal *thing* wore the face of Gozzo, but it couldn't be the kindly old fisherman. Not the man who'd given Logan so much advice, who'd guided them across this perilous island.

Could it?

"You know, things were going so well until that damned boy got himself killed." Gozzo mused. Crossing his arms, he tapped at his elbow. "Now *he* had a spirit I could get behind. He wouldn't have hesitated like all of you. He would have destroyed it by now, and the consequences be damned."

"Rob." Logan swallowed. "That's when you appeared to us."

He could not tear his eyes from Zachary. The man was still on the ground, all colour drained from his face, his eyes ringed by shadows. He looked like he already had one foot in the grave.

"Come, who will be the first to take up the power?" Gozzo asked again.

Dustin too had been staring at Zachary, but he blinked at the creature's words. "What will you do if we refuse?"

Gozzo chuckled. "Then I will destroy you, Pathfinder, and wait for more to come. You are not unique."

"Yet he spoke the truth, did he not? You cannot use the power yourself."

There was a long pause. "Do not test my patience, Pathfinder."

"Very well, shade," Dustin replied. "I will do it."

Behind them, Willow cried a warning. Caspar reacted instantly. Her Tame was almost as quick as well. A deep glow began to spread through its body, shining from its tusks —but the Pluff was faster still. A dozen replicas branched off the original fox, and before Willow's Tame could strike it found itself surrounded. Its tusks brightened, the light spreading out to touch the ring of Caspars. They glowed in turn, but did not vanish.

Gozzo laughed. "Nice, Pathfinder. That trick might pierce lesser illusions, but not Caspar in the flesh." He made a gesture with his hand.

Snarling, Caspar leapt, dragging Willow's Tame to the ground.

A lump lodged in Logan's throat as Willow crumpled along-side Zachary. His every hair stood on end as he stared at

Caspar. The Tame's eyes glinted a terrible silver...but it was not the silver of Hope or Eiliah. No, there was a depth to its eyes, a glimmer of something greater. Not silver at all, but...diamond?

"I said I would do it," Dustin spoke again. "Leave the girl be."

Gozzo's eyes narrowed and he studied Dustin, as though expecting some fresh trick. But finally he gave a wave of his hand, and Caspar retreated from its prey. The boar-like Tame remained motionless on the ground, rendered unconscious, just as Daze had been.

"Dustin..." Logan started.

His brother reached out and placed a hand on his shoulder. "Do not worry, brother," he said with a smile. "This is what I was born to do. If there is a price, I am willing to pay it."

Logan frowned at his brother's words, but already Dustin was turning away. His eyes took on the glassy look as his mind joined with Eiliah. The dragon Tame had settled nearby, but now it gave a rumble from deep in its throat. Rising, it looked from Gozzo to the crystal suspended over the waters. Light danced on its scales as it drifted towards the island's heart.

Watching his brother's Tame, Logan held his breath. This was wrong. And yet...again he imagined Amilyse's fiery eyes opening. His heart clenched. Couldn't they just have one moment of happiness, one win?

But no. Not if it cost them everything.

"Stop..." Logan breathed, barely able to bring himself to speak the words. Merged with his Tame, Dustin did not hear the words. Logan spoke again, louder. "Dustin, you have to stop!"

Still Dustin did not return. Eiliah was nearing the crystal now. Its scales were practically aglow, shining in the light of the crystal, almost as though it was not a reflection at all, but...

Logan frowned. *What—*

A roar shook the chamber as Eiliah swung suddenly in the air. Energy crackled, dancing across the dragon's scaled skin. Concealed by the light of the great crystal, it had gathered its power in preparation for an attack. Now, with a howl that echoed up into the darkness far above their heads, it unleashed its attack.

Boom.

Thunder shook the earth beneath Logan's feet as the lightning slammed into the fox-like Pluff. He stumbled, falling to his knees as the world turned to light. Power surged through him, and he sensed Hope at his side, placing itself between its human and the attack.

A heartbeat later, stillness returned to the world.

Blinking the stars from his eyes, Logan struggled to rise, to see what his brother had wrought. His heart swelled as he saw the blackened patch of earth where Caspar had been standing. There was no sign of the diminutive Pluff and its terrible eyes. He must have been wrong about its strength, and Zach was right, if it had been destroyed by a single attack...

"Impossible," Dustin whispered. Eiliah had alighted at his side, but he was looking not at the Tame, but the nearby shadows.

Laughter echoed from the walls of the chamber as Gozzo appeared from thin air, Caspar still at his side—apparently untouched by the power of Eiliah's lightning.

"Truly, you creatures of fresh and blood are incorrigible."

Ice spread through Logan's veins as the old fisherman came to a stop before them. He and his Tame were untouched—if they were even here. Who knew what a creature as powerful as Caspar might be capable of? They might be far from here, or exist only in spirit, or crystal.

"I must say, I am disappointed Dustin," Gozzo admonished. "I had expected more of my favourite."

A sound that might have been laughter, might have been a long, drawn out moan, came from the ground nearby. His face ashen, Zachary pushed himself to his feet.

"It must be something," he gasped, swaying where he stood. "To be immortal, all powerful—and yet still trapped." This time there was no mistaking his laughter. "Tell us, Gozzo, what would you give for the joys of the flesh now. How long has it been since you felt something in that crystal heart of yours?"

Gozzo said nothing. His face remained impassive as he stared at the thief, but at his side the Tame advanced a step. Zachary ignored it.

"Let me tell you a story, Gozzo," Zachary continued. "About a thief who traded all he possessed to save his life, only to look back and find he had lost everything he'd cherished about his life in the first place." The man paused. "That's it, that's my story. I imagine it must look a lot like yours. What is left for a creature like you, after all this time like *that?*"

A rumble came from the old fisherman's throat. "There is immortality," he growled. "Freedom from death. What else is there, mortal?"

"Love. Life. Joy." He waved a hand. "I wouldn't expect you to understand—"

Caspar struck without warning, slamming into Daze again. This time great chunks of crystal slouched from the Tame. It slumped to the ground, its inner light flickering, almost going out. Zachary fell without a sound beside his Tame.

"That's better," Gozzo muttered. "You were always my least favourite, Zachary." He turned back to where Dustin and Logan stood, their faces pale. "Now, where were we?"

A tremor slid down Logan's throat. He swallowed and opened his mouth.

"Ah yes," Gozzo spoke over Logan's words. "The brothers grim. Just as I had hoped, both of you together. Though I had hoped you would not need the extra motivation."

At his words, Caspar struck again. Not at Zach or Willow this time, but the great, dangerous form of Eiliah. It shouldn't have been a contest. The dragon-Tame was four times the size of the little Pluff. It didn't even use illusions this time, only surged at the Tame in a terrible burst of speed.

Crack.

Eiliah reeled back from the blow. This time, there was no fine network of cracks where the blow had struck. Instead, great chunks of crystal splintered and broke from the Tame, crumbling as they struck the ground. For a heartbeat, Eiliah swayed on its delicate legs, its colour taking on a sickly green. Then that light flickered and began to fade.

"No!" Logan cried as Dustin fell to his knees.

He reached his brother, but it was already too late. Dustin's face went white as a ghost. His eyes stared blankly into the distance. He didn't react as Logan screamed his name, didn't blink as Logan dragged him into his arms.

With a final hiss of exhaled breath, Eiliah crumbled to dust. The Tame's inner light lit the cavern for a heartbeat longer, then went streaming into Caspar.

And the spark of Dustin Kaine's life was snuffed out.

"I offer you one last chance, Pathfinder," Gozzo's voice rang through the chamber. "Take up the crystal, use its power to save your brother. Or refuse, and rest forever at his side."

❧ 46 ❧

LOGAN

"**N**o, no, no!"

Logan was on his knees beside Dustin. His brother's body was still, unmoving. There was no response as Logan shook him. The warmth of life remained, but Dustin had already fled.

Just like Amilyse.

Just like Rob.

Just like their mother, all those years ago.

"Get up, Dustin, you have to get up!" he croaked.

He squeezed at his brother's fingers. Hope nudged his side, whimpering softly. It's coat had darkened to the deepest blue of grief. But the Tame could not help Logan now. Eyes clenched closed, he begged and pleaded and prayed to whichever of the Old Gods might restore Dustin to life.

But no one answered.

No one but Gozzo.

"Take up the crystal, use its power to save your brother."

Logan shuddered. The man—if he could be called that—stood nearby, hands clasped behind his back. There was no emotion in his eyes now. No joy or laughter or anger. Only disdain. He knew this game was won. It was no coincidence that of all those he could have killed, he'd chosen Dustin. The others might have been strong enough to refuse his demands.

But not Logan. Not the naïve, innocent boy who'd stumbled onto this adventure by accident.

Worst of all was that he was right. Staring down at his brother, Logan knew he would do whatever it took to bring Dustin back.

He came to his feet and turned towards the crystal, Hope at his side. He reached out a hand and rested it on the Tame's head, sensing its warmth. Its power was reassuring, but it was not enough.

"Logan."

The voice belonged to Zachary. Somehow the old thief was still conscious, though he was on his knees. Their eyes met…and the man gave the slightest nod, as though to acknowledge Logan's choice. Or rather, his lack of choice. Zachary could read the cards as well as anyone. There was no victory here. Caspar had defeated their Tames with ease. Hope could not stand against it. Gozzo wasn't lying. He would kill every one of them to get what he wanted.

"Choose, Pathfinder."

Logan exhaled. "I choose life."

Closing his eyes, he merged with Hope. There was no hesitation now. He hardly noticed the crackling of power as they approached the crystal across the swirling pool. There was no time to linger, no time to think.

The energies of the island's heart bathed Hope as they alighted along-side it. Paws hovering just above the racing waters, they reached out to touch the enormous crystal.

Light burst before Logan's eyes. Suddenly he was no longer Hope, no longer Logan. He wasn't even human. His mind expanded, racing outwards from the crystal cavern, his consciousness growing, fed by the infinite energies. He saw all, *was all.* Intricate lattices filled the world, converting power, connecting all, binding man and nature and crystal.

And still he grew, spreading to encompass the island, the ocean, the continents. Far to the south, he witnessed the great lions of the savanna as they brought down a gazelle, saw in the north bears emerging from the freezing waters onto shelves of ice, watched as armies clashed in the east, brother peoples warring over some insignificant peninsula.

Time passed, and civilizations rose, then fell and rose again. Coasts changed and rivers broke free of their constraints, raising enormous plateaus, before carving new channels through the weathered stone. He witnessed the slow attrition of mountains, and the growing darkness as it claimed the world.

But even as he witnessed the end of all things, a slice of Logan remained. A tiny sense of self that clung to the infinite, binding him to that long-forgotten chamber. Without it, that moment, that tiny slice of time, would have been lost. He was almost surprised when he found the thread leading back to man and Tame.

Intrigued, he found himself standing again in the chamber of the crystal. Memories flooded him as he saw the old thief on his knees. Zachary had been his name. There was a woman too, lying unconscious. He recognised her as well, but the name was longer in coming…Willow.

Then his eyes found the dead man.

All at once, Logan's purpose came rushing back.

Dustin. He'd come here for Dustin, to bring his brother back from across the veil. He could see it too. It was hung like a mist over everything, a shadow at the edges of the eye, lingering, waiting for each new soul to cross. No man could see beyond its silky tendrils.

But Logan was no longer a man.

Silhouettes waited just beyond the mists. The souls of all he had loved, and lost. Dustin, Amilyse, Rob. His mother. Power burned within him, the energies of a thousand lives. The power that had fed this island for a millennia. He had only to slash across that veil, and they would be restored to him.

It would consume his power. The part of him that had grown used to the infinite feared that, but the fragment that was Logan rejoiced, that he would once again draw breath, know life.

So he gathered the power to him, drew its tendrils back from across the world and the void, readying to do what must be done.

Yet as the energies reformed, Logan noticed something he had missed. A shadow that lingered on the edges of the chamber. Wrapped in power, it had thought to hide, to conceal itself in the shadows. It wore the guise of a man, but like himself, this creature had long ago discarded the trappings of humanity. The creature seemed to realise it had been seen.

Congratulations, brother. It pulsed the words. Though it used no recognisable language, Logan understood. *You have ascended. Now, undo the chains the traitors cast upon me.*

Logan saw that it was true. Bands of light wrapped the shadows of his brother spirit. They bound it tight to the physical realm, holding him to the tiny island. Sadness touched him at the thought of being so constrained. He reached out to break the chains of fire.

Only at the last moment did he pause. A memory drifted to him, not of Logan or the infinite, but that of his crystal companion. Of a thousand souls crying out as one.

Why are you chained? he found himself asking.

Because of weak minds, came the reply, *and weaker spirits.*

Logan frowned. *Surely no...mortal could do this.*

They are treacherous beings, brother. Grant them power, and they will turn upon you. They must be ruled.

The words gave Logan pause. There was truth in what the creature said, but it was not an entire truth.

And you would rule them?

We can rule them together, brother.

A few minutes before, he might have been tempted. On his travels, he had often found himself wondering how the chaos could be tamed, how he might bring peace to the disorder. Yet with each passing moment in the chamber, his mortal memories grew stronger. Emotions he'd thought long wilted were returning. Wonder and excitement, love and…pain.

Logan shivered, looking to where his brother lay. Dustin was why he'd taken up the power in the first place. He could still sense the veil, hovering just out of sight, its host of faceless shadows waiting beyond.

And if I choose not to free you?

Silence followed his words. **It matters not,** the shadow replied at last. **Already you have consumed much of the crystal's power. Free me, or do not. I will have my freedom regardless.**

Again, Logan saw that it was true. The great crystal that hung above the whirlpool had dulled now, the power drained away, diminished.

But not yet exhausted.

Logan looked again at the darkness Gozzo had become. He had led them here, bid them use the crystal, knowing that in doing so they would consume the very power that kept him trapped. But all of that relied on the one who took up the crystal making the selfish choice. Of using it to bring back their brother, their lover, to restore their health. It was what Dustin might have done, Zachary as well.

But it was not the only choice.

The last of the crystal's energies gathered within Logan. Gozzo had returned to his human form now. The face of the old fisherman began to glow as the last chains of power faded, freeing him of his bonds. A roar began on Gozzo's lips as he stretched out his hands in triumph.

In that moment, Logan unleashed the power of the crystal.

Not on the veil, not to pierce the underworld and bring back his brother.

But on Gozzo and his shining Tame.

ZACHARY

Z ach was in agony. Not the kind that came from a twisted ankle or the ache that found its way into his bones on a cold day. This wasn't the sort of pain where he could just grit his teeth and get by. This was the pain a man felt only once or twice in his life—if he was lucky. He'd taken an arrow through his shoulder once. That had left his arm in such agony that it was a struggle just to rise each morning.

But even the memory of those months seemed just a scratch to this agony. All the worse that it came not from his own body, but Daze. If this had been his own body, he would already be dead and free. As it was…he could barely think, barely do anything but beg for the end to finally come.

Yet he clung on, watching as the crystal lit up Logan's Tame out above the waters, as the energy played its way across Hope's shaggy fur. He didn't know what he was waiting for, what he expected. Gozzo had won. Zach had thought himself so smart, uncovering the man's secrets, exposing his plans. But he'd been a fool. They had only ever been mice before the tabby cat, spared its claws for a brief moment of hope, before it struck.

The glow of the crystal faded, dying to a spark—then burst suddenly to renewed brilliance. The new light flowed from the crystal into Hope.

And with a roar, the Tame unleashed the gathered energies.

Light pulsed through the cavern, casting back the shadows, burning up the darkness. Gozzo's eyes grew wide, his crystal face reflecting the power of that light. He raised a hand, as though he might hold it back. Snarling, Caspar leapt to intercept the energies, a dark glow burning in its tiny body.

The chamber shook as the twin forces collided. If Zachary hadn't already been on the ground, he would have fallen. A deep rumbling began in the earth, and the air crackled with spent energies. Blinded, Zach blinked, struggling to see through the stars, to see what had become of Logan and Gozzo.

When the light finally faded, he lay alone in the darkness. He blinked again, adjusting to the dark. Shadows began to make themselves known. Despite their injuries, a faint light still glinted from Daze and Zahra and...yes, there was Hope's light too. His spirits lifted at the sight. It meant that Logan and Willow still lived.

A strange stillness hung over the cave. It took Zach a long while before the source became apparent.

The roar of the whirlpool had ceased.

Gathering his strength, he stood. Stumbling to his Tame, he placed a hand on Daze and concentrated. The bond tugged within, and a trickle of his energy flowed into the Tame. The spark at its core flickered, then brightened, casting back the shadows further.

By its light, he saw that he was right. The whirlpool had drained away, leaving a dark hole in the centre of the chamber.

Shivering, he looked for the others. Logan lay nearby. Zach went to him first, crouching beside the young man. Despite knowing Hope lived, he checked for a pulse, and was thankful to find it strong. Only then did he turn his attention to Gozzo.

Zachary circled the chamber twice before he allowed himself to relax. There was no sign of the fisherman or his Tame. Not even dust remained of the crystal pair. Whatever Logan had done there at the end, both had been destroyed.

It was over.

Thank the Gods. He paused, his gaze lingering on Logan. *No, thank the kid.*

He was about to return to the young man's side and try to wake him, when he glimpsed a glimmer from the corner of his eyes. His heart lurched, thinking for a second that Gozzo had returned after all. But no, this light was dim, barely visible against the glow of his Tame. He crossed the chamber and came to a stop beside the source of the light.

It was a fragment of the crystal Logan had used to destroy Gozzo. The heart of the island, he'd called it. Its light was almost gone, just a spark really. No longer enough to create the water that had fed the island.

But might it be enough for something else?

He turned his mind inwards. The tendrils of the cancer threaded through his chest, dark, twisted things. How long did he have now? A few weeks, no more, he would guess. Unless...

He reached for Daze. Warmth swept over him as they merged. He looked again at the crystal from the eyes of the Tame. There was power there. Enough to heal him? Daze reached out and touched a paw to the shimmering light.

Power. They gasped as the crackling, burning energies filled them. This was only a fraction of what Logan had held? How could he have given it up, used it against Gozzo instead of keeping it for himself?

Zachary could never have been so selfless.

Could he?

He found himself looking across the chamber at the unconscious young man. If not for Logan, he would already be dead. They would all be dead. And Gozzo would be free. The kid had saved more than the lives of those in this chamber. He'd saved everyone.

His gaze passed from Logan to the body that lay beside him. Dustin. Zach had not known the man long. But he had tried to stop the old fisherman, in the end. He meant everything to the kid. And Logan had given that up.

Zachary swallowed, looking again at the sickly tendrils of his cancer. The energy could burn them away, cleanse him of his sickness, restore his youth. He could return to Margery and live out the rest of his days in peace. Thanks to Logan.

Holding the power in his hands, he could sense the veil to the after world, the shadows of the seven hells beyond. Without the crystals magic, he would join them soon. Days or weeks, it was inevitable. It would all end.

A curse slipped from Zach. Before he could second guess himself, he gathered the power close. Instinctively, he knew what he had to do. With a final rush, he sent the power into Dustin's still form, setting his heart to beating, his lungs to breathing, filling him with the energies of the island.

Then, with the last spark that remained, he hurled it at the veil.

And the spirit of Dustin Kaine stepped back into the land of the living.

EPILOGUE
LOGAN

Logan woke at the same moment as his brother. He could not have said how he knew, only that one moment he was dreaming of Dustin, of the pair of them speaking across the veil, just as they had in their dreams.

The next moment he was gasping in ice cold air, back in the crystal chamber, back in the dark beneath the island. And his brother was crying out beside him.

He stilled at the sound of Dustin's voice. The chamber was dark, but as he blinked, a light grew, and he watched in wonder as light gathered above. Piece by piece, the dragon form of Eiliah took shape, until with a harsh roar, it flashed a final time and settled beside them.

Logan pushed himself to his hands and knees and crawled to where his brother lay. Dustin's eyes were wide and he clutched at his chest, gasping in great lungfuls of air, as though he'd forgotten how to breathe. Logan clutched him by the arm.

"Dustin! Dustin, it's alright, you're alright."

Tears brimmed in his eyes. He could hardly believe what he was seeing. He had given this up, hadn't he? When he'd chosen to destroy Gozzo. Movement came from nearby. Zachary stepped into the light. Their eyes met.

"You did this," Logan whispered.

The thief shrugged.

Logan swallowed. "But you'll die."

"We all die, kid," Zachary replied, the faintest of smiles crossing his lips.

He started to turn away, but a groan from the earth beneath their feet gave him pause. The earthquake struck seconds later. Zach cried out as he was almost thrown from his feet. Logan clutched at his brother.

The shaking ceased, but the noise continued. Sharp groans came from somewhere above, followed by the crackling of breaking stone and crystal.

"Lowlanders, quickly, this place is going to collapse."

Willow's voice called from across the chamber. Logan's heart pounded hard in his chest as he stumbled to his feet, dragging Dustin with him. His brother still hadn't said a word. He was shivering as Logan drew him towards the entrance. He wondered just what his brother had experienced, on the other side. But questions would have to wait.

Above, the noises grew louder—then with a sharp tearing sound, a chunk of the ceiling crashed down in front of them. Logan cried out and Zachary flinched, while Willow leapt backwards out of the boulders path. Dustin barely moved.

"We'll never make it up that tunnel before it collapses," he gasped. It had taken them a quarter hour to descend, and that had been without the ground trembling and the ceiling closing in.

Zachary grimaced. "Don't worry, I've got an idea."

A few minutes later, the silhouettes of four Tames burst from the mountainside. Dust clung to the humans on their backs. The four coughed and spluttered as they dismounted, stumbling as the earth shook yet again. Logan slumped to his knees and looked back up at the cave mouth.

With a final *roar*, an explosion of dust and crystal burst from the cave. When it settled, only a sliver remained, a harsh scar on the mountainside. Rocks and boulders had piled up within, barring any passage back into the depths. But they had survived.

Logan looked at the others. Despite his stupor, Dustin had thankfully held on to his Tame. Willow and Zachary seemed to have coped with the ride a little better than Logan or his brother. Apparently they'd already ridden their Tames once before.

Reaching out, Logan placed a hand on his brother's shoulder. "Dustin…" he said, unable to keep the concern from his voice. The man had still not said a word.

Dustin turned slowly, and Logan saw now the pain in his eyes. "You should not have brought me back, brother."

The words struck Logan like a bullet to the heart. He reeled back. "I…I didn't. It was Zach."

"I see," Dustin murmured. He looked away. "It wasn't meant to happen like this," he whispered. "It was meant to be *her* we brought back. Not me." He hung his head. "All this time, all that I have sacrificed, and in the end, I failed."

Logan swallowed. He tried to speak, to say something, but there was nothing. What could he say? Amilyse was still gone. He felt the pain of that loss sharp in his heart. And he'd only known her for a fleeting moment. How long had Dustin known his highland girl?

Nearby, Zachary bent in two and began to cough. It was a bad one, going at least a minute. Logan hadn't seen him suffering like that since their first day on the island. His stomach twisted. He rose and went to his friend.

"You didn't have to do that for us," he said as the thief straightened.

The man waved a hand as he removed a cloth from his mouth and tucked it back into his pocket—though not before Logan saw the blood staining the white satin.

"Call it payback for the mistake I made in the forest," Zach said with a smile.

Logan hesitated, but finally he nodded his thanks. What more could he say? That he would rather Zach had saved himself than Dustin? After everything they had been through, the man deserved better than a lie.

"What about your wife?" he asked instead.

"I…"

Zachary trailed off as the crunch of stones carried to their ears. A moment later, Cordelia and the other sailors appeared. Relief touched Logan to see them alive. With only one Tame for protection, that had been far from a sure thing.

The two groups exchanged greetings as the sun began its inevitable dip towards the horizon. Watching its light fade, Logan could hardly believe his journey up the mountainside had only been that morning. Less than a day had passed since Amilyse gave her life to save them. After all he had experienced, consumed by the power, it seemed eons must have passed…

…but already those last memories were fading. His mortal mind could not handle such a vast knowledge; that much he could recall. A part of him longed to return to the infinite, but it was a small part. The rest of him, the mortal, joyed in the breeze upon his skin, the weight of his body, even the metallic taste of blood in his mouth from biting his cheek in the wild flight from the cavern.

A gasp of inhaled air brought Logan's attention back to the present. The others were all on their feet, looking towards the north and east. His heart began to race as he saw what had caught their attention.

Beyond the shores of the island, the ever-present clouds were lifting. The dark banks drifted away, rising, fading away.

In their place, island after island stretched out towards the north.

"He said there were others," Logan found himself saying. The light shone from the distant shores, reflecting from crystalline sands and stone.

"Then there will be more magics." For the first time since his resurrection, Dustin's voice carried a note of hope.

Logan swallowed. He couldn't help but feel the same quickening of his pulse, though it was not just because of Amilyse. It was that tiny sliver of him that desired the infinite, that dreamed of regaining those powers he'd held for just an instant.

"Looks like the armada will be joining us," Cordelia spoke up.

Looking to the south, Logan saw that she was right. With the clouds gone, they could now see the ships of the King's Council. Tall smokestacks filled the horizon and wind billowed in sails as they turned towards the crystal shores. They would make landing within an hour. What then? What would become of this place once the King's Council gained a foothold?

But none of that was Logan's concern. He turned his eyes to the future. A narrow strip of sand led from the shores of their island to the next.

"Let them come," he said softly.

"They'll try to stop you," Zachary remarked.

Logan frowned at his words. "You aren't going to join us?"

The old thief let out a sigh. "I've had enough of crystal magic for this lifetime, kid," he replied, a sad smile crossing his lips. "I think I'll return to Leith. If I have only a few weeks left, I'd like to spend them with the one I love." He paused. "If she'll still have me."

A lump lodged in Logan's throat. He found he could not speak, so instead he only nodded, hoping the man would understand. The smile Zachary gave by way of reply said that he did.

"I'll join you, Sicario," Cordelia said softly. "My men and I are done with crystal too. Past time we put some proper salt-water beneath our feet again." She glanced at Logan. "We'll try and delay them as long as we can."

Logan nodded his thanks. That left one last Pathfinder. He looked around for the highland woman, but Willow had disappeared while they had been speaking. A curse slipped from his lips. Dustin chuckled and slapped Logan on the back.

"Looks like we've got some competition, brother," he said. "Come, we'd better not let her head start grow too large."

Logan nodded. He clasped hands with Cordelia, then each of the remaining sailors. Only when he reached Zachary did he hesitate.

"Are you sure about this?"

"I'm sure," Zach replied, then hesitated, his eyes flickering to where Dustin stood waiting on the trail down the mountain. "Just be careful, kid. I…"

"…don't trust him," Logan finished for him. "Don't worry, Zach. You taught me well. But I'll choose my own path. And right now, I'm choosing to help my brother."

Still Zachary hesitated. He stared down at Logan, as though looking for something. Finally, though, he nodded. "Very well," he said. He placed a hand on Logan's shoulder. "Then I bid you good luck, Pathfinder."

Here Ends Book One
of
The Untamed Isles:
The Path Awakens

APPENDIX

Skelt — Defense Tame   **Burrl** — Vitality Tame

Thoona — Special Attack Tame   **Brackis** — Attack Tame

Pango   **Guang** — Luck Tame

Guppy   **Pluff** — Agility Tame

YOUR FEEDBACK

Thank you so much for reading this book! I hope you've enjoyed it. Read on through the next sections for more about this world and other opportunities to explore its history and future. However, at this very moment, some one else is considering taking a leap of faith on this book, but they need your help! Please don't forget to head on over to the Amazon page and post your review if you've enjoyed the story. Every review and rating helps make a successful new series fly.

YOUR IN-GAME REWARD

In case you weren't aware, the Untamed Isles are more than just a book series—they're also a monster hunting and taming MMORPG online game! **And the team over at Phat Loot Studies would love to reward you for joining in our adventures**. In honour of the occasion, we're giving away a unique, in game prize for everyone who purchased a copy of the book—whether in electronic, paperback or audio format. **Simply contact the team at rewards@untamedisles.com with proof of purchase to receive your prize by 31st December 2021.**

JOIN THE COMMUNITY

The Untamed Isles are more than just a book or a game. Come join our community on Discord and discuss the adventures of Zachary, Logan and the other Pathfinders. Discuss fan theories and what comes next for this exciting new world.

Join the Discord Community

NOTE FROM THE AUTHOR

Well that's the Untamed Isles! This book was a few firsts for me. Its the first time one of my drafts has cracked 100,000 words for a single book (even if that dropped to 97,000 words on the final edit!). It's also the first time I've worked actively with an outside team to write a series. Definitely a bit of a different project working with Josh and the team, but all up a good one I think!

Hopefully you the reader agree—but I guess the reviews will tell that in time.

Write on!

Aaron

FOLLOW AARON HODGES

Join Aaron Hodges on his Patreon for exclusive sneak peeks into his current works in progress and **a free digital copy of all upcoming novels!**

https://www.patreon.com/aaronhodgesauthor

OR

Join his newsletter to r**eceive TWO FREE novels and a short story!**

https://aaronhodgesauthor.com/newsletter

Book 1: Warbringer

Book 2: Wrath of the Forgotten

Book 3: Age of Gods

Book 4: Dreams of Fury

The Alfurian Chronicles

Book 1: Defiant

Book 2: Guardian